Evening Stars

Also available from Susan Mallery

THREE SISTERS
BAREFOOT SEASON
ALREADY HOME

SUSAN MALLERY

Evening Stars

A Blackberry Island Novel

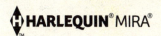
HARLEQUIN® MIRA®

ISBN-13: 978-1-61129-169-8

EVENING STARS

Printed in U.S.A.

Evening Stars

To the women in my life.
Thank you for becoming my 'sisters of the heart.'
Thank you for the love and support, for the friendship, the laughs, the advice, the caring. Thank you for being there, for believing in me and for telling me straight, when I'm heading in the wrong direction. This is for you. With all my love.

Chapter One

۶۲৩

IN A BATTLE between Betty Boop and multicolored hearts, Nina Wentworth decided it was going to be a Betty Boop kind of day. She pulled the short-sleeved scrub shirt over her head and was already moving toward the bathroom before the fabric settled over her hips.

"Don't be snug, don't be snug," she chanted as she came to a stop in front of the mirror and reached for her brush.

The shirt settled as it should, with a couple of inches to spare. Nina breathed a sigh of relief. Last night's incident with three brownies and a rather large glass of red wine hadn't made a lasting impression on her hips. She was grateful, and she would repent later on an elliptical. Or at least vow to eat her brownies one at a time.

Ten seconds of brushing, one minute of braiding and her blond hair was neat and tidy. She dashed out into the hall, toward the kitchen where she grabbed her car keys and nearly made it to the back door. Just as she was reaching for the knob, the house phone rang.

Nina glanced from the clock to the phone. Everyone in her

world—friends, family, work—had her cell. Very few calls came on the antiquated landline, and none of them were good news. Nina retraced her steps and braced herself for disaster.

"Hello?"

"Hey, Nina. It's Jerry down at Too Good To Be True. I just opened, and there's a lady here trying to sell a box of crap, ah, stuff. I think it's from the store."

Nina closed her eyes as she held in a groan. "Let me guess. Early twenties, red hair with purple streaks and a tattoo of a weird bird on her neck?"

"That's her. She's glaring at me something fierce. You think she's armed?"

"I hope not."

"Me, too." Jerry didn't sound especially concerned. "What's her name?"

"Tanya."

If Nina had more time, she would have collapsed right there on the floor. But she had a real job to get to. A job unrelated to the disaster that was the family's antique store.

"You let your mom hire her, huh?" Jerry asked.

"Yes."

"You know better."

"That I do. I'll call the police and ask them to pick up Tanya. Can you keep her there until they get there?"

"Sure thing, kid."

"Great. And I'll be by after work to pick up the stuff."

"I'll hold it for you," Jerry promised.

"Thanks."

Nina hung up and hurried to her car. After her cell connected to the Bluetooth, she called the local sheriff's department and explained what happened.

"Again?" Deputy Sam Payton asked, his voice thick with amusement. "Did you let your mom hire this employee?"

Nina carefully backed out of the driveway. Jerry's humor she could handle. He'd lived here all his life—he was allowed to tease her. But Sam was relatively new. He hadn't earned mocking rights.

"Hey, tax-paying citizen here, reporting a crime," she said.

"Yeah, yeah. I'm writing it down. What'd she take?"

"I didn't ask. She's at the pawn shop. Too Good To Be True."

"I know it," Deputy Sam told her. "I'll head out and see what's what."

"Thanks."

She hung up before he could offer advice on hiring policies and turned up the hill. The morning was clear—odd for early spring in the Pacific Northwest. Normally the good weather didn't kick in until closer to summer. To the west, blue water sparkled. To the east was western Washington.

As she climbed higher and higher, the view got better, but when she parked across from the three Queen Anne houses at the very top of the hill, pausing to enjoy the spectacular combination of sky and ocean was the last thing on her mind.

She hurried up the steps to the front porch that was both her boss's home and her office. Dr. Andi, as she was known, was a popular pediatrician on the island. Make that the *only* pediatrician. She'd moved here a year ago, opened her practice in September and had been thriving ever since. She was also a newlywed and, as of two months ago, pregnant.

Nina unlocked the front door and stepped inside. She flipped on lights as she went, confirmed the temperature on the thermostat and then started the three computers in the front office.

After storing her purse in her locker, she logged in to the scheduling program and saw that the first appointment of the day had canceled. Andi would appreciate the extra time to get herself moving. She was still battling morning sickness.

Nina did a quick check of her email, forwarded several items to the bookkeeper/office manager, then walked to the break room for coffee. Fewer than five minutes after she'd arrived, she was climbing the stairs to her boss's private quarters.

Nina knocked once before entering. She found Andi, a tall, pretty brunette with curly hair, sitting at the table in the kitchen. Her arms cradled her head.

"Still bad?" Nina asked, walking to the cupboard.

"Hi and yes. It's not that I throw up, it's that I feel like I'm going to every single second." She raised her head and drew in a breath. "Are you drinking coffee?"

"Yes."

"I miss coffee. I'm a wreck. I need to talk to my parents about my ancestors. Obviously I don't come from hardy stock."

Nina took down a mug, filled it with water and put it in the microwave. Then she collected a tea bag from the pantry.

"Not ginger tea," Andi said with a moan. "Please. I hate it."

"But it helps."

"I'd rather feel sick."

Nina raised her eyebrows.

Andi slumped in her seat. "I'm such a failure. Look at me. I'm carrying around a child the size of a lima bean and I'm throwing a hissy fit. It's embarrassing."

"And yet the need to act mature doesn't seem to be kicking in."

Andi smiled. "Funny how that works."

The microwaved dinged. Nina dropped the tea bag into the steaming water and crossed to the table.

The eat-in kitchen was open, with painted cabinets and lots of granite. The big window by the table took advantage of the east-facing views in the old house. The mainland shimmered only a few miles away.

Andi had bought the house—one of three up on the hill—when she'd moved to Blackberry Island. Undeterred by the broken windows and outdated plumbing, she'd had the house restored from the framework out. During the process, she'd fallen in love with her contractor. Which had led to her current tummy problems.

"Your first appointment canceled," Nina told her.

"Thank God." Andi sniffed the tea, then wrinkled her nose and took a sip. "It's the ginger. If I could have tea without ginger I think I could get it down."

"The thing is, the ginger is the part that settles your stomach."

"Life is perverse like that." Andi took another sip, then smiled. "I like the shirt."

Nina glanced down at the pattern. "Betty and I go way back."

One of the advantages of working for a pediatrician was that cheerful attire was encouraged. She had a collection of brightly colored fun shirts in her closet. It wasn't high fashion, but it helped the kids smile and that was what mattered.

"I need to get back downstairs," she said. "Your first appointment is now at eight-thirty."

"Okay."

Nina rose and started toward the stairs.

"Are you busy after work?" Andi asked.

Nina thought about the fact that she was going to have to go by the pawn shop and pick up what Tanya had tried to sell, then spend several hours at Blackberry Preserves, her family's antique store, figuring out what had been stolen, then tell her mother what had happened and possibly lecture her on the importance of actually following up on a potential employee's references. Only she'd been lecturing her mother for as long as she could remember, and the lessons never seemed to stick. No matter how many times Bonnie promised to do better, she never did. Which left Nina picking up the pieces.

"I kind of am. Why?"

"I haven't been to Pilates in a week," Andi said. "It's important I keep exercising. Would you go with me? It's more fun when you're along."

"I can't tonight, but Monday's good."

Andi smiled. "Thanks, Nina. You're the best."

"Give me a plaque and I'll believe it."

"I'll order one today."

Nina counted out the number of happy fruit and vegetable stickers she had. Just enough, but she would have to order more.

Since opening her practice, Andi had started a program of inviting local elementary school classes into her office as a field trip. Kids learned about a basic exam, were able to use the stethoscope and check their weight and height in a nonthreatening atmosphere. Andi's goal was to make a visit to the doctor less stressful.

Nina handled the scheduling and conducted the tour. Each student left with a small goodie bag filled with the stickers, a small coloring book on different ways to exercise and a box of crayons.

Normally the gift bags were filled by their receptionist before the event, but she had forgotten the stickers last time, so Nina had taken over the task.

She was in the middle of lining up the open goodie bags for quick filling when her cell phone buzzed. She pulled it from her pocket and checked the name, then pushed speaker and set it on the break-room table.

"Hi, Mom."

"Sweetheart! How are you? We're fine, but you were right, as you usually are."

Nina grabbed crayons from the big bag of them on the chair. "Right about what?"

"The tires. That we should have replaced them before we left. We had snow last night."

Nina glanced out the window at the sunny skies. She could see a few clouds pilling up against the horizon. Rain later that afternoon, she thought.

"Where are you?"

"Montana. It was coming down like you wouldn't believe. We had about four inches, and the tires just couldn't handle it. We skidded off the road. We're fine now. Bertie found a Les Schwab store and the man there was just as nice as the one back home."

Nina sank onto the only free chair in the break room. "You were in a car accident?"

"No. We skidded. Not to worry. We're fine. The new tires are very nice. We went to several estate sales and more antique stores than I can count. We're filling the van with so many beautiful things. You're going to love what we've found."

She kept talking. Nina closed her eyes and rubbed her temples, telling herself that her commitment to eat her brownies one at a time had not made any reference to wine, and when she got home that night, she was taking a bath and having a glass. Then she'd have her breakdown.

Bonnie Wentworth had given birth to her oldest at sixteen. She hadn't settled down when she'd become a mother, and she sure wasn't settled now. Bonnie and her partner, Bertie, traveled the country on "buying trips" for their antique store. Antique being defined very loosely in this case. Junk was probably more accurate, but even Nina avoided the "j" word as much as possible.

She drew in a breath as her mother talked about a hand-made doll Bertie had found.

"Mom, Tanya was caught trying to sell inventory to Jerry this morning."

Bonnie paused. "No," she said, sounding stunned. "I don't believe it."

Nina resisted the need to point out that Bonnie never be-lieving it was the main problem.

"This is why I want to do the interviewing. Or, if not me, then at least let Bertie do it."

"Are you sure she wasn't selling something of her own?" Bonnie asked. "She seemed like such a nice girl. I hate to think of her doing something like that."

"Me, too. You know this means the store's closed." Again.

There was silence. "Do you want us to come back? We could be there in a couple of days."

"No. I'll find someone."

Nina knew that if she asked, her mother would come home and run the store while they found someone. But then Nina would feel guilty, like she did now. And for the life of her, she couldn't figure out why.

"Sweetheart, you take on too much."

Nina opened her mouth and closed it. Right. Mostly be-cause no one else was here to do it. "Mom, it's fine. But we need someone in the store who's responsible and can work without stealing."

"You're right. There must be someone, and I'm sure you'll find her."

"I will. Did you call on the roof? Is the guy coming out to fix it?"

"I did call." Her mother sounded triumphant. "It's taken care of."

"Great. Thanks."

"You're welcome. I love you, sweetheart."

"I love you, too, Mom."

"I'll call in a few days. By then we should know when we'll be home. Bye."

Nina heard the click and knew her mother had hung up. Before she returned to the goodie bags, she called the local paper.

"Hi, Ellen, it's Nina Wentworth."

The old woman cackled. "Let me guess. You need someone to work at Blackberry Preserves. I have the information from the last ad, which is the same as the one before and the one before that. Want me to run it?"

Nina glanced out the window again. The storm clouds were closer. She could see a bit of the Sound and wondered if she got on a boat right now, where she would end up.

"That would be great," she said instead. "Thanks, Ellen."

"You know, Nina, you've got to stop letting your mama hire people for that store."

Nina tightened her grip on the phone. "Yes, I know."

Nina stared at the items in the box. The candlesticks were silver and actually worth something. There were also several pieces of jewelry, a few with gems. The painting was a cheap reproduction and worth less than the frame, but still…

Jerry nodded as she inventoried the haul. "I was thinking the same thing," he told her. "How could a girl smart enough to know what to steal be dumb enough to come to me? Why didn't she just drive over the bridge and head toward Seattle? Another forty minutes in the car and she could have had the cash and been on her way."

"That's exactly what I was thinking," she admitted. "But I'm glad she was impatient. Was Sam Payton by?"

"Yup. He took pictures. He said he needs to know what the candlesticks are worth." Jerry, a chubby, balding man in his sixties, nodded knowingly. "If it's over five grand, then Miss Tanya has committed a Class B felony. If she gets the maximum, it's a ten year prison sentence with a twenty thousand dollar fine."

"You're very knowledgeable about felonies and the law."

"In my business, it pays to know that sort of thing."

Nina picked up the box of items from the store. "I'm going to have to call Sam, aren't I? He's going to tell me I can't sell these until the case against Tanya is settled, right?"

"I wouldn't be surprised," Jerry told her.

Great. So the only items of value in the store were now going to be held hostage. She started for the door. "Thanks, Jerry."

"You're welcome. Hire better people."

"I'll do my best."

He buzzed the door so she could get out.

Nina crossed the small parking lot and opened her trunk. As she walked around to the driver's side, she felt the first drops of rain.

Although the house was only a few blocks away, she was going to have to go by the store and put up a sign explaining it would be closed for the next few days. She should also see what else might have been stolen. This may not have been Tanya's first attempt. Tomorrow she would talk to Sam and find out what charges were being brought against the former employee.

Nina started her car and headed for the bay. Blackberry Preserves might not be classy, but it had a killer location, right across from the small beach. In the summer, there was lots of tourist traffic, which was what helped the business survive the slower winter months. But this time of year—

Two things happened at once. The rain went from light to pounding, and her car engine died. Completely.

Not sure what to do, Nina steered to the side of the road and pulled onto the shoulder before she lost all momentum. After putting the car in gear, she started it again, or tried to. The engine turned over, but wouldn't catch. She checked the fuel, and her tank was just over half-full. What on earth?

Beyond how to put in gas and where to take it for service, what she knew about cars and their systems could fill a shot glass and still leave room for the shot. She was stuck.

She glanced down at her shirt. "You've failed me, Betty."

The cartoon didn't answer.

Nina got out her cell phone only to see she was in one of the dead spots on the island. Between the somewhat-isolated location and the hilly terrain, there were cell phone wastelands, with no signal to be had.

So much for phoning a friend or Mike's Auto Repair. Because while Mike would come get her and give her a lift home, he wasn't psychic.

She leaned her head back and tried to tell herself that a walk in cold rain wouldn't kill her. She only needed to get to a part of the island with a signal. Later, when she got home, she would have that bath and glass of wine. But being rational didn't take away her desire to scream or cry. Or just once want to hand this problem over to someone else. But there wasn't anyone else, there was her.

She couldn't remember a time when it hadn't been her. She'd been taking care of her mother since she'd been old enough to ask, "Mommy, are you okay?" She'd taken care of her baby sister and the family business, and now she was still

doing it all. Worrying about the store, picking up crap stolen
by employees her mother had hired and…

She gripped the steering wheel with both hands and tried
to shake it. "Drive, you stupid car! Drive!"

She stopped when her hands started to hurt, then separated
her car key from the house keys on the chain and tucked the
car key under the driver's seat. Then she put her purse over
her shoulder and stepped out into the rain. She was soaked in
a matter of seconds.

The good news was, if anyone she knew drove by, he or
she would stop and give her a lift home. The bad news was,
it was dinnertime on a very small island and the odds of rescue were slim.

Nina started the long walk toward some kind of signal.
With each step she told herself this was good. Forced exercise. Plus shivering burned calories. It wasn't cold enough that
she had to worry about hypothermia. But her clothes clung
to her in a way that wasn't flattering, and her pants were rubbing on her thighs. She was pretty sure she was going to get
a rash. That would be attractive. Too bad she wasn't a blog-
ger, because this would make for a great blog. She could title
it Nina Wentworth's Very Bad Day.

Fifteen minutes later, Nina had started working through
the five stages of grief. She'd quickly moved from denial to
anger and thought that might be a good place to stay. Her entire body was chilled except for the friction where her thighs
rubbed together. She was shaking, dripping and more miserable than she'd ever been in her life. She checked her cell,
but there still wasn't a signal. At this rate, she would be home
before she picked up reception.

She heard a car coming up behind her and turned quickly.
She didn't care who it was—she would happily get in with a

stranger, if necessary. Not that there were many on the island this time of year.

She squinted against the rain, trying to figure out if she recognized the vehicle. It was blue and shiny. A new BMW, she thought, as the car slowed. No one she knew drove one of those. The driver pulled up next to her and rolled down the passenger window.

"Hey, are you—" The man stared at her for a second. "Nina?"

Although she'd been reaching for the door handle, now she pulled back. The unfairness of the situation made her want to raise her hands to the sky and ask what she could possibly have done to deserve this.

"Nina?" he asked again. "You're soaked. Get in. I'll take you home."

But she couldn't, she thought, staring into those green eyes, remembering how they'd softened when he'd promised he would love her forever. Only he hadn't. Dylan Harrington instead had abandoned her and their forever love his third year of college. He'd left the island and never come back. Well, he'd visited his family occasionally. But he'd never bothered with her again. Not once. Worse, he'd said *she* was the reason he'd ended the relationship. Yet another person in her life who had been unwilling to take responsibility for his actions.

"Nina, get in. It's freezing."

"I'd rather walk," she said and turned away.

Lifting her head proudly, ignoring the rain stinging her eyes and the burning of her chafed thighs, she proceeded to do just that.

Chapter Two

✦

"NINA, GET IN the car."

She wanted to ignore him. Really she did. But his tone was insistent, and the Dylan she remembered had a way of taking matters into his own hands.

She closed her eyes and wished him away. But the steady hum of the car creeping alongside proved that plan didn't have much chance of working.

"Do you know how ridiculous this is?" he asked loudly.

Unfortunately, she did. She also knew that in the end she would get in the car because she couldn't stand to be this wet and cold any longer. But why did it have to be him? Why not some well-dressed, quiet serial killer? Other people got strangled, but not her. Nooooo. She got the ex-love of her life.

"Fine," she said, turning and walking over to the passenger side. The door opened smoothly, and she plopped her wet self on the leather seat.

For a second she was engulfed in the scent of new-car smell and the warmth blasting from heating vents. Bliss, she thought, pushing her dripping hair out of her face. Then she turned and once again met Dylan's green eyes.

His expression was an uncomfortable combination of concern and amusement. Damn him, she thought. Whenever he had crossed her mind over the past decade, she'd envisioned their first meeting would be something she could plan for. That she would be perfectly dressed and answer questions with smooth but subtle one-liners that would leave him impressed by her wit and chagrined about letting her go. She hadn't thought she would be dripping wet and fighting thigh-burn.

"What happened?" he asked.

To them? To her?

"To your car," he clarified when she didn't speak.

"I have no idea. It stopped running. I'll call the garage when I get home."

"Then, let's get you there."

He didn't bother asking where she lived. No doubt his parents would have kept him informed on the small island's permanent population. Had he asked he would have been informed that, yes, she was still living with her mother. Not that she couldn't afford her own place. She could. It was just that when it came to her mother and taking care of the store and everything else that fell on her shoulders, somehow it had seemed easier to stay put.

They drove in silence for about two minutes. She shifted uncomfortably, aware of her wetness on his pristine leather seats.

"So, you're back," she murmured into the awkward silence. At least it was awkward on her part. She had no idea what he was thinking.

"Uh-huh. I finished my fellowship a few weeks ago. Went to Europe for a vacation, then came here."

A European vacation? She thought about how she'd spent

the past month—as she'd spent the past seven or eight years. Working, dealing with whatever disaster her mother created, checking on the store. She had friends she hung out with, and she'd recently joined a book club, but now that she thought about it, her life lacked any level of excitement.

Not that she cared about impressing Dylan Harrington, she told herself. She didn't.

"You're still going to join your dad's practice?" she asked, already knowing the answer to the question.

"Yes."

"I thought you might change your mind."

"Me, too." He flashed her a smile. "But I didn't want to break his heart."

Because Dylan's dad had spent the past decade waiting to say, "My son, the doctor." Once he could, it was something he repeated endlessly. He'd told everyone who would listen that Dylan would be joining his practice. She supposed most fathers wanted their sons to go into the family business. Doctor and Son, she thought, imagining the sign outside the front door.

"You stopped working for him," he said.

She glanced at him, then away. "Yes."

Until last fall, she'd been one of Dr. Harrington's nurses. Mostly because he was the only doctor in town and she'd hadn't wanted to commute to the mainland. But with Dylan potentially returning, she'd wondered about job security. Fortunately, Andi had moved to town and decided to open her pediatric practice, giving Nina the perfect job.

"Like working with kids?" he asked, obviously aware of where she'd landed.

"Yes. There are enough families on the island to keep us busy, but not so many that we're swamped. Andi's great to work with."

"Did you leave because of me?" he asked, stopping at the corner and checking before making the turn.

A blunt question she hadn't expected. "I was excited about the opportunity with Andi," she said, sidestepping the issue. In truth, she would have left regardless. There was no way she could spend day after day with Dylan. Talk about weird. He'd been her first boyfriend, her first time, her first broken heart. He was a good-looking guy, a doctor, and it was just a matter of time until he fell in love and got married. Not that she wanted him for herself, but she sure didn't want anyone thinking she was hanging around, pining.

She leaned back in the seat and sighed. Why hadn't she planned better? This would be so much less awkward if she'd married some rich guy, preferably with a yacht. Or moved to Tibet to open an orphanage. Something remarkable and important. She could at least be studying to be a neurosurgeon. Instead, she was a nurse in a pediatrician's office, and her romantic past had little to recommend it. She had been married once. For five days. Not exactly her proudest moment.

She and Dylan were supposed to have been doctors together, she thought grimly. That's what they had talked about. Going to medical school and opening a practice. She hadn't decided on her specialty, and he'd thought he would go into emergency medicine.

But then they'd broken up, and somehow finding the money to follow her dreams had become impossible. Between dealing with her mom and her baby sister, the store and everything else, she'd lost her way. Nursing school had been so much more practical. She'd only needed two years away at a four-year university. She couldn't remember making the decision—somehow life had happened.

Dylan pulled into the driveway of her house. Rain still pounded on the windshield, and she wasn't looking forward to the dash into the house. Not with her scrubs clinging to every bulge and him watching. Just as unfortunate, she could see the general shabbiness of the house from where she sat. It hadn't changed at all in the past ten years. It needed paint and a new roof. She'd had plans for both, but a plumbing disaster last October had pretty much sucked up her savings.

"Thanks for the ride," she said, turning to him and offering a smile she hoped looked pleasant and confident. "Great timing. It would have been a long, ugly walk home. I'm sorry for dripping on your seats."

"They'll be fine. Come on. Let's get you inside."

Before she could respond, he was getting out of the driver's side and walking around the car. What? He was coming with her?

She quickly scrambled out and met him on the walkway. "I'm fine. You don't need to come in. Seriously. Go on with what you were doing. You saved me from the long walk home. That should be enough for one day."

He gave her an easy smile and put his hand on the small of her back. "For someone soaking wet and cold, you're sure arguing a lot."

Then they were moving toward the front door, and she was opening it. As she stepped inside, she kicked off her soggy shoes. Dylan moved past her. She tugged off her socks and dropped her purse on the tiles of the foyer before walking barefoot into the living room.

She was aware of several things at once. First, there was a suspicious dampness in the stained ceiling in the corner. As she watched, a single drop fell onto the carpet below. Which meant her mother *hadn't* called about the roof. Tim, their general handyman, was always timely about taking care of whatever crisis they had. So if the roof was still leaking, he hadn't been told he was needed.

Second, she realized she couldn't remember the last time a man had walked into their house. Well, a man-man, not a service guy. Dylan looked tall and masculine. Very out of place in a room crowded with too much furniture and "treasures" from the store. Every corner, every shelf and all surfaces were littered with figurines, wooden or glass boxes, picture frames and vases that her mother couldn't stand to sell. In Bonnie's mind, some objects were meant to be shared with the world and others were meant to be saved for family.

Last, and maybe most unsettling, was how having Dylan standing in the living room made *her* see just how scruffy everything had become.

The sofa was old and worn, with permanent dents in the cushions where they sat night after night. Nicks and dings marred the coffee table. The lampshades had faded from cream to a dingy yellow.

Nina stared at the room as if she'd never seen it before, shocked by how she'd ceased to see what was all around her. For a second, she had the realization that her hopes and dreams had suffered the same kind of neglect, becoming invisible due to inattention. Sadness swept through—the loss nearly painful enough to make her gasp.

"I'll wait while you get changed," Dylan said, walking over to one of the chairs and sitting down, as if he planned to stay a while.

She blinked at him. Why? Then she felt the damp chill of her clothes and water dripping down her back from her hair.

"Sure," she told him, then hurried toward the hall, feeling the burn of wet cotton rubbing against her skin.

Ten minutes later she was in jeans and a sweatshirt. She'd done the best she could with her hair, towel drying it before combing it. She wasn't going to take the time to blow-dry it. That would imply… She wasn't sure what, but either way, she wasn't going there. She shoved her feet into flats and went back to the living room.

Dylan sat where she'd left him. He stood as she came into the room. "Better?"

"Much." She shoved her hands into her pockets. "You didn't have to stay."

"I thought we could catch up. I haven't seen you in a long time."

Simple words that genuinely confounded her. The obvious question was why? Why would he want to catch up? They hadn't seen each other in forever, and aside from living on the island, they had nothing in common. Not anymore. Maybe not ever.

If only he wasn't so tall, she thought, gesturing to the kitchen. Back in high school, Dylan had been what her mother had called dreamy. Now he was successful, polite, employed and still good-looking. The green eyes and strong jaw, not to mention broad shoulders, probably ensured he had a flock of available women at the ready. She wondered why he hadn't married one of them.

She paused in the middle of the kitchen. No way she was going to bother feeling ashamed of the worn linoleum or ancient cabinets. There had been enough humiliation for one day.

"Wine?" she asked, heading for the small rack on the counter. She pulled out a bottle of red before he could reply. "Or I could make you coffee."

"Wine sounds good."

She collected the opener, but before she could do more than reach for the bottle, he was at her side.

"Allow me."

Such a gentleman, she thought, not sure if she was impressed or annoyed. His mother must be so proud.

He pulled out the cork with a lot less effort than she usually needed, then poured them each a glass. Nina had a brief thought that she should keep some kind of snacky thing around to offer guests. She had kept the leftover brownies, but she wasn't about to share those. The wine would have to be enough.

She led the way back to the living room and claimed a corner of the sofa. She kicked off her shoes and tucked her feet under her. Dylan took the chair opposite and raised his glass. "To old friends."

She raised her eyebrows. "I assume you mean that in the spirit of friends you haven't seen in a while and not 'old' friends."

He grinned. "Exactly." He took a sip of the wine. "Nice."

"Thanks."

"So how are things?"

She thought briefly of Tanya and the inventory theft, of the leak in the roof and how she still had to call about getting her car towed. "Great."

"I heard your sister moved out of state."

"Averil lives in Mischief Bay. That's in California, south of Santa Monica."

"Right. Is she in college?"

Nina smiled. "She graduated a long time ago, Dylan. Averil's married. She's a writer for *California Girl* magazine."

One brow rose. "Married? Little Averil? I can't believe it."

"I know, but it happened."

"Any kids?"

"Not yet." She gazed at him over her glass. "You're not married."

"Was that a question or a statement?"

"A statement." She gave him a genuine smile. "Are you forgetting where we are? This island is the definition of a small town. Of course I know everything about you."

His expression turned wry. "I hope not *everything*."

Probably not, she admitted to herself. But there had been a time when she had been the keeper of his secrets and, in theory, his heart.

She'd been fifteen when she'd fallen in love with Dylan. A sophomore in high school. He'd been a senior. She'd tried to conceal her crush, but she'd been unable to look away whenever he was near. One day, at lunch, he'd walked up to her.

When's your birthday? he'd asked.

In three weeks.

His green eyes had crinkled with laughter. *You'll be sixteen? Uh-huh.*

I'll wait.

Because fifteen is too young? she'd asked. *You do realize that nothing about me will change in the next three weeks. I'll be exactly who I am.*

He shrugged. *I'll wait.*

He had, and on her sixteenth birthday he'd asked her out. And he'd kissed her, like no one else had.

There'd been a couple of other kisses before him. Fumbling, stupid kisses at parties where games were used to hide the awkwardness of adolescence. Those kisses had been insignificant. Kissing Dylan had rocked her world.

From that date, they'd been a couple. He'd graduated and gone to college and they'd stayed together. It was when she'd been a few months from graduating high school herself that the trouble had started.

"When do you start work?" she asked as her mind returned to the present. Polite questions for a safer topic.

"Monday."

"Are you excited?"

His eyebrows rose. "I'm not sure I would describe myself as excited."

"Your dad is."

Because there was nothing the senior Dr. Harrington wanted more than his son to join his practice. He'd talked about it from before Dylan was born. Or so the Harrington family lore went.

"I know. He's been telling me over and over." Dylan sipped his wine. "He's already designed new business cards."

There was something in the way he said the words. "Didn't you want to come back?"

"Sure."

She studied him, not sure she believed what he was saying. "You had an obligation. There's a difference."

Dylan glanced around the living room. "Where's your mom?"

"In Montana, on a buying trip."

His mouth curved up at the corners. "I remember those and her love for the treasures she found."

"She does like going through other people's stuff."

"She runs an antique store."

An exalted name for Blackberry Preserves, but her mother would enjoy it.

"She's bringing back less junk these days," she admitted. "Bertie helps with that. She has a good eye for a bargain."

"Who's Bertie?"

Nina raised her chin. "My mom's lover."

Dylan's expression didn't change. "I thought I heard something about that from my parents. I'm impressed. When did she come out?"

Nina had been hoping for a little more reaction. Something that could make her dislike him. His acceptance was disappointing. "Just over ten years ago. Bertie started coming over.

Averil and I thought they were friends. Then Bertie stayed the night a few times. One day Bertie took me aside and said she wanted to move in. She asked if that was okay."

She smiled at the memory. "I like Bertie a lot. She's very stable."

"Meaning you don't have to be the only grown-up in the room?"

She nodded. Dylan would know all about that. He'd seen what she'd gone through. Sometimes she wondered if knowing about how difficult her family had been was one of the reasons he'd broken up with her.

"It helps." She shifted on the sofa. "Enough about what's going on in my family. What about you? Are you staying with your folks?"

He shook his head. "I came to the island a couple of months ago and bought a condo by the marina. I closed on it last week. I'll be moving in over the next few days."

He continued talking about the move, but she wasn't listening. A condo at the marina? No doubt one of those new, fancy ones. With granite counters and a full-time concierge.

Ridiculous, she thought, her gaze dropping to the brown shag carpet that had to be at least fifteen years old. This was Blackberry Island. The UPS guy just left the packages on the porch.

She was aware that he was clean and smelled good. He looked better. Dylan had left and followed his dreams and now he was a successful, happy doctor. She was stuck in a rut, and for the life of her, she couldn't say exactly how that had happened. How had ten years passed? How had she never made her break? Was it circumstances, or was she responsible? She had a bad feeling it was the latter.

"It's late," she said abruptly, coming to her feet.

Dylan looked startled for a second, then put down his wine and rose. "Sure. It was good to see you, Nina."

"You, too. Thanks for the ride home. I really appreciate it."

"No problem."

She walked him to the door, murmured the appropriate polite goodbye, then shut the door behind him. When she was alone, she returned to the sofa and sank onto the cushions. Her life was a disaster, she thought grimly. Or if not a disaster, then at least pitiful, which might be worse.

Chapter Three

❧

THE ART OF The Perfect First Kiss. Averil Stanton paused to reflect on the headline, then shook her head. No way. *California Girl* magazine catered to girls, ages thirteen to nineteen. Talking about a *first* kiss was too limiting.

She continued to stare at the screen, then tried again. Every First Kiss is Different. Better, she thought. Because there was always a new first kiss. At least for them. Once you got married, the odds of a new first kiss were slim. So was the chance of a new first anything. Though she wouldn't share that with her readers. They were young and hopeful and why depress them?

She paused to sip her tea. Not that she wasn't happily married, she thought. Kevin was great, and she loved their life. She lived six minutes from the Pacific Ocean, in Mischief Bay—an eclectic Southern California beach town. She had her work and her friends and—

"Stop it," Averil said aloud, then slammed her laptop shut and stood. She crossed to the window and stared out at the view of the side yard. It consisted of little more than the neighbor's fence and the recycling bin, but was apparently more fascinating than her work.

She couldn't focus, she thought grimly. Couldn't write. Whatever was causing this was happening more and more. In the past few months, she'd turned in every article closer to deadline. Her boss hadn't said anything, but Averil knew she would eventually. Digital content had to be produced regularly, and if Averil didn't step it up, there were a hundred younger hopefuls ready to take her place. The print version of the magazine only came out once a month, but the online presence needed daily updates.

She walked to the battered armchair in the corner and dropped onto the mashed cushion. Maybe she should go see her doctor. Vitamins might help. Or hypnosis. Lately nothing had felt right. She was restless and couldn't say why. Uneasy without a cause.

She glanced outside again. Maybe a run would bring her out of her funk. She'd already exercised that morning, but a run on the beach might clear her head. Or she could go to the mall and—

"Averil?"

She looked up and saw Kevin standing in the doorway to her small office. After dinner she'd excused herself, saying she had to work. Something she was doing more and more, she thought. Disappearing to her private space, only to realize she still couldn't focus, couldn't think, couldn't do anything.

Now she saw there was a tightness to his face. She came to her feet. "Are you okay?"

"I decided to sharpen the knives in the kitchen."

Her gaze dropped to his hand where a fresh bandage covered his middle finger. "Is it deep?"

"No. It's fine. But while I was looking for a bandage, I found something else." He stepped more fully into her office and held up a small, round, plastic container. "We'd agreed to start trying for a baby, Averil. Why are you still taking birth control pills?"

Averil felt instant heat on her cheeks as she instinctively looked for a place to hide. Or a way to escape. As Kevin stood between her and the door and she wasn't willing to try leaping out the window, she was trapped.

"It's not what you think," she said loudly, even as she knew it was. "Having a baby is a big decision. You can't expect me to get pregnant just like that. It's not fair or reasonable."

She tried to stop the words, knowing they could come back to bite her in the butt later. Because Kevin was nothing if not fair. They had talked…endlessly. For weeks and weeks. They'd made lists of the pros and cons and had mutually agreed it was time to start their family. Only she couldn't seem to stop taking the pills. Every morning she told herself she was ready, and every morning, she carefully swallowed the next tiny pill.

"You're still on birth control."

He made the words a statement, but she nodded anyway. She braced herself for the fight, but instead of saying anything, he turned and left.

Averil stood in her office, trying to steady her breathing, wondering what would happen now. Finally she went down the short hallway and into the other spare bedroom. The one he used as his office.

He sat at his desk, the disk of pills next to his keyboard. He wasn't typing, but he didn't look up at her, either.

She'd met Kevin six years ago. She'd been in her senior year of college. A journalism major, sent to report on a street fair in Mischief Bay. Not her usual assignment. Averil had been the go-to reporter for her college newspaper, accustomed to hard-hitting stories on criminals or cover-ups. But one of the junior reporters had flaked out, and she'd agreed to fill in.

She was just pretty enough to be used to a lot of male attention. Tall and blonde, which made her practically an indigenous species on a California beach. She'd been taking notes and shooting pictures, when a guy had approached her.

He'd been kind of cute, about her height, skinny, with the intense look of someone with more intelligence than the average man-on-the-street. He'd held out her camera bag and said, *You left this on the bench back there.*

She'd smiled and thanked him, then had playfully asked, *Are you going to hit on me now?*

He'd shaken his head. *No, but I will tell you that you shouldn't use autofocus in this setting. It's letting in too much light, and you'll lose contrast in the scene.*

An unusual response. She'd studied him more closely, taking in the gold flecks in his brown eyes and shape of his mouth. He'd lacked the deep tan of a surfer—no surprise there. Engineer, she thought. Or computer science major.

You do like girls, right? she'd asked.

He'd smiled at her, then. A slow, sexy smile that had made her toes curl in her Keds and caused the noise around them to fade into the background.

I'll take the pictures, he'd said, reaching for the camera. *You make your notes.*

I'm writing an article for The Daily Bruin. She paused. *That's the paper at UCLA.*

I know what it is.

You're out of college?

Yup. Just got a job at a software company here in Mischief Bay. He'd slipped the strap around his neck and started making adjustments on the camera. *I went to MIT.*

Smart, great smile and he had a job. Things were looking up. *I'm Averil,* she'd said.

Kevin.

He hadn't hit on her, but he had asked her out. It had been three dates before he'd kissed her and nearly four months before they'd had sex. The day after she'd graduated, he'd proposed. She'd said yes to him and a full-time job at *California Girl* magazine.

"About the pills," she said, stepping into his office.

"You said you were ready. You said you wanted to have kids. Have you changed your mind?"

"No. It's just..." She took a step forward. "There's a lot going on."

"What's going on now that isn't going on all the time? We're settled in the house, we have money in the bank. You have your job and your novel. What are you waiting for?"

She wished he hadn't mentioned the novel. The one she was supposed to be writing. The one that was little more than a few notes and a hundred and forty-seven false starts. Saying you were going to write a novel was easy. Actually writing it—not so much.

"I'm feeling pressured," she said, hearing the defensiveness in her voice and not liking it. "It's so soon."

"Our fifth anniversary is in a few months. It wasn't exactly a shotgun wedding."

"No, but..."

He looked at her then, his brown eyes filled with what could only be betrayal. He looked as if she'd cut out his heart.

"Kevin, no," she breathed as she started toward him. "I'm—"

He waited. "You're what?"

"I'm sorry."

"Nina told you to wait, didn't she?"

Averil had to hold back the overpowering need to stomp her foot. "You always bring up Nina. Why do you hate my sister?"

"You know I like Nina a lot. I bring her up because she's always with us."

"That's ridiculous. She's a thousand miles away."

"No, she's not. She's the voice in your head. You talk to her every day for weeks until you two have a fight, and then you complain about her every day until you two make up. She's the opinion you care about most." He returned his attention to his computer screen. "It's never you and me making a decision. It's always the three of us."

She wanted to tell him he was wrong, but he wasn't. Her and Nina's last blowup had been about three weeks before, and they hadn't spoken since. Funny—Averil couldn't even remember what they'd been fighting about.

She looked at Kevin. She could feel his pain. He wanted more, and as much as she wanted to give it to him, she couldn't. The problem with Kevin was that he saw her as more capable than she could ever be. But how was she supposed to tell the man in her life to expect less of her?

"I need more time," she told him. "Please, stop pressuring me."

She waited, expecting him to say that asking her to keep her word wasn't exactly applying brute force, but he only nodded.

"I love you," she whispered.

He looked at her then. "Sometimes I'm not so sure."

The next morning, Nina woke without the alarm. One of the perks of a Saturday morning. She'd had a restless night. While she'd avoided the brownies calling her name, she'd given in to the wine. Worse, she'd dreamed of Dylan on and off. Probably the result of seeing him and then watching *The Day After Tomorrow*.

She would guess that most women remembering a breakup went for a more classic romantic comedy or a movie that would make them cry. She would have, as well, but it was right after seeing *The Day After Tomorrow* that Dylan had broken up with her. She'd been making a point on global warming, and he'd announced he wasn't going to be coming back to the island on weekends anymore.

Now the shots of ice and snow were firmly linked in her brain with the pain of losing the only man she'd ever loved. In her pathos, she'd noticed that the sheer size of the storm had matched the vastness of the emptiness filling her heart. Dylan had filled so much of her world, and now he was going to be gone.

All this time later, he was back. Not that it was going to be an issue for her, she told herself as she sat up and stretched. It wasn't as if he'd sought her out. Their meeting had been completely random. Even on an island this small, she was unlikely to run into him very much.

For the best, she thought, standing by the bed. She would simply—

"Crap. My car!"

She'd never called Mike about it. Never asked him to tow it to his shop and start work on it. All because she'd been distracted by a handsome man from her past. Dylan had a lot to answer for.

She glanced at the clock and saw it was nearly eight-thirty. Which meant Mike's repair shop had been open for an hour. Saturdays were busy for him, and she was pretty sure someone else would have gotten the beat-up truck that was his loaner car.

She walked into the kitchen and picked up the phone. Mike's business card was one of a dozen held to the refrigerator by a tacky magnet designed for the tourist trade. No surprise to anyone, Nina's mother collected them.

Mike answered on the third ring. "What?"

"It's Nina Wentworth."

"Hey, listen, I'm good but I'm not that good. I'll get to it later today. I'm guessing the fuel injector, but I mean it. That's a guess."

Nina blinked several times. "Excuse me?"

"Your car. That's why you're calling, right? You're not going to try to sell me any damn magazine subscriptions, are you?"

"What? No." She walked over to the kitchen table and sat down. "My car is there?"

"Sure. I got a call yesterday just before closing to go pick it up. I had Benny drop off the loaner last night. You telling me you don't know about this?"

She stood and walked into the living room. As she looked out the front window, she saw a battered pickup in the driveway.

Dylan, she thought, unable to believe he would have bothered. But there wasn't another explanation.

"I, ah... Thanks, Mike," she said. "I'm sorry to bother you. Let me know when it's ready and I'll be in."

"Sure thing. Probably Monday. You can come on your lunch break."

"Sounds great."

She hung up, more than a little confused by what had happened. She checked the window again. Yup, there it was. The loaner.

She put down the phone and walked into her bedroom. She had a mile-long list of things to get done today, and none of them had involved mulling over an old boyfriend. Dylan had been nice. That spoke well of his character. The fact that she didn't *want* him to be nice was her own issue.

By nine-thirty, Nina had arrived at Blackberry Preserves. As it was a Saturday, she changed the sign to read Open—not that she was expecting many customers. It was too early in the season for a lot of tourists, and locals tended not to browse on the weekends. She flipped on the light switch by the door, then walked through narrow pathways to the office in the back. After tucking her purse into a desk drawer, she turned up the heat and started a pot of coffee.

In theory, the shop's inventory was supposed to be computerized. In reality, more than half the stock moved in and out without ever being accounted for. Bonnie's buying trips were done with cash and accounted for with mostly handwritten receipts. Nina had known that one day she was going to have to tackle the problem, but she'd been putting it off as long as possible. And that was going to continue, she thought, returning to the front of the store.

To the left, old wooden shelves held an impressive collection of vintage lunch boxes. Everything from Hopalong Cassidy to early Batman to My Little Pony. Some were battered and worn, but others looked as if they'd never been used at all. A couple still contained their thermoses.

Bonnie loved lunch boxes because children were generally happy. That was her actual logic. She bought the lunch boxes to share her joy in that fact with others. The knowledge that they collected more than they sold didn't seem to bother her.

Three large display cabinets held figurines of all kinds. Lladro and Hummel, along with those from more obscure artists. Even as a kid, Nina hadn't liked the tiny statues. She'd always thought they were watching her with evil intent. The same with the antique dolls. But the vintage clothes were fun. They were dusty and smelled funny, but she and Averil had enjoyed playing dress-up.

She walked to a rack of ball gowns from the 1940s. She'd loved dancing around, a rusty tiara on her head.

You be the queen and I'll be the princess, Averil had told her.

Nina had resisted, saying there could be two princesses. Even at nine, she'd understood that being the queen meant taking responsibility. All she wanted was to escape for a few minutes. But Averil had been stubborn.

You're my queen, Neenie. You'll always be the queen.

She touched another dress, remembering her sister claiming she could tell whether or not the wearer had been happy simply by the scent of the fabric. As everything smelled dusty to Nina, she couldn't decide if her sister had been telling the truth. But Averil would only wear castoffs from happy people and carefully inspected all new inventory.

Nina supposed that everyone had strange memories from his or her childhood. Hers were about pockets of chaos followed by blissful periods of calm. Bonnie had been big on love, but not so much on structure. If there was no one to watch the girls, she thought nothing of taking them out of school for weeks at a time when she went on her buying trips.

When Nina turned twelve, she informed her mom that she was old enough to be left alone. She'd been armed with a list of reasons why she should be trusted by herself, but Bonnie had simply agreed with her. The following year, Bonnie had deposited Averil in her care, as well. She'd made sure the house was stocked with food before she headed off. There was money in the drawer and the checkbook. Nina had been faking her mom's signature on checks for years, so paying the bills wasn't a problem.

Nina paused by a desk lamp that Bonnie swore was genuine Tiffany and touched the smooth, colored glass. Memories lurked in this store, she thought. Hiding in corners like dust bunnies. As she couldn't figure out how to get rid of them, she avoided them and this place. Which probably explained why Tanya had stolen. There was no one watching her.

The front door opened. Nina tensed, wondering if Dylan

would be stopping by. She'd phoned to thank him for his help, but her call had gone directly to voice mail. She still wasn't sure if she was disappointed or relieved.

But he wasn't the one who walked in. Instead, it was a well-dressed woman with short, dark hair. She was about five-five, with dark blue eyes and a wide smile.

"Are you Nina?" she asked.

"Yes."

"Great. I'm Cindy Yoo. I'm here about the job. I saw it online last night, and I'm very interested."

In reality, shutting down the store made the most sense. Unfortunately, that wasn't Nina's decision to make. She didn't feel prepared for an interview, but they had to hire someone.

"Thanks for coming by," she said. "There are application forms in the back."

Cindy withdrew a folder from her large leather bag. "I brought a copy of my resume, along with several letters of recommendation."

Nina took the papers. "That's very professional of you," she said slowly. As far as she knew, no applicant had ever come in with a resume before.

"I've got coffee going in the back," she said, motioning to the open doorway. "Want some?"

"Sure."

Cindy followed her into the office. Nina cleared a stack of invoices off the spare chair, then poured them each a cup.

"Black is fine," Cindy told her, then reached for the mug.

Nina poured her own and settled behind the desk. "I didn't know the ad had gone up already."

"I was online checking when it popped up." Cindy smiled at her. "I'll just say it. I don't have retail experience, but I'm open to learning."

"It's not a complicated business," Nina murmured, studying the other woman. She didn't know all that much about fashion, but she would guess Cindy's clothes were expensive. Her bag seemed to be real leather, and her wedding band was a row of sparkling diamonds.

Cindy pointed to the folder. "I can get more recommendations if you need them. I'm very excited about this opportunity."

Maybe a little too excited? Nina opened the folder and studied her resume.

Cindy had graduated with a degree in history from a university in the San Francisco area. From there she'd become a secretary in a law firm. Four years later, she had been a paralegal in the same firm. That had been followed by a move to Seattle, where she'd done more of the same.

Behind the resume were a half dozen letters of recommendation. All glowing. Each had a phone number and a vow that he or she would hire Cindy back in a second if she was interested.

"Impressive," Nina said, then looked at her. "I'm looking for someone to run the store. It involves managing inventory and selling to customers. I can't help but think you're overqualified."

Cindy clutched her mug in both hands. "To be completely honest, I really need this job. My husband is a few years older than me. I'm his second wife. Our children just left for college. One is at MIT, the other is at Stanford."

So it was a money thing, Nina thought, able to relate to that.

"My husband is Korean. My mother-in-law, while a lovely woman, has a very traditional interest in the life of her only son. Apparently his first wife was also traditional. Perfect, according to my mother-in-law, chosen by the family. She died and he fell in love with me." Cindy paused. "Have you heard about the Tiger Moms?"

Nina frowned. "I think I read a couple of articles. They're focused on their children succeeding."

"Multiply that by a thousand and you'll understand what I'm dealing with. I'm never good enough, and while she doesn't come out and say it, I'm certain her daily prayers include me being dead." Cindy flashed a smile. "Or at the very least, having her son come to his senses and kick me out."

"That could be uncomfortable."

"Yes, it is, and she's coming to live with us." Cindy swallowed. "This week. He's helping her pack right now. I want to be nice to her. But to keep myself sane, I need a job. A place where I can go and think about something else. A place to pour my energy. I swear, I'm highly motivated to learn everything I need to know."

Nina felt her concerns melting away. "You don't have a criminal record, do you?"

Cindy's eyes widened. "I assume that's not a prerequisite?"

"No. Our last employee stole from us. We wouldn't have known except she went to a local pawn shop to fence our property."

"The pawn shop on the island?"

"That's the one."

Cindy leaned back in her chair. "Seriously, that's just dumb. But lucky for you. As to the question, no. I've had two speeding tickets and that's it. I'm a good person. Ask anyone."

Nina grinned. "Except your mother-in-law."

"Right."

Nina handed Cindy the application. "I'm going to check inventory while you fill this out."

She left Cindy in the office. She would ask Sam at the sheriff's office to run a background check on Cindy, then call a couple of references. If that worked out, she was going to hire the woman and consider herself lucky to have found her.

Chapter Four

❧

AVERIL HAD GROWN UP in the Pacific Northwest where the ocean temperature rarely climbed past sixty and that was in the summer. California wasn't all that different. Right on the beach the water warmed up a little in July and August, but only a few hundred yards from shore, the ocean floor plunged and the water was chilly. She'd visited a friend in Florida over a summer break from college and had been shocked by the shallow, warm gulf lapping at the sand. Somehow it just seemed wrong.

Now, as the wind picked up, she tightened the sail, then secured the line. The sun was high in the sky, the brilliant blue reflected in the endless ocean. Once they were on course again, she glanced at Kevin. His sunglasses hid his eyes, and if she couldn't see them, she didn't know what he was thinking.

He'd been quiet lately. If it were anyone but him, she would say pensive.

"Kevin," she began. "Are you mad at me?"

He turned to her, his sunglasses hiding the direct line of his vision. "No. Not mad."

"Then what?"

"Disappointed."

The word was like a slap. She'd always been the object of desire in their relationship. The one who was chased and caught. She loved her husband and did her best to be good to him, but he was the one who came to her. Now she felt the foundation of her world shifting under her.

"About the baby?" she asked, her voice small.

"Some."

The wind whipped her hair around her face. She'd pulled it back in a braid, but a few strands had worked loose. She pushed them out of her eyes and stared at him.

"Are you disappointed in *me?*"

"Yes."

She felt the air rush out of her lungs—as if she'd been kicked in the gut. Panic seized her, making her want to say whatever was necessary for him to take the words back. She couldn't stand for him to reject her.

"I know you're not happy," he continued. "I wonder if I'm the reason."

Relief made it easier to breathe. This wasn't her fault. Okay, she could deal. "You're not," she assured him. "I'm not sure what's wrong."

"Do you still love me?"

"Of course. Don't be silly. We're married."

"What does being married have to do with anything?"

"I don't know. It just does. We're together."

He looked away, then, and the panic returned. This time joined by fear.

"I don't know what you want," he admitted.

"I don't, either. It's not about you, it's about me being uncomfortable and…" She paused as the truth settled over her. A truth she'd been avoiding for a long time now.

"I want to go home."

She said the words without thinking about how they would sound. How *he* would read them. His expression didn't change, but his hand reached for the line, and seconds later the jib collapsed. He pulled in the large sail, keeping it from sinking into the ocean.

"Kevin, no," she said, grabbing his free arm. "Don't do this. I didn't mean right this second."

Because by "home" she'd meant Blackberry Island. They'd both understood that.

He secured the sail, then turned to her. "It's always been home. I've known that. You need to see Nina. What I don't get is you two can't be in the same house for more than a day without fighting. It happens whether she comes to see us or you go to see her. Yet, you can't seem to make a decision without her. Why?"

She didn't have an answer. She wanted to tell him he was wrong, only he wasn't. Nina was... She swallowed. He was right. Nina was the voice in her head.

"I'm sorry," she whispered.

"It's not about an apology. I've given you all I have, Averil. All I am. If it's not enough, I've got nothing left. Maybe I'm not supposed to make you happy. Maybe you're supposed to figure that out on your own."

She wanted to tell him she didn't know how. Didn't understand what being happy meant. Contentment was relatively easy, but happy? Who could say that?

"I don't want you mad at me," she murmured.

"I'm not. I've loved you from the first day I met you, but I can't live in this half life any longer. I need you to be in this with me, or I need you to leave."

The fear returned, but she held on to it, enduring the sense of having her heart ripped into pieces.

"Go see your sister," he continued. "Figure out what you want. I'll wait."

"For how long?"

He removed his sunglasses then. She gazed into his eyes, seeing a combination of sadness and determination. "I don't know. I'll let you know when I'm done wanting you to come home."

Which was fair, but terrifying. What if she waited too long? What if...

And with the questions came the realization that she'd already made up her mind. That whatever the price, she needed to go back home, to find answers. She felt as if everyone else had grown up and moved on, while she'd been stuck.

"I'll be back," she promised. "Please, don't give up on me."

Nina confirmed the charts had been pulled for that day's appointments while she waited for the coffee to fill her cup. She'd had a restless night, no doubt brought on by the phone call from her sister. Averil was coming home for a visit. By herself.

Nina placed the files back on the shelf, then walked toward the break room. Kevin was such a great guy. She could only hope her sister wasn't being an idiot over something inconsequential. Averil could be flighty—a characteristic she had inherited from their mother. Or maybe their father, who had walked away shortly after Averil had been born.

At the time, Nina had been too young to know much more than he was gone. Later, she'd blamed her mother for driving him away. Now, as an adult, she wondered if he had somehow sensed that in her heart, Bonnie preferred to play for the other team. Not that the news excused him for abandoning his daughters.

"Wow—where did all that come from?" she asked aloud.

Obviously she'd been spending too much time on her own, she thought, shaking her head.

She poured a cup of coffee and took a restorative sip. The door at the top of the stairs opened, and Andi appeared.

"Morning," Nina called. "You're looking like you feel better."

"I do! I ate breakfast without having to throw up. I call that progress." Andi reached the main floor and grabbed Nina's mug. She inhaled deeply. "God, I miss coffee. More than wine. I would have thought the wine would be the hardest to give up, but it's not."

She returned the mug and glanced at the stack of files. "Looks like a busy day."

"We had a fairly light schedule, but there were a few last-minute calls."

"There always are on Monday."

They talked about who had phoned for an emergency visit, then Andi led the way to the break room.

"Guess who we had dinner with last night?" Andi asked as she filled a mug with water, then set it in the microwave. Her green eyes danced with amusement.

Nina took a step back. "No way. I don't want to know."

"But I want to tell you and you have to listen." She grinned. "Dr. and Mrs. Harrington and their son, Dylan." Andi clapped her hands together. "I can't believe I've been on the island nearly a year and this is the first time I'm meeting the infamous 'my son, the doctor.'"

Nina groaned. "Seriously? They had you over?"

"Uh-huh. It was great. He's handsome. I wasn't expecting him to be so ruggedly good-looking."

"He's okay."

Andi hesitated. "Is this hard for you? Should I not fill you in on the details and tease you?"

Nina wanted to say yes, but that was ridiculous. She squared her shoulders and instead said, "Of course it's fine. Dylan and I were over years and years ago. I never think about him." Or she hadn't until this past weekend. Which was his fault. If he hadn't stopped to help her, she would have been completely fine. And happy not to have him on the brain.

Because he'd never called back. Not that she wanted him to. She didn't. She wasn't interested. But she would have enjoyed having him call so she could have told him that to his face. Or at least his ear.

"He's single," Andi announced. "I asked if he was seeing anyone."

Nina leaned against the counter and clutched her coffee. "You didn't."

"Why not? I've never met him before. Asking questions is a part of polite conversation. He didn't have a date, so I asked if he'd left someone special behind, and he said no. It was a natural bridge to 'Are you seeing anyone?' He said he wasn't." Her smile was smug. "So it's a clear field."

Nina held in a groan. "I don't want a clear field. I'm not interested. What part of 'it's been decades' doesn't make sense to you?"

"It's been only one decade and you were both young." Andi pulled the mug out of the microwave and dropped in her tea bag. "Oh, and his parents mentioned that they'd been instrumental in your breakup. They feel bad about that."

Nina felt a tic starting under her right eye. "You talked about me?"

"Not a lot. But I think it's interesting, don't you?"

"That my boyfriend let his parents dictate his love life? No. That's not interesting." Not that she was surprised by the admission. Dylan's parents hadn't worried at first. Nina would guess they'd assumed, once he got to college, the relationship would naturally end. But it hadn't. He'd come home on weekends, and they'd spent breaks together. By the summer after his second year of college, the elder Harringtons had been pressuring them both. Nina hadn't been about to give in, but Dylan had finally ended things with her.

Which she supposed she could accept. What had really hurt was he'd tried to make it *her* fault. He'd said… She reminded herself it didn't matter what he'd said.

Andi pulled out the tea bag and set it in the sink. "He was a kid."

"He was twenty."

"Still, he wasn't completely mature or he wouldn't have let you go." She smiled. "I liked him. He seems intelligent without being annoying about it."

Nina knew that was a reference to Andi's parents, who were both brilliant. "I'm not going to be dating Dylan."

"Why not? You're single. He's single. What if the flame still burns?"

"There's no flame. There's not even ash. I'm sure Dylan is a great guy." After all, he'd stopped to help her long before he knew who she was. Which meant he'd been willing to have a stranger drip on his expensive leather seats. "But I'm not looking to get involved with him."

"You never date," Andi started. "It would be fun for you to go out. I'm not trying to be pushy, but why not—"

"You are being pushy. I can find my own guy."

Her boss shook her head. "I'm just trying to help."

"I appreciate that, but you can let this one go. Dylan and I are long over."

In the end, it wouldn't matter, Nina told herself. Dylan hadn't called, wasn't going to call and she didn't want him to call. Problem solved.

Andi's smile faded. "You're my friend and I want you to be

happy. Your whole life is work. Either here or dealing with the store. You take care of everyone all the time. It's exhausting, and I'm just watching. I thought maybe a good-looking guy might be a nice break."

"I agree with the theory, but not with the guy."

Andi's smile returned. "You're saying if a handsome stranger swept you off your feet, you'd be open to it?"

Nina thought about how long it had been since someone had shown interest in her girl parts. "I'd be begging." A safe statement considering how few single men there were on the island. It was a family place. Most visitors came as part of a couple.

"Then I'm on the lookout for a handsome stranger," Andi told her.

There was a loud bang as the upstairs door slammed. Andi sighed.

"That's Carrie's bedroom door. She's running late again."

Nina couldn't remember a morning when the teen hadn't been running late.

Sure enough, there was the sound of someone rapidly descending the stairs, followed by a loud, "Mom? Where are you?"

"Back here," Andi called.

Carrie, fourteen and still gangly, burst into the break room. She flung herself at Nina and hung on tight.

"Morning," Nina said, putting down her coffee and hugging her back. "I heard you're late."

Carrie grinned at her, then turned to Andi and hugged her. "I know, I know," the teen said cheerfully. "I need to get up earlier. See you guys later."

With that, she was flying toward the front door.

When Andi had moved to the island, she'd bought the large Queen Anne that now housed her practice. She and her contractor, Wade, had fallen in love. Carrie had been a bonus, settling into her new life as a stepdaughter.

The front door slammed. Andi sighed. "I need to have Wade check the hinges. One day she's going to pull that door out of the frame."

"I think it's a little sturdier than that."

Andi glanced at the clock. "Nearly showtime. Are we still on for Pilates after work?"

"I have my stuff in the car."

"Great."

With that they went into the hall. Andi turned toward her office, while Nina went up front to make sure the computers had booted up correctly. Out the window she saw Carrie climbing into the SUV next door. Deanna, Andi's neighbor, took her girls to school every morning, and Carrie joined them.

Shared responsibilities, Nina thought. Balance. She understood the concept, even if she didn't get to practice it much. Maybe in her next life she wouldn't be the one who had to hold it all together.

"Point your toes, Andi. A little higher, Nina. Now slowly roll back down and breathe."

Nina collapsed back on the mat. The way her stomach muscles were protesting, a slow roll to the starting position wasn't an option. She was hot and sweaty and knew she was going to be sore in the morning. Had it really been that long since her last Pilates class?

She placed her hand on her rib cage and told herself that layer between her skin and the bones was necessary padding. Or maybe she should start walking on her lunch hour. The weather was going to get nice in the next few weeks. She could take advantage of that. Become fit over the summer.

She rolled to her side and struggled to her feet. Andi was already up and smiling, as if the class hadn't been difficult at all. Nina gasped for breath as she finally gained her balance.

The workout room had an entire wall of mirrors. She made the mistake of turning sideways, taking in both her butt and her stomach. It seemed that extra ten pounds she'd been carrying since puberty had morphed into fifteen. She thought of the last of the brownies she'd consumed the previous night and vowed not to replace them. And she would start coming to mat class twice a week for sure.

Too weak and sore to change back into street clothes, she shoved her bare feet into her sensible, white athletic shoes and shuffled to the parking lot. Andi walked with her, practically bouncing with extra energy.

"I'm feeling so much better," her friend said. "I'm glad that trimester is over. Now I have my energy back, and I'm eating. I love being pregnant."

"You look great," Nina murmured, trying not to sound surly. It wasn't Andi's fault that she was tall and *thin* and beautiful. Even with a baby on the way, her stomach was still flatter than Nina's. Talk about unfair.

"And I'm sorry I guilted you into coming to Pilates with me today."

"No, you're not."

Andi grinned as she paused by her SUV. "No, I'm not. Thursday?"

"I'll be here."

Nina got into her car, grateful to have it back from the auto repair shop. One fuel injector doodad later, her wheels were running and her checkbook was lighter. Not her favorite kind of compromise, but stuff happened and Mike had to earn a living, too.

She started the engine and thought longingly of heading

home. Only she'd just hired Cindy and she needed to check on her progress.

She drove down to the main road that circled the island, then turned left. As she sped north, she saw a familiar BMW coming in the other direction. Dylan.

She thought of how she looked—hot and sweaty and not in a sexy kind of way. Her workout clothes weren't the least bit flattering, and she was pretty sure she smelled. But it turned out not to be an issue. Dylan simply gave her a wave and kept on going. The truth was clear. Whether or not he was single, he sure wasn't interested in her.

Something she could live with, she told herself. It wasn't that she desperately wanted to spend time with him. She supposed the deep-in-her-heart fantasy was that he would come crawling back, so she could dump him as heartlessly as he'd dumped her. Not mature, but at least somewhat honest.

She turned into the parking lot by Blackberry Preserves. Cindy's was the only car there. Nina walked over the gravel and went into the store.

The first thing she noticed was the light. There was a lot more of it. Also, the air was fresher, without that heavy stuffiness that seemed to cover everything like mold. Prince's "Kiss" blasted from an iPod plugged into portable speakers. Cindy was up on a ladder, a microfiber duster in one hand. As Nina watched, she expertly swirled the cloth around the crystals dangling from the chandelier.

Rather than call out and startle her new employee, Nina walked to the speakers and slowly turned down the music. Cindy glanced over and grinned.

"Yes, I love Prince. I admit it." She scrambled down the ladder. "How's it going?"

"Good. This is impressive," Nina said as she looked around. "The store looks great."

"I took down the drapes," Cindy admitted. "They were blocking the light and more than a little dusty. There were some very suspicious holes in them. I folded them up into a box, in case you want to keep them, but I think they should be tossed."

"Not a problem. Toss away."

Cindy had pulled her dark hair back with a headband, and she wore jeans and a sweater rather than her stylish interview clothes. Still, she managed to look put together and elegant. Nina thought maybe years of wearing scrubs had squashed her fashion gene, assuming she'd ever had one in the first place. Her appearance had never much mattered to her. If she was clean, she was happy. Growing up, she'd never had time to pore over fashion magazines or worry about what was in style. Now she wondered if she'd missed her chance.

Cindy pointed to the chandelier overhead. "I've been doing research. From what I can tell, that bad boy is Italian and maybe three hundred years old. If I'm right, it's worth about ten thousand dollars."

Nina felt her mouth drop open. "I'm sorry, did you just say—"

Cindy grinned. "Yup. Ten thousand. I could be wrong, of course. I was thinking of making a list of what could be high-end pieces, then talking to you about having a professional come up from Seattle and appraise them."

Nina stared up at the crystals and shook her head. "I doubt my mom paid more than twenty bucks for that. She's not a big spender when it comes to inventory."

"She has a good eye."

"She got lucky. Let's remember what else we have in here. It's good Tanya didn't know or she would have carted it away. Any other finds?"

"A couple of sets of Depression glass. One is in amethyst.

It's beautiful and rare. I'm still working up a price. I also found a wonderful collection of cameos. Some of them look really old. Like I said, I'll have a list put together for you."

Nina couldn't believe there was a chance the store could actually be a moneymaker. Talk about an unexpected turn of events. Of course, it hadn't happened yet.

"I'm going to need some more cleaning supplies," Cindy told her. "And the vacuum broke. I think I killed it with dust."

"Can you buy what you need and give me the receipts?" Nina asked. "I'll write you a check the same day."

"Sure. I'll stop by the store tomorrow on my way in." She smiled. "So, you're not going to secretly go behind my back and reclean what I've already cleaned?"

"No." Nina tilted her head. "Let me guess. Your mother-in-law does that."

"Yes, but with her, there's no attempt to hide what she's doing. And she loves to bring a cleaning rag out to my husband and show him the speck of dust or dirt she found." Cindy sighed. "She really loves her son, but she doesn't make it easy. I tell myself she can't help it."

"I'm sorry about that." Nina knew that in-laws could be difficult, but there was a line that shouldn't be crossed.

"It's fine." Cindy shrugged. "I tell myself she secretly adores me. It may not be true, but it helps."

Chapter Five

‿✑

"I'LL STILL WRITE ARTICLES," Averil said, wondering if she looked as guilty as she felt.

Maya, her boss, waved her hand. "Of course I want to keep getting articles from you, Averil. You're one of my best, but we're talking about your *novel!* I'm so excited." Maya, a petite brunette with brown eyes and an easy smile, leaned forward. "OMG, I can't believe it. You're going to go away and write. I'm so envious. You're from Blackberry Island, right?"

Averil did her best not to squirm. She had asked for an indefinite leave of absence on the pretext that she needed time to finish her novel. Not a total lie, if one ignored the fact that before she finished, she needed to actually start it.

"I grew up there."

Maya sighed. "Returning to the family home. You'll be able to take long walks on the beach and write and just be in your head. I envy you. Not that I have any plans to write a book. Dear God, do you know how long they are? I have trouble with a three-part essay." She smiled. "We'll keep in touch via email, of course. And when you're famous, I can say I knew you when."

Averil tried to smile, but she was feeling too much like a fraud. Still, she needed the time away to figure out what was wrong with her. Kevin was a great guy, she loved her job, so why wasn't she happy? And why didn't she want to start a family?

Questions to explore over the next few weeks, she told herself as she rose.

"I appreciate this," she said. "You've been so good to me."

Maya dismissed the compliment with a shake of her head. "You're talented, Averil. This is a great opportunity. I know you'll use it to the fullest. We can always use your freelance articles. You know that."

Averil nodded. "And when I come back?"

Maya hesitated only a second. "You'll be a famous novelist."

"Right," Averil said, ignoring the sinking sensation in her stomach. Because while her articles would always be welcome, her *job* was less secure. In this business, there was always someone talented waiting in the wings. Something she worried about, but knew in the end she didn't have a choice.

Averil thanked her again and left. As she walked to her small office to pack up a few things, she thought how Nina would have rolled her eyes to hear that kind of praise. Her sister knew the truth. That any opportunity handed to Averil had a fifty-fifty chance of being tossed aside and wasted and that what others saw as determination was merely a smoke screen to hide the truth. That Averil was simply one bad decision away from disaster.

What she couldn't help but wonder was if the decision to go home was going to make things better or worse.

Nina sat in the car in her driveway. After a very long day at work she was tired and cranky. Steady rain danced on the windshield. It wasn't the best time to be on the phone with Deputy Sam Payton.

"Seriously?" She leaned her head back and closed her eyes. "She was wanted?"

"Uh-huh. In Spokane, mostly. An assault, passing bad checks and, of course, stealing. We're looking at four or five felonies. She was being held on half a million in bail, and then was released due to a clerical error. Now that we've got her back in custody, we're sending her over to Spokane, assuming you don't want to press charges."

"She's going away for a long time?"

"My guess is close to ten years."

"I can put the stuff she tried to sell back in inventory?"

"You can."

"Sold." Nina opened her eyes. "Please, don't let her escape again."

"I didn't let her escape the first time. She'll be driven to Spokane tonight, in custody." Amusement crept into his voice. "You might want to run a background check on your next new hire. You can do it online for a few bucks."

Nina thought about Cindy, happily pricing and cleaning. There was no way she would believe the woman was other than what she said, but still…

"Any sites you recommend?"

"Sure." He gave her a couple of names.

Nina wrote down the info, thanked him and hung up. As soon as she got inside and changed, she was going to check Cindy Yoo and confirm she wasn't a secret serial killer. Or wanted by any law-enforcement agency.

She grabbed her bag and then dashed toward the porch. She was congratulating herself on not getting too wet when she stepped into the living room, only to be confronted by a steady drip in the corner.

"No!"

Nina dropped her bag on the floor and kicked out of her shoes. She crossed the carpet in sock-covered feet, stopping only when she felt the dampness seeping across the floor.

The roof leak. The one her mother had sworn she'd had fixed. The one Nina had forgotten about because of the shock of seeing Dylan. First, her car and now, the roof. This was not her week.

She detoured into the kitchen and pulled a card off the refrigerator. She used the landline to dial.

"Buffet."

"Hey, Tim, it's Nina Wentworth. I have a roof leak. Did my mom call you about it a couple of weeks ago?"

"Lemme look here." Paper rustled. Tim was old-school and had not embraced the electronic age. He kept all the info on his customers in a ratty notebook that fit into his shirt pocket. "She called and left a message, but didn't say what it was. I called her back and never heard from her again."

Nina leaned against the wall and sighed. "Right. I'm not even surprised. We have a leak. It's pretty serious. A steady dripping that looks like it's getting worse."

"I'm in Seattle, Nina. I can be there in the morning, but not before. Any way you can get somebody to cover it?"

This was when the concept of female equality and independence really sucked, she thought. "Sure. I'll get a tarp on it. The back door will be open, if you need to get inside."

"Sure thing. Then I'll leave the invoice on the kitchen table."

"Thanks, Tim. You're the best."

Ten minutes later, Nina had changed into jeans and a long-sleeved T-shirt. She pulled on a waterproof jacket, then went to the garage where she collected a tarp and four bricks. She'd done this drill before.

After dropping her supplies into a bucket for easy carrying, she leaned a ladder up against the house, close to the leak. She held the bucket in one hand and used the other as she climbed.

The rain was steady and damned cold. It got in her eyes and trickled down the back of her neck. As she reached the roof, her left foot slipped, and for a second, she nearly lost her balance.

She hung on and regained her footing. She pushed the bucket onto the roof, then scrambled up next to it.

The second she sat, water seeped into her jeans. Pine needles poked her fingers and covered much of the roof. They were going to have to be removed, Nina thought, thinking it was a job for another day. The shingles themselves were wet and slick. Nothing about this was very much fun.

It was also desperately unfair, she thought grimly. Bonnie had sworn she'd arranged to get the roof fixed, but hadn't. Nina knew that when she complained to her mother about that, Bonnie would have a good excuse, or get so wounded that Nina would end up feeling like the biggest, baddest bitch in the West. If she didn't complain, then once again her mother got away with being irresponsible while Nina took care of business. There seemed to be no win and in the end, the roof was still leaking.

Rain continued to pour onto her. She shifted to her hands and knees and moved slowly to the leaking corner. She pushed the bucket in front of her as she went. As she got closer, she tested the boards below her, not wanting to plunge through to the living room. About three feet from the actual leak, she pulled the tarp from the bucket and threw it over the shingles. She settled bricks into place and hoped it would hold until Tim arrived. Then she turned to make her way back to the ladder.

Later, she would try to figure out what had gone wrong. Maybe there was an extra coating of needles. Maybe patches of moss made the surface even more slick than usual. Maybe it was simply bad luck. But as she turned to crawl back to the ladder, her hand slipped, then her knee. Before she knew what was happening, she was sliding toward the edge of the roof, with nothing between her and hard ground but about ten or twelve feet.

Not enough to kill her, she thought as she screamed, but enough to—

"Got you."

She landed hard but not on the ground. Instead she was caught by a man she'd never seen before. He held her in his arms and smiled down at her with an expression that made no sense. If she had to guess, she would say he was thinking he'd just won some kind of prize. And not just any prize. He looked as if he'd won a PGA tournament, NASCAR race and Quarter Finals all in one.

He was tall and strong enough to save her ass. His eyes were blue, and he looked good when wet.

"Hey, Nina."

The voice was low and sexy, but not the least bit familiar. "Who are you?"

"You don't remember?"

No, she didn't, and he was still holding her.

She struggled a bit, and he quickly set her on her feet. She swayed as she found her balance and was about to take a step back when he put his hands on her waist, drew her against him and kissed her. Just like that.

She was so shocked, she didn't move. Couldn't move. Couldn't breathe. His lips were warm and gentle, the kiss was brief and then he released her and moved back. She stood there, in the rain, unable to feel anything. Not the kiss, not the dripping, not the cold.

"You kissed me!"

His grin was unrepentant. "I know. I couldn't help myself."
He studied her for a second, still way happier than the situation warranted. "You still don't know who I am, do you?"

"No. That's why I asked the question." She had asked the question, hadn't she? Maybe she really had fallen. Like on her head and now she was in a coma, imagining all this.

"I'm Kyle Eastland. The last time I saw you, I was twelve years old. It was August. A Tuesday. You were so beautiful."

Kyle Eastland? "I used to babysit for the Eastland family," she said slowly, as the memories returned. "There was a little girl and a son from a previous marriage—" She stared harder, suddenly remembering that preteen son. The one who had followed her around like a puppy, telling everyone who would listen that he was madly in love with her.

Her mother had said his devotion was sweet and that she should be flattered. Nina remembered being completely humiliated by the attentions of a very determined kid.

"You're Kyle?"

"I knew you'd remember me."

"That was years ago."

"You're more beautiful than I remember."

Maybe he was the one who'd hit his head, she thought, aware of her wet hair plastered to her face and the dripping clothes. Or he was insane. A crazy stalker who had, until recently, been locked away.

He flashed her an amused smile. "Don't be scared. I'm a normal guy."

"I'm sure all serial killers say that."

He chuckled. "I have proof." He pulled out his wallet and showed her his military ID. Kyle was in the Navy and he was an officer. She was pretty sure the Navy would do a mental evaluation.

"Okay, then," she murmured. "We're getting soaked. Come inside."

As he followed her into the house, she had the strangest sensation of déjà vu. In the past couple of weeks, she'd gotten drenched twice and been rescued by two men she hadn't seen in forever. Was this a horoscope thing? Cosmic humor?

She checked the ceiling as she entered the living room and was pleased to see the dripping had stopped.

"Stay there," she said, pointing to the small tiled foyer. "I'll be right back."

He gave her the kind of slow, sexy grin that had, for centuries, caused women to make very bad choices. "Now that I've found you, I'm not going anywhere."

"You think statements like that are comforting?" she asked.

"I'm telling the truth."

"Yeah, not good news."

She hurried to her bedroom where she locked her door before changing for the second time in fewer than thirty minutes. She left her hair wet, which was *exactly* what had happened with Dylan. Was it the rain? Should she move to Phoenix?

Still perplexed by the bizarreness that was her life, she returned to the living room and found Kyle exactly where she'd left him. Only he'd removed his jacket and hung it on the coatrack. Which meant he was wearing a thin sweater that illustrated the man enjoyed working out.

Even damp he was pretty, she thought, taking in the square jaw, dark blond hair and blue eyes. He was about six feet, maybe six one, lean, but strong. She knew the latter because he'd caught her without gasping for air.

"Why are you here?" she asked pointing to the sofa. "Everything okay with your family?"

He looked up, scanning her face. "I'm not here for help, Nina. I'm here for you."

"Yeah. Okay, then. Have a seat."

When they were sitting across from each other, she drew in a breath. First things, first, she thought. "Thank you for saving my life."

"You're welcome."

"I doubt the fall would have actually killed me, but I would have been hurt."

"That's true."

He was staring at her as if trying to memorize her features. The intensity wasn't scary, it was just strange.

"So, what brings you to Blackberry Island?" she asked.

"You."

"You keep saying stuff like that. What does it mean? I haven't seen you in forever. Kyle, you did get over your crush, didn't you?"

"If I say yes, will that make you feel better?"

"A little."

He leaned back against the sofa and stretched his arm along the back cushions. The relaxed, open posture of a man who was supremely confident.

"I got over you, but I never forgot you," he told her. "I remember everything about you, Nina. You were my dream girl."

"You were twelve." He'd also been persistent, she thought, remembering him re-creating the scene from *Say Anything,* and standing outside of her house with a boom box. Only it had been about six in the morning, on a Sunday. The neighbors hadn't been amused.

"Making you the older woman." The grin returned. "You were so hot. You used to wear these really short shorts and when you bent over to pick up my sister—"

She held up her hand. "You were twelve," she repeated, wondering if anything about this conversation was illegal.

Back then she'd done her best to ignore him, while taking care of his baby sister. Kyle had been a friendly kid. When he wasn't trying to convince her to run off with him, he'd been busy hanging out in his room or having friends over. Normal stuff.

"How long ago was that? How old are you now?"

"Twenty-six."

"So, fourteen years ago. I was sixteen. I was saving money for college."

"I know. I kept telling you to wait for me, but you didn't listen."

"Do you blame me?"

"No. Back then the age difference was too big. I figured that out eventually. After we moved away, I really missed you. But then I got to high school and discovered girls my own age." Humor brightened his eyes.

"Uh-huh. So much for me being 'the one.'"

"You were, but I thought it best to practice so that I would be—" he coughed "—ready for you."

"How generous."

"I'm that kind of guy."

A player, she thought. Not that it mattered to her. He was still too young. "I know you're not really here on Blackberry Island because of me. Is your family still in the area?"

"No. We moved years ago, and they've never been back. I'm stationed in Everett." He leaned forward and rested his forearms on his thighs. "I'm a fighter pilot."

She felt her eyes widen. "What?"

That grin was back. "F18s. I'm doing training. Part of a joint task force. I'm good at what I do. I'm on track to join the Blue Angels."

With five simple sentences, he'd started her head spinning. She knew about the Blue Angels. They were stars at air shows all over the country, maybe around the world. Their precision flying was practically the stuff of legends. "You're a fighter pilot?"

"Yes. I was offered a couple of different assignments. I picked Everett because of the location. I thought it would be fun to check out the island and see if you were still here."

She ignored that. "You fly multimillion-dollar planes?"

"That's me. And if the government is willing to trust me with that kind of equipment, you can trust me, too."

She chuckled. "Right. Does that line usually work?"

"All the time."

"I apologize for women everywhere."

"No need. So, what about you? What do you do?"

"I'm a nurse."

He raised his eyebrows. "So, if I'm hurt, you can take care of me."

Which was just like a guy, she thought humorously. "Not everything is about you."

"Sure it is. Have dinner with me."

"What? No. You're too young."

"It's only four years and you know you're curious. We'll catch up."

"We were never friends, Kyle. There's nothing to catch up on."

"Then we'll get to know each other. I meant what I said. You're the girl I fantasized about, Nina." There was that smile. "You're even better than I remember."

She thought about the extra twenty pounds, the wet hair, the lack of makeup. "Are you sure they're checking your vision regularly?"

He stood up and crossed to her, then pulled her to her feet. His large hands held hers. His skin was warm, and although she didn't want to admit it, there was a distinct tingle low in her belly.

"Nina Wentworth, I have wanted you and been waiting for you for fourteen years. The least you can do is have dinner with me."

Her breath actually caught in her throat. She could say with certainty that had never happened before. Not even once. She'd been nervous and interested and aroused, but never... fluttery.

Suddenly Kyle seemed like a *man,* in the best possible sense of the word. Gone was the preteen who had stalked her. This new and improved version got her attention in a big way. His gaze never left her face as he dropped her hands, cupped her cheeks and kissed her again.

This time she was warm and dry and had the wherewithal to notice the gentle warmth of his mouth on hers. He didn't push, didn't move, but he lingered, as if he wanted this moment to last forever.

Or maybe that was her.

He raised his head. "Dinner," he murmured. "Say yes."

"Yes."

"Day after tomorrow?"

"Sure."

He put his hands on her shoulders. "I'll be here at six. We'll have dinner. You'll have a good time."

"You know that for sure?"

That sexy smile returned. "I do."

"You're a player."

He raised his eyebrows. "Your tone says you don't mean that as a compliment."

"I don't. You enjoy women, and for some reason, now you want to enjoy me." She winced, wishing she'd chosen another phrase.

"I do," he said easily. "Very much. All of you."

Because he'd had a crush on her years ago.

"Reality never lives up to the fantasy," she said.

"You're right. Sometimes it's better."

Oh, he was good. Way out of her league. He hadn't denied her charge. Given the chance, he would seduce her before she'd had a chance to catch her breath.

Instead of being dismayed by the thought, she had to admit to a little tingle of anticipation. She hadn't ever been with anyone like Kyle. He was easy to look at, funny and charming. So what if she would be one among no doubt many notches on his bed post? If she knew what she was getting from the outset, then she wouldn't get emotionally involved and she wouldn't get hurt. Didn't she deserve a little "me" time?

"Dinner," she said firmly. "At six."

"I'm looking forward to it," he told her as he crossed to the door.

"I am, too."

He paused to study her. "For real?"

"Yes, Kyle. For real."

The smile turned boyish. For a second, she could see the kid he'd been. Then the man returned and winked at her.

"Good," he said, before he disappeared into the rain.

She shut the door behind him, then leaned against it. "What have I done?" she asked aloud.

Fortunately, there was no answer.

She wandered toward the kitchen thinking that dinner would be nice. She could use a man adoring her. It would perk up her spirits and brighten her complexion.

Her cell phone rang. She answered it without checking who it was.

"Hello?"

"Hi, Nina, it's Dylan."

Dylan? Her nose wrinkled. Hearing his voice was a bit like taking a bite of broccoli after tasting a hot fudge sundae. Because that's what Kyle was, she thought humorously. A forbidden dessert.

"Did I catch you at a bad time?"

"What? No. Sorry. I just got home from work and I'm still figuring out my evening. How are you? How are you settling back into island life?"

Guilt, she thought with disgust. She always babbled when she felt guilty. Not that she owed Dylan anything, but here she was, talk, talk, talking.

"It's smaller than I remember," he admitted. "My parents are closer."

"And you're the favorite son."

"The only son. It's intense."

"I bet."

There was a moment of silence.

"I have to go to Seattle this weekend," he said. "But I was wondering if you'd like to have dinner next week, after I'm back."

Nina knew for a fact she hadn't been on a date in nearly eighteen months. Now she'd been asked out twice in one day. Why couldn't this have been better coordinated? One date last year, one date this year?

Dinner with Dylan. Although she hadn't recognized Kyle, she knew everything about Dylan. While she was over him, she was still the tiniest bit bitter about the way things had ended. Which brought the guilt back again, which annoyed her.

"It wasn't supposed to be a hard question," he said quietly.

Ack! "Sorry, sorry. Sure. Dinner would be great."

"You sure?"

"Absolutely. Give me a call when you're back and we'll set

up a night. I'll bring you up to date on all you've missed since you've been gone. That will take at least fifteen minutes."

He chuckled. "I look forward to it. Talk to you soon."

"Sure. Have fun in Seattle."

She hung up and tossed her phone on the counter.

If ever there was a time to have wine with dinner, tonight was the night, she thought, heading for the open bottle on the counter. But she would pass on the cookies she'd bought. And go to Pilates at least one more time a week.

Not that Kyle was ever going to see her naked. But still. A girl could dream.

Chapter Six

THE DRIVE FROM Mischief Bay to Blackberry Island was direct. North on I-5 for about 1100 miles, then a left at the arrow pointing to the bridge. Easy enough.

Now, after spending the night just this side of Sacramento, Averil carefully pulled into a rest stop south of Medford, Oregon. At the rate she was going, she was going to get to the island before dinner, which seemed both good and bad. On the one hand, she was happy to be escaping her life. On the other, she knew she was running away, and that was hardly a situation to make anyone proud.

She parked her car and got out. The rest area was quiet. There were only a couple of big rigs parked on the other side. Hers was the only passenger vehicle. After using the restroom, she washed her hands and walked outside.

The morning was crisp and clear. The rain would start farther north. She could see her breath and was grateful for her jacket. Deciding to stretch her legs for a few minutes, she started to circle the building.

She really needed to use her time away to get her life in

order, she thought. She was too old to be running away, and yet here she was. Escaping from unpleasant reality. She missed Kevin already, and at the same time, she was glad to be away from him. As if that made sense. She had no direction, no novel, no anything. She was lost, plain and simple. Which was probably why she balked at having a baby. If she wasn't sure she could save herself, how could she be responsible for someone else?

Just past the men's room, she saw something move by the trash can on her left. She paused and watched. She saw the movement again. Her stomach clenched when she realized a small dog was huddled by the can.

The animal looked to be maybe twenty or thirty pounds, with matted gray-and-brown fur and big eyes. She could see it was shaking and, as she approached, the dog cowered.

She glanced around, but there were no other cars. The animal looked terrified, torn between running and wanting to be rescued.

"I know the feeling," she murmured in a low voice as she slowly approached. "It's okay, little dog. I won't hurt you." She crouched down and held out the back of her hand. The animal flinched but didn't move. She gently touched its shoulder.

The animal shuddered, then seemed to collapse on itself. Averil shifted closer and patted its side. She could feel bones everywhere.

"Oh, honey, you're starving," she said, realizing some jackass had simply abandoned the animal. There was no collar, and with the dog sticking close to the rest area, it should have been easy for an owner to find.

She continued to pet the animal, trying to gain its trust. After a few minutes, she stood. "Okay," she said, patting her leg. "You want to come with me?"

The dog rose and stared at her. It continued to tremble.

"I think we're close to Medford. I'll take you to a vet and have you checked out. If you have a chip, we can find your owner. If not, at least you'll be warm and fed."

The dog stared at her.

"It's all right," she said. "I'm a good person. I'm confused and emotionally stunted, but I won't hurt you."

The dog seemed to accept that and walked along with her.

It turned out the animal was too weak to jump into the backseat, so Averil lifted her. She was shocked at how little the dog weighed. She poured water into her hand and the animal drank greedily. She had part of a scone from the Starbucks where she'd stopped earlier, and the dog gulped that down.

When Averil slid behind the wheel, she started the engine and turned up the heat. It only took her a couple of minutes to use her phone to find a vet in Medford. She called and got directions, then drove back onto the highway.

"She's about three years old," the vet—an old guy with a kind expression—told Averil. "I would guess she's been on her own for a month. She has a few bruises and she's malnourished. I doubt she's had a decent meal in that time."

The technician looked up from the computer. "There aren't any reports of missing dogs in the area," she said with a shrug. "Without a chip, there's no way to find her owners."

"She was dumped," the vet said. "Unfortunately, it happens." He left the room.

Averil stroked the dog huddled on the examination table. The animal had been examined and bathed. She'd also been given a small meal.

"There's a no-kill shelter in town," the technician said. "She's pretty cute and it shouldn't be long until she's adopted. You did a good thing, bringing her here. She'll be fine."

Averil stared into the dog's brown eyes. She was white with

brown spots after all. Part King Charles Spaniel, the vet had said. Part who-knows-what. She'd endured the exam and the bath without protest and seemed resigned to whatever fate had to offer. Averil knew the most sensible solution was to leave her at the shelter.

She fingered the dog's soft fur. "I'll take her," she said. "Can I do that?"

"Sure." The other woman smiled. "She seems like a sweetie. Do you know what you're going to name her?"

"Penny." Averil touched the dog's head. "Hey, Penny. Want to come live with me?"

Brown eyes regarded her solemnly.

"You'll need some food," the tech said. "We have a brand that's good for sensitive stomachs. That will help her ease into having regular meals. Feed her about half a cup, four times a day for the first few days. Then you can go to a cup twice a day. Maybe mix in a little canned food. If you want to change brands, do it over time or she could get sick."

The woman wrote down a few instructions. "Once you get where you're going, she'll need to be vaccinated. She's already been spayed. I think there's an old collar and leash in the lost and found box. Let me go grab them."

She left the room. Averil continued to pet Penny. "It's okay. You're going to live with me now. I'm pretty sure I can handle a dog."

Penny stared at her, her expression still fearful, but at least she'd stopped shaking. Soft brown eyes seemed to ask if that was the best Averil could offer.

"You're right," she said quietly. "I need to make a commitment. I *will* take care of you. I promise."

The tech returned with a leash and cloth collar, along with a couple of old towels. Averil thanked her, paid the bill and walked to her car. Penny had accepted the collar and leash without complaint and now walked beside her. When they reached the car, Averil opened the back door.

Penny looked from her to the seat.

"Come on, Penny. Can you jump?"

Penny did as requested.

Averil laughed. "Good girl," she said. "You're smart, you know that? All right. Let's make you a bed."

She folded the towels into squares and placed them on the seat. Then she unfastened the leash. She patted the soft fabric.

"Come on, Penny. This is for you."

Penny placed one paw on the towel.

"Good girl. Yes, you get comfy for the rest of the drive, okay?"

Penny turned twice on the towels, then laid down with a sigh. Averil stroked her a couple more times before closing the door and walking around to the driver's side. By the time she pulled onto the freeway, the dog was asleep.

The afternoon had started to wane by the time Averil made her way over the bridge leading to Blackberry Island. Penny had slept for most of the drive north. They'd stopped at a couple of rest stops so they could both use the bathroom, and Averil had given the dog light meals. It turned out that Penny was also a big fan of burgers, so they'd shared lunch at a Mc-Donald's just south of Portland.

Now they were nearly done with their drive.

Averil was both relieved and oddly tense as she took in the familiar sights on the island where she'd grown up. As a kid she'd ridden her bike over nearly every foot of road here and had explored vineyards and coasts. She'd swum in the ocean, eaten at most of the restaurants and stands and knew at least one kid from all the local families.

Blackberry Island had always been home. It was the place

that made the most sense to her. It was where she always knew who she was.

She supposed that was part of the problem. In Mischief Bay she had many roles. She was a reporter, a writer, a wife. In Mischief Bay, she was a grown-up. Here she was Nina's little sister. Bonnie's youngest. There weren't expectations.

In her head she knew that running back home wasn't exactly a testament to her maturity, but she could live with that. The truth was, somewhere along the way, she'd gotten lost, and now she didn't know what she wanted.

About a mile from the house, she pulled off the main road and parked by the beach. She collected Penny's leash and walked around to the passenger-side back door. Penny sat up, waiting for her. Her long tail thumped steadily.

"So you like me now, do you?" Averil asked with a grin. "It was the burger, wasn't it?"

She clipped on the leash, then stepped back. Penny jumped to the ground and started to sniff.

"There's a doggie area over there," Averil said as she pointed to the square of gravel just off the beach.

Penny used the facilities, then the two of them went for a walk along the rocky sand. The air was warm, the sun bright in the sky. Due west was the Strait of Juan de Fuca. That body of water separated Washington's northwest peninsula from Vancouver Island. Somewhere in the middle of the strait was the line between the United States and Canada. About sixty miles due west was open ocean.

Averil remembered her friends staring out at the strait and talking about getting on a boat and sailing away. To see what was out there. She'd been less interested in leaving and found little appeal in the thought of days or weeks at sea. Nor had she wanted to go to UCLA. That had been Nina's dream for her. But she'd made it sound so wonderful that Averil had agreed.

Now she was home—whatever that meant.

"I'm not making much sense, am I?" she asked Penny.

The dog glanced at her and gave a tentative tail wag.

"Come on, Penny. Let's go face the music."

They walked back to the car. Penny settled on her bed, and Averil started down the familiar road.

When she saw the house, her eyes began to burn. Nothing had changed, she thought with relief. Not the street or the neighborhood. Everything was as she remembered.

Emotions tore through her. She fought against them, not sure if she was happy, sad or desperately confused. By the time she'd parked the car, she was crying.

Nina opened the front door and walked out. Averil stumbled to her feet and rushed toward her.

"Hey, it's okay," her big sister told her. "You don't have to cry."

But it was too late. Averil hung on tight, sobs tearing through her. She cried without knowing why, but now that she was home, that was okay, too.

Nina stood in the center of the bedroom. Averil had been home all of thirty minutes. She'd carried her suitcase into her old room, changed into PJs and climbed into bed. From the looks of things, she didn't plan on getting out any time soon. Nina had brought her water and a sandwich. Averil had consumed both, then stretched out with her eyes closed.

"Thanks Nina," she said, her voice sleepy. "You've been great. I feel a lot better."

Nina sat on the edge of the bed, still not sure why her sister was home and what would happen now that she was. Nina stroked Averil's hair and felt a rush of affection. They were sisters. They loved each other. Despite how they fought like cats and dogs, that wouldn't change. And speaking of which…

"Tell me about the dog," she murmured.

Averil opened her eyes and smiled. "Her name is Penny and she's sweet." She explained about finding her. "I've fed her and she went to the bathroom before we got here. I'll set my phone to wake me up so I can take her out in a couple of hours."

"What about bowls and a bed?"

Averil yawned. "She's been on her own for at least a month. She isn't expecting much. I've got food and I'll get the rest tomorrow. I love you, Neenie."

Nina smiled. She hadn't been called that in years. "I love you, too, kid."

With that, she rose and walked out of the room.

Once in the hall, she hesitated. Should she shut the door? Penny followed her, watching with her big, brown eyes.

"You're unexpected," Nina told the dog.

Penny's tail wagged, and she followed Nina into the kitchen.

Averil had left her luggage in a pile in the living room. One suitcase was open, with half the contents spilling out over the floor. In the kitchen was a bag of food and some instructions.

"You'll need to eat soon," Nina said as she read over the notes. "Small meals several times a day. Canned would be good." She looked through the luggage Averil hadn't dragged to her room. There were a couple of ratty towels and a jacket, but no dog food beyond the small bag that was about a third gone. No bed, either.

"My sister isn't much of a planner," Nina told the dog. Penny thumped her tail.

Nina grabbed her purse and headed for her car. While there wasn't a pet store on the island and she didn't have time to make the drive across the bridge, there was a large general store with a decent pet section.

She bought canned food, a bed and another bag of the dog

food. While she was heading toward the checkout line, she grabbed a couple of chew toys and a ball.

A sizeable credit card purchase later, she was on her way home. The usual evening traffic jam caused her to watch the clock in the car nervously. Her date with Kyle was in an hour. She'd already showered, and her makeup wouldn't take long, but she would need some time to obsess about what to wear. She needed to look good without being overly dressy. It was cool enough that she would need long sleeves, or a jacket, or both.

Ten minutes later, she parked and grabbed her purchases. Penny met her at the door.

"Hey, you," Nina said, giving the dog a pat. "You now have possessions."

She put the bed in the living room and the dog dishes in the kitchen. After filling a bowl with water, she measured out a little canned food and the permitted amount of dry. Penny waited patiently until she was served, then gobbled down her dinner. She followed Nina into the back bedroom and watched as she went through her various clothing options.

"I was thinking blue," she said, holding up a cobalt-blue dress. "I know it's plain, but I have these great shoes that go with it."

Penny stared at the dress. Nina did, as well. The neckline was slightly scooped but didn't flash any cleavage at all. Still, the tailored lines were flattering and it was long-sleeved, which meant she could avoid the whole ugly coat issue.

The shoes—black and cobalt-blue suede—were three-inch heels and had cost more than the dress. Even at Nordstrom Rack, where they'd been marked down 70 percent.

She put the dress back in her closet. "There's also basic black."

She pulled out a sleeveless classic LBD. The hemline was

a tad shorter than she thought her thighs could handle, but if she put on black tights, they would look firmer.

Penny stretched out on the carpet and yawned.

"Too predictable?" Nina asked. "I'm not really a dress person. But I doubt Kyle wants to see me in cartoon scrubs."

She looked at her two best options. "What if I wear the suede pumps with the LBD?"

She dug out the tights and shimmied into them. They had a control top which would cut into her ability to eat dinner, but made the dress look great. She shrugged on a robe and went into the bathroom to touch up her makeup. When she came out, Penny was standing in the hallway, staring intently.

"What?" Nina asked. "He can't be here yet."

Penny started for the kitchen, then looked back at Nina, as if inviting her along. Nina trailed after her. At the back door, Penny scratched the small rug.

Understanding dawned. Nina opened the back door and let the dog out. The backyard was fenced. Even so, she waited until Penny had done her business and hurried back in. Together, they retreated to the rear of the house.

"You're impressive," Nina told the animal as she brushed out her straight hair. "Maybe you can teach Averil responsibility."

When her hair was smooth, she slipped on the dress and pulled up the zipper. She added gold hoop earrings, lip gloss and a ten-year-old cropped leather jacket. Fortunately, it was plain enough that it didn't look too out of date.

She'd barely had time to smooth her skirt when the doorbell rang.

Nina was surprised to feel her stomach lurch. The slightly tingly feeling of anticipation was sadly unfamiliar, she thought as she crossed the worn carpet and opened the front door.

Kyle, all six feet of blond godlikeness of him, swore under his breath.

"What's wrong?" she asked.

"You're not supposed to look that good. I thought I'd prepared myself. I wasn't close."

This guy was too much, she thought to herself. She reached for the small clutch she'd left by the door. At this point, she didn't even care if he was lying. He was exactly what she and her battered ego needed. For one night she was going to forget about all the responsibilities in her life. She was going to go on a date with a hot, younger guy and toy with the idea of letting him sleep with her. If there were consequences— and there always were—she would face them in the morning. She'd been doing the right thing for a very long time, and she deserved a reward. Kyle was just the man to make sure she got one.

Chapter Seven

❧

NINA CHECKED TO make sure the door was locked, then started down the two stairs to the walkway. As she moved, Kyle stepped next to her and put his hand on the small of her back. The light pressure was unfamiliar, reminding her that it had been months and months since her last date. Nerves kicked up in her belly, as she realized this night might not be as easy as she'd first thought. Inappropriate guy or not, little Kyle had grown up into a handsome man.

She spotted his car and laughed out loud at the low-slung two-seater convertible.

"Seriously?" she asked with a chuckle. "That's what you drive?"

"A land jet," he told her. "Chicks love it."

"I doubt you need the car to get the girls."

He stepped in front of her to open the passenger door. "Every little bit helps. Especially with you. I need to keep my edge."

"Very smooth," she told him. "You've had a lot of practice."

She'd thought he might protest, but instead he grinned.

"All the better for you," he said easily. "You get to take advantage of all I've learned."

"A man who loves women. And whom women love back."

He shrugged. "It's a flaw, but one I can live with." He moved a little closer. "Tonight is all about you, though."

She could see the blue of his eyes and his thick, blond lashes. He's shaved, she thought, studying his tanned skin. He smelled good, too. As if he'd showered. She liked thinking he'd taken his time getting ready. That he'd made an effort for her. In truth, he'd probably done the same thing a thousand times, but that was okay. Tonight she would rather be one of the many than all alone.

She lowered herself into the seat, aware it was going to take every muscle she had to climb out gracefully. A problem for later, she told herself.

He settled next to her. Their seats were close enough together that his shoulder brushed hers. There was something intimate about the way the dashboard seemed to wrap around them. He rested his hand on the gearshift as he turned toward her.

"About dinner," he began, his voice low and teasing.

For a second she thought he was going to suggest they pass on the food. And for that same second, she considered saying yes. She'd never been one to have sex with a stranger, but while she didn't know much about Kyle, she knew some things. Like his parents' names and that he had a baby sister. So they weren't exactly unknown to each other.

"I thought we'd go to Marianna's."

She raised her eyebrows. "Really?"

"Is that okay? I made reservations, but I can cancel them."

"Marianna's would be lovely."

She wanted to add, if he was sure he could afford it. Because while Marianna's was known for exquisite food, the prices weren't exactly bargain. She'd only been there a couple of times, most recently with Bonnie and Bertie to celebrate the ten-year anniversary of Bertie moving in and Bonnie coming out.

But instead of checking on Kyle's financial viability, she decided that if he'd had it together enough to make a reservation, he'd probably checked on the menu. Besides, it wasn't as if she was going to order the most expensive item on the menu. She knew how to be a thoughtful date.

He started the car, then turned back to her and smiled. "This is nice. Having you so close."

He leaned toward her and lightly kissed her. Just a quick brush of mouth on mouth, but it was enough to leave her flustered.

When he straightened, she turned to face front, then nervously smoothed her skirt.

"You're good," she told him as he shifted into gear and backed out of the driveway. "You sure you're only twenty-six?"

"It's not the years, Nina. It's the miles."

"There have been a lot of miles?"

He chuckled as he drove down the street. "Enough, but they weren't you."

She laughed. "Who were they, then?"

He looked startled for a second, as if he hadn't expected the direct question. "I'd rather talk about you."

"My brilliance and beauty? Will there be poetry later?"

"You're mocking me."

"A little. Come on. You haven't thought of me once in the past ten years."

He glanced at her, his expression serious. "You're wrong."

"You were just a kid."

"Some things never change."

"It's a great line."

"Maybe, but it's also the truth." He flashed her a smile. "You're going to have to trust me on that."

"I don't trust so easily."

She spoke without thinking, then wished she could have called back the words. Not exactly first-date conversation, she told herself.

He took her hand in his and brought it to his mouth. After kissing her knuckles, he placed her fingers back on her lap. "Not to worry. We'll go as slow as you need us to."

Something she was a lot less sure about than he was, she thought. She got that this was a game to him, but there were also flashes of sincerity. So, which Kyle was real? Or was he like everyone else on the planet—not any one thing, but a combination of traits that were both good and bad?

He drove around the island and across the bridge. Once they were on the mainland, he headed south. A few miles later was the turnoff to the restaurant.

He drove up to the valet. Nina made sure both feet were on the ground before throwing herself up and out of the low car. Kyle circled around and guided her into the building.

The sun was still relatively high in the sky, and from the foyer, they had a view through the restaurant, out onto the water. The setting was perfect, she thought, once again aware of Kyle's hand at the small of her back. Soft music, white tablecloths on tables, quiet conversation.

The hostess, a petite twentysomething, walked toward them.

"Hello," she said, her gaze on Kyle. "Welcome to Marianna's."

Kyle winked at her. "We have a reservation," he said and gave his name. He leaned toward Nina and pressed his lips to her ear. "I asked for a table by the water."

She shivered at the erotic sensation of both his mouth touch-

ing her and the warmth of his breath. The hostess shot her a
death stare, but Nina was too busy thinking Kyle was out of
her league to much care.

With the age difference, she should be the one taking
charge, sexually. But obviously that wasn't going to happen.
She could only hope he was making an effort to seduce her,
because if this was all unintentional, she was in trouble.

The hostess led them to a table by the window. She flashed
Kyle a smile, then lightly touched his arm, but he didn't bother
with another wink, and she left with a sigh.

Kyle moved the menus to the side of the table and leaned
toward Nina.

"Thanks for coming out with me," he said, gazing into
her eyes. "You know, I've been planning this night since I
was twelve."

A line that made her want to roll her eyes. "You're not serious."

He smiled. "I loved the shirt you wore all the time, the one
with little white starfish on it. When you bent over to pick up
my sister, I could see down the front of it. You painted your
toenails red. The color was called Cherries in the Snow. Your
favorite song that summer was Cher's 'Believe.'"

Nina stared at him. "I remember you following me around
like a puppy, so I'll accept you used to *know* all that, but how
could you remember it now?"

"I meant what I said," he told her. "You were the one I
wanted, Nina. I loved you." He shrugged. "As much as a
twelve-year-old kid can. You don't forget that kind of stuff."

"This is crazy. I barely remember you. I'm sorry, but it's
true."

His smile widened. "Probably for the best, what with me
barely having reached puberty then. It's okay that we were in
different places because now we're both adults."

"Maybe, but you're talking dream girl and that makes me nervous. No one can live up to that." Especially not someone with a brownie problem. Nina considered herself pretty and funny and nice, but she wasn't fantasy material.

"Then we should get to know each other," he said. "Take it from there. You're here with me, Nina. This night is already a win for me."

She stared into his blue eyes and held back the need to sigh. "Damn, you're good."

He chuckled.

The server appeared, and he ordered a bottle of wine. When they were alone again, she leaned back in her chair.

"All right. Enough with our mutual past. Tell me about yourself. When did you know you wanted to be a pilot? Was it because of that movie? What was it? *Top Gun?*"

He made a face, and she realized it was probably before his time. "I was more an *Independence Day* kind of guy. But what really got me interested in flying was when we left the island. Our new house was close to a private airport. The guy who ran it lived next door, and I hung out with him a lot, got interested in planes. My grandmother thought I should have the chance to learn so she paid for lessons. By the time I graduated from high school, I had my instrument rating and I was hooked."

"Why the Navy and not the Air Force?" she asked.

"You've heard of the Blue Angels? They're the Navy's flight demonstration squadron. They were formed in 1946 and perform all across the U.S. and around the world. I want to do what they do."

"Okay," she said slowly. "You wanted this before you joined the Navy?"

"Uh-huh. I studied hard in college, got on track to be a pilot."

She thought about what she knew about the military, which was very little. "Are there tough math classes?"

"I was motivated. I'm a big believer in being focused. Having a goal and going after it." He smiled. "Let me be clear. You're a goal."

"Nice to know where you stand," she told him. "How long does this goal last?"

"I'm going to be in Everett a few months."

She waited, but there was nothing that followed. The message was pretty clear. He remembered her from his past, and he'd looked her up to see if she was still what he visualized. She had a feeling she wasn't, but Kyle didn't seem to notice, and, hey, why not go with that?

He obviously wasn't looking for a long-term relationship. He wanted to sleep with her, and he was willing to put in the effort required to seduce her. He might be playing a game, but he'd made the rules clear up front. She respected that.

"Do you have a serious girlfriend?" she asked.

"No. I wouldn't be with you if I did."

She raised her eyebrows. "Really? You're completely faithful to every woman?"

He leaned back in his chair. A smile pulled at the corner of his mouth. "If you're going to get technical," he began, then shrugged.

There was always bad to balance out the good, she thought. As long as she accepted her relationship with Kyle in the spirit he meant it, she would be fine. Because right now a short-term sexy fling sounded like exactly what she needed.

The server returned with the bottle of wine. It was from a local vineyard. When he'd poured, Kyle raised his glass.

"To old friends."

"Old friends," she repeated. "So, tell me about life in the Navy. Have you ever landed a plane on an aircraft carrier?"

"Sure."

"Seriously? How is that possible?"

He grinned. "Lots of practice. When the carrier's at sea, every landing is different. It's not like an airport because the runway itself is moving, as is the plane. There's almost no time between landing and stopping. It's a rush."

To her it sounded more like torture, but she'd never been overly adventurous. "You're deployed for months at a time, right?"

"I've seen the world." The smile returned. "I like it."

"A girl in every port?"

The smile returned. He shrugged, but even without words, the message was clear.

"But I don't get involved at work. When I'm on the ship, I'm a pilot."

She reached for her glass. "But when you're home, you play?"

"Something like that." He studied her. "What about you, Nina? You said you're a nurse. Do you work for a hospital?"

"No, in a doctor's office. Andi, my boss, is a pediatrician. She's great. I like working with kids."

"You stayed on the island."

"That was never the plan," she admitted. "I wanted to get away, but somehow it never happened. Money was tight, so I went to community college. Then I had two years at UW."

"You didn't want to stay in Seattle?"

"I thought about it, but there was a job waiting for me at home, and I had a younger sister in college."

He frowned. "You were raised by your mom, right?"

"Uh-huh. My dad took off when I was still really young. I don't know if you remember, but my mom has an antique store. Blackberry Preserves. It's small and not a huge money-maker. I helped pay for Averil's college. She went to UCLA."

"So, she got away and you didn't."

"You could say that." Nina thought about her sister's recent arrival. "She just came back today. There's something going on, and I have no idea what it is. She's married. Kevin's a great guy. He adores her. I hope Averil isn't screwing things up with him."

"Does she do that?"

"She's not big on taking responsibility."

"While you take responsibility for everything."

"Yikes. What makes you say that?"

His blue eyes were thoughtful. "A guess. Am I wrong?"

"No. Yes. Well, not on purpose. Averil found a dog at a rest stop on her drive up from California. Someone had abandoned her. So Averil took her. I think she made the right choice, but within five minutes of arriving home, she was in bed. I had to go get dog food and a bowl and all that stuff. I don't want to be the one taking care of everyone, but somehow I am."

He reached for her hands and took them in his. "They know you'll pick up the slack. Like when you were fixing the roof."

His thumb rubbed a slow circle on her palm.

"When you saved my life."

"That's right. You owe me."

"And how would you like to be repaid?" she asked without thinking.

His gaze dropped to her mouth. "You know exactly how."

"Right. I should probably warn you that wanting is frequently better than having."

"Not in this case."

"I hope that's true. I wouldn't want you to be disappointed."

"Not possible," he told her.

He was so sure, she thought. So determined. While she'd dated before, she'd never had a guy flat-out tell her he wanted her. It was oddly appealing.

"Ever been flying?" he asked.

"On a big plane, sure."

"I'm going to take you up and show you the island from how I see things. Seeing the world from a few thousand feet up in the sky has a way of changing your perspective."

"I look forward to it," she told him.

Dinner passed more quickly than she would have thought possible. Kyle enjoyed current events, read mysteries and had a surprising working knowledge of the plot of *Pride and Prejudice*.

"I dated an English major in college," he said with a shrug as they drove back to her place. "It was her favorite book and movie."

"Mr. Darcy *is* dreamy," Nina said, her voice teasing.

"I'm not convinced," he told her. "I think Elizabeth is in love with his estate more than the man."

"How can you say that?"

"She started to fall for him after seeing the house. The change in her feelings makes sense. He's a rich man, and back then, a woman needed a man with money to be safe."

"Whereas today we want good looks and a great car?"

He grinned. "You wouldn't be swayed by a car. Not even mine."

"True. Does that break your heart?"

"A little, but I'm resilient." He turned into her driveway.

Nina had enjoyed the evening more than she'd thought she would, but now that they were back at her place, she found herself fighting nerves. She doubted he expected anything on their first date, but what if he did?

"I mentioned Averil is visiting, right?" she asked, hoping she didn't look as nervous as she felt.

"You did. Along with her new dog."

"Penny. She's very sweet."

He parked behind Averil's car and turned to her. "Thank you for dinner," he said.

"I think that's my line. I had a good time."

"Me, too."

He leaned in and kissed her. Just once and lightly. But she felt the contact all the way down to her toes. There was something about the way he took charge, she thought, sighing softly. He wasn't overly aggressive, but he made her think she could relax. That he would handle things. That didn't happen very often to her.

"I want to see you again," he murmured, kissing her again, this time lingering.

She let her eyes drift closed. His mouth was warm and firm. Knowing, she thought, feeling the heat grow between them. With each brush of his lips, nerve endings fired. It wouldn't take much more for her to figure having Averil in the house didn't matter at all.

"I'm going out of town for four days," he said.

She opened her eyes. "For work?"

He chuckled. "Yes, for work. I'm taking the jet with me. I won't be able to call, which is why I'm telling you I'm going to be gone. I don't want you to think I'm one of those guys who promises to call and then doesn't. Can I see you when I get back?"

"Yes."

He grinned. "As easy as that?"

"I think maybe we should avoid the word *easy*."

"Absolutely."

He wrapped his arms around her—something of a trick considering how small the space was in the two-seater. His hands were large and strong as he traced the length of her spine. He kissed her again, this time brushing his tongue against her bottom lip.

She parted for him, welcoming him as he deepened the kiss. Nina put her hands on his shoulders and leaned in. She half expected him to start to feel her up. After all, her breasts were right there, practically begging to be touched. But he didn't. Talk about disappointing.

He drew back and sighed. "I'll call as soon as I'm back in town."

He opened the door and got out of the car.

Nina wasn't about to spoil the moment by struggling to her feet. She kicked off her heels, then stepped out in stocking feet. They walked to the front door. From the other side, she heard a faint whining.

"The mystery dog," he said.

"She probably needs to go out."

"Four days," Kyle told her. "Then I'll be back." He kissed her one last time before turning and jogging back to his car.

Nina let herself inside. She petted Penny, then led her to the back door. The dog trotted out into the yard and took care of business. When she returned, Nina gave her another small meal before heading to her bedroom.

She leaned against the door frame and smiled as she thought about the handsome fighter pilot who very much wanted to sleep with her. It had been, she thought happily, a very good night. Kyle had impressed her—something that didn't happen very often. He'd made his goal extremely clear. After tonight, she was ready to admit that as far as making his dreams come true—she was all in.

Chapter Eight

❧

THREE DAYS AFTER arriving back home, Averil opened her eyes and knew she was ready to face the world. She'd done little but sleep for the past three days. She'd grabbed a couple of snacks, made sure Penny was fed. They'd taken daily walks. Then Averil had returned to bed. She now found herself completely rested and totally starving.

She sat up and glanced at the clock. It was a little after seven in the morning. At the foot of the bed, Penny raised her head and looked inquiringly.

Averil laughed. "Yes, to answer your question. I *am* getting up. How are you? Good?"

Penny's tail wagged. She jumped off the bed and walked to the door. Averil stood and stretched, then walked with her to the kitchen. She opened the back door and let out the dog.

A few feet away, a coffeepot sat on the counter. A cup was missing from the carafe. No doubt Nina had taken it for herself before stepping into the shower. Averil was sure her sister would pour in grounds and water the night before, then set the timer. Nina was nothing if not organized.

After filling a mug, Averil added a little milk, then let Penny back into the house. She paused to study the backyard. There was a patch of grass beyond the deck and a tidy bed of plants that had to be Bertie's doing. None of the Wentworth women had a green thumb.

"Breakfast," she said firmly, closing the door.

She fed Penny, then opened the refrigerator to figure out what she wanted for herself. There were eggs and a few leftovers. She pulled out a plastic container with what looked like mac and cheese and dumped the contents into a bowl. After sticking it in the microwave and setting the timer, she grabbed a pad of paper from by the phone. She had articles due in a couple of days and needed to be thinking about them.

She scribbled out a few sentences. Maybe she could write something about relatives visiting and the stress that caused teenagers.

"So you're up," her sister said as she walked into the kitchen.

Averil ignored the accusing tone. She was happy, and she wasn't going to start her day with a fight.

"Good morning," she said brightly. "It's not raining. That's nice."

Nina didn't bother glancing out the window. "It's been three days. You've been in bed for three days."

"I was tired."

"You walked into this house and dumped everything on me." *Like you always do.* Nina didn't say that part, but she didn't have to. It was implied.

"What responsibilities?" Averil demanded. "My God, when did you get so dramatic? My sleeping doesn't impact you at all."

"No, but your dog does."

"I let her out," Averil said, glancing at Penny. "I've been

feeding her three times a day. Starting today, I'm cutting back to twice a day. That's what the vet told me."

Nina pressed her lips together. "You've been feeding her that much?"

"And walking her. What did you think? That I went to bed and completely forgot about her?"

Nina's tight expression said that was exactly what she *had* thought.

Averil glared at her. "She's a living creature. How irresponsible do you think I am? You just assumed the worst about me." She glanced at Penny, whose tail was wagging as she glanced between them. "So, you took care of things, like you always do. Sorry, my dog friend, those six meals you've been getting are ending starting now."

Nina glared at her. "I took care of things because there was no way to know what you were doing. All you had was a bag of dry food. What about the canned food that miraculously appeared? Or the extra bag of dry food? And that bowl she's using for her water. Where did you think all that came from?"

The microwave beeped. Averil ignored it as she realized Kevin was right. Being with Nina was always such a great idea…at a distance. But in close proximity, they didn't do so well.

"Thank you for buying her food and a bowl," she said through gritted teeth. "But it wasn't necessary. I'm dealing with her."

"So you say."

The unfairness was like a slap. "Jeez, Nina, angry much? Maybe if you'd gotten your ass off this island, you wouldn't be so mad all the time."

"Maybe if you'd stop running away from your life, you'd finally grow up. Why are you here? And where is your husband?"

Questions she couldn't answer. "Go to hell," she snapped and stomped out of the kitchen. Penny followed her.

When Averil reached her room, she waited for the dog to enter before closing the door behind her. She sank onto her bed and realized she'd left her breakfast in the microwave. Dammit. She was hungry, and she couldn't go back out there until Nina left for work. At least that would be relatively soon.

"Your Aunt Nina is not a nice person," Averil told the dog. Penny jumped up and sat next to her. "You know I've been taking care of you, right?"

Penny wagged her tail in agreement.

She hugged the dog, then opened her laptop and logged on to the internet. There was nothing captivating in her email so she typed out a quick note to Kevin.

Hey, it's me. I'm doing okay. I slept for about three days, which I guess I needed. Now I'm going to do some work and get going on my novel. The novel she really had to start before she could get going on it, she thought.

Nina is her usual domineering self. She's upset I brought a rescue dog with me. I found her at a rest stop, where she'd been abandoned. She was in pretty bad shape. I took her to a local vet and just couldn't give her up. Penny's so sweet—I know you'll love her.

She paused, then decided she didn't want to admit he'd been right about her sister. Again.

I hope you're doing okay. How's work? I miss you.

She sent the email, then heard the front door close.

"She's gone," Averil told Penny and hurried back to the

kitchen. Her mac and cheese was on the counter. She took a bite, then another.

After finishing her pasta and eating a banana, Averil wandered back into the bedroom. She saw she had mail waiting and clicked on the icon. Kevin had written her back.

I'm fine. Work is busy. I've been staying later than usual and getting caught up. As for Nina and the dog, I'm not surprised she's upset. Unless you asked her if it was okay if you brought a dog into the house, she has every right to be annoyed. It's not like you asked me if I wanted one. Instead you announced you'd found one and were keeping it.

Averil glared at the screen. "That's not fair," she mumbled. "What was I supposed to do? Leave her in the parking lot?"

But she knew that wasn't what Kevin meant. Averil could have called and asked him if he agreed with her decision. Or she could have taken Penny to a shelter.

You do that, his letter continued. You make decisions that affect other people without talking to them first. Without talking to me. You're the first one to blame others for what goes wrong in your life, but you don't want to think about anyone else when you make a decision. Like changing your mind about wanting a baby.

There was more, but she didn't want to read it. She slammed her laptop shut and crossed her arms over her chest. First, Nina and now, Kevin.

"I hate my family," she said aloud. Penny looked at her. "Not you," she told the dog.

Penny returned her head to her paws, but Averil would swear she saw something in the animal's eyes. As if her new pet was asking how long it would be until Averil blamed her for what was wrong in her life.

★ ★ ★

Nina typed quickly on the keyboard, blocking time on the future schedule. As Andi's pregnancy progressed, she would need time to rest during the day. It made sense to get the blocks in place now, before appointments were made, rather than trying to fit them in later. She'd already checked the supply order that was going out and rescheduled a rep visit. A busy morning, she thought. Just like all the others.

Their afternoon was light—which was unexpected. She and Andi were going to discuss temporary replacements for the few weeks Andi wanted to take off for maternity leave.

The phone buzzed.

Nina reached for it. "Hello?"

"You have a visitor." Holly, their receptionist, sighed. "A very handsome visitor. Tall, blond. Great blue eyes. If you don't want him, can I have him?"

Nina grinned. "You're married."

"I know, but as I was pretty sure you were going to say no, I figured it was safe to ask."

"Unusual strategy. I'll be right there."

Nina hung up and saved her work. She sat for another couple of seconds, telling herself the sudden fluttering in her stomach wasn't excitement or even nerves. She hadn't eaten lunch yet. She was hungry, nothing more. The fact that Kyle had stopped by didn't mean anything.

As he'd warned her, he'd been gone for four days. She hadn't heard from him. She'd thought she might get a call or a text later in the day, but she hadn't expected him to stop by. Yet here he was.

She stood and smoothed the front of her scrubs. She had gone for angels in pastel colors that day, with dark green pants. Not exactly a sexy look. Her work clothes were supposed to be functional, and until today, she hadn't cared one way or the other. How just like a man to make her worry about her appearance, she thought, fluffing her bangs before walking down the hallway.

Andi stuck her head out of her office. "A man? Can I meet him?"

"Not yet."

She opened the door to the waiting room and saw Deanna Phillips with her two youngest. The twins were watching Kyle as he waved his hands over their heads, then pulled a quarter out of Sydney's ear.

"Look!" Savannah said, clapping her hands. "Can we learn magic, Mommy?"

Deanna saw Nina and grinned. "I'm sure there's a class. I'll check with the summer camp. Learning new tricks is always fun, isn't it, Nina?"

Nina rolled her eyes. "Hello, Kyle. I see you've met Deanna and her daughters."

"I have." He handed the quarter to Sydney. "They're as beautiful as their mom."

A loud sigh came from the reception area. This was getting out of hand.

She walked over to him. "We should take this outside so we don't disrupt everyone's day."

"Don't leave on my account," Holly called.

"Uh-huh." Nina held open the front door. "I'm taking lunch."

Kyle followed her onto the porch. "Sorry I didn't call before stopping by, but I wanted to see you."

Once again, she didn't care if it was a line—it totally worked for her.

"How was your trip?"

"Busy. Good."

"A lot of flying?" she asked as they went down the stairs.

He grinned. "Yes, I flew a lot."

"Is there a better way to ask the question? Am I showing my ignorance?"

They'd reached his car. The ridiculously small two-seater. He took both her hands in his and drew her close. "You're showing how charming you are. I like the angels on your shirt."

Before she could respond, he pulled her against him and kissed her.

His lips were warm against hers. She instinctively tilted her head and wrapped her arms around him, even as she parted her lips. He brushed her tongue with his. Her eyes sank closed, and she gave herself up to the seduction that he offered.

The deep kisses made her weak with longing. She honest-to-God couldn't remember the last time she'd had sex with someone other than herself, let alone a man-induced orgasm. Kyle moved his hands up and down her back, touching her with a confidence that made her wonder if the front seat of his silly car really was too small.

He drew back and rested his forehead on hers. "I've missed you," he murmured. "I thought about you while I was gone."

"I missed you, too," she admitted. "Even if you are too young and completely inappropriate."

He grinned. "Think of me as a temptation."

"Sure. That's easy."

He straightened. "I brought lunch."

She stared at him. "Excuse me?"

"Lunch. It's noon. I brought a picnic."

"That's so sweet. I would have been happy with the kissing."

He chuckled. "Good to know."

He popped the trunk and pulled out several bags of food, along with a thick blanket. The day was clear and the temperature in the high sixties. Not exactly beach weather, but it was warm enough for an alfresco meal.

Nina led the way to the side yard, away from most of the windows and whoever might be watching. They spread out the blanket, then settled on it. Kyle passed out sandwiches and cans of soda.

"I brought one of each," he said, showing her both regular and diet soda.

"I'm a girl," she said, reaching for the can of diet.

"I noticed. It's one of my favorite things about you."

"Me being a girl?"

His blue eyes crinkled at the corner. "Uh-huh. It makes for intriguing possibilities." He glanced around, then lowered his voice. "There are anatomical differences between us."

She did her best to keep from smiling. "Are there?"

"Several."

"Does it make things confusing?"

"It can, so let me know if you need me to explain them to you."

She took the sandwich he offered. "I'd like that. Or you could show me."

The teasing was fun, and as with the sex issue, she was woefully out of flirting practice. She was about to joke about diagrams when she noticed Kyle staring at her with an intensity that made her want to squirm. Gone were the humor and the playful grin. Instead he looked at her the way a man looked at... Well, a woman.

A second later, the passion was gone, and the Kyle she knew returned. But the moment reminded her he wasn't the kid she barely remembered. He was a soldier and very much an adult. Despite the four years between them, if anyone was going to be playing catch-up, it was her.

"I can't see you for a few days," he said, unwrapping his

sandwich. "That's the other reason I stopped by. There's a drill, and I'm going to be on base."

"Military life is complicated."

"It can be."

She took a bite of her sandwich and chewed. "I looked up the Blue Angels online. You have to have 1250 tactical jet flight-hours. They keep track of how many hours you fly?"

"Uh-huh, along with the number of carrier landings. Bigger is better."

"You're such a guy."

"We already discussed that anatomy thing."

"Yes, we did and we're not going back to it. The average age of a pilot on the team is thirty-three. So you still have a ways to go."

"I'll get there by thirty," he said, sounding confident. "I'm always ready to take a flight. I work hard."

"It's a different world than the one I'm used to," she admitted. "You're dedicated."

"I know what I want and I go after it." One corner of his mouth turned up. "In every aspect of my life."

She admired his focus as much as she worried about not living up to his vision of her. "So, once you've had me, you'll move on?"

"Not even close."

"Maybe you will. Maybe it's a one-time thing."

"I'm going to enjoy having my fantasy fulfilled for more than a little while. I mean that figuratively and literally. Like I said—I'm in Everett for a few months. Why not spend them with you?"

In bed. He didn't say that part, but she hoped he was thinking it. Because she was.

"The Mariners are having a good season," she said, thinking baseball had to be a safer topic. "They're in second place in their division."

"Can't take the heat?" he asked.

"I'm making a strategic retreat."

"Don't know the meaning of the word. I gotta keep moving forward."

"So you're relentless."

"I'm determined."

He overwhelmed her, she thought, wondering if she was getting aroused or having her very first-ever hot flash. With Kyle there was no maybe. No almost. After years of being the one who decided, it might be nice to put her fate in someone else's hands...so to speak.

"When are you back?" she asked.

The slow, sexy grin returned. "Early next week. I'll call the second I'm free."

"You do that."

Averil got over her annoyance with the world in time to bang out an article. It was about surviving a bossy older sibling, complete with breathing exercises and escape plans. She would edit it later and then send it in. As long as she stayed on her writing schedule, she would keep her manager happy. Right now Maya seemed to be the only person still on Averil's side. Best to keep things that way. Besides, steady freelance work paid.

After lunch, Averil loaded Penny in the car. She drove across the island and parked in front of Blackberry Preserves.

The store had been in her family for a couple of generations. Averil had grown up in and around the store. She and Nina had played dress-up with the old clothes and made forts out of moth-eaten cushions. Later, in high school, Averil had worked shifts to earn money, although she'd preferred her job

at the local diner. At that point, getting away from her demanding older sister had been a priority.

Averil and Penny walked into the store. It was as crowded
as she remembered, with stacks of furniture, overflowing
shelves and boxes of yet-to-be-discovered treasures. There
was a musty smell, which was familiar, mingling with the
scent of what she would swear was an orange-scented cleaner.

"Hello," she called. "Anybody here?"

A pretty woman with short dark hair walked around a
shelving unit and smiled. "Hi. Can I help you?"

"You work here?" Averil asked.

"Yes. I'm Cindy. I'm new."

Averil smiled. "Averil Wentworth. Nina's ne'er-do-well
baby sister." She nodded at the dog. "This is Penny."

"Oh, hi. Nice to meet you. Nina didn't mention a sister."

"I live in Mischief Bay. I'm visiting for a few weeks." She
sniffed. "Have you been cleaning? It smells good in here."

"Yes, and it's daunting, but I'm getting there."

"You sure you want to take on a project this big?"

Cindy laughed. "I'm also unearthing treasures as I go. Just
this morning I discovered several quilts that are handmade.
I've been online trying to figure out their ages. If I'm right,
a couple of them are valuable."

"I'm not surprised. My mom only buys what she likes. She
searches for beauty and then either keeps it in the family or
shares it with the world. Bertie is more practical and generally has a good idea of what's valuable." The first year Bertie
had worked in the store, sales had been up fifty percent. They
hadn't moved any more merchandise, but nearly everything
sold had been more expensive.

"How long have you worked here?" Averil asked.

"Only a week. There were some issues with the woman
who was here before."

No doubt Nina had run her off, Averil thought.

"I have tea brewing in the back," Cindy said. "Want some?"

"That would be nice. Thank you."

They walked into the crowded back room. Averil could see how Cindy had already made changes. While there was still furniture everywhere and plenty of boxes, the counters were clean and the floor had been swept.

Cindy poured two mugs of tea and offered cookies from a box.

"Thanks." Averil took a sugar cookie, broke it in half and gave the smaller piece to Penny.

"There's so much to do," Cindy said. "Most of the inventory isn't in the computer. I'm splitting my time between cleaning and organizing. I start to go crazy if I'm on the computer too long. I guess it comes from all the years I spent typing on mine. I was a paralegal in my past life."

"What brings you to the island?"

"My husband retired. He's a little older than me and has worked hard, so he deserves it. But I just can't stay home. My mother-in-law lives with us."

"Oh." Kevin's mother was a lovely lady, Averil thought, but she wouldn't want the other woman living with her. "That could be difficult."

"It's rarely boring," Cindy said with a grin. "She hates me, but I think she's accepted that, after twenty-five years, I'm not going anywhere." She lowered her voice. "I'm the second wife. His first wife died."

"And your husband's mother has turned her into a saint."

"Pretty much. But that's okay. I would never tell him, but he's worth it. And I have three great kids. One from his previous marriage and our two. I've been lucky. Now I have this job. I love it, except for the obvious stress."

"What stress?"

Cindy laughed. "Selling a chair for ten dollars only to have it pop up on *Antiques Roadshow* with an auction value of twenty thousand."

"I wouldn't worry about it," Averil told her. "Bertie is good, but she's not that good."

"I don't know. I've found a few amazing pieces. Speaking of which, I should get back to work. I'm not trying to kick you out. I just need to be cataloging."

"I understand." Averil took a sip of her tea, then followed Cindy back into the store. "What are you working on now?"

"The lunch boxes. They're easy enough. I look them up on eBay, figure out a good price and then enter them in the computer."

Averil thought about the novel she had yet to start, the angry email from Kevin and the fact that Nina wasn't speaking to her.

"Want some help?" she asked. "I can sticker or enter in inventory."

"Thanks. It will go faster with two of us. If you're sure you don't mind."

"I don't," Averil assured her. "Any old blankets around?" she asked, motioning to Penny.

"In the box in the corner."

Averil collected a couple. "I'm going to make a bed for her." She thought about how long they'd been out. "Let me take her on a short walk and then I'll be back to help."

"Sounds great."

Averil smiled. See? She could be responsible, she thought, heading for the front door. Kevin and Nina were wrong about her.

Chapter Nine

NINA PUSHED A piece of chicken around on the plate. This was ridiculous, she told herself. How could she and Averil not have anything to say to each other? They were sisters who hadn't seen each other in months. They sure had enough to talk about on the phone, but there was silence when they were in the same room.

Averil was pouting, no doubt because Nina had snapped at her about Penny that morning. Though maybe Averil hadn't been as careless with Penny as Nina had first assumed, but why go there? This family was exhausting, she thought. If it wasn't her mother forgetting to get the roof fixed, it was her sister picking up stray dogs.

She drew in a deep breath and decided she would remember her lunch with Kyle instead. That had been perfect. The man was funny and charming and just intense enough to be irresistible. If she could bottle his brand of determined flirtation, she could make a fortune.

The phone rang. She reached for it and glanced at the caller ID.

"It's Bertie," she said, pushing the speaker button and setting the receiver in the middle of the table. "Hi, Bertie."

"Hello, my sweet. How are you?"

"I'm good. Guess who's here?"

"Hi, Bertie," Averil said from across the table.

Bertie laughed. "What brings you to Blackberry Island, Averil? Did we know you were coming?"

"No. I'm just here to do some thinking." Averil stuck out her tongue at Nina. "I have a dog. She's beautiful and her name is Penny."

"I can't wait to meet her," Bertie said. "Bonnie, Averil has come home for a visit."

There was a squeal in the distance, then they heard Bonnie's voice. "We'll be home in a few days. You'll still be there, won't you?"

"I promise," Averil said. "Tell Nina to be nice to me, because she's been surly."

Nina told herself to act like the adult. That she had to believe in karma and that she would be rewarded in a later life.

"Nina, be patient with your sister," Bonnie said. "We all aspire to be more like you and we all fail."

Nina felt the slap from over a thousand miles away. Did it occur to Bonnie that Averil was the problem? Of course not. But she didn't say that. "Have you had a good trip, Mom?"

"The best. The van is full of wonderful treasures."

"Tell her about the painting," Bertie said.

Bonnie laughed, the sound carrying clearly over the phone lines. "I found the most hideous painting. There was an estate sale of an old man who bought storage unit contents. There were crates and crates of them. We bought two of the crates."

Nina held in a groan. "Let me guess. Without knowing what was inside."

"Of course. If you know what you're getting, where's the

fun? Anyway, mostly there was junk but there was also a painting. It's truly ugly, but the frame is beautiful. I wanted to toss
the picture right away but Bertie said you had to see it. So
we're bringing it home."

"Lucky us," Nina murmured.

There was a muffled noise, then Bertie was on the phone
again. "We should be there in less than a week, my loves. Be
good until we get there. Oh, Nina. How's the new girl working out at the store?"

"Cindy's great," Averil said. "I met her. I really like her.
Don't believe anything Nina says about her."

Bertie sighed. "I wish you girls wouldn't fight. Family matters."

Nina glared at Averil and mouthed the words, "Stop it."
Averil glared right back.

"We're not fighting," Nina assured her. "Drive safely. We'll
see you Saturday or Sunday."

"Yes, you will. Night all."

There was a click and the call disconnected.

Nina replaced the receiver. "Seriously? You have to act like
that? What are you, twelve?"

She half expected Averil to flounce out of the room. Instead her sister leaned back in her chair and nodded slowly.

"You're right. Sorry. It's really easy to fall back into bick-
ering when I'm here."

Nina studied her sister, taking in the long blond curls and
big eyes. "Okay," she said slowly, not sure she could believe her
sister to be that rational. "Maybe I jumped to conclusions about
Penny. I should have asked what your plans were for her."

Averil cleared her throat. "Me sleeping for three days made
it hard to talk."

This was good, Nina thought cautiously. "So, why are you
here?"

Averil stared at her. "So, the thirty seconds of détente was too much for you?"

"I just asked a question. You showed up with no warning. It's a little strange. I'm concerned. Is everything okay back home?"

Averil pushed her broccoli around on her plate. "I needed to get away. I have to think."

"About Kevin? Is everything okay with him? He's such a great guy."

Averil shook her head. "Right. It has to be my fault. He can't have done anything wrong. Poor, perfect Kevin, stuck with a wife like me."

Nina felt the beginnings of a headache. It was always like this with her sister. No matter how she tried, Averil misread everything she said. Averil had no idea how lucky she was. She kept risking everything she had, and for what?

She forced herself to take a breath and speak in a slow, non-threatening voice. "I'm sorry you felt things were so difficult that you had to leave home to work through the issues. Want to tell me what's going on with you and Kevin?"

Averil studied her, as if trying to decide whether or not to believe the conciliatory tone. "He wants to start a family," she admitted.

Nina found herself pressing her hand to her belly. A baby, she thought longingly. She'd always wanted a family. A couple of kids. Maybe three. A rambling house, a few pets. Nothing crazy. It wasn't as if she aspired to be on the cover of the *Sports Illustrated* swimsuit edition. She'd always assumed her dreams were achievable. But she'd taken the more affordable path of being a nurse rather than trying to get into medical school. She'd never fallen in love after she broke up with Dylan. Here she was, thirty, living at home with, as Elizabeth Bennett would say, no prospects.

Except for Kyle, she thought wistfully. Although he wasn't looking for anything permanent.

She was supposed to have left the island. Every now and then she thought about starting over. Sometimes she even made progress. Like taking her MCATs a couple of years ago. But, so what? She'd done great on the medical school entrance exams. It wasn't as if she was really going to start medical school now. She was settled. Or maybe the correct phrasing was she *had* settled.

"What do you want?" she asked her sister.

"I don't know." Averil shook her head. "I want kids. I really do. Just not right now. I'm lost. I know he's upset because I'm still not sure. We've been married nearly five years. He doesn't know what I'm waiting for."

Nina was pretty sure that Averil wasn't ready to have someone else be the center of attention. Her little sister was good at getting people to take care of her. A baby would make that whole dynamic shift. But she also knew better than to mention that.

"Do you know what's wrong?" she asked instead.

"No. That's why I'm here. I want to figure it out. I like my job, but I don't love it. I love Kevin, but there's something missing in our marriage. I feel like I'm always waiting for something to happen. I just don't know what it is."

Nina tried to be sympathetic, but all she could think about was how much she'd sacrificed so Averil could follow her dreams. And here she was, saying she'd picked the wrong dreams.

"Are you sure you still love Kevin?"

Averil grimaced. "Yes. He's wonderful and adores me. I don't want to be with someone else. I just want to feel..." She shrugged. "I don't know. I can't explain it. I'm not leaving Kevin."

"You kind of already have," Nina pointed out.

Averil jumped to her feet. Penny jumped up as well, obviously startled. She looked between the two women.

"Why do you have to do that?" Averil demanded. "Why do you have to turn everything into the worst possible scenario?"

She stalked off toward her room. Penny trailed after her.

Nina stood and began to clear the table. She remembered when she and Averil had been more like real sisters. Back when it had been the two of them against the world. But since college, everything was different. Averil was always coming to Nina for advice and direction, but then got mad at her when she gave it. Nina wasn't sure who was at fault, nor did she think it mattered. The bigger problem was they were caught in a cycle of blame and misunderstanding and she didn't know how to change that.

She knew she loved her sister, but sometimes loving someone wasn't fun.

"Hi," Dylan said with a smile.

Nina smiled back, wondering why she'd agreed to a date she didn't actually want. She'd spent most of the day dreading her evening plans and had nearly called him a couple of times to cancel. But she figured she was just putting off the inevitable. She would go out with Dylan, they would talk about the past, come to terms with the fact that they were both living on a very small island and then be done with it.

If only he were Kyle.

He looked good, she admitted grudgingly. Tall, with dark hair and deep green eyes. He wore jeans and a button-down shirt, and his clothes emphasized the strength in his body. He was older than Kyle and looked more mature. Solid, she thought. Kyle was a low-slung convertible. Dylan was more like all-wheel drive. Not sexy, but reliable in bad weather.

"My sister's back in town," she said to fill the silence. "She's out walking her dog, but she said to say hi."

"How is Averil?"

"Honestly, I have no idea. She showed up with her dog and hasn't said much about what's going on with her. I hope she's not going to do something foolish and leave her husband. Kevin is a good guy." She winced. "Wow, that was an emotional dump you didn't need."

"I can handle it." He motioned to his car. "Shall we?"

They walked toward his BMW. Dressing for this date had been a lot simpler than her dinner with Kyle, she thought. She, too, wore jeans, with a silky blouse. She'd put on a little makeup and earrings.

She slipped into the passenger seat, remembering the last time she'd been in his car.

"Any permanent damage to the leather?" she asked when he settled next to her.

"None at all."

"Good. So, where are we going?"

"It's a surprise."

"A good surprise or a bad surprise?"

He grinned. "A good one, I hope."

"Now I'm nervous."

"Don't be." He started the engine and pulled out of the driveway.

Because he would take care of her, she thought. That was Dylan's style. Comfortable and dependable. When they'd first started dating, she'd been mature enough to appreciate those qualities. While other girls had craved the bad boys, she'd wanted to feel safe.

She remembered the first time he'd taken her sailing. The ocean had been so big, the swells had made her uncomfortable. But he'd been careful and had obviously known what he was doing.

He'd never driven drunk or partied too hard. He'd gotten her home on time, he called when he said he was going to. With Dylan, she'd been able to relax, to be a teenager. That had been nice, she thought wistfully.

And then he'd left her.

Best not to go there, she told herself, returning her attention to the road. She watched as he drove through town, then started to laugh when he pulled into a small, gravel parking lot. "No way."

"We're not eating here, if that's what you're asking. I know a great place with a view. But I thought we'd pick up sandwiches, first."

They were at Arnie's—a low-rent kind of food place with the best pulled-pork sandwiches in three counties. People drove all the way from Seattle to eat here. The food was messy and delicious.

They walked up and placed their orders. When everything had been packed into paper bags, they returned to the car. Dylan headed for the marina.

For a minute she thought they were going to go out on a boat. Maybe his dad's. But instead, he headed for the new luxury condos and pulled into the underground parking structure.

"Your place," she said.

"I figured we could watch the sunset and talk without being interrupted. I do have to warn you I don't have much in the way of furniture right now. But I did dig up a blanket to put on the floor."

"You know how to show a girl a good time."

As they walked to the elevator, she wondered if he had anything else in mind. But as the thought formed, she dismissed it. This was Dylan. He would never presume that sex was on the table. Besides, they hadn't seen each other in years and years. They were barely friends. They'd been in love once, but that had been so long ago.

For a second she allowed herself to wonder what it would have been like if things had been different. If they'd stayed together. They would now be Dr. and Dr. Harrington. Maybe with a couple of kids. The concept was so at odds with her life, it was like envisioning living on Mars.

They walked out of the elevator and toward a large wooden door. Dylan opened it, then motioned for her to go first.

A short hallway forced a left turn, then she stepped out into an open-concept condo with floor-to-ceiling windows and a view of the Sound and the Strait of Juan de Fuca.

In the early evening, there were just enough clouds to block the sun. Patches of blue sky showed through. She could see the peninsula and boats. The water was smooth, reflecting light that seemed to shimmer.

"Amazing," she murmured. "That doctor thing is working out for you."

He chuckled. "It has its advantages."

He set their dinner on the granite countertop, then collected a comforter from the corner. As he'd warned, there wasn't much in the way of furniture. There were a couple of folding chairs, a coffee table and a massive TV mounted above the fireplace.

"You made sure you have a TV but you don't have a sofa?" she asked as she helped him smooth out the blanket.

"I have priorities. Actually the TV came with the unit. I've ordered furniture. It's supposed to be here in the next few days."

He walked over to the refrigerator and pulled out a couple of beers. She took the food to the comforter and sat down.

Her second picnic meal in a week, she thought, knowing that it wouldn't be polite to compare the two men or dates.

"How are you adjusting to being back?" she asked as she passed out food.

He opened the beers and joined her. "It's going to take a while. The practice is pretty typical for the suburbs. Any trauma cases go to the hospital on the mainland."

Dylan had graduated from medical school several years ago and done the usual residency, but then he'd taken a fellowship. Two years working with poor families in Appalachia.

"Not used to having a hospital to fall back on?" she asked.

"For a while, I was all there was." He unwrapped his sandwich. "Poverty makes it difficult to stay healthy. A lot of homes lacked the basics, like clean running water and sanitation. Not like here."

"Are you questioning your decision to come back?"

"It's done now," he said, picking up his beer. "I told my dad I'd return, so I did."

"But if you hadn't?"

He gave her a wry smile. "I wouldn't mind trying something different. Maybe becoming a trauma specialist."

"You're right, that's different."

"What about you? Happy with your work?"

"Most days. It's satisfying. I like working with kids. Andi's great. You met her, right?"

He nodded. "My parents had her and her husband Wade over for dinner. I remember Wade and his brother. Zeke was a senior when I was a freshman. He was a football god."

She laughed. "That made an impression on you?"

"Sure. I was scrawny and picked-on. I wanted to be a football god."

"Your parents would never have allowed it. What if your

precious brain had been damaged?" She smiled. "My son, the doctor. They're your dad's favorite words."

Dylan's green gaze settled on her face. "I hope he didn't talk about me too much."

"It was fine. By the time I went to work for him, I was long over you." She picked up her sandwich. "You weren't all that."

Actually he had been, and he'd broken her heart, but why go there?

"I handled our breakup badly," he admitted. "I'm sorry about that."

She was saved from answering by having to chew. When she swallowed, she said, "It was years ago, Dylan. Don't sweat it."

"I want to apologize. We'd been together a long time. We'd talked about getting married, and then it was over."

All true, she thought, preparing to be magnanimous about the whole thing when he added, "Just because you changed the rules doesn't mean I shouldn't have behaved better."

She put down her sandwich. "Excuse me? How did I change the rules?"

He frowned. "We were going to be together, Nina. You said you'd come to Seattle for college."

"I couldn't. Not for four years. There wasn't enough money." Not to mention the responsibilities she had at home. "We don't all have rich parents able to foot the bills."

"It was more than that. We had plans, and then you changed your mind."

"I didn't. I wanted to be with you. I wanted you to wait."

"I'd been waiting. You changed your plans without talking to me. That's why I broke things off."

He was taking the past and twisting it, she thought furiously. How could he blame it all on her? She'd been working her butt off, saving for college, taking care of her sister, working in the store and handling school.

His mouth twisted. "I don't want to fight about what happened. You're right. I ended it. I'm sorry for that."

A peace offering. She picked up her sandwich, then put it back down. "You'd gone off to college. It was bound to happen. Having your parents pushing you to find someone else didn't help."

His expression softened. "They never expected us to stay together as long as we did."

Because for the first two years of his college career, he'd stayed faithful. He'd come home on weekends, had her visit him. They'd still been wildly in love. But the summer after she graduated, everything changed.

"They had to step up their campaign," Nina said, poking at her potato salad. "They didn't know there was no way I could join you at UW." She started to say again that she'd been struggling with a lot of things at home, but held back. She was still trying to put together the pieces. Did Dylan really believe *she'd* been the one to change the rules?

"I'm sorry," he repeated.

"Apology accepted. It's not like we both didn't move on, right?" She reached for her sandwich.

"It took a while for me. After college, I came back for you."

She dropped her sandwich onto the paper bag and stared at him. "What are you talking about?"

"It had been two years, and I still missed you."

"You never came to see me."

He picked up his beer. "You were getting married. To Serge."

She groaned. "No. You didn't."

"I was there that weekend." He took a drink, then raised his eyebrows. "Serge?"

"I have no excuse."

"You married him."

"Something I still can't explain." Nina thought about her lone impulsive act. She'd met a tattooed biker on Wednesday, had sex with him on Thursday, eloped with him on Friday. By the following Tuesday, she'd been filing for an annulment.

"I was looking for something," she admitted.

"A guy named Serge."

"Will you please let that go?"

"No. I plan to hold it over your head forever."

She laughed. "Okay, then. As long as we're playing fair." She studied his face. "Did you really come back for me?"

"Yeah, I did."

She felt a whisper of regret brush across her heart. "Then you went off to medical school and forgot all about me."

"You forgot about me in Serge's arms."

She sighed. "For what it's worth, I was never impulsive again."

"As long as you learned your lesson."

"I did."

She took another bite of her sandwich. As she chewed, she wondered what would have been different if there hadn't been a Serge. If she and Dylan had done what they'd always talked about. Become doctors together.

Sometimes, like when she'd taken the MCAT, she told herself it wasn't too late. That she could walk away from her life and follow her dream. But then something happened. Something mundane and silly and she got distracted. Which made her wonder if her dream was all that important to her. Did she really want to be a doctor or did she just want to talk about it? If she meant what she said, why hadn't she done anything about it?

She raised her bottle of beer toward him. "A toast," she said. "To you. You did what you said you would do."

"That's not so hard."

"Sometimes it is. Welcome home, Dylan."

"Thanks."

Their bottles clinked.

"How are your folks?" she asked.

He groaned. "My mother's already talking about grand-children."

"In general, or does she want you to get married first?"

"She wants a big wedding."

"Any prospective brides on the horizon?"

"No, but that doesn't seem to bother her. She bought me towels. They were green, with flowers."

"To match your eyes?" she asked sweetly.

"Hey, whose side are you on?"

Nina laughed. As she bit into her sandwich again, she remembered that she'd been dreading her evening with Dylan. Now that she was here, she wasn't sure why. Whatever had happened between them, they'd always been friends. He was a good guy. Wrong about their past, but still fun to be around.

"Thanks for inviting me over," she said impulsively. "I'm glad we did this."

"Me, too."

Averil walked into the kitchen. She wasn't sure of the time, but it was obviously after seven-thirty because Nina was gone. There was still coffee in the pot and boxes of cereal on the counter. Penny lay in a patch of morning sun—her relaxed state attesting to the fact that she'd been let out and had her breakfast.

"You really don't need me here, do you?" she asked the dog.

Penny thumped her tail on the floor.

Averil poured coffee, then sat at the table. She hadn't slept well and didn't know the reason. It wasn't that she was overly tired. She wasn't doing much of anything. She'd written all the articles due for the next three weeks. She couldn't bring herself to look at her novel. Which left her, tragically, with nothing to do in her day.

Telling herself she needed time to think, to discover her inner self, made her feel like a self-indulgent child. But what else was there?

She carried her coffee with her to the bathroom and showered. After dressing and eating breakfast, she looked at the clock. It was nearly nine. The rest of the day stretched out endlessly.

"Fine," she muttered and collected her car keys. After grabbing Penny's leash, she called to the dog and together they made their way to her car. Five minutes later, she pulled into the gravel parking lot of Blackberry Preserves.

Cindy was by the cash register. She smiled when she saw Averil.

"Hi. What brings you here this morning?"

Averil drew in a breath. "I wondered if you needed any help in the store. With the cleanup or data entry or whatever."

She braced herself for questions. Why would she feel the need to ask in her own family's store? Didn't she have anything better to do with her time? Had she really run away from her life, driving over a thousand miles to do it, only to end up in here?

But all Cindy said was, "Sure. I'd love some help. Where would you like to start?"

Chapter Ten

NINA COULD BARELY breathe. She was tingling and fluttery and about to jump out of her skin. "Insanity," she murmured, slipping into flats before dashing out of her bedroom.

The afternoon had crawled, and now it was five to six and she didn't know how she was going to survive the next three hundred seconds.

What if he was late? What if he had to cancel? She shook her head, refusing to consider the possibility. Kyle had been released or relieved or whatever it was that allowed him to leave the base. He'd called and was on his way. She was going to see him in a few minutes. They were spending a casual evening together. Alone. Until then she could—

The doorbell rang.

"I'll get it," she yelled as she hurried toward the door. She flung it open and saw him standing on the porch. His grin was easy and welcoming, his gaze appreciative. It was all she could do not to throw herself into his arms.

"Hi," she said, suddenly nervous and unsure of what to do with her hands.

"Hi. I can't believe I had to wait so long to see you again."

Which was the exact right thing to say, she thought as she shoved her house key into her purse and stepped out to join him.

"Me, too," she admitted.

His grin turned triumphant. "So, you missed me."

"Yes."

"A little or a lot?"

She laughed. "More than I wanted."

"I'll take that." He put his arm around her and drew her against him. "Ready to go?" he asked before kissing the top of her head.

"Yes."

They walked to his ridiculous car. He opened the passenger door for her, but before she could slide inside, he turned her so they were facing, then leaned in and kissed her.

His mouth was warm and welcoming, his tongue insistent. She parted for him and felt the instant heat that flared in her body. It was as if she were melting from the inside out. She had no choice but to wrap her arms around his neck and hang on for the ride.

He settled his hands on her waist, as if to hold her steady. The way the world was spinning right now, she needed an anchor, she thought, savoring the need pulsing through her in time with her rapidly beating heart.

He drew back slightly. The grin was gone, as was the easy acceptance. Instead he looked dark and dangerous, a man on the sexual edge.

He swore under his breath. "You're not supposed to get to me that much," he told her.

Words to make her breath catch. "I thought I was your dream girl."

"You are, but I figured I'd stay in charge."

She smiled. "Silly man."

"I guess." He sucked in air. "Okay, then. Dinner. There's a place up the coast where they serve—"

She put her hand over his mouth to silence him. He stopped talking and looked at her. One eyebrow rose inquisitively.

She knew the sensible course, knew what was supposed to happen. There was a sequence to these sorts of things. Rules existed for a reason—mostly to keep everyone...rational. Appropriate. Only she didn't care about that. She didn't care about saying no or waiting or what she *should* do.

She wasn't fooling herself. She knew Kyle wanted a fling—if she could use that term. He wasn't looking for an actual relationship. She was someone he wanted to have sex with. He was charming and honest and really good at making her feel like a princess. These days, that was fairly extraordinary.

"I'm not that hungry," she told him.

Kyle's expression tightened. She felt the muscles moving under her fingers. She dropped her arm to her side and held his gaze. "And I'd love to see your place."

There was a shift in his eyes. Something hot and male flared before being tamped down but not extinguished. "Dinner can wait," he told her, his voice low and full of anticipation.

She started to get into the car, only to pause. "You have condoms, right?"

One corner of his mouth turned up. "I have condoms."

The drive went by faster than Nina would have thought. They went over the bridge connecting Blackberry Island to the mainland, then south toward Everett. She would guess he had a small apartment near the base.

Sure enough, he pulled up to a four-story building. There was a nice garden out front and big windows, but otherwise it was unremarkable.

It wasn't until they were in the elevator that she felt the first of the nerves start to kick in. Her chest was tight, and her hands felt as if they were shaking. She thought about her last Pilates class, when she'd been forced to admit she was desperately out of shape. Her thighs were flabby, her tummy too fat and her breasts hadn't been perky in at least three years.

She wasn't having second thoughts, exactly. Because the truth was, she wanted to have sex with Kyle. She wanted his kisses on her mouth, his hands on her body. She wanted to feel him inside of her and mostly she wanted that soul-clearing moment of release.

If only she could use a better body to get there.

He led the way to the apartment door, then used his key to let them in. She stepped inside, half expecting some scary bachelor pad filled with pictures of lingerie models and beer cans. Instead she found herself in a large light-filled living room dominated by a black leather sofa. There was a TV above the fireplace and a glass coffee table but nothing else. The carpet was vacuumed, the surfaces clear of clutter.

Kyle dumped his keys and cell phone onto a small table by the door. His actions seemed automatic. She wondered if it was a fighter pilot thing. He had to be ready to leave at a moment's notice and couldn't spend valuable time looking for his keys.

She could see a bit of the kitchen, and it looked as clean as the living room. She could guess he didn't spend a lot of time in his apartment, but when he was here, he wasn't making a mess.

"Your mom taught you well," she murmured.

He smiled. "I'll tell her you approve."

"I'm not sure that's a good idea."

He faced her. "Nervous?"

"Very."

"Me, too."

She shook her head. "No way. You're the great-looking younger man. You win just by showing up."

His expression turned serious. "There's no win, Nina. There's just me wanting to make love with you. This isn't a game to me. I want you. I want to touch you and please you, but I also want you to be comfortable with me. I want you talking and laughing. This isn't just about getting laid. I hope you believe that."

Nina realized she didn't care if he was lying. Suddenly her flabby tummy was a whole lot less important than being held by this man. She walked into his embrace and pressed her mouth to his. She was going to take whatever he was offering.

Three hours and two orgasms later, Nina knew this was as close to floating as she'd ever gotten. She was boneless, sated, happy and all those other words used to describe the glow of mind-clearing sex.

She lay on her side, tucked next to Kyle. Her fingers rested on his rock-hard abs. She could actually trace the individual muscles. The man worked out, she thought, her eyes drifting closed. Something she should think about doing later. And she would. When her strength returned.

He ran his hand up and down her side, drifting over her hip, then back up to her shoulder. He had nice hands, she thought. Hands that knew right where to touch her. Skillful hands that had understood what a clitoris was for.

"Want to order a pizza?" he asked, as he nuzzled her neck. "I'm going to need to eat before round three."

She opened her eyes. "Round three?"

He flashed her that sexy grin. "See. I knew you'd get into the younger guy thing." He sat up. "I have a menu. Let me go grab it and we'll figure out what we want."

Then he was standing and walking across the room. Naked.

Her gaze dropped to his impressive ass as he left, then took in the full frontal as he returned.

He paused by the side of the bed. "Are you staying?"

The tone was questioning but tentative. So at odds with his usual cocky attitude. She looked at his face.

"The night?"

He nodded without speaking.

She would have guessed he preferred to sleep alone, so the question surprised her. "Do you want me to?"

He looked at her then. Something filled his blue eyes. Something that looked a lot like sincerity. "Yeah, I would."

In that heartbeat, she realized he wasn't out for a piece of ass. That, despite the attitude and good looks, he was just like everyone else. Looking to connect, to belong, to be accepted. Maybe not forever. Maybe, as he'd said, for the few months he was in town. But right now, that was plenty for her.

"Only if I get to be on top next time," she said.

He grinned. "You just keep getting better and better."

Saturday morning Averil worked in the store. Cindy took care of the customers, leaving Averil to sort through the box of jewelry they'd unearthed.

She knew almost nothing about how to tell real stones from fake. Cindy had found an old loop so Averil could look for a stamp that might indicate an artist or designer. Or if the metal was gold or silver. Very nice people actually stamped a piece when it was sterling silver or fourteen- or eighteen-karat gold.

Penny strolled around, exploring. She had settled into her new life easily. Averil couldn't figure out why someone would have dumped her. She was housebroken, friendly and affectionate. She supposed there were awful people everywhere, and she should be happy she'd been able to save Penny.

She opened another shoebox filled with jewelry and began

to sort them by type. Those with flaking stones or settings were obviously not the genuine article, but there were several gaudy pieces she thought might be the real thing.

The front door opened. Averil looked up and saw Nina walk in. Her sister looked slightly bemused, as if she hadn't yet figured out it was morning. Not a surprise, considering Nina hadn't come home the night before.

Nina glanced around the store, spotted her and came over. Penny hurried toward her, her long tail wagging. Nina paused to pet her.

"I didn't know you were seeing someone," Averil said, picking out a pair of earrings. The blue stone could be glass or it could be sapphire. She put them in the "maybe" pile.

Nina pulled out a stool and sat down. Her hair was combed, but she wasn't wearing makeup and she had that "I haven't showered yet" air about her.

"I'm not seeing anyone," she said, then shook her head. "All right. I guess I am."

"Can I assume the someone is a guy? Unless you're taking after Mom these days. You didn't come home. Or call."

She waited for her sister to snap that it wasn't her business, but instead Nina flushed. "Yes, well, I should have called. I'm sorry."

Curiouser and curiouser, Averil thought. "So where were you?"

"Out. With a friend." Nina paused. "A male friend."

"Thanks for the clarification. Anyone I know?"

"I don't think so. You, ah, did…." She cleared her throat. "No, you don't know him."

"Okay, then. You still have the glazed look. It must have been quite the night."

Nina's mouth twitched. "It was." She picked up a brooch in the shape of a large rose. "This is hideous."

"I agree. But I'm thinking the stones might be pink sapphires and rubies. I'm sorting as best I can. I thought we'd take everything to a jeweler and get a price on appraising it all."

"If you think it's worth it."

"Some of the gold is stamped, so we know that's genuine. A few of the items around here are valuable. Mom hated to price anything above twenty bucks. Cindy's been doing research. Not everything is going to make the center stage of *Antiques Roadshow,* but some of it is worth more than it's been priced."

Nina rolled her eyes. "Are you sure that's not wishful thinking?"

Just then Cindy walked past them carrying a box with three dolls poking out.

"Now, three hundred is for all of them, right?" the customer was saying.

"Yes. I'll write up the invoice. Will that be cash or credit card? We don't take checks."

Nina turned back to Averil. "Three hundred dollars for dolls?" she asked in a low voice.

"I know. It's crazy. Some of the lunch boxes are worth hundreds, too. There are some beautiful quilts, and we found several boxes of linens. I called Boston and asked her to stop by to give us her opinion on them and—"

Nina's expression sharpened. "What do you mean you called Boston? Boston King?"

"She's the only Boston I know."

"You can't call her."

"Why on earth not? She's a textile artist. I don't expect her to know the value of anything, but I'll bet she can spot which ones we need to be careful with and also give us the names of some local experts."

Nina stood and put her hands on her hips. "You can't *impose* on people like that."

"I'm asking a friend."

"Since when are you and Boston friends?"

"I've known her for years. I've taken art classes with her. We email every now and then. How can you not know this?"

"You *email* with her?"

Averil didn't get the problem. "Why are you so upset?"

"She's *my* friend. You're talking to my friends."

"Do you realize this is the third sentence in a row where your voice has gone up? You're getting shrill. You're also acting like a crazy person, Nina. I suppose I should tell you I also asked Deanna to come in and look at a few of the antiques. They might carpool, and I'll be talking to them together. Can you stand it?"

"Go to hell," Nina said loudly. She turned on her heel and left the store.

Averil stared after her until the front door of the store closed, then slowly shook her head. "That was the weirdest thing ever," she told the dog. "Your Aunt Nina is turning into a loon. Sex is supposed to make you mellow. She must be doing it wrong."

Penny wagged her tail.

Averil turned back to the box of jewelry, but instead of studying the next piece, she pulled her cell phone out of her pocket and texted Kevin.

Just had a run-in with the evil queen. She makes me tired.

What were you fighting about?

A good question, she thought. I have no idea. She's in a mood. You know how she gets.

I also know how YOU get.

Averil decided to take the comment in the spirit she was sure her husband meant it. You're saying I can be difficult.

That's one word for it. Gotta go.

Okay. I love you.

She waited, but there was no response. Because he was busy, she told herself. There couldn't be another reason.

Nina stepped out of the shower still annoyed with herself for letting Averil get to her. She shouldn't be surprised, she told herself as she toweled off and reached for her body lotion. Of course her sister would start invading every aspect of her life. That's what Averil did. Soon she would be working part-time at Andi's office and pretending to be a nurse.

Averil had always weaseled her way in to whatever Nina was doing. Whether it was getting her own tiny uniform and flags for drill team or visiting nearly every weekend while Nina was at UW for the last two years of college. Everyone adored her sister. Everyone asked about her. Averil became the favorite.

Nina reminded herself that she and her sister had a strange sibling/maternal relationship, and of course there would be friction. That all those years ago, Averil had only been trying to fit in and be important to Nina. She wasn't trying to make everyone like her better.

She reminded herself to relax. That she was an adult now and could handle what was going on. Her knee-jerk reaction wasn't something she should allow herself to continue. Her friends would stay her friends, whether or not they had anything to do with Averil.

As Nina dressed, she remembered her ambivalence as a child. She'd been responsible for her sister and therefore wanted the best for her. But sometimes Averil made that difficult...or impossible. Complications, she thought, reaching for the blow-dryer. And because of her annoyance, she'd just burned through the last lingering tingles of well-being left over from her night with Kyle.

Unfair, she thought, picking up her brush. Last night had been so amazing. And unexpected. Kyle was an attentive lover and sure knew what he was doing. She'd felt cherished and satisfied. He'd been funny and easy to be with. She'd thought she might worry about her less-than-perfect body, but he'd seemed happy enough with her, so she'd decided not to care, either.

She finished with her hair and tidied up the bathroom, then made her way into the kitchen. Of course Averil had left her breakfast dishes in the sink, along with bowls and pans. Apparently carrying things all the way to the dishwasher, three inches away, was just too much to ask. There were...

Nina saw the plate on the kitchen table. On it were a stack of dark, chocolate brownies covered in plastic wrap. There was also a note, "I'm hoping you're staying out all night with a man, big sis. So these are to keep up your strength. Xoxo."

Nina closed her eyes and swore, then reached for one of the brownies. They were soft and nearly melted on her tongue. How was she supposed to stay mad now, she wondered as she ate the brownie, then thought about having a second.

Before she could figure out the complexity that was her relationship with her sister and her own need for sugar, the doorbell rang.

She crossed the living room, aware that her heart was pounding and she couldn't stop smiling. Kyle, she thought happily. He'd said he was busy this weekend but maybe he'd—

She opened the door and was surprised at her visitor. "Dylan," she said, stating the obvious.

"Hey, there's a wine tasting down by the marina. Want to come with me?"

She thought about the dishes in the sink and how, aside from cleaning the house, she had no fun plans for the weekend beyond eating a batch of brownies her hips and thighs really didn't need. Then she looked at her former lover and remembered how she'd felt in *his* arms all those years ago.

The unexpected image was nearly as potent as remembering her night with Kyle. Great—a couple of orgasms and she'd turned into a total slut.

"I'd love to," she said. "Let me get my keys."

She collected her purse, keys and a hoodie, and followed him out the door.

The late morning was sunny, but still cool. Summer was slow to arrive in the Pacific Northwest. The weather gradually cleared and there was less rain each month, but real warm temperatures often didn't show up until late July or even August.

Despite the nip in the air, Dylan had the top down on his convertible. She laughed.

"Seriously? It's barely sixty."

"But it's sunny," he said with a shrug. "I have to take advantage of that."

"You are such a guy." She slipped on her hoodie and zipped it.

"Are you going to complain about your hair? Because I can put up the top."

"You'd rather give up your car's reason for being than listen to a woman complain about her hair?"

"Pretty much."

"I can't decide if that is noble or very, very sad."

He grinned as he held open the passenger door. She got in and then twisted her long hair into a coil and tucked it under her hoodie.

"Leave the top down," she told him. "I hate it when men over thirty start to sob."

"But it's okay if they're twenty-nine?"

"They're still maturing."

He chuckled as he got into the driver's side and started the engine. "Okay, young lady. Let's get you drunk."

"We sip at a wine tasting. We do not get drunk."

"It's okay to cry if you're younger than thirty, and you can't get drunk at a wine tasting. Are there other rules?"

"Dozens. I can send you a pdf later."

They drove to his condo building and parked in his spot. They took the elevator to the ground floor, then walked out into the bright sun.

The grassy area between the marina and the duck boat rides had been roped off and there were booths and tables. Nina counted at least a dozen Washington wineries in attendance, some from as far away as Walla Walla.

Dylan led the way to the entrance and paid for the two of them. They were given colored bands for their wrists and handed a wineglass decorated with an event logo.

"I never get asked for ID anymore," Nina said, as they strolled to the first booth. "It's been years. Isn't that sad?"

"You want to look twenty?"

She stared at him. "All women want to look younger."

"Why? You're what? Thirty? Talk to me when you're pushing fifty."

"Hey, what happened to the sympathetic guy who was worried about my hair?"

"I don't get the age thing. You are what you are. Who cares about the number?"

"So speaks a man who has never read a fashion magazine."

His green eyes crinkled with humor. "And yet I feel completely satisfied with my life. You look great. Why sweat it?"

"Just stop talking or I'll hit you."

"Violence. Unexpected and a little exciting."

"Oh, please." She was still laughing when they reached the first booth.

"Hi," the woman behind the makeshift counter said. "Today we're pouring our Merlot and our Malbec. The grapes are grown in the state. The weather in the Columbia Valley is perfect, with long sunny days and cold nights."

Five minutes later Nina knew she was a fan of Malbec. "I know way more about growing grapes than I should," she admitted as they moved toward the next booth. "I hate that it's science. Winemaking should be a mystery with a hint of magic. It's like finding out what's in the secret sauce."

"Add it to the rule book," he said. "I have a lot of extra memory on my computer. I can take it."

They went to a couple more booths before stopping at a food cart and buying a fruit and cheese plate. There were picnic tables set up by the water. They settled across from each other and opened their boxed snacks.

"How's work?" she asked when they were settled.

"Good. My parents are already planning a trip to Australia and New Zealand next year."

"Leaving you in charge?" she asked teasingly.

"I'm sure I'll be supervised. There's office staff to keep me in line."

She studied him. "You still miss your fellowship work," she said.

He nodded. "Some. I've been talking to a couple of doctors I know at the university hospital. I might be able to get in to some studies there."

"Interesting research?" she asked.

"And a lot of choices. Did you know the Pacific Northwest has the highest incidence of MS in the country?"

She nodded. "I've heard one of the theories is our chronic vitamin D deficiency. A result of all those gloomy days." She smoothed some cheese on a cracker. "You're saying you won't be happy with flu shots and annual checkups?"

"Family medicine serves a purpose. People need help with the little things and I'm the first line of defense against the bigger problems."

She waited.

He nodded slowly. "I'd like to be more challenged. Coming back to work with my dad was something we always talked about. Now that it's here, it's not how I imagined."

"But he's loving it."

"Yes, he is." He smiled at her. "Now it's your turn to be tortured. How's your mom?"

"Good. She and Bertie are on their way home from one of their buying trips. God knows what treasures they'll have with them."

"Your mom has eclectic taste. Is she still holding on to the most precious items for the family?"

"Yes. You're so well-mannered, and that's a very polite way to say we have a lot of crap in our house."

"I like your mom. She was always on my side."

Until he broke her heart, but why go there? "You'll have to come by the store and check out her latest finds. Although I do have to admit, with Bertie along, the quality is improving. I hired a new person to help at the store. Cindy has found a lot of potentially valuable merchandise in our inventory. We're going to get some pieces appraised."

She thought about Averil asking Boston and Deanna for help. The request made sense. They were smart, successful women who knew a lot. With a bit of distance and some wine tasting to mellow her mood, she wondered why she'd jumped all over Averil. They were both adults now. Averil wasn't going to take her place or suddenly become the "fun" friend.

"Where'd you go?" he asked.

"Sorry. I had a fight with Averil this morning. It was stupid. That's one of the tough things about having her home. I regress. Actually we both do. I become bossy and she acts like she's twelve. I should mention that to her. She could use it in an article for her magazine."

"That's one way to deal with it. I remember she used to hang around a lot. She wanted to be like you."

"No, she didn't. She was always complaining about the rules." Bonnie would have let Averil do whatever she wanted. It had been up to Nina to give her sister structure.

Dylan shook his head. "She used to watch you and dress like you."

"I don't remember any of that." Most of her memories were of trying to be a parent when she was still a kid herself. Except she'd thought the same thing herself, earlier that morning. She'd seen it as trying to steal her life, but maybe Dylan was right. Maybe it was about wanting to be closer.

"You were too busy raising her to see it. I like your mom a lot, but she didn't make it easy on you." He picked up his glass. "Come on, we're supposed to be having fun, not talking about subjects that make you uncomfortable. Let's go figure out the difference between a Syrah and a Cab."

Chapter Eleven

✦

IT WAS NEARLY three when Dylan drove her home. Nina leaned back in the seat, enjoying the wind in her hair and the sun on her face. Of course what she might have been enjoying was all the wine tasting, but that was okay, too.

"I had a good time," she told him as he turned onto her street. "We should—" She saw the big white van parked in the driveway and started to laugh. "They're back, so if you want to drop me off on the corner, I'm okay with that."

"Are you kidding? I can't wait to see what treasures they found."

"You are using the word *treasure* in the loosest sense of the meaning, right?"

"Have a little faith. What if they found something great?"

"You have obviously never been here to unload from one of their trips."

He pulled up in front of the house. Bonnie, Bertie and Averil turned toward them. Nina paused to take in the family resemblance of the Wentworth women. They were all tall, with blond hair. Averil's was curly, while Bonnie's hung straight down her back. Their blue eyes were the same color. Only Bertie was dark-haired and petite, with delicate features.

All three women wore jeans and sweaters. Bertie had tied a bright red scarf around her neck.

Nina found herself smiling as she hurried out of the car. "You're back!"

"We are!" Her mother hurried toward her, arms outstretched. They hugged, then Bertie joined them.

"We missed you," Bertie said, kissing her cheek. "We had a wonderful time, but it's nice to be home."

"We have so many wonderful things to show you," Bonnie said, glancing over Nina's shoulder. "But first, who's your young man?"

"Mom, you know Dylan."

"Do I?" Bonnie's tone was almost flirtatious. "I remember a gangly boy. This is a handsome man."

She moved toward Dylan. He surprised Nina by hugging her mother. Bertie watched with raised eyebrows.

"The infamous doctor who broke your heart?" she asked, her voice low.

"That's the one," Nina told her. "He's back to go into business with his dad."

"You're dating?"

"No, we're friends. We've been hanging out a little, but it's not romantic." She thought about Kyle. "But I do have fun news in the man department." She glanced at Dylan, then at her sister. "I'll tell you about it later."

Bertie squeezed her. "Good. I can't wait."

Averil was speaking to Dylan. "I didn't know you were back." She shot Nina an accusing glance. "It's great to see you."

"You, too. You're all grown up."

Nina pressed her lips together. If Averil really was an adult, she would be back with her job and her husband instead of hid-

ing out up here. But she didn't say that. There would be plenty
of fighting later. She didn't have to go looking for trouble.

Dylan walked to the back of the van. "May I?" he asked,
reaching for the handle.

"Be my guest," Bonnie told him. "As long as you're prepared
to be amazed."

"I am."

He opened the door, locking it in place before unlatching
the second door. Nina and Averil moved in behind him. Nina
stared at the jammed contents and wondered, as she did after
every trip, what on earth they'd been thinking.

There were boxes, a few chairs, a couple of small tables,
stacks of clothes and several paintings. The end of what could
have been a coatrack was balanced on a stack of old dishes.
A hat hung on the edge of a frame. It was as if the store had
given birth to a smaller, less organized version of itself.

"Impressive," Dylan said. "Is there a method to any of this?"

"It should all go to the store," Nina said firmly, aware she
was fighting a losing battle. But she had to at least try.

Bonnie and Bertie exchanged a glance. Nina didn't know
what the silent communication meant, but was sure it wasn't
flattering to her. She sighed.

"We don't have a lot of room in the house," she added.
"There isn't any space on shelves or tabletops." She turned to
Bertie. "You're the one who always says a cluttered environ-
ment isn't healthy."

"Then you're a little late with the advice," Averil told her.

"I know, but we have to start somewhere," Nina murmured.

Bonnie's expression turned wistful. "It would be nice to
have a few things here." She shook her head. "No, Nina is
right. Oh, but Dylan, you must see the ugly painting we
bought."

Dylan winked at Nina. "You bought an ugly painting on purpose?"

"Of course not," Bonnie said as she patted his cheek. "We bought a container and it was inside. Trust me, it's spectacularly awful, but I adore the frame. It's there." She pointed.

He reached for the painting. Nina moved in to help, holding the end of the coatrack, while he tugged on the frame. A couple of boxes tumbled out, along with a stack of books.

"Haven't you heard of e-readers?" Averil asked, catching several of the books before they hit the driveway.

"Some people like the smell and feel of paper," Bonnie said with a sniff.

Bertie reached for the hat. "This one is mine." She perched the lace-and-straw hat on her head.

"I love it," Nina told her. Bertie was pretty, in a pixie kind of way. The old-fashioned hat made her look like a heroine from an E. M. Forster novel.

Dylan continued to pull at the frame, and it eventually cleared the back of the van. He turned it toward them. Nina stared at what she assumed was a portrait of a very weird-looking person from a planet not in this solar system.

The picture was mostly done in reds and blacks. She was pretty sure the subject was a woman. Her face was a series of boxes with too many ears and eyes. She had claw hands, and the background was a swirl of colors. The body part looked normal enough, but it was really tough to get past her box face. Nina couldn't read the artist's name. She caught a few letters. The first name started with an *E* and the last name was *S-t*...something.

Averil started to laugh. "Mom, what were you thinking?"

"That it's a beautiful frame. It's wood, and the carving is lovely. You have to admit it's stunning."

Nina pulled her attention away from the picture itself

to study the frame. It was elegant and obviously expensive. Wood, hand carved. There was a sheen to the wood, as if it had been hand polished for hours.

"I give you a thumbs-up for the frame," Averil said. "But that painting…"

Her mother laughed. "I know."

"Where do you want it?" Dylan asked.

"Back in the van," Bonnie said, putting down the box she'd rescued. "I'm going to take the picture out of the frame. I have no idea what to do with the canvas. I hate to throw it out, but seriously, who's going to buy it?"

"You did," Nina murmured.

Bertie grinned. "Actually we bought a numbered lot of undetermined contents. It was one of those storage unit auctions."

Where people who hadn't paid and couldn't be contacted lost their stuff. The contents were sold in lots, often sight unseen.

"What else did you get?" Nina asked.

"Nothing good. There were a couple of mirrors. We sold those to a dealer in the town. Your mom kept a few books and a couple of other things. You just never know with those auctions. Sometimes we do well. This time, it was kind of a mess."

Dylan looked at the van. "Are you going over to the store now? I could come with you and help unpack it all."

"You're sweet," Bonnie said and hugged him. "I've missed you so much. Why did we stop seeing you?"

"He dumped Nina, Mom," Averil said.

Dylan winced. "Not how I would have put it." He held out his hands, palm up. "I was young and foolish."

"As long as you regret what you did," Bonnie told him.

"I do." He winked at Nina.

She told herself that with the joy, family came with a very

particular hell, and this was hers. She had to give Dylan credit, though. He was being a sport. Especially considering he'd made it clear he blamed a lot of the breakup on her.

"Okay, then," she said, moving toward him. "Time for Dylan to go."

"What about all the stuff?" he asked.

"We'll deal with it. The two of them managed to load the van. The four of us can unload it." She lowered her voice. "Seriously, we're talking about my mother. Imagine what else she's going to say."

"You have a point." He bent down and kissed her cheek. "I'll see you."

She nodded and watched him leave. When he'd gotten in his car and driven away, she turned to find all three of them watching her.

"What?" she demanded.

"He kissed you," Bonnie said with a sigh.

"On the cheek. We're friends. Nothing more."

Any sparkage was firmly in the Kyle column, she thought, wishing she could run off and spend another hour or seven in his bed. That was the healing magic she needed.

Bonnie walked toward her. She put her arm around Averil and Nina. "My girls," she said with a sigh. "It's so good to be home and with you."

Nina held out her arm to Bertie and the other woman joined them. Together they walked into the house.

The afternoon passed in a flurry of helping Bonnie and Bertie settle in. Then the three of them took the van over to the store, while Bertie stayed behind to start dinner.

Nina was curious as to how Cindy would react to her mother. Just as important, she wanted Bonnie to like Cindy. The woman had worked miracles in the store.

Cindy came out when they pulled up and hurried toward the van.

"Hello," she said, clapping her hands together. "Nina told me all about your trips around the country. They sound amazing. I'm Cindy, by the way." She paused, then smiled. "Bonnie, you look just like your beautiful daughters. You could be the older sister."

Averil sidled close to Nina. "A side of Cindy I haven't seen before."

Nina nodded. "I know. She was a paralegal. My guess is she's used to working with crazy clients."

"Then she's gonna love Mom."

Averil was right. In a matter of minutes, Cindy and Bonnie had linked arms, and Cindy was showing her the changes she'd made to the store. That left Averil and Nina to unload the van.

They carried in boxes and small tables. They argued briefly over who had to drag in the ugly painting. Averil finally agreed, and Nina went to find an old easel to put it on.

"What do you think?" Bonnie asked Cindy, then told her the story of how she came to own it. She pointed to the tiny writing on the frame. "Evening Stars. That's the title of the painting. Which is ridiculous. There aren't any stars."

Cindy frowned. "I agree it's not my taste, but there's something familiar about it. I should do some research." She peered at the signature. "Hmm, I wonder who did this."

"Someone famous would be nice," Averil told her. "Please find out it's worth more than a dollar."

Cindy smiled. "I'll do my best."

They finished unloading the van. Just before they climbed in to head home, Nina grabbed Averil's arm.

"I'm sorry about before. Snapping at you. Sometimes with my friends…" She felt herself flushing. "It's just you're so fun and I have a lot of rules."

Averil studied her. "They're *your* friends. They're not going to like me more."

"You can't know that."

"You're a nut."

"Yeah, well, speaking of that, thanks for the brownies."

Averil smiled. "Later you can tell me the details of your hot monkey-sex night."

They returned home to find the house smelling of roast and baking potatoes—a traditional Wentworth celebration dinner. There would also be glazed carrots, homemade rolls and, since Bertie had joined the family, German Chocolate Cake.

"I'm going to weigh five pounds more in the morning," Averil said with a sigh. "But it will so be worth it."

Nina had to agree. She quickly changed into clean jeans and a short-sleeved T-shirt, then went into the kitchen.

Bertie and Bonnie stood next to each other, Bonnie's hand on her lover's shoulder. They looked like what they were—a happy couple spending an evening together. Nina supposed there were some who would be uncomfortable with a lesbian mother, but Nina was pleased with Bonnie's choice. Bertie added a level of stability to their family that had been missing. Her only regret was that Bertie hadn't shown up sooner.

"We bought wine," Bonnie said, holding up an open bottle. "We're all going to get a little tipsy tonight."

"I like it when we party," Averil said as she walked into the kitchen. "I'll pour."

When everyone had a glass, they toasted each other.

"We have about a half hour before everything is ready," Bertie said. "Let's go in the living room and talk."

They did as she suggested, each taking their proscribed places. Bertie and Bonnie next to each other on the sofa, Nina in the overstuffed chair and Averil on the ottoman. These had been their places for years, Nina thought. Like most family traditions, these were well-worn and difficult to escape.

Bonnie tucked her feet under her. Nina studied her mother. Bonnie was young—forty-six. She'd gotten pregnant while still in high school. Babies having babies, Nina thought. She supposed it wasn't Bonnie's fault she hadn't been ready to be a parent. Of course she'd never bothered growing into the role, either.

Nina recognized that she was at the other end of the spectrum. Thirty and still not married. Not even close to finding someone. While Kyle was the answer to every spinster's dreams, he wasn't exactly a long-term proposition. His stay was temporary, and when he moved on, she wasn't going with him. Not that he'd asked, but her life was here. And even if it wasn't... Not a subject for tonight, she thought.

But if not Kyle, then who? Dylan? He was swoon-worthy, in his own way. Successful, dependable. Not that he was begging to sweep her off her feet, either. No, a man wasn't the way out. She had to find her own happiness.

She sipped on her wine and wondered where she'd gone wrong. If she'd been asked ten years ago, she would have said that of course by now she would have the career of her dreams. That she would get married and have kids. She would never have believed that she would be in exactly the same place. How had that happened?

"When did you get here?" Bonnie asked, patting the cushion next to her so that Penny jumped up and joined her. "And where did this beautiful little girl come from?"

Penny gazed lovingly into Bonnie's eyes.

Averil told the story of finding Penny at the rest stop and rescuing her.

"You poor thing," Bonnie told the dog. "What horrible

person would have done that? Bertie, do we know anyone who does curses? Whoever abandoned her should be cursed."

"I'll see what I can do," Bertie said calmly. "You never said why you came for a visit." Bertie directed that comment to Averil. "Is everything all right?"

"Ask Kevin," Nina murmured, which earned her a glare from her sister.

"I needed some time to think."

Bonnie continued to stroke Penny. "Without your husband? Is there a problem at home?"

Averil deliberately turned away from Nina. "Everything is fine," she said brightly. "He's okay with me being here. I just need to figure some things out."

"Like what?" Nina asked, not sure why she was bugging her sister, but finding pleasure in the act.

Averil sighed heavily. "Just things, Nina. You wouldn't understand, what with not being married or even in a relationship."

"At least I'm not running away."

Averil turned toward her. "No, you're not. But that would require you leaving the island. Something you seem unable to do."

Bonnie looked at Bertie. "Help," she said. "They're fighting."

Bertie sipped her wine. "Girls, is this necessary on our first night back?"

"Of course not," Nina said, wishing she'd kept her mouth shut. She didn't know why she felt compelled to needle Averil. It never accomplished anything. Yet the urge was often powerful.

"Nina started it," Averil said.

"That's mature," Nina told her.

"There you go again. You start it, then have to have the last word. Don't you have enough to do in your life? I'd think you were too busy already, what with being critical of everyone and then telling them what to do. With all your free time, you should think about volunteering."

"My free time? I have a job with responsibilities. A lot of us can't simply disappear when the mood strikes. What are you thinking, taking off like you did? Kevin's a great guy."

Averil spun to face her. "Better than I deserve, right? That's what you think."

"He's certainly patient. You've already been gone a week. How long are you staying?"

"You don't get to ask that. This is my home as much as yours."

"I'm not saying you should leave," Nina told her. "I'm asking how long you expect him to wait for you to discover yourself. Because that's what this is about. You and your needs. When is it about Kevin?"

"Stay out of my marriage," Averil told her. "It's not your area of expertise."

Nina watched as Bonnie and Bertie got up and left the room. Penny trailed after them.

"Great. Now you've driven them away."

Averil turned and stared at the empty sofa. She returned her attention to Nina. "Right. It's my fault. For someone so big on everyone else being responsible, you sure don't see what's lacking in yourself."

"And you're so quick to blame me for what's wrong, just like you used to. Can't figure out if you should have a kid? I'm the reason. Don't know what to do about your marriage? It's big, bad Nina who messed that up. Let me guess—I'm the reason you're not writing your novel, too. I come into your room at night and suck out all your creative energy. It must be nice to never have to take personal responsibility."

Averil sprang to her feet. Tears filled her blue eyes. "I can't believe you threw having a baby in my face. That's low, even for you."

She stomped out of the room.

Nina stayed in her chair, aware that all she wanted was to feel connected, and all she'd done was drive everyone away.

"I hate her," Averil said into her cell as she wiped away tears. "She's so sanctimonious."

Kevin was quiet for a second. "What happened?"

"She's mean and blames me for everything. I don't understand. What is her problem? Do you think it's because she doesn't have a life? She steps in and handles everything for everyone else all the time. Which would be nice, but there's a price. You have to do it Nina's way or else."

"Maybe that's an easier solution. You get to do what you want and have a scapegoat."

She sniffed. "Do you mean in general or are you talking about me?"

"You don't like taking responsibility."

Averil stiffened. "That's not fair. What don't I take responsibility for?"

"You told me you were ready to start a family, and then you accused me of pressuring you. You keep talking about your novel, but I'm not sure you've even started it. You're running away from our relationship, and I have no idea why."

She sucked in a breath as fresh tears spilled down her cheeks. "What? Do you keep a list of my flaws in your pocket?"

"I was answering the question. Averil, think about it. You do like to blame other people for your mistakes."

"Fine. If I'm so awful, why do you want to have a baby with me?"

"And now you're trying to distract me from the main point."

"I have to go."

She pushed the end button on her cell phone and tossed it on the bed. She'd already pulled the box of tissues close, and now she pulled two free and blew her nose.

What was wrong with everyone? Was it "be mean" day? She stared at her phone, waiting for it to ring. The seconds ticked by. She grabbed the cell, hit the call button and waited for Kevin to pick up.

"I'm here," he said, sounding weary.

"What is this about?" she demanded. "What's really going on? If you don't want to be with me, just say so. I don't want to play these games."

She braced herself for him to say she loved the games, which might be true but wasn't the point. Instead he sighed.

Something cold and snakelike coiled in her belly. The sensation made her want to run hard and fast, and it was only when she stood up to bolt that she realized the chill came from fear.

Because until this second it had never occurred to her that she could lose her husband in all this. That Kevin might not wait for her forever. That he might be weary of the drama and actually like that she was gone.

"Kevin?"

"You like to make excuses, and I get tired of that," he told her. "You're a good person, Averil. Just look at how you took on Penny. But I want you to be a grown-up with me. I want us to have a partnership. I want to know I can depend on you, Averil. I love you and I want to stay with you. But I don't know if that's what you want and I won't be in this alone. You need to think about what's important. I know you need time and I'm willing to give it to you, but I won't wait forever. Good night."

With that, he was gone. She dropped the phone on the bed, then stretched out next to it. There were still tears, but there was also confusion and a nagging sense of having missed something very important.

Chapter Twelve

✥

"I'M SORRY," NINA said later that evening, after the dishes had been washed and Averil had retreated to her room.

She was once again curled up in the big chair with Bonnie and Bertie on the sofa. Penny lay next to Bonnie, her new BFF.

"I let her get to me and I don't know why," Nina continued.

"She frustrates you," Bertie said. "You're used to taking care of her, and that's hard to let go. Now that you're both older, you want to simply be sisters, but the old patterns creep into your conversations. You get parental, she rebels and there's fighting."

"It's my fault," Bonnie said, petting Penny's side. "But as you both know, I'm not entirely stable."

Acknowledgment followed by excuses, Nina thought, unable to summon any energy on the topic. She had a feeling her mother would never change. Everybody loved Bonnie— she was fun to be around and always game for whatever was exciting and new. A great trait in a friend, but a lousy one in a mother.

Nina knew she reacted by being the opposite. Not fun and

disinterested in anything spontaneous. Which made her sound like the best date ever, she thought grimly.

"Either way, it's good to have you two back," Nina said, hoping the change of topic would get those kinds of thoughts out of her head.

"It's good to be back," her mother told her. "I adore Cindy. She's done so well with the store. She has a good eye." She nudged Bertie. "I told you those dolls were worth something."

"Yes, you did."

Bonnie tucked her hair behind her ear. "We saw dolls on this trip, but they were too scary for me. Those little porcelain hands. You know they're going to come alive in the night and scoop out our brains."

"I assume you mean the entire doll and not just the hands."

Bonnie wrinkled her nose. "It's not like one is better than the other." She turned to Nina. "Did I tell you that you were right about the tires? As soon as it started snowing, I told Bertie 'Nina was right. We should have replaced the tires.'"

Bertie nodded. "I was trying to keep up on the road, but when it's slick, that old van drives like a bathtub."

Bonnie smiled at her. "You kept us safe. You always do."

"Thank you." Bertie looked at Nina. "How are you holding up? There have been a lot of changes."

"Just Averil and Penny. And Penny isn't any trouble."

Bertie laughed. "Meaning Averil is? She can be a handful. But I didn't mean just that. What about Dylan being back?"

Nina thought about seeing him. "I knew he was returning. I didn't know when." She told Bertie about her car and the rescue. "I was humiliated, but he was nice."

"Any chemistry?" Bonnie asked. "Chemistry is important."

"So is stability," Bertie said gently. "Finding someone you can depend on."

Bonnie sighed. "Yes, that's important, too."

"No chemistry," Nina said. "Dylan and I are friends. What we had was a long time ago."

Bertie studied her. "You'd promised to tell me about the new man in your life. If not Dylan, then who?"

Nina did her best not to squirm. "His name is Kyle." She felt herself starting to smile. "It's crazy. He's four years younger and a fighter pilot. I used to babysit his sister. He was maybe twelve. For a whole summer he followed me around and told anyone who would listen that he was in love with me. It was kind of a joke. I barely remembered him."

Bonnie straightened. "I remember that boy. It was very sweet. He had such a crush on you. What's he like now?"

"Yummy. Irresistible. He showed up and said I was his fantasy."

"That's a lot to live up to." Bertie grinned. "He asked you out?"

"He did. I've seen him a couple of times."

"Good for you," Bonnie told her. "How was it?"

Nina laughed. "He's gorgeous and sexy and has made it clear he wants to sleep with me. Heady stuff. I know it's not serious, but I'm okay with that. Right now hot, meaningless sex sounds really good."

"You have had a dry spell," Bertie admitted. "Are you sure it's meaningless?"

"He's too young and very driven. He wants to be a Blue Angel."

"I'm sure Blue Angels can be married."

Nina rolled her eyes. "Yes. I find it unexpected that you're so traditional. You want me married. What about you, Mom?"

Bonnie considered the question. "I want you to be happy," she said. "That's enough for me."

"What about her having babies?" Bertie asked. "I never wanted to push, but I'm fifty. It's time for me to be a grandmother. I never got to have children, so I have unmet needs. I expect you and Averil to fulfill them."

Bonnie took her partner's hand.

"I'll do my best, but not with Kyle." A Navy wife? She wasn't the type.

"But someone," Bonnie said. "You do want that."

"I do. I was thinking earlier that I thought I would have it all together by now. I'm not sure where everything went wrong. I guess part of it is living on the island. There aren't a lot of single guys here."

"And now there are two." Bonnie grinned. "I'm so proud. Who will win your love?"

Nina shook her head. "This isn't *Twilight*. I don't have to pick a guy."

"That's true." Bertie nodded in agreement. "I want you to be happy, and it's not like I can offer any advice. I've always found relationships with men complicated and perplexing. Which is why I've avoided them. Well, that and being gay."

Nina laughed. "The latter is probably the bigger reason." She paused. "You were never with a guy?"

"No. I always knew. I dated a little, but the first time a boy kissed me, I was horrified. It was so disgusting." She shuddered. "After that I stopped trying to pretend. I had my first girlfriend in college. It was a revelation. I never looked back. When I met your mom, I knew I'd found the one."

She and Bonnie shared a look, and Nina knew this one had nothing to do with her.

She remembered how Bonnie had introduced Bertie as her friend. There hadn't been an explanation of their relationship. One night Bertie hadn't gone home. Nina hadn't said anything, but Averil had asked about it the next morning.

"Are you a lesbian, Mom?"

Bonnie had looked up from her bowl of cereal. That's what

Nina remembered most. The fact that they were having perhaps one of their most significant conversations over cereal
and orange juice.

"Yes, I am. Bertie is going to be with me now."

And she had been.

"You were a welcome addition to the family," Nina said,
shaking off the memories. "It's been nice having you around.
You take care of things."

Bonnie frowned. "What does that mean? Nina, not everyone can be like you."

"I'm not asking you to be. But there are times…" She
paused. "Like the roof. You called once, but only left a message. You never returned Tim's call, so it didn't get fixed. I had
to deal with it. You said you'd taken care of it, but you didn't."

Bonnie pouted. "It's not my fault he didn't pick up when
I phoned."

"We still had a leaking roof. It's hard when you promise to
deal with something, then don't." She felt herself starting to
get upset. Not tonight, she told herself. She'd already alien-
ated Averil. Did she want the same with her mother?

It wasn't fair. In the end, it was all up to her. If she complained, she was a bitch. If she didn't, she got stuck doing it
all while everyone else went off and had fun. It had always
been like that. She was, as she'd realized a couple of weeks
ago, trapped in a situation with no win for her.

"You expect too much," her mother told her. "That's always been your problem."

Bertie touched her lover's arm. "You know I think you're
wonderful, but making the decisions and following through
isn't your strength. You shouldn't offer to do something and
then not take care of it."

"But I…" Bonnie nodded slowly. "You're right. I know
you're right. I'm just used to Nina taking care of things."

Right, Nina thought bitterly. When her mother didn't have to try to be responsible for anything.

Bonnie rose. "I'm going to bed," she said.

"I won't be long," Bertie told her.

Bonnie walked to Nina, then bent down and hugged her. "I do love you, daughter of mine."

"I love you, too, Mom."

Love wasn't the problem, Nina thought.

When Bonnie had left, Penny trotting at her side, Bertie turned back to Nina. "I'm glad you found someone for the store."

Nina accepted the change in subject the same way she accepted her mother leaving the room. It was what they did as a family. Things only went so far, then there was a strategic retreat. No one was willing to push to the point of clearing the air. From fear, she supposed. Of what the other person would say.

"Cindy seems to be working out," Nina said. "She's organized and willing to learn about antiques. And she doesn't have a criminal past."

Bertie sighed. "Tanya might not have been the best choice."

"Sadly, she wasn't the worst one, either."

Bertie looked at her. "I'm willing to help out more than I have," she said slowly. "I've been open to it for a while, but I haven't wanted to push."

"Please, push," Nina told her. "I don't like having to worry about everything going on in the store, along with my job and the house."

"If you're sure."

"I am."

Bertie nodded. "Then I'll start stepping in. You could also expect a little more from your mother. She's stronger than everyone thinks."

"I don't doubt her strength, it's her follow-through I have trouble with. Like the roof."

"She's a work in progress."

Nina smiled. "You love her and that's great. I'm glad she has you. But Bonnie is a complete flake. We're all guilty of taking care of her, so she never had to grow up. Now I think it's too late."

"I'm not so sure. I'm seeing signs of progress."

Nina hoped she was right, but she had a feeling that love made Bertie blind. Which would be nice to experience, she thought.

Bertie stretched her arms toward the ceiling, then stood. "I'm tired, which makes no sense. All I did today was drive."

"That's stressful. You have to concentrate."

Bertie smiled and moved toward her. "I'm glad we're back. We both missed you."

They hugged.

Nina went into her room. She was glad they were back, too. With her mother around, life was never boring.

She glanced at her phone and saw she'd received a text.

Just wanted to say hi.

It was from Kyle. Butterflies hatched in her stomach. She typed back, asking if he was still doing his government thing.

Nope. Back for the night. Thinking of you. Don't suppose you could get away?

It was very close to a booty call, she thought, studying the small display. She was pretty sure that the correct response was to make him actually ask her out. Or beg a little harder.

She wasn't interested in being his go-to sex partner whenever it was convenient for him.

Only just thinking about being in his arms was enough to get her heart racing. If she lingered on the memories of all he'd done to her body, she found herself not caring about potential damage to her feminist side. A good orgasm or two healed a lot of ills.

"Happy clothes?" Cindy asked, sounding doubtful.

Averil opened the second box and started pulling out vintage dresses and jackets. "I can't explain it more scientifically. Some of it is the smell. Old clothes have a scent, which is fine. But sometimes they have an odor that is gross."

"Like body odor?"

Averil laughed. "No, it's different. I'll let you know if I find any unhappy clothes. We can't sell those. They need to be destroyed or at least thrown out."

"Because the unhappy cooties will be passed on to the new owner."

"I'm not making this up," Averil said as she pulled out a flapper-style dress and shook it. "This is fabulous. Look at the beading. I'll bet it was all done by hand."

Cindy fingered the fringe. "Expensive. Check to see if there's a label. I'll bet it was couture."

They were sorting through the boxes unloaded from Bonnie and Bertie's van. Cindy had already put the books aside to look for first editions. The chairs were sorted and tagged already. Which left the clothes and accessories.

"I'm going to ask your mom to look for more vintage beaded purses on her buying trips," Cindy said, holding up a lace wedding gown that looked to be a size two at most. "They would sell like crazy. Especially on eBay. This is beautiful."

Averil reached for a hanger. "I have no idea how old that

one is." She hung up the dress, sniffing as she worked. "But it's happy."

"Good to know. For the right bride, this is a real find." Cindy put it on the rack. "Now that your mom is back, is she the boss or is it still Nina?"

"Good question. I'm not sure. Nina's the bossy one. Bertie sometimes handles things."

Cindy looked up. "Bertie's your mom's…partner?"

"The romantic kind."

Cindy pulled another dress out of the box and held it up. But her gaze was on Averil. "You're comfortable with your mom being gay?"

"Uh-huh. It explains dad leaving her all those years ago," she joked.

"You're comfortable with the idea."

"It's not like my family was ever normal. I was in high school when Mom told us. I liked Bertie a lot. Having her around made things easier. Bertie's always been a buffer between Nina and me." Something she'd forgotten in her quest to come home.

She loved her sister, but they did better from a distance. Which made her need for Nina's approval confusing. Kevin always complained Nina was the voice in her head. Averil wasn't sure she could dispute that, but why would she want the voice of a person who made her crazy?

They continued to unpack clothes. There were several minidresses from the 1960s which made her think that she could write a fun article on finding hot, fresh looks in grandma's closet. She paused to scribble down a few notes.

Cindy watched her. "That's right. You're a writer, aren't you?"

"Articles, mostly. I write for *California Girl* magazine."

"You must be very talented." Cindy laughed. "In my previ-

ous life, all my writing was legal based. It sucked my soul dry.
Now I can barely scratch out an email. Ever write any fiction?"

Averil thought about the novel that was unstarted, let alone
not finished. "I think about it," she admitted. "Which turns
out not to be the same as doing it."

Her phone rang. She pulled it from her pocket. "It's my husband," she said, pleased to see Kevin's picture pop up. "Give
me a second."

"Sure. Take all the time you need."

Averil stepped out the back door of the store. "Hey," she
said. "How's it going?"

"I need to talk," Kevin said. "Do you have time?"

"Sure. What's wrong?" There was tension in his voice,
which in turn made her tense. Had he been in an accident?
Had he figured out she wasn't worth the trouble?

"It's James," he said.

"James, your friend from work?"

"Yeah. He just told me…" Kevin sighed. "He's having an
affair with his assistant."

Averil walked to the low stone wall by the parking lot and
sat down. She knew James, she thought, stunned. And his
wife. They'd been to their house for barbecues and had gone
out to dinner.

"Does Melissa know?"

"I don't think so. What the hell is he thinking? He just
told me." He swore under his breath. "I don't want to know.
I like Melissa. I like my friends being happily married. This
is all Don's fault."

"Your boss? What does he have to do with anything?"

"He cheats all the time."

"What? No way. I've met him. And Jan." His wife was a
pretty fiftysomething who obviously adored him. She baked

cookies and volunteered and always had something funny to say. "They have four kids."

"Don always has something on the side. That's what it's like here. The guys talk about it like it's no big deal."

Averil was grateful she didn't have to stand right now. She pressed her hand against her stomach. "Is this your way of telling me something?"

"What? No. I'm not that guy. I love you, Averil. I don't want anyone else. That's not the point."

A relief, she thought, wondering if she could believe him.

"It's James. Now he's one of them. The thing is, they don't understand the consequences. If Melissa finds out, she's going to leave James. She's not an idiot. She'll make sure his life is hell, and then she'll be gone. He's going to wake up and wonder how he lost it all. I've told him that, but he says he can't help it."

"What are you going to do?" she asked.

"Nothing. I can't make him see what he's doing. He'll have to live with the consequences. I just wanted to hear your voice. You're the one I talk to about this kind of stuff."

Averil relaxed a little. Because she and Kevin were each other's best friend. Because he wasn't completely comfortable with everyone else's feelings, and she was his emotional barometer. Now his reason for calling was clearer. He wasn't threatening. He needed her. Just like she needed him.

She sighed. "Poor you, having to deal with this."

"Tell me about it. Men are idiots."

"Not you."

"I try not to be." There was a pause. "I have to get back to a meeting. I just wanted to hear your voice."

"I like hearing yours, too."

"I love you, Averil."

"I love you, too, Kevin. Very much."

★ ★ ★

"I thought you were dating Dylan," Bonnie said, as she sat on Nina's bed and watched her daughter get ready.

Nina pulled the hot rollers from her hair. She hadn't stayed long at Kyle's the night before, mostly because she hadn't wanted to be caught sneaking in the house at five in the morning. But he'd claimed his "Nina needs" hadn't been met by their quick encounter, and he'd asked to see her again the next night. Only this time they were going to have a date and he was picking her up. Something she would have been fine with, if it hadn't meant Kyle meeting her mother.

"Dylan and I are friends," she said, thinking of the friendly text he'd sent her that morning. "It's nice that after all this time we can still talk to each other."

"You used to be in love with him."

"That was ages ago."

"I know he broke your heart, but that only makes him more significant. I've never understood exes becoming friends. If Bertie left me…" She paused and shook her head. "I can't even think about it."

"Bertie loves you. Don't worry about it."

"I know. I'm so lucky to have her. She did mention your new young man." Her mother smiled. "I heard you come in last night."

Nina finger-combed her hair. "Sorry. I tried to be quiet."

"You were. I happened to be up. I never sleep well the first night we're back. I'm too happy to waste a whole eight hours unconscious." She watched as Nina pulled on a lightweight sweater and then slipped into heels.

"Nice," Bonnie said, surveying her. "Sexy but not obvious. Your sister would be in black leather."

"My sister has the body for it." Averil had always been thin, Nina thought with some resignation. And willing to take risks. Although when she thought about how eagerly Kyle touched her, maybe she should think about a little black leather for herself.

She was going to spend the evening with Kyle. She would enjoy their dinner and their post-dinner. In the morning she would be smug and have glowing skin. If that wasn't the end to a perfect weekend, she didn't know what was.

The doorbell rang.

Nina glanced at the time and groaned.

"You did warn him about us, didn't you?" Bonnie asked.

"I said who you and Bertie were," Nina told her. "There's no need to warn him about anything."

Her mother grinned. "So he knows we're witches?"

"Very funny. Come on. You can meet my young man." *Young* being the key word.

She and Bonnie walked into the living room. Bertie had already let Kyle in. Nina crossed to him and took his hand. "Hi," she said.

"Hi, yourself. You look amazing." He smiled at Bonnie. "I can see where Nina gets her best qualities."

Bonnie laughed. "Yes, those are all me. Everything else comes from her father."

"Okay, then," Nina said. "On that note, we're going to go."

"Do you have to?" Bonnie asked. "We'd like to get to know you."

"Don't be frightening," Bertie told her. "Middle-aged lesbians take getting used to."

"We're not middle-aged," Bonnie said, sounding horrified. "That's so old."

"Unless you plan on living past a hundred, I'm afraid it's too late for that."

Nina shook her head. "Okay, and for the second time, on that note, we're out of here."

"Have a good time," Bonnie said. "Stay out as late as you'd like. We know you're having sex. There's no need to try to hide it. You can come back here, if you'd like. Nina's room is in the back of the house. No one would hear you."

Kyle looked stunned. "That's very thoughtful," he managed to say.

Nina pulled him toward the door. "Escape while you still can," she told him. "They will suck you in and trap you, if you're not careful."

When they were out front, he glanced back at the door. "I like them," he admitted.

"Sure. From a distance, they're hilarious. But on a day-to-day basis, they're a challenge."

"You like that they're back."

"I do. It makes me as twisted as them, but I can live with that."

He opened the passenger door. "So dinner and then sex?"

She laughed. "A man with a plan. I like that."

Chapter Thirteen

❧

NINA ARRIVED HOME Tuesday after work to find the house filled with Calypso music and the blender running in the kitchen. Averil met her in the living room.

"We're playing *Practical Magic*," her sister said with a laugh as she handed over a margarita glass rimmed with salt and brimming with a slushy pale green mixture.

Nina admired Averil's open Hawaiian shirt. The white tank top underneath matched her shorts. A necklace of tiny shells hung around her sister's neck.

Nina took a sip of the drink and gasped as the tequila settled on her tongue. "Okay, Bertie made these."

"You know it."

Bertie made the best margaritas on the island, but she was more than a little heavy-handed.

"We're all going to have a hangover in the morning," Nina murmured as she danced along to the beat. "Okay, let me get changed and I'll be right out."

"We'll be getting drunk while we wait."

Nina made her way down the hall. Once in her room, she

stripped out of her scrubs before pulling on jeans. In the back
of her closet, she had a bright pink T-shirt that was decorated
with sequined flip-flops. She pulled her hair back in a braid
and slipped on plastic palm tree earrings. Because costumes
were required on *Practical Magic* night.

The movie was one of her mother's favorites. Some families watched Christmas movies in December. In the Wentworth household, the women watched *Practical Magic* on both
nights of the solstice. When she was twelve, while her friends
had been pretending to be models, Averil had tried to convince everyone she was a witch. Her complete lack of magical
powers had made the process difficult, but Averil had given
it her best shot.

Nina took her drink with her and arrived in the kitchen
in time to watch Bertie and Bonnie dance to Harry Nilsson's
"Coconut" song.

Bertie wore a sarong as a skirt and a bikini top. Nina toasted
her moves, along with her trim body.

"We should all look so good at fifty," Averil said in Nina's ear.

"I wish I looked that good now," Nina told her.

Bonnie wore a grass skirt over shorts and a T-shirt. Both
women had silk flower leis around their necks. They each held
a margarita in one hand and linked fingers with the other. The
sisters moved their hips and sang along with the familiar lyrics.

The smell of limes and margarita mix mingled with the
mouth-watering tang of teriyaki chicken that was already on
the grill outside. Bertie had perfected a low temperature recipe that had everyone begging for more.

Nina turned to her sister to mention the chicken, but found
Averil obviously thinking about something other than the
party. Instinctively, she grabbed her by the arm and pulled
her into the living room.

"What's wrong?" she asked.

"Nothing. I'm fine." Averil pulled free of her grip.

"It's not nothing. You're upset."

"Then you should be happy. Nothing makes you feel more useful than telling other people what they've done wrong."

Nina felt the familiar frustration and annoyance welling up inside of her. The road to this argument was so well-worn, neither of them had to think before arriving at a disagreement.

She took a quick swallow of her drink and drew in a breath. This time she wouldn't react, she told herself. This time she would listen and be supportive, no matter how annoying Averil became.

"I'm sorry you think that," she said honestly. "I really am interested in what's bothering you. Is it Kevin?"

Averil hesitated, then nodded. "He called me a few days ago because of something going on at work. He found out one of his friends is having an affair. It really bothers him. We know James and his wife, and this isn't going to end well for either of them."

Nina didn't understand why that would make Averil so sad. "You're worried about the other couple?"

"Some. Maybe. Mostly I wonder about Kevin. Not that he would cheat on me. I believe he loves me. It's just I'm here and I miss him." She held up her hand. "Please, don't tell me to just go home. I know that. But before I go back I need to figure out my life."

Nina gulped more of her margarita and told herself that she was going to continue to find patience and be a supportive sister. Because what she really wanted to say was, "Why go looking for trouble?"

"Every time I'm around Kevin, I notice how much he loves you," she said instead. "It's so clear in what he says and how he acts. You're exactly who he wants to be with. Maybe think-ing about that will help."

Averil sighed. "It does. He's great and we're talking more. I just—"

The doorbell rang.

Averil looked toward the sound. "Are we expecting some-one else?"

Bonnie stepped out of the kitchen and laughed. "Oh, good. It's your young man. I called and invited him."

"You have a young man?" Averil asked, as Nina moved toward the door.

"The one she's sleeping with," Bonnie said loudly. "Kyle. He's adorable. Remember how he used to follow Nina around years ago? I'd nearly forgotten all about him. Apparently he still adores your sister."

Nina felt herself flush.

"*He's* the guy who has you staying out all night," Averil said with a grin. "I remember him from school. He was okay, I guess, but he and his family moved before I realized boys were anything other than annoying. Wow, a younger man."

"Not that much younger," Nina said between gritted teeth.

Averil grinned. "Look at Nina, robbing the cradle."

"You will all be quiet and behave," Nina told them before hurrying to the door. She opened it and found Kyle standing on the front porch.

He looked good in jeans and a Hawaiian shirt. He held out a bag of frozen coconut shrimp. "As per the invitation."

She sighed. "My mom invited you to dinner *and* asked you to stop at the store on your way?"

"I don't mind," he told her. "I would have brought wine, but she said that would be a waste."

"That's my mother."

He stepped into the house and turned to Averil. "Hi. Kyle."

"Averil. The baby sister. We've met. You accidently stood outside of my bedroom window when you pulled your *Say Anything* move that summer."

"Sorry about that," he said with an easy grin.

"No problem."

They shook hands.

Nina relieved him of the bag of frozen shrimp and led the way to the kitchen. "We're getting drunk. I hope you can handle it."

"I'll do my best."

Rather than risk the deep fryer, Bertie cooked the shrimp in the oven. By the time they sat down to dinner, they were on their second pitcher of margaritas, and it wasn't taking much to send at least one of them into hysterical laughter. Nina did her best to pace herself. She had to be prepared to throw herself between Kyle and anyone in her family. That meant keeping some control of her faculties.

In addition to the shrimp, there was a huge platter of teriyaki chicken and a couple of salads. The windows in the dining room were pushed open to allow in a light breeze.

Kyle was next to Nina. They sat on the same side of the old table. Every now and then, he dropped his hand to her thigh and squeezed gently. She liked having him around, and she liked how he touched her. He was a man who knew his way around a woman's body. He seemed to enjoy the process as much as the endgame—or he was good at pretending. She was content either way.

"Tell me about your road trip," he said as the food was passed around. "Nina mentioned you go out to estate sales and find inventory for the store."

"We look for treasure wherever it is," Bonnie said. She was flushed and gesturing broadly, but still speaking in complete sentences. "Beauty calls to me. This time we bought the contents of several storage units at an auction. That was exciting. One man bought one with a gun safe in it. We were all waiting to see what was inside."

"Guns?" Averil asked.

"If only," Bertie murmured.

"What was it?" Kyle asked. "Jewelry?"

Bonnie stared at him. "Bones."

Nina took a chicken breast and passed the platter to Kyle. "Excuse me?"

"Bones. Animal bones. Hundreds of them."

"That is so gross," Averil told her. "Why would you put animal bones in a gun safe?"

"Are we sure they're animal bones?" Kyle asked. "Maybe he was a serial killer."

Nina shook her head. "Please don't encourage them. Tell him about the ugly painting."

Bonnie looked confused, as if she wasn't sure of the change of topic, then she nodded. "It's the ugliest painting ever, but the frame is lovely."

"Good one," Averil mouthed.

Bertie smiled at them. "Have some potato salad," she told Kyle. "I understand you're a fighter pilot."

He managed to take the salad and answer the question, without appearing thrown by the odd juxtaposition of statements.

"I am. I fly jets for the Navy."

"That's so manly," Bonnie said, reaching for the margarita pitcher. "A manly man."

"You need to eat," Bertie told her. "Try the chicken. It's your favorite."

"Is it?" Bonnie asked, staring at her plate. "All right." She picked up a leg and took a bite. "It's delicious," she mumbled.

"Don't Navy pilots have long deployments?" Bertie asked.
"You're assigned to a carrier group?"

"Usually," Kyle told her. "Right now I'm assigned to a task
force here in Everett."

"You know about carrier groups?" Nina asked, impressed.

Bertie shrugged. "I know things."

"Obviously," Averil said. "Bertie's the deep one in the family. Do you like serving in the military?"

"Sure. I was born to fly."

Nina waited, wondering if he would mention his ultimate
goal. But he never said anything about the Blue Angels and
shifted conversation back to her mother and Bertie.

Unexpected, she thought. She supposed that meant he'd
told her what he did on their date as a way for her to get to
know him. He hadn't been bragging. Not that she needed
him to have even more nice qualities. He was already tempt-
ing enough.

"It must be nice to know what you're supposed to be doing,"
Averil said, her voice wistful. "I was never sure."

Nina stared at her, not sure if that was the tequila talking,
or if Averil was about to spill an unexpected truth.

Her sister picked up her fork, then put it down. "I might
as well tell you—there's no novel."

Kyle looked confused. Nina leaned close to him. "Averil
has been writing a novel for a few years now."

"Not writing," her sister corrected. "I've taken classes and I
have an online critique group. I rarely send pages. I've started
it a dozen times and I pretend to write, but there's nothing."

Bertie and Bonnie exchanged a glance, then Bonnie sighed.
"Is it something I did wrong that's preventing you from writing?"

Averil's brows drew together. "No, Mom. This is all me.
I keep starting projects, but none of them feel right. I get

input from different people and then I read their comments and I question my own judgment. Maybe I'm wishing for the moon."

"Don't say that," Bertie told her. "You'll write a wonderful book someday."

"I was hoping for something a little sooner than that."

Bonnie patted her daughter's hand. "You'll find your way. You write those great articles. I love reading them."

"It's not the same," Averil told her. "I told everyone I was going to write a novel. Was I lying? Aren't I willing to do the hard work? And what about the baby?"

Now Nina was the one putting her hand on Kyle's leg. Talk about an emotional dump.

"You're pregnant?" Bonnie asked, obviously thrilled.

"No." Averil sighed. "Kevin wants to and I'm not ready. Why aren't I?"

"Children are such a job," Bonnie said with a sigh. "Of course, I love both of mine."

"They change your lifestyle," Bertie added. "It's a lot to think about."

"I want to feel like I have it all together," Averil told them. "But at this rate, I'll never get there."

"Don't worry," Bertie told her soothingly. "No one has it all together. As you age, you get better at faking it. That's the only difference."

Kyle picked up his margarita. "Or you figure out what you wanted all along. Like when I was crazy about Nina before. I was right to stalk her. She was totally hot then and she still is."

"An unrequited love," Bonnie said with a sigh. "That's nice."

"Especially as it's plenty requited now," Averil murmured.

"Do I need to start kicking you under the table?" Nina asked sweetly.

Averil grinned.

"So many men from your past," Bonnie said. "How un-expected."

"Men?" Kyle raised his eyebrows. "I have competition?"

Not a question Nina planned to answer. Saying yes meant more explanations. Plus, Dylan wasn't competition. Not exactly. They were friends with a past. She'd loved him once, and losing him had been harder than anything she'd ever been through. But she wasn't going to say that.

Averil solved the problem. "Nina's first serious boyfriend moved back to town. Dylan. He's a doctor."

"The other man, huh?" Kyle smiled at her. "I should meet him."

"I'd rather you didn't," Nina said. "We're friends, nothing more."

He studied her for a second before nodding. "Okay."

"It's not like you don't have plenty of old girlfriends," Bertie pointed out. "How interesting if some of them are living on the island. Are they?"

Kyle was drinking as she asked the question. "No," he started to say, then began to choke.

Averil laughed. "Was that helping, Bertie? Because I'm not sure."

Bertie wrinkled her nose. "Oh, dear. I think I've had too many margaritas."

Bonnie raised her glass. "Is that possible, my love? To us, family and friends."

They all repeated the phrase and took a drink. Kyle leaned over to Nina. "You have a great family."

"You're not terrified?"

He gave her a quick kiss—one that promised more to come. "Never."

★ ★ ★

Nina had always been a baby-lover. She liked how they smelled and the way their little bodies felt when she rocked them in her arms. But after a morning of crying babies, she was starting to rethink her career choice.

As yet more shrill cries carried through the office, she hurried into the break room and pulled open the cabinet door. The ibuprofen bottle looked less full than it had a few days ago. Obviously she wasn't the only one with a headache.

She took the two pills, then walked into the hallway. Andi stepped out from an examination room.

"Never again," she said. "I know it was my idea, but next time, tell me no."

"You know I will," Nina told her.

Andi had thought it would be good to have all the babies come in on the same day. Vaccinations, well-baby visits and the like. The theory was the visits would go smoothly because everyone was dealing with a specific age group. The reality was one baby started crying, which set the others off.

Holly, their receptionist, entered the hallway.

"Can you come help?" she asked Nina. "Boston is here and says her little girl won't stop crying."

"I can see her," Andi said.

"You have three more appointments." Nina pointed toward the first examination room. "If I can't handle it, I'll come get you."

Andi hesitated. Nina understood—Andi and Boston were friends. But they were packed with appointments and already running about twenty minutes behind.

"Trust me," she said.

Andi nodded and went in to see the next patient. Nina followed Holly to the waiting room.

Two other mothers sat there, crying babies in their arms.

The sound seemed to vibrate off walls and furniture. Nina wasn't a big believer in auras and energy, but she was wondering if baby day was cursed somehow.

"I don't know what to do," Boston said, her face pale. "She won't stop crying. She doesn't have a fever, and she's eating all right, but I'm getting scared."

A reaction Nina understood. Boston and her husband had lost a baby a couple of years before. He'd had an undiagnosed heart condition and had passed away in her arms. When their little girl had been born, she'd been tested for nearly everything possible, but under the circumstances, Boston was more sensitive than most to anything out of the ordinary.

Nina took the baby and rocked her. She gently slipped her finger into the little girl's mouth and rubbed her gums. The crying faded.

"What did you do?" Boston asked frantically.

"She's teething. It's a long, ugly process, I'm sorry to say. Let me get you some information on what's happening and how to soothe her."

Nina handed the baby back, and she instantly began to cry louder.

Boston's face crumpled. "She hates me."

Nina's headache clicked up a notch. This had the potential to be a very long day.

"She doesn't hate you," Nina told her.

She was saved from having to figure out what else to say by the front door opening and Dylan walking in. He smiled when he saw her, but quickly turned his attention to Boston.

"Sounds like someone's unhappy," he said.

"She hates me," Boston said, tears filling her eyes.

"No, she's probably teething." He moved toward her and shifted her hands on her baby. "Hold her this way. There are pressure points that help infants relax."

As he spoke, he shifted Boston's hands a few millimeters and then pressed on a few of her fingers.

"Like that," he said, as the crying softened.

"Oh, wow. Look. She feels better." Boston sniffed. "Thank you."

Dylan nodded and moved to another mother. He showed her the same move. The third baby quieted on his own.

Nina stared at him. "Where did you learn that?"

He grinned. "Where I learned everything I know about babies and childbirth. From a midwife. She had to be at least ninety. I stayed with her for about three months. She was crotchety, but for some reason she took a liking to me and taught me more than I ever learned in medical school."

"You are so hired," Andi said, from the entrance to the waiting room. "And you're going to come by later and show me how to do that."

"Sure thing, if I can borrow Nina for a couple of minutes now."

Andi nodded, even as she raised her eyebrows. Nina knew there would have to be an explanation later.

"What's up?" she asked as she led Dylan into the break room.

He surprised her by closing the door behind them, then turning to her. She was about to ask what was going on, but suddenly his hands were on her waist and he was pulling her toward him.

She went because she was too surprised to move away. Without meaning to, she found herself putting her hands on his chest, which was broader and more muscled than she re-membered.

He'd filled out, she thought hazily. Finishing growing up in the time they'd been apart. He felt nice and—

His mouth settled on hers. She didn't have any warning,

and once she realized he was kissing her, she couldn't figure
out if she minded or not.

This was Dylan. Her first love, her first time, her first broken heart. Familiar and different all at once. His mouth explored hers with a thorough easiness that had her relaxing.
Her fingers found their way to the back of his neck. Her body
leaned into his, even as she let her lips soften and accept the
warm pressure of his.

He tilted his head. She felt the first brush of his tongue
against hers, not exactly sure how things had gotten that far.
They weren't dating, so why were they kissing?

But as he explored her mouth, she felt heat pouring through
her. Once again, as she remembered and yet completely different. This Dylan was just different enough to keep her off
balance.

He drew back and sucked in a breath. "That's not why I
stopped by."

Nina found herself wanting to ask "Why not?" Talk about
baffling. She dropped her arms to her side and retreated to the
safety of the counter. She leaned against it in an effort to re-
gain her balance. She wasn't sure which was more surprising—
that Dylan had kissed her or that her head was spinning.

She was with Kyle. *They* were the dating couple. She and
Dylan were friends. Just friends. Friends didn't kiss like that.
At least she didn't.

"Okay," she said slowly. "I'm guessing it wasn't to show off
your baby whisperer skills, either."

That earned her a smile. "No," he admitted. "I came by
because of the painting."

"What painting?"

"The ugly one with the great frame. I kept thinking about it."

"Why? Are you saying you're scarred by the hideousness
of it?"

"No." He pulled his phone out of his jeans pocket and touched the screen. "There was something about it that seemed familiar. It took me a while to find what it was."

He turned the phone toward her and showed her a picture of another painting. One that looked eerily similar to what Bonnie had purchased on her trip. The colors were in the same family, but what really caught her attention was the face made out of boxes.

"There's more?" she asked. "Why would anyone do that? It's so weird. Are there like six ears?"

She realized that maybe she was missing the point. "Where did you find that?" She felt her eyes widen. "You're not saying it's by someone famous. It can't be, can it?"

He shrugged. "I think it is."

She drew in a breath and emotionally braced herself. "Who painted that one?" she asked, pointing at his phone.

"Emilion Stoicasescu."

"Who?" she asked, even as the name nibbled at the back of her mind. She held up a hand. "He's dead and was sort of a famous artist. He has a daughter or granddaughter who does maybe sculpture?"

"Caterina is his granddaughter. Emilion was a protégé of Picasso."

"Okay, well, good to know."

Dylan touched her arm. "You don't get it, Nina. Emilion Stoicasescu isn't in Picasso's league, but he's well-known. His paintings are worth a fortune."

She swallowed against the sudden tightness in her throat. "How much is a fortune?"

"From what I found online, his last painting to go to auction sold for ten million dollars."

Chapter Fourteen

AVERIL WATCHED AS Nina carefully locked the front door of the store. Her sister had called earlier and said they had to talk. Privately. Which meant not at home where Bonnie could bounce into one of their rooms at any moment.

Averil wasn't sure which was the most troubling—Nina's insistence on absolute privacy or describing their mother as "bouncing." Bonnie moved with enthusiasm, but it wasn't as if she were spastic.

Of course a greater point could be made that Bonnie wasn't at the store. As she was the owner, one would think she would spend her days here. But she never did—which was part of the reason Blackberry Preserves had never done much more than lurch along. No one had cared enough to provide continuity.

Averil's laptop sat open on the counter. She'd decided to try writing in the store, to see if some of the old pieces would inspire her. So far she'd managed to write five pages which could have been the start of a novel, only she'd deleted them all. The problem was she didn't know what she wanted to write about. The old advice of "write what you know" seemed ridiculous.

What did she know that was anything anyone would want to read? Or even different? Her life was just like everyone else's. Where was the special in that?

Nina crossed the now-closed store and stood in front of the counter. "I have to tell you something."

"I guessed that. You're eloping with Kyle."

Her sister—blond and curvy with a quiet sex appeal Averil had always envied—stared at her as if she'd suddenly started speaking in German.

"What? No. Kyle? I wouldn't elope and I certainly wouldn't elope with him."

"Why not? He's adorable. All that energy. Plus he's crazy about you. And you have all that history."

"He had a thing for me when he was twelve. That's not exactly a foundation for a solid relationship."

Averil smiled, aware she was pulling her sister off topic. While it wasn't an amazing achievement, it was still satisfying. Nina was always so damned together. It helped to take small victories wherever possible.

"He never forgot you," Averil pointed out. "Doesn't that say something about his emotional staying power? I can't speak to his other attributes, although based on how your skin is glowing, I'll guess they're pretty good, too."

Nina flushed. "I'm not discussing sex with Kyle."

"No, you're just having it."

Nina groaned. "I meant I'm not discussing me having sex with Kyle with you."

"But he's good, right?"

"He's—" Nina pressed her lips together. "I asked to speak to you for a specific reason."

"Yes, I know. We don't usually have clandestine meetings. Although I'll admit it's hard to take you seriously while you're wearing a shirt covered with Disney characters."

Nina glanced down at her scrub shirt. "I came directly from work."

"It must be nice not to have to worry about what to wear every day. With all the running around you do, you have to be practical. Wear things that wash well. But your scrubs are still cute. You always look so friendly."

"It's important with our patients," Nina said. "Sometimes they're really sick or scared."

"Or both." Averil held in a smile as she silently gave herself another point for the second distraction. She was on a roll. If only she could use her powers for good.

Nina started to say something, then shook her head. "Okay, about the reason I called you." She opened her purse and pulled out several folded sheets of paper. "Dylan came to see me today."

Averil started to make a comment about him, figuring she could go three for three, but something in Nina's eyes stopped her. It wasn't that her sister was frightened so much as she looked…unsure.

"What's wrong?" she asked, not wanting to hear anything horrible. No one could be dying, she decided. Or even sick. Not right now.

"Nothing's wrong exactly. It's more of a situation."

Averil relaxed. A situation meant logistics. Something her sister excelled at. "Okay, and it is what?"

Nina unfolded the papers and spread them out on the counter. Averil stared at them.

They were color copies of the ugly painting Bonnie and Bertie had bought. Only they were different. Similar colors and subjects, but not the same. There were different faces and poses.

"This is part of a series?" she asked. "Part of the 'I'm the weirdest painter of my generation' collection?"

"I've been looking at the signature." Nina tapped the last sheet where that part of the painting was enlarged. "Mostly because of what Dylan said."

Averil touched the sheet, studying the letters. "We saw this before. Em something."

"Emilion Stoicasescu."

"Why is that name familiar?" Averil squinted as she tried to place it.

"He studied with Picasso," Nina told her. "Dylan figured it out. He said there was something about the painting that looked familiar. He started doing research online, and this is what he came up with."

"Okay, so Mom bought a painting from a guy Picasso knew? Big whoop."

Nina put down another article. Averil scanned the headline, then read it more slowly as the words sank in.

Emilion Stoicasescu Original Sells for Ten Million at Auction.

"Oh, my God."

"I know." Nina wrapped her arms around her midsection. "It's crazy, right? Mom found this painting and nearly tossed it because it was ugly, but, hey, she liked the frame."

"No way. I don't believe it. It's a copy or a print or whatever they call an imitation in the art world."

"Maybe. Maybe not. There are missing paintings. Some not seen in decades." She nodded toward Nina's laptop. "Look it up yourself. He wasn't nearly as prolific as Picasso, and no one is really sure how many of his paintings are out there. But the consensus is there aren't that many. Which increases the value."

Averil typed on the keyboard automatically. Her brain was offering a dozen other explanations to the ugly painting question. There was no way Bonnie had bought some important painting. But even as she struggled to reconcile what was possible with the framed piece currently parked in their living room, she wondered if it was in any way probable.

If someone was going to stumble on an art find, it would be her mother. Bonnie went out into the world with an open heart. She was like a puppy, assuming everyone would like her and want the best for her. She didn't worry about details like being on time or paying bills. Those mundane activities were for others—mostly Nina. She was meant to be free to find beautiful things and share them with the world.

As a result, she rarely suffered. People did take care of her and look out for her. Over the past decade, that job had fallen to Bertie who sheltered her with love and devotion.

The pictures came up in rows. Various paintings by Emilion Stoicasescu, all strange and unusual. Several were enough like the painting Bonnie had bought to make her wonder if maybe, just maybe, everything was about to change.

"I know," Nina said, shaking her head. "It's amazing and horrifying at the same time."

"What if it's real? Do you have any idea what it's worth? As much as that one that sold for ten million?"

"I have no idea. I guess it could be that much. Or it could be nothing. We need a plan."

"First, find out if it's real," Averil said.

"Absolutely. But if it's what we both think it is…" Nina drew in a breath. "That's where I get overwhelmed."

Millions, Averil thought. That would be a life-changer. Bonnie and Bertie would be able to buy the biggest antique store ever. Or travel the world. Or save the spotted owl. She supposed she would leave some to her daughters.

Averil wondered what would change then. A million or two meant no worrying about the mortgage. Not that Kevin would ever quit his job. He loved it. She would…

She realized she had no idea what she would do differently. If anything. As for Nina, Averil wasn't sure her sister had dreams.

"We need to make a list," she said, pulling herself back to the moment at hand. "That's what you always taught me. Break the problem down into manageable pieces. Step one. Is it real? How do we find that out?"

Deanna Phillips lived in a restored Queen Anne home next to Andi's house and practice. The downstairs was a combination of period-appropriate furniture and pieces that reflected the on-the-go lifestyle of a busy family with five growing daughters.

Nina perched on the edge of a tufted chair. She'd refused the offer of tea, mostly so she could keep her hands pressing down firmly on her shaking knee. In the past two days she felt as if one part or another of her body was always vibrating. Nerves, she told herself. Or a breakdown.

She didn't have time for either. In addition to her regular life, dealing with her mother and worrying about her sister, she might now have the headache of a valuable painting. An undiscovered or missing Emilion Stoicasescu was one definition of a blessing and a curse, she thought. Because Bonnie was involved, nothing about this was going to be easy. She'd decided to go to the closest thing to experts she knew. Boston and Deanna.

"You look on edge," Deanna said with a smile. "You're stressed."

"A little," Nina admitted. "Mom's back and she can be a handful."

Boston laughed. "You know I adore your mom."

"Everyone does. Bonnie's the life of the party."

Deanna's gaze sharpened. "Always a challenge for her daughters. How can we help?"

Nina and Averil had discussed the best way to explain the problem without actually going into detail. "We think Bonnie might have picked up an original painting on her trip. I was wondering if either of you knew a reputable art expert in the Seattle area who could tell us."

"Your area of expertise, not mine," Deanna told Boston.

Boston motioned to the beautifully decorated living room. "You're the antique queen. You have contacts."

Nina wanted to smack them both. Yes, they were good friends. Love to all—she needed an answer to her question.

But instead of saying that, she forced herself to smile and breathe.

"We're talking a painting," Deanna said. "Who comes to mind?"

Boston leaned back against the sofa and nibbled at her brownie. "Do you have a century?" she asked.

"Twentieth," Nina told her. Based on her limited research, if the painting was an Emilion, it seemed as if it would have been done in the 1930s or 1940s.

"Twentieth century art." Boston thought for a second, then nodded. "Ambrose Priestly. He's the best. Pricey, but worth it. I have his card in my studio. He travels, but he's based in Seattle. I'm sure he would be happy to make the trip here, as long as you pay for his time."

"Thank you," Nina said.

Boston made no move to get up, which meant they were going to visit before she got what she'd come for. Something she would usually enjoy. Just not today.

Ambrose Priestly looked like a cross between a butler from a Jane Austen novel and a British host of PBS. He was tall, thin and dressed in a three-piece suit. Custom made, Nina thought as she escorted the man into their house, based on what he'd charged to make the trip to the island.

Nina told herself that peace of mind and knowledge were worth the cleaning-out of her savings account. The sooner she knew what they were dealing with, the better. And if it turned out the painting was a fake or an imitation or worthless, everything would go back to what it had been before that much quicker. She would be out five grand, but, hey, it was only money, right?

"I haven't been to the island before," Ambrose told her as he stepped into the living room of their house. "It's charming."

"We like it. There are a lot of tourists in the summer, but as they pay the bills for much of the island's population, we make do."

Averil had taken Bertie and Bonnie to lunch. They'd left a half hour ago and wouldn't be back until after one. That gave Nina what she hoped was enough time with Ambrose and his expertise.

He crossed to a small display case and studied the tiny figurines inside. Nina was sure she saw him flinch.

"You know those aren't valuable," he murmured, turning toward her.

"Yes, but my mother likes them."

"I see."

His dark gaze swept over the lumpy sofa and ancient carpet. She couldn't tell what he was thinking, but if she had to guess, he was hoping the check cleared and wishing he'd asked for cash.

"The painting is over here," she said, pointing to the easel and painting Averil had brought from the store.

Ambrose walked toward the painting. She'd positioned it by the window, so it got a lot of light, but away from the doorway. He had to circle around to see it.

"My mother travels the country looking for antiques," she explained. "Not that many of them are valuable. She has unusual tastes. We have a small store here and sell to the tourists. Every now and then she finds a real treasure. This painting is probably nothing, but it seemed prudent to check it out and—"

She was aware of the art appraiser going completely still. She doubted the man was even breathing. His brown eyes were focused on the canvas. As she watched, his pupils dilated, and his fingers fluttered slightly.

"My dear girl, do you have any idea what you have here?" he asked.

"No. That's why I wanted you to see it."

He gave her a faint smile. "I meant that rhetorically."

"Oh."

He picked up the painting. "I need more light."

"Sure. The kitchen is through here."

She led the way and turned on the overhead light. Ambrose held the frame steady and studied the piece.

"It's stunning. Look at the mastery, the brilliance. There's complexity in every stroke."

Nina looked down at the face made of boxes and the claw hands. Maybe she should have taken an art appreciation class in college or something.

"Okay," she said slowly. "Is it…"

"Genuine? I'm sure of it. There are tests that would have to be done, of course. You'll want an official appraisal. An Emilion Stoicasescu here on Blackberry Island. I never would have guessed."

Ambrose took the painting back to the easel and set it in place. "Beautiful," he murmured. "All right, let's get to the paperwork."

"Right," she said, pulling the check from her back pocket.

"Yes, my fee. Of course, but there are some forms to be filled out, and I have some information for you."

They went back to the kitchen and sat at the large table. Ambrose pulled several papers out of his briefcase.

"Research will have to be done," he told her. "As I mentioned before, tests to confirm it's genuine. Does your mother have a receipt for the purchase?"

"I think so. It was in one of those storage unit auctions."

He winced. "I will not think about that treasure in a storage locker." He picked up a pen. "Document the purchase. Make copies of everything. Now to the painting. You'll need to keep it somewhere secure with temperature and humidity control. There are several places in Seattle. I assume you have a safe here you can use until we secure a proper home for it?"

"Ah, sure."

They had an old vault at the store, but it hadn't been used in years. Nina wasn't sure where the key was. Averil might know.

"Do you have a preliminary value?" she asked tentatively.

Ambrose tapped his pen against the table. "It's hard to say. The more important works have gone for quite high sums. Given the subject matter and age, the size." He pressed his lips together. "I'm going to be guessing."

"That's fine."

"I'm not guaranteeing this is a certain amount."

Nina nodded and told herself hitting the nice art appraiser wouldn't help her situation. "I understand."

"I would say ten million."

The room shifted ever so slightly. "Dollars?"

"Yes. You'll need to insure it for at least that amount."

Nina nearly choked. Insure it? For ten million? How much would that be? Her car insurance was about four hundred a year. She could replace her car for maybe ten thousand dollars.

She wasn't sure how the numbers compared, but she knew for a fact there was no way to afford whatever the sum might be.

Wasn't worrying about the store, the roof, her mother and her own job, not to mention her sad little life, enough? Now she had the painting. A ten-million dollar Emilion Stoicasescu original that was currently sitting in her mother's living room.

She felt something heavy pressing down on her shoulders and knew it was the knowledge that she would never escape. Never be able to walk away. Not that she had a destination, but she hadn't intended to live her life on this island. Not the way she was.

"My fee sheet," Ambrose said, passing over a paper. "Assuming you want my help as you wind your way through the process of selling the painting. You are selling?"

"I have to talk to my mother," Nina told him. "With Bonnie, one can never know."

"Won't it be a family decision?"

"It's her painting. Hers and Bertie's." She looked at the list of his services. Ambrose would handle everything from authenticating it to working with the auction house. There were costs for each item and most of them were in the five figure range. And that didn't include pennies.

Ambrose touched the paper with his pen. "If you sign with me, I'll be paid when the painting is sold. Obviously if I'm acting as your agent, the authentication and appraisal will be done independently." He pulled out another sheet of paper and signed it with a flourish, then handed it to her.

"My confidentiality agreement. Everything is standard. I won't tell anyone about your find."

Confidentiality? "You mean we should keep this quiet."

"Absolutely. You don't want a bunch of thieves and opportunists sniffing around. Not only will they make your life miserable, but you'll risk losing the painting. Best to keep everything quiet until all the decisions are made." He handed her his card. "That is my cell-phone number. Call me at any time."

His expression softened. "You've made a wonderful find, my dear. But owning something that special is never easy. Nor is the selling process. I will be happy to help you in any way I can. You'll want your ducks in a row before you make any moves."

She nodded and they stood.

"Thank you for everything," she said as she walked him to the door.

"Give yourself a few days to absorb it all," he suggested. "Then call me. You and your family are about to be a part of history."

"Yay us," she murmured.

When he was gone, she closed the door behind him and leaned against it.

His suggestion was a good one. She should get her ducks in a row. If only they were talking about ducks, she thought, this would be a whole lot easier.

Chapter Fifteen

꧂

"CAN YOU BELIEVE IT?" Averil asked, stretched out on her bed, her cell phone to her ear. "An Emilion Stoicasescu. Stuff like that doesn't happen to our family. I wish you were here to see it. The camera picture I sent you doesn't do it justice. The painting is so strange. How can something like that be famous? I guess I don't understand art."

She paused and waited for a response. There was only silence.

"Kevin? Are you still there?"

"I'm here."

He didn't sound excited or happy. Or even interested.

"What's wrong?" she asked. "Don't you think this is at least kind of cool?"

"I don't care about the painting, Averil. Why can't you see that? It doesn't matter. There are more important things to talk about."

She sat up and tightened her grip on the phone. "What do mean?"

"Us. Our relationship. How long are you staying up there?

Why did you go in the first place? Are you spending any time thinking about us or our lives together? Are you so caught up in your family and the damn painting that you've forgotten you're married and that you left me?"

Her breath caught. "I didn't leave you," she told him. "How could you say that? We agreed I needed time away to think."

"No, we didn't. You said you needed the time and were leaving. I didn't stop you."

"That's not what happened," she said, even as she knew he was telling the truth.

"Do you miss me at all?" he asked, his voice quiet.

"Of course. All the time."

"It's hard to tell if that's true or not. You never talk about coming home. I don't even know what you're waiting for. Is progress being made?"

"I don't know," she admitted, feeling her eyes start to burn. Without wanting to, she heard her mother's voice. The gentle, but insistent whine that she "didn't want to have to decide. I can't make up my mind."

It was genetic, she thought sadly. Not that Kevin would think much of that excuse.

"Things are complicated," she began, then stopped. What was complicated? The decision as to whether or not she wanted to be with her husband? "I love you, Kevin. I want us to be happy."

"I believe that. What I don't know is if you think that happiness is going to come from being together. I keep thinking I'm going to lose you, and there's nothing I can do to stop it from happening. Am I supposed to show up and fight for you or give you space? What do you want from me? How can I make things better?"

Tears filled her eyes. "I don't know. It's not about you. I'm the one who messed up. I'm sorry. I'm trying to figure out what's wrong. Can you give me a little more time?"

"Do I have a choice?"

"Are you telling me to come back?"

"You know I'd never do that," he told her. "That's why you're asking. You get to say that you wanted to make sure I was okay with what you were doing. Then no matter what, it's not your fault. Neatly played."

And with that, he hung up.

Nina had debated the best way to handle the painting situation. Who would ever expect her mother and Bertie would find a piece of art worth ten million dollars? If she didn't know better, she would think there were secret cameras from a reality show, monitoring her soon-to-be-experienced breakdown.

She'd decided on a direct approach, after certain safety precautions were in place. With Averil's help, they'd unearthed a key to the big safe in the store and put the painting in there. The key was now in her safety deposit box at the local bank.

"You're up for this?" she asked her sister.

Averil nodded, then climbed off her bed. "Sure. We have to convince Bertie to act normal, which shouldn't be too difficult. Then she can be the one to keep Mom in line."

All things they'd discussed before, only Averil didn't sound very enthused. "Are you upset?" Nina asked. "Did you want to talk about another plan?"

The last thing she needed was her sister going over to the dark side in the middle of the conversation. The best way to corral Bonnie was to present a united front.

"I'm fine with it," Averil told her. "I swear. I've got some other things on my mind."

Nina wasn't sure she could handle another crisis, but she knew her role in the family. "What's wrong? How can I help?"

"You can't," Averil told her. "I need to handle this one myself."

Nina wished that were true. Eventually all problems led to her door. But for now, she would take the words at face value and be grateful.

"Okay, then let's go." She headed for the door, then paused. "You agree that we can't say it's a four-way decision, right? It's not our painting."

Averil shook her head. "This is Bertie and Mom's windfall. Not ours. Not that I would say no to a large cash settlement." Her mouth turned up in a smile, although her eyes were still sad.

Nina nodded. She agreed with her sister. This wasn't like a family inheritance or grandmother's legacy. They were interested parties, but not the principles.

The sisters made their way into the living room where Bertie and Bonnie were already waiting on the sofa. Nina smiled as she saw them. The women were different in every way. Bonnie was tall and curvy—Nina had inherited her body type, if not her personality. With long blond hair and blue eyes, Bonnie looked more like a California surfer than a Blackberry Island native. Minus the tan, of course.

Their personalities were different, too. Bonnie was impulsive and generous, but not a detail person. She loathed planning, thought responsibilities were like dirty toilets—best left for others to deal with. She loved the world and assumed that was enough to cause others to overlook her flaws.

She loved her children, yet thought nothing of burdening her oldest daughter with the responsibilities no child should ever have handled.

Both women looked up as she and Averil walked into the living room. Bonnie laughed.

"A family meeting. I'm so curious. Nina, are you running off with your young man?"

"Dylan and I are friends."

Bonnie's eyebrows rose. "I meant Kyle."

"Oh. No, we're not running off."

"Keep using him for sex," Bertie said with a smile. "You deserve it."

Bonnie leaned into her partner. "I'm not sure you should be giving advice on men, my love."

"Why not? All relationships have certain aspects in common. Although I'll admit to a complete lack of knowledge when it comes to men."

Averil took one of the chairs and Nina sat in the other. Nina laced her fingers together as she tried to figure out how to start.

"You look serious," her mother said, her smile fading. "Is it bad? I don't want to hear anything bad."

"We're all fine," Nina told her quickly. "No one is sick or anything. It's about the painting."

"The ugly one?" Bonnie asked. "We can't sell it. That would be wrong. No one should pay good money for something that ugly." She shuddered. "It violates everything I believe about life being beautiful."

Bertie's gaze sharpened as she studied Nina. She took Bonnie's hand in hers. "Let's hear her out."

Nina smiled gratefully, then drew in a breath. "Dylan came to see me last week. He said there was something familiar about the painting, but it took him a while to place it. He showed me some pictures on his phone and said he thought it might be by an artist who was a disciple of Picasso. Emilion Stoicasescu."

Both women stared at her blankly.

"Of course I know about Picasso," Bertie said. "But I've

never heard of his friend. The last name sounds familiar, though...."

Bonnie nodded. "Catherine or something. Are they related?"

"Caterina is his granddaughter, but that's not exactly the point." Nina did her best to look casual. "I found an art expert to come up and look at it. His name is Ambrose and he agrees the painting is by Emilion, and is probably an original. Ambrose is knowledgeable and was really helpful. Based on his suggestion, I've locked the painting in the safe at the store for now. Until you two decide what you want to do."

"Oh," Bertie murmured. "You mean we could sell it?"

"Yes. You could. In the meantime, Ambrose suggested we insure it for ten million dollars."

Bonnie collapsed back on the sofa. Her shoulders started shaking and soon she was laughing. The happy sound filled the room.

"Is she slipping over the edge?" Averil asked quietly.

Nina shrugged.

After a few more seconds, Bonnie straightened and wiped her eyes. "How wonderful. Nina, whenever I start to worry about you, you surprise me with something like this. So funny. Thank you, darling. That was exactly what I needed this morning. A wonderful joke for all of us."

Bonnie started to stand. Bertie pulled her back to the sofa. "She's not kidding."

"Of course she is. Don't be ridiculous. We couldn't possibly have found a painting worth..." The humor faded, along with Bonnie's color. "No. We didn't. That doesn't happen in real life. It was a storage unit auction. Who would put something that valuable in a storage locker?"

"Somebody did, Mom," Nina told her. "Like I said, it's

safe for now. I wanted to let you know what I'd done and get your permission to—"

"Our permission?" Bonnie shook her head. "Mine and Bertie's? No. This is a family thing."

"You two are the ones who bought it. It's yours."

Bertie took Bonnie's hand again. "What is the next step?" she asked.

"Ambrose gave me the name of a few banks in Seattle where we can safely store the painting while we're working through the process. The painting needs to be authenticated. We'll have to confirm it wasn't stolen from a government or museum that will want it back. After that, you can pretty much do anything with it."

"We could give it to orphans," Bonnie said happily. "Although it's ugly and would frighten them. Oh, I know. We can open a little museum here in town. Charge two dollars for people to go through and see it."

"Or we could sell it," Bertie said drily.

"That's not very fun."

"We can't afford to keep it," Bertie told her. "None of us can afford the insurance, let alone whatever special display would be required. A painting that valuable doesn't fit into our lives."

"Neither does ten million dollars." Bonnie shuddered. "That's too much money."

"Not divided four ways and after taxes. The girls would be set for life, as would we."

"I wouldn't say no to the check," Averil said. "But you two need to do what you think is right with the painting."

"I agree," Nina told them. "But whatever you decide, for now we need to keep this quiet."

Bertie nodded, but Bonnie's expression turned stubborn.

"Why?"

"We have the painting secured. We don't want to risk it being stolen or hurt in any way."

"She's right," Bertie said, facing Bonnie. "You know how much I love you."

Bonnie sighed. "You always say that right before you tell me something I don't want to hear."

"Yes, I do, because you don't like to hear the truth. We need to be responsible about this. Nina has gone to a lot of trouble for us, and we have to honor her hard work. She's right about the painting. We must keep the secret for now. I'm worried if you tell someone, you'll be taken advantage of."

Bonnie's mouth blossomed into a pout. "You're treating me like a child."

"Yes," Bertie said. "I wonder why that is."

"Fine," Bonnie said with a huff. "I won't tell anyone."

With that, she stood and stalked out of the room. Bertie watched her go, then turned back to Nina.

"You've put a lot of thought into this. Thank you. You're right about moving the painting to Seattle. I don't think there's a big rush, but I think it should happen in the next couple of weeks."

"I was going to take a day off next week, but I can talk to Andi if you think it should be sooner."

Bertie smiled. "I think your mom can hold off for that long. I'll talk to her." She rose and crossed to Nina. She touched her shoulder. "It always falls to you, doesn't it?"

"I'm used to it."

"I'm sure you are." Bertie left.

Nina turned to her sister. "You okay with all this?"

Averil nodded. "I have no idea what they're going to do

with it. I hope they sell it, but I wouldn't put it past Mom to give it to orphans, like she said."

"It's a tax deduction she'd be living off for the rest of her life."

After the painting discussion, Averil returned to her bedroom. She booted her laptop, but instead of opening the file for the article she'd been writing, she went to her picture file and started a slide show.

These were photos she'd scanned in from when she was a kid. They showed her in costumes, her with a neighbor's dog, her in school plays and other events. Nina was with her in some, but mostly her sister was behind the camera.

Nina had always handled things, just like she'd done today. She'd taken care of the details. No matter what, Averil knew she could depend on her sister.

Bonnie opened her door and walked in.

"Hi," her mother said, walking over to her desk and staring at her computer. "Oh, look at how adorable you were."

Averil glanced at the screen. She was maybe seven or eight, dressed as a pumpkin, for Halloween. Bonnie had made the costume herself—it had taken days.

Her mother crossed to the bed and sprawled across the comforter. "I remember trying to convince you to be something else," Bonnie said. "But you wanted to be a pumpkin."

Averil smiled. "I could be stubborn."

"Yes, you could. You always had such a strong personality."

Not like Nina. Bonnie didn't make the statement, but she didn't have to. Bonnie loved her firstborn, but sometimes Averil wondered if her mother had resented her, too.

Bonnie had been sixteen when she'd gotten pregnant. She'd refused to marry the boy, despite pressure from both sets of parents. They'd broken up and gone their separate ways.

Four years later love, or at least sex, had flared between them again and Bonnie had gotten pregnant for a second time. Twenty and a single mom with a four-year-old, she'd accepted her boyfriend's proposal this time. Averil had been born a few months later.

But within a year, he'd been gone, and Bonnie had been living with her mother. Averil did the math and realized that when Bonnie had been *her* age, Nina had already been nine and running the household.

Bonnie rolled toward her. "Remember when you were little and we used to pretend we were princesses held in a tower?" She laughed. "We would plot our escape and then travel all over the world. I wonder if those old maps are still up in the attic. Remember how we always looked for the most exotic countries and cities with the strange names?"

Averil nodded. While Nina had taken care of things like cooking and urging her mother to go grocery shopping, Bonnie had been content to play pretend and dress-up with her youngest. All those years ago, Bonnie had insisted they were both princesses. When Averil had tried to tell her that Bonnie needed to be the queen, she'd gotten upset. She didn't want to be the queen.

Averil realized now that there had been a message in that protest. Being the queen meant being the grown-up in the room. Worse, the escape they had planned had been from Nina—a child herself who was simply trying to survive.

Their grandmother had helped out, Averil thought. But after she died, it had all fallen to Nina. Bonnie had resisted the rules imposed by her oldest daughter even as she'd looked to her to handle things. It had been an impossible situation for all of them. Averil had survived with a relatively normal childhood, but she'd been left with a confusing relationship with both her mother and her sister.

Bonnie sighed. "What do you think about the painting?"

"That you got lucky."

"I suppose that's one way to look at it. All that money if we sell it. Or we could keep it. Or give it away. Bertie will decide." She sat up. "We could get a reality show. That would be fun."

"I don't think I'm ready for reality television," Averil told her. She had a feeling that if there was a camera trained on her 24/7, she might not come off in the best light.

"What are you ready for?" Bonnie smiled at her. "Why are you here, Averil?"

"I don't know. I needed to think, but I'm not spending much time doing that. I'm at the store or writing my articles."

"Is it Kevin? Are you escaping him?"

"No. I love him."

"From a distance? Is he easier to love from up here?"

An unexpectedly insightful question, she thought wryly. "Maybe. He's so good to me and I'm not sure I deserve that."

"Of course you do. We all deserve to be loved. Is it because he wants to start a family?"

"Some. I thought I was ready, but I'm scared. I don't want to mess up. Being a mom will change everything."

Bonnie continued to smile without comment. Averil wondered if that was because, for her mother, little had changed with her children. There had always been someone there to take care of the details. Averil didn't want to be like her, but she also wasn't ready to sacrifice herself the way Nina had. Of the two of them, Nina had been the one who'd wanted to escape the island, yet here she was. Stuck.

"Did you discuss children before you got married?" Bonnie asked.

"Sure. I do want them. I just don't know how they'll fit. Or how I'll change."

"Love makes us stronger," Bonnie told her. "You're such a gentle spirit. Your children will be a blessing." She laughed. "Besides, I'll be a great grandmother."

"They will adore you, that's for sure."

Bonnie clapped her hands together. "They can stay with Bertie and me for the summer. We'll love it."

Averil thought about how Bonnie would allow her grandchildren to do anything they wanted, which was both good and bad.

Bonnie's smile faded. "What do you want, Averil? Deep in your heart, what moves you?"

Averil considered the question. "I want to be with Kevin. I love him and he's a good man. I want to make him happy."

"Happiness comes from inside. You can't make anyone happy. That's their choice."

"Okay, then I want to be a better wife. I want him to be proud of me."

"Isn't he now?"

"I don't know. I keep talking about writing a book and I'm not. I can't seem to start it. Every time I think I have a great idea, it falls apart."

"Write about a family that finds a famous painting. How it changes them."

"You think it's going to change us?" Averil asked.

"No," her mother told her. "Because we're strong. But it would change others."

An arrogant statement clothed in charm, Averil thought. The painting had already changed things.

Her mother stood and crossed to her. After hugging Averil, she straightened. "Find your own way. Follow that path to wherever it leads. That's where you'll be happy."

Averil wasn't sure what her mother meant, but she nodded. Bonnie left.

Averil clicked on her word processing program, then stared at the blinking cursor. Its unceasing urging reminded her of Nina. How her sister had insisted she leave the island and go to school somewhere else. Averil had decided on UCLA mostly because of the location. And because she'd heard of the paper. Majoring in journalism had seemed her best option.

But she hadn't really wanted to go. She'd wanted to stay on the island, at least a while longer. She unexpectedly saw the connection to her mother in not wanting to be the queen. Because staying on the island meant not having to grow up so quickly. But life wasn't like that, and eventually every young girl had to grow up. There came a time when one had to stop pretending to be a princess and accept the role as queen. At least of one's own life.

The picture of a princess lodged in her brain. Her hands moved to the keyboard.

No, not a princess, she thought. A rich teenager in a house full of staff. A cliché, maybe, but one she could work with. And not a teenager. Maybe twenty-three was a better age. Post college. Assuming she'd made it through college. Unless that was what the fight was about.

"We're cutting you off."

Averil paused, wondering if that was really where she wanted to start her story. Then she told herself it didn't matter. At this point it was all about getting the pages down. Or in her case, page.

Tracy Galloway rolled her eyes. It was a threat she'd heard a thousand times before.

"I know you're not happy about Bryce," she told her father. "But seriously Daddy, you can't cut me off. What will your friends say?"

Averil paused to read what she'd written. She carefully deleted everything after the first line. For a second, she thought about tossing her computer across the room, but stopped herself. She said she was going to write a novel, and by God, she was going to do it. Word by word, if necessary. Word by frigging word.

Chapter Sixteen

❧

ANDI LOOKED AT the vacation spreadsheet. "I feel bad about making everyone take time off while I'm giving birth," she said.

"It makes sense." Nina flipped to the second page. "You're only going to be home a month. We'll take the first two weeks and then come back and get things going." There was plenty to keep everyone busy, even if they didn't have as many patients as usual.

Andi had been careful to let everyone know about her pregnancy and when she would be taking off to have the baby. Most parents were getting their well visits done before then. While the office was closed, Dr. Harrington would pick up the slack. Then a contract doctor would come in for a month—two weeks while Andi was still home and for her first couple of weeks back.

"You've helped me organize all of this," Andi said with a sigh. "I'm not sure I could have done it without you."

"You would have been fine," Nina told her.

"I like to think so, but I'm not sure. How are you doing? You look tired."

Nina tried to take the comment in the spirit she was sure Andi meant it. "There's been a lot going on. Bertie and my mom are back. They're fun but exhausting. Averil's here, too." Then there was the painting, but she wasn't going to mention that. Even if Boston and Deanna had talked about their meeting, she hadn't been very specific with them, beyond her need for an art expert.

"Dealing with my family is like herding cats," she continued, thinking Kyle was a bright spot. He was good for easy conversation and better sex. He'd been on one of his task force ops and away for a few days, but he was due back anytime now. She had to admit that she and her girl parts were looking forward to spending time with him.

Andi smiled. "Family is tough. I know mine makes me crazy, so you're in good company. We do what we have to and we love them anyway."

"Mostly because we don't know any better."

Her boss laughed.

"Bertie helps," Nina admitted. "She's great. I wish she would just take charge, but she doesn't want to step on any toes. I keep telling her to step away. I won't mind."

"You take on too much," Andi said. "God knows I let you run my life. But it's not healthy. Who takes care of you?"

"I'm like the cats. I'm very self-sufficient."

Andi raised her eyebrows. "Will we be seeing more of Dylan?"

"I have no idea."

"You're not dating him?"

"We're friends. He came by the other day to talk to me about a few things."

"He's very handsome."

He was, Nina thought. And dependable. Sometimes, the latter was a whole lot more appealing.

Andi nodded slowly. "Okay, your silence on the subject is very clear. I won't meddle. I'm just pointing out that he's a great guy."

"Thanks for the update."

Nina threw herself onto a sofa, then coughed as dust billowed out from the tufted piece.

"Bad day?" Averil asked. While Nina did show up in the store from time to time, it wasn't usually at three in the afternoon.

"No worse than any of the others. Mom called."

Averil sat on a stool and waited. She had a feeling she knew what her sister was going to say.

"She wants to wait to move the painting to Seattle," Nina told her. "She's not ready to sever the connection." Nina's eyes closed as her mouth twisted. "It's a painting, not an umbilical cord. Sever the connection? Why can't I have a normal mom? They have to exist, right?"

Averil had spoken to Bonnie earlier and had the same conversation. Bonnie claimed to have been dreaming about the painting, and she felt she had a spiritual connection with the work. Until she understood what it wanted from them, she couldn't allow it to be moved.

"Have you talked to Bertie?" Averil asked. "She can reason with Mom."

"She can, but she usually won't." Nina opened her eyes. "I can't blame her. She doesn't want to always be fighting, so she picks her battles. But still. I have no idea what message is going to come from that painting. I only know it's going to be a pain in my ass."

Averil was pretty sure Nina was right. If there was a mess that needed cleaning, it generally fell on Nina.

No one had ever expected much from her, she thought. Nina took care of things, including her baby sister. Averil had just been along for the ride. She'd been able to go hang out with her friends, to have free time and not have to worry about things like getting food in the house or keeping the lights on.

"Remember when we used to play dress-up?" she asked. "That was always fun."

Nina looked around the store. "Some of my best memories are in this store. We did have a good time."

"You told me what to do," Averil mused. "What to wear and what my lines were."

Nina, still dressed in her scrubs, shuddered. "Okay, I'll admit it. Today is not a day when I can deal with everything I did wrong back then."

Averil stared at her. "No," she said quickly. "I didn't mean it that way. You always took charge, so all I had to do was have fun. It was nice."

Nina didn't look convinced. "Yeah, right. Bossy older sisters. Everyone wants one."

"You took care of me, Nina. When Mom was off doing whatever, disappearing to buy stuff for the store, you were here. I knew you wouldn't leave me. I depended on you."

Nina relaxed. "Okay. Thanks. Sorry to be so sensitive. I didn't take the call very well. I'd just gotten out of a meeting with Andi when she phoned to explain why we had to keep the painting here." She touched the side of her head. "I'm still throbbing. Apparently I got shrill and pale. Andi told me to take the afternoon off."

Averil was surprised. Nina didn't usually let herself be managed by other people. "You're tired," she said, taking in the dark circles under her sister's eyes.

"My boss said that. I need to start wearing concealer. Or any makeup." Nina smiled ruefully. "You, on the other hand, are as beautiful as ever."

Averil shook her head. "I'm not, but thank you." She stood and crossed to a small box on the counter. "Cindy and I found these yesterday."

"Where is Cindy?" Nina asked, taking the offered box.

"Taking her mother-in-law to the doctor. It's the gynecologist. Apparently not a place her son can take her."

Nina shook her head. "Cindy deserves a medal for dealing with that woman."

"I think they have come to an understanding. At least I hope so."

Nina opened the box and stared down at the brooches. "Where did you find these?"

"In the back on a shelf. I thought you'd want them."

The collection was made up of brightly colored bugs. Butterflies and ladybugs, dragonflies and bumble bees. Their grandmother had worn them with everything.

"After she died, I tried to find them," Nina admitted, turning a butterfly over in her hand. "I couldn't. I was afraid Mom had thrown them out, but when I asked she swore she hadn't." Her eyes filled with tears. "Grandma said I could have them when she was gone. How silly. They're worthless, but I wanted them so much."

Averil smiled at her. "Now you have them."

She didn't remember much about the older woman. She'd only been seven when their grandmother had died. But the other woman had been a much larger presence in Nina's life. A stable force who'd kept Bonnie's waywardness in check.

One thing Averil remembered clearly was her grandmother's final days. She'd been hovering in the hall, not sure what was happening, but knowing it wasn't good. Nina hadn't been afraid. She'd gone right into the bedroom.

You know I'm dying, don't you? their grandmother had asked. Averil hadn't heard Nina's reply.

It's all going to be up to you, now. Take care of your mother and sister.

Again, Nina's words had been too quiet for Averil to hear. At the time she'd been relieved to know that little about her life would change. Nina was the one who took care of things and that would go on. Now, looking back, she realized what a burden that must have been for an eleven-year-old girl. Bonnie should have been the one to deal with her mother's passing. But she hadn't.

"You did a good job raising me," she said impulsively.

Nina looked at her. "I can't take credit for that. Not really. We raised ourselves. I say we did a decent job." Nina stroked Penny as she walked by. "I wish Mom had found Bertie about ten years earlier. That would have helped."

Averil bent over to rub Penny's ears. "We would have been the only 'two mom' family in our school."

"It would have been worth it."

Averil was sure Nina could have used the help. "Remember when Mom decided there was too much inventory and she priced everything at a nickel?"

Nina closed the box with the brooches and groaned. "It was horrible. I couldn't begin to figure out how much money we lost. People kept leaving more money because they felt bad, but going from a nickel to a quarter on something worth twenty dollars isn't much help." She looked around the store. "I'm amazed we made it. There were days I expected Social Services to show up and take us away."

"Really?" Averil asked, surprised that would have been a worry.

"Sure. Mom would disappear for weeks at a time on her buying trips."

"She always came back."

Nina's hands fluttered over the box. "We were twelve and eight. You're not supposed to abandon your kids while you drive around the country buying junk."

Averil realized her perspective was different. Life had gone on pretty much the same whether or not Bonnie had been in town. But it hadn't been like that for her sister.

"Was it easier or harder when Bonnie was gone?" she asked.

"Both. There was less to worry about and more to do. I don't know. It doesn't matter now."

Averil wasn't sure she agreed. It might matter a lot. Nina had been the one who'd wanted to leave Blackberry Island. She'd been the one with dreams.

"Am I the reason you didn't go away?" she asked. "So you could look after me?"

Nina rose. "You can't think about that," she said firmly. "I made my choices for a lot of reasons." She crossed to Averil and hugged her. "You're worrying about nothing."

Averil nodded, because she wasn't sure what to say. That she was sorry her sister had to take care of her? She was for Nina's sake, but not her own. She'd always known her sister loved her and would be there for her. But at what cost to Nina?

Nina left the store and drove down to the marina. She parked and started walking along the boardwalk. It was a beautiful sunny day. Not hot, but warm enough that she didn't need a jacket. She supposed she should have gone home and gotten changed. Her scrubs meant she stood out from the few tourists on the island on a weekday in mid-May. Not that she cared. She needed to think.

Or maybe not, she thought as she strolled. What was there

to consider? She'd made her decisions a long time ago. Had lived with the consequences. There was nothing to be done about the past now.

"Nina!"

She turned and saw Dylan walking toward her. She paused and smiled. "Shouldn't you be at work? Playing hooky already? That can't be good."

"I had a furniture delivery. I took off to let the guys in. Then my last two appointments canceled, so here I am. What about you?"

"A rare afternoon off. I came down here to walk by the water."

"Come on," he said, motioning to a small restaurant across the street. "Their bar is open. I'll buy you a drink."

Five minutes later they were seated on the deck, in a warm, sunny spot. She sipped her glass of chardonnay.

"I could get used to this," she admitted. "Sitting around in the afternoon with nothing to do."

He smiled at her over his beer. "You're lying. You hate being bored."

"I know, but it's nice to pretend."

"I doubt you go on vacation without a plan."

"Hey, don't be critical."

"I'm not. I'm stating the obvious. There's nothing wrong with a plan."

She thought about her mother. "Some people thrive on being spontaneous."

"Let 'em. You enjoy your rules."

He was telling the truth, but... "That makes me sound boring. And old."

"You're neither. You're solid and trustworthy."

"Ah, like a faithful dog. A large dog. Like a Lab or a Saint Bernard."

He leaned toward her, placing both forearms on the table. "You're determined to make me the bad guy in this."

"No, I'm not. Sorry. I'm in a mood. I was supposed to drive to Seattle tomorrow with the painting. I've found a bank where we can keep it while Mom and Bertie figure out the next step."

"And?"

"And my mother is having a spiritual moment. She feels we should keep the painting around until she understands what she's supposed to do with it."

Dylan's green eyes flashed with surprise. "The painting is speaking to her?"

"Apparently."

"They have medication for that. Have her come in and I'll write a prescription."

"Very funny." She sipped her wine.

"I'm a funny guy." His humor faded. "You're worried."

"I have no idea what she's going to do, but the odds of it being sensible seem small. I'm terrified she's going to tell someone she shouldn't."

He touched her arm. "You know I'm not going to say anything."

"I do. Thanks. To be honest I never thought to call and tell you to keep quiet. I knew you would." Which was unexpected, she thought. When things were complicated, she'd always been able to trust Dylan. Except with her heart.

"Thanks. Do you have any idea which direction her spiritual connection is going to take?"

"No. She's mentioned everything from opening a museum to display the painting to burning it so it would return to the artist."

He grimaced. "I hope she decides against burning it."

"Me, too. I'm pretty sure Bertie will keep her at least close to normal." She wondered if banging her head against the table would make her feel better. "I was really hoping for a calm summer."

"It could happen."

She smiled. "Unlikely. Okay, let's talk about something else. How are you enjoying working with your dad? Is it still boring?"

"Hey, I never said it was boring."

"You implied it was less than satisfying." She tilted her head as she studied him. "Sorry you came back?"

"It's more difficult to adjust than I thought it would be. Everyone deserves to have access to health care. Both here and there."

She knew him well enough to be able to complete the thought. "But there you make a more tangible difference. Here they can simply drive to the mainland and see another doctor."

"Thanks for making me feel special."

"Sorry. You know what I mean."

"I do." His gaze settled on her face.

There was something about the way he looked at her. It reminded her of his kiss—the one she'd nearly forgotten about because of the painting. Something else her mother had to answer for, she thought humorously. Not that she planned to go around kissing Dylan. It had been nice and all, but they were friends.

"Is leaving an option?" she asked.

"I don't know. I promised my dad."

"He'd want you to be happy."

"I'm pretty sure he thinks I can be happy here."

"Maybe if you were to settle down," she said. "Get married and all that."

"Proposing?" His voice was teasing.

"That would freak out your parents. They worked so hard to break us up."

"They were wrong."

She studied him for a second. When he didn't speak, didn't add the obvious "And so was I," she drew in a breath.

"You really do think it's my fault we broke up."

"No," he said easily. "It was both of us. You had your family. I knew that. I kept thinking that you'd walk away from them, but how could you? You were the one holding it all together. I was angry because I thought you were changing plans without discussing it with me. You were angry because I, from your perspective, wouldn't understand."

When he put it like that... "We were doomed?"

"Maybe."

"I thought we'd get married," she admitted. "I thought we were going to be together always."

"Me, too."

So, what did their joint admission mean, she wondered. Maybe that they could stay friends for a long time.

She had to admit he was right. She *had* changed the rules in their relationship.

She touched his hand. "It was literally a decade ago. What do you say we release the topic into the cosmos? Maybe it will meet up with Emilion Stoicasescu and tell him we have his painting."

He turned his wrist so their fingers were laced together. "I wish you'd managed to get away."

She was so caught in the unexpected feel of his skin on hers that she nearly missed his words.

"From the island?"

He nodded. "Not that I don't like hanging out with you, but..."

There could have been so much more to her life. Heat

burned on her cheeks. She started to pull away, but he held on to her hand.

"It was too hard to leave," she told him, avoiding his gaze.

"Not good enough."

"I had responsibilities. My mom, Averil."

"Averil moved to California when she was eighteen, and Bonnie met Bertie."

She tugged free of his grip and dropped her hands to her lap. "I was scared," she admitted. "I knew what it was like to be here. I kept telling myself that once everything got settled I could go. I meant it, but then time passed and suddenly it was yesterday."

"You could go now," he told her. "Especially if your mom sells the painting."

She didn't have anywhere to go, she thought. No dreams left. Medical school, but that was from a long time ago. Was it possible now?

"Have you changed your mind?" he asked. "About being a doctor?"

"I've picked what I want to do."

"I don't believe that," he told her. "You picked what was expedient. Are you happy?"

His tone was gentle enough that she didn't feel threatened, and she appreciated the questions.

"I guess I've been stuck for so long I forgot to keep moving forward. This is easy."

"Like working for my dad," he said. "It seemed like a good idea at the time. Tell you what—you jump and I'll jump."

"We're not in this together," she reminded him. "Plus, I've already been on the outs with your family. I don't want to go through that again."

"You made up. Hell, you worked for my dad for years."

"Yes, and sometimes it was awkward."

He studied her for a second. "So, you're staying?"

She nodded.

"Me, too."

Information that shouldn't have mattered, she told herself. Yet oddly, it made her feel better. As if she wasn't going to face everything happening right now on her own.

Chapter Seventeen

✣

AVERIL SAT ON her bed as she scanned through the comments from her online critique group. They were universal, she thought, her stomach tightening. No one liked her opening. Two people thought her main character was selfish, the rest thought she was uninteresting.

"I would never read past the first page," someone had written. "Does this story ever get going? You haven't posted anything in weeks and this is what you give us?"

The harsh criticism surprised her. She hadn't thought her story was the best thing ever written, but it had kept her up late; she'd been excited to be putting words to paper, so to speak.

She scrolled to another set of comments.

"What happened to the teenager who was gang raped?" another person posted. "Now that was a story. I really liked the part where she was blamed when they were persecuted by the town."

She stared at the screen, frowning. "I never wrote that,"

she murmured. Why would anyone? It sounded awful. Talk about depressing.

She picked up her cell and pushed the button to dial Kevin.

"Hey," he said a second later. "How's it going?"

"I don't know. I just got the feedback from my online group."

"And?"

"They hate it. Mostly they think it's boring and has no purpose. One of them wants to know why I don't go back to the gang rape story."

"The what? I don't remember that one."

"I never wrote it." She sighed. "I don't know. Maybe they're right. Maybe this is boring."

"Is that what you think?"

"I didn't. I can't seem to find a story I'm excited about. I feel like I'm going through the motions. Maybe I'm not a writer. What do you think?"

"Enough about me. What do you think about me," he said.

His tone was light enough, but she got the point. "I'm sorry," she said, feeling herself flush. "You're right. I do talk about myself. How are things at work?"

"Good. I'm avoiding hanging with James."

"Is he still having his affair?"

"Uh-huh. That's going to blow up in his face."

She thought about how Kevin had been on his own for a while now. How she'd been gone. "I'm sorry to be away from you. I miss you."

"That's nice to hear. I miss you, too."

"I know you want me to come home," she said. "I want that, too."

"But you're not ready yet."

He wasn't asking a question. Still, guilt flooded her. Guilt that she was gone. Guilt that she couldn't seem to write the novel she'd told everyone about. Guilt for being unable to commit to having a baby.

"Why can't I be mature like everyone else? Did I miss some vital part of my development?"

He was silent.

"Don't want to comment?" she asked.

"You already know what I think."

She did. He believed she listened to Nina too much. That she substituted her sister for her own judgment.

"You're wrong," she told him. "I don't even like Nina half the time."

"That doesn't change the fact that you're always trying to prove yourself to her. What I can't figure out is why. Are you showing her that her sacrifice had value or is it about being unwilling to break the bond by being a well-rounded adult? If you don't need her, then she ceases to exist?"

Averil straightened her legs and shifted the phone to her other ear. "That's harsh."

"It's not inaccurate. Nina is the voice in your head."

"You're saying I hear voices?" she asked, her tone teasing. Anything to get him off this subject.

"I'm saying you can trust yourself. You won't wake up and be your mom."

Ouch. She pressed her lips together, uneasy with the sense of being exposed on more levels than she could count.

"Okay, then," she said. "Thanks for the insight."

She half expected him to apologize or ask if she was all right. Instead he drew in a breath.

"I'll talk to you later," he said.

"Sure. Later. Bye."

Then he was gone. Averil flopped back on the bed and closed her eyes. Tears burned, but she ignored them. Kevin was wrong, about all of it. Just like her critique group was wrong. Maybe that story hadn't been her best work, but it wasn't as crappy as they said. Besides, who wanted to read a book about a gang rape? Not her. She wanted to lose herself in something that was an escape.

She sat up, not sure if she should go to the store or quit her critique group or start another project. Indecision made her limbs heavy.

Penny raised her head from her place at the foot of the bed. Her brown eyes were warm and affectionate. Averil stretched her hand toward her and rubbed her back.

"You know exactly what you're supposed to do, don't you? There aren't a lot of questions in the dog world."

She stretched back out on the bed and closed her eyes. Penny moved next to her.

Kevin's comments nipped at her, making her uncomfortable. She wanted to say he was wrong, but she wasn't sure. About anything. And she supposed that was what it came down to. How much of her life was chosen by her and how much was chosen *for* her? Of course a case could be made that no one really got to choose. In a perfect world...

She opened her eyes. That was it, she realized. She didn't know what a perfect world looked like. She didn't have a clue as to what she wanted. Not with her writing or her work or even her marriage. Certainly not about whether they should have a child now.

How ridiculous, she thought. Wasn't it time to figure this all out?

"The wind direction is key," Kyle was saying.

There was more plane talk. He didn't usually go on about the technical aspects of his job, but every now and then he couldn't help himself. Nina did her best to follow along, but when he started in with words like *G-force,* she was totally lost.

Not that her inattention was his fault, she thought. With everything going on these days, she was having a lot of trouble focusing. She kept thinking about the painting. That having it was going to change everything. Sometimes she worried it was all going to be a pain in her ass, but every now and then she allowed herself to think about possibilities. That maybe it would work out.

The money was hard to grasp. That amount. Who had ten million drop in their lap? Certainly not her. And even though the money was her mom's and Bertie's, it wasn't unreasonable to think they might share.

A hundred thousand would pay for medical school, she thought wistfully. A hundred and thirty would cover the tuition and her living expenses, if she was careful. Assuming she could still get in. She wasn't twenty-two anymore. Did she actually want to be a doctor, or was that something left over from—

"Earth to Nina."

She looked at Kyle and saw him watching her.

"Sorry," she murmured. "I was dealing with stuff."

"I could tell. That or my lift-thrust ratio explanation needs work."

She smiled. "It's perfect. Don't change a thing."

He reached across the table and took her hand in his. "What's going on? You've been distracted all night."

"Family stuff," she admitted. "Having my mom home is sometimes stressful. With Averil here, it's more complicated than usual."

The real problem was the painting, but as she'd asked the others not to mention it, she wasn't going to say anything, either.

She watched his fingers stroking her hand. For once the feel of his skin against hers didn't send waves of longing through her. If she was completely honest with herself, she mostly wanted to go home and spend the evening losing herself in mindless television.

"I missed you," he said, staring into her eyes. "That was a long six days."

"It was," she said, even as she realized she'd been too busy with painting trauma to do much more than notice he was gone. "You have a lot of responsibilities with work."

He shrugged. "Just national security."

She smiled. "All on your shoulders? Impressive."

"I can handle it." He lowered his voice. "Want me to prove it to you?"

An invitation to his bed, she thought with a sigh. Because he wanted to sleep with her. They always had sex after dinner on their dates. Sometimes they had sex before. That's what they did together. They ate and they had sex.

While the situation had never been dissatisfying before, tonight she wasn't in the mood. Only it had been six days, and saying no seemed unfriendly. Or at least not girlfriendlike.

Only she wasn't his girlfriend. This was a fling. Hot monkey sex with a cute guy. It was perfect. Right up until she wasn't in the mood for sex. Because what exactly did she and Kyle talk about?

Fortunately he didn't hear the convoluted conversation inside her head. And he took her silence as agreement. He waved their server over and paid the bill, then rose and walked her to his car.

Thirty minutes later they were at his place. Nina followed him into his apartment. He closed the door behind her, then turned and pulled her into his arms.

She went willingly, wanting to feel his mouth on hers. His lips were gentle but insistent. His hunger burned through her, as it always did, and she kicked off her shoes in anticipation of the wanting that would start her melting.

She wrapped her arms around him and brushed his tongue with hers. All sexy things. But instead of getting lost in growing sensations, she was aware of the faint taste of coffee and mint and the sound of the furnace clicking on. Somewhere outside, she heard a car horn.

She closed her eyes more tightly and rubbed her belly against Kyle's erection. He was hard, she thought, picturing him naked. That was arousing. Naked hunky guy. Yum.

Only it wasn't yummy or even appealing, she thought. And when he put his hand on her butt, she found herself stepping back.

"I'm not really..." She paused when she saw the passion in his eyes.

He was so adorable, she thought. Eager. Really sweet to her. The man had caught her when she'd fallen off the roof.

"I've got a lot going on right now," she told him. "Let's just make this about you."

His eyebrows drew together. "What do you mean?"

Was the concept that difficult to understand? "I don't think I can focus enough tonight."

He moved toward her. "Sure you can. I'll make it good." He put his hands on her breasts and lowered his head to her neck. "I know what you like."

He kissed his way along her neck to her ear. After nipping on her lobe, he licked the sensitive space right below it. At the same time, he cupped her breasts and rubbed his thumbs against her nipples.

But what should have been arousing only made her uncomfortable. It was as if someone had severed the connection between her head and her body. She knew what he was doing but didn't really feel it. Not in a sexy way.

He dropped his hands to her hips, then reached for the waistband of her jeans. She stepped back.

"Kyle, I can't." What she meant was *I don't want to,* but that sounded harsh. She put her hand on his erection, rubbing him through his jeans. "I'll go down on you." Oral sex was a regular part of their play, although usually it was mutual. Still, tonight, she couldn't summon the interest.

He grabbed her wrist, stilling her movements. "You first."

Annoyance joined exhaustion. "Kyle, I'm trying to make this as clear as I can. I'm not interested in having an orgasm tonight. Seriously. Maybe it's hormones, maybe it's stress. Whatever the reason, I don't want to come."

"We should try." He wrapped an arm around her waist and pulled her against him. "I can make it good."

"No," she snapped, and pushed away. "No."

She fought anger, but could see he was only confused. Jeez, it was like arguing with a puppy.

"I'm sorry," she murmured. "I want to please you."

"Then, let's go to bed. Once we get started, you'll like it."

They were arguing in circles. "What part of me saying I'm not interested is confusing?"

"You're not really trying."

"So, you know what I'm feeling better than I do?"

He looked more wounded than upset. "No. But I need it to be good for you."

"Why?"

He shrugged. "I just do."

"Because sex is about winning, and you don't win if I'm not begging for more?"

He have her that slow, sexy grin she usually adored. "Something like that."

For the first time since he'd blown back into her life, she

felt the age difference. What had been quirky and fun seemed ridiculously self-absorbed.

"I need to go," she told him and started for the door.

"Nina, wait." He touched her arm. "What's wrong?"

She drew in a breath. Most of this wasn't his fault, she reminded herself. Until a few minutes ago, she'd been just as interested in a sex-centric relationship.

"I'll be better in a few days," she told him. "There's some family stuff I have to deal with. When that calms down, I'll be back to normal."

She knew she was being a complete wimp, taking all the responsibility on herself. That if she expected to have a relationship with Kyle, she needed to be honest with him. They needed to communicate. But it was all so exhausting, and this was a fling, right? No serious communication required. Wasn't that the point?

He crossed to her, then lightly kissed her on the forehead. "You know I'm here for you, right?"

She nodded, then leaned into him. "I know. Thanks." Then, before he could try to seduce her again, she picked up her bag and left.

Once she was in her car, she started the engine, then leaned back against the seat. She was unsettled, both physically and emotionally. Her skin didn't feel right. Not too small or scratchy, but just uncomfortable. Like that half second before breaking out in goose bumps.

She glanced back at the apartment building, battling guilt. She'd done nothing wrong, she told herself, then wished she could believe herself.

Her phone chirped, letting her know she had an incoming text. Not Kyle, she thought as she dug out her phone and glanced at the screen.

It wasn't from him. Instead the message was from Dylan.

Get to the store right away. Urgent.

She put the car in gear and headed out of the parking lot. From Kyle's apartment she was maybe three minutes from the freeway. From there it was a short drive to the bridge and back to Blackberry Island.

At the stoplight by the on-ramp, she tried Dylan's number, but it went right to voice mail. Next she tried Averil, but her sister didn't answer. By then, the light was green, and she had to merge onto the freeway.

It was nearly eight in the evening. Rain fell, but it was still light enough for her to see without headlights. She crossed the bridge, then headed for the west side of the island. As she turned onto the main road, she found herself watching for an accident or smoke. Panic twisted in her chest and made her hands slippery on the steering wheel. She was just about to try her sister again, when she saw them.

Bright lights and news vans. Three of them, lined up on the side of the road. A crowd had collected to watch whatever was going on.

Nina parked as close as she could, then got out of her car and hurried toward the throng of people gathered around the lights. Nina pushed her way through until she could see her mother standing in front of Blackberry Preserves. The painting was on an easel, on full display for everyone. Apparently the key she and Averil had for the safe wasn't the only one.

"Oh, no!"

She turned and saw Bertie had joined her. The other woman looked as shocked as Nina felt. Averil appeared, as well.

"She didn't," Averil breathed. "She couldn't."

Bertie shook her head. "We talked about this yesterday. She mentioned wanting to share the painting with the world, but I said we should wait. That we needed a plan in place.

That it would be irresponsible…" Her voice trailed off. "I'm sorry, Nina."

"Me, too."

Because there were three reporters—one for each news van, she thought. All from Seattle. Which meant as soon as the story played on the local news, it would be picked up nationally. How long did they have until CNN showed up? Not to mention crazy people and shysters.

A warm hand settled on the small of her back. Irritation flared. Seriously? He couldn't give her fifteen minutes to deal with this?

She turned, prepared to take Kyle on, only to find herself looking into Dylan's concerned eyes.

"Hey," he said. "I heard a teaser while I was watching the game. Something about a discovered painting and I knew. I came right away."

Of course he had, she thought, relieved to have him there. No doubt he'd been in his parking garage when she'd tried to call. He wouldn't have a cell signal there.

"Now what?" he asked.

Bertie's eyes filled with tears. "How could she do this to all of us?"

Averil sucked in a breath. "Is anyone actually surprised?"

"No," Bertie admitted.

Nina turned back to her mother. Bonnie was smiling, obviously enjoying the attention. The reporters were calling out questions—some about the painting, some about how she'd found it.

"We can't keep it in the store anymore," Nina said. "The safe is old. I'm sure it would be relatively easy to pick. We'll have to take it home tonight."

"Then to Seattle tomorrow," Bertie said firmly. "You have the places that can store it?"

Nina nodded. She still had the list from Ambrose. "There are a couple in Seattle."

"I'll drive," Dylan said. "I'm on call this Saturday, so I have tomorrow off."

"You don't have to," she told him.

"I know."

"Thank you."

He moved his hand to her shoulder and squeezed. "No problem. I'll be at your place at eight tomorrow. We'll be in the city by ten and back the same day."

"I'll be calling the banks by nine," Bertie said firmly. "Then I'll let you know where I've made arrangements for storage." She looked at Bonnie. "All right. This has gone on long enough."

She walked past the reporters and stepped next to Bonnie, standing directly in front of the painting.

"That's all for tonight," she said firmly. "Thank you so much for coming."

Bonnie looked at her, as if she was going to say something. Then her smile faded, and worry pulled at the corners of her eyes.

"Oh," she mouthed, as if suddenly remembering that this was not what they'd agreed to do. She looked like a toddler who had just realized she'd done something very, very wrong, and that there would be punishment. What was adorable on a three-year-old was less appealing on a woman pushing fifty.

"Bonnie has some explaining to do," Dylan said as they moved away.

"Don't worry about her. Bertie doesn't hold a grudge." In a few days, all would be forgotten, Nina thought. By each of them.

"See you in the morning," Dylan said before he left.

When he was gone, Nina moved next to her sister. "This is a mess."

"A big one, even for Mom." Averil's mouth twisted. "I would offer to take the painting in for you, but I suspect you'll be more comfortable doing it yourself."

"I will. I can't help being overcontrolling."

"In this case, it makes sense."

The TV lights turned off one by one. As twilight closed in, the crowd began to disperse.

"So much for having time to think," Averil said. "Now we have to figure out what to do with the painting and fast."

"Lucky us," Nina whispered, thinking it was going to be a very long night.

Chapter Eighteen

❧

DYLAN ARRIVED ON TIME. Nina couldn't remember when she'd last been so happy to see a man—and that included date anticipation for her nights with Kyle. Even better than his reassuring presence, Dylan had brought his father's Suburban. The giant SUV held the painting easily and could also be used as a tank in case there was a sudden attack from Canada.

"Can you make the climb?" Dylan asked as he held open the passenger seat. "Want me to get a stepladder?"

"Very funny. I'm not short and I take Pilates."

"Impressive."

She scrambled into the seat, and he closed the door, then walked around to the driver's side. She didn't bother looking back at the house. While Averil had gotten up early to have coffee with her, she hadn't seen her mother since the previous night. Bertie had briefly shown up to offer support, without saying anything about Bonnie. Loyalty, Nina thought as Dylan headed across the bridge to I-5. From there they would go south to Seattle.

But instead of merging, he pulled into a Starbucks drive-thru.

"Coffee will help," he said as they got in line.

"Is my lack of sleep that obvious?"

"Of course not."

She thought about the shadows she'd seen under her eyes that morning. "I appreciate the gentlemanly lying." She leaned her head back against the seat. "I stayed up until one, then Averil got up and took over. I'm not sure what we were waiting for or how we expected to ward off an intruder."

"Did you call the sheriff?"

She nodded. "He sent by regular patrols. I want to say I can't believe my mother did that, but it's actually very her. How she loves to share beauty with the world." Although in this case, everyone agreed it was an ugly painting. "Or maybe she just wanted the attention."

She tried not to think about the media people in front of the store and everyone who now knew about the painting.

Dylan pulled up in front of the speaker and glanced at her. She told him her order, which he repeated. Then he ordered a latte for himself.

"Ambrose is going to meet us at the bank," she continued when they'd moved forward a car length. "I have all the signed paperwork for him to manage the painting. He'll take care of getting the painting officially appraised and then we go from there."

She refused to think about how they were going to pay the man if there weren't proceeds from a sale, but that was a problem for another day. Right now she simply wanted the painting as far away from her mother's house as possible.

They got their coffees, and then Dylan merged onto the freeway. Nina sipped and waited for the caffeine to drift into her bloodstream and increase her energy level.

She glanced at Dylan, taking in his handsome profile. "Did I thank you for driving me to Seattle?"

"You did."

"Okay, well, I'm going to say it again."

"Happy to help."

She smiled. "You just wanted to get out of dealing with vaccinations and hemorrhoids."

"I'll admit that hemorrhoids aren't my favorite thing to look at." He kept his gaze on the road. "Spending the day with you has its perks."

"My sparkling conversation?"

"I like that we have a history."

"Me, too."

She wouldn't have thought they would become friends, but they had. They'd both grown up, and with maturity came change. But the essential core of who they had been hadn't shifted very far from center. As much as she'd loved Dylan, she'd also always liked him. Apparently a decade apart hadn't changed that.

He was nice and decent and had a way of taking charge that she totally respected. She could depend on him. These days, having someone else help with the decision-making was really nice.

She wasn't sure what that kiss had meant. Dylan hadn't ever asked her out—not the way Kyle had. Of course, Kyle had made his intentions clear from the first second she'd landed in his arms.

She sighed. He was turning out to be a complication, she thought. Last night had been a disaster. She briefly wondered about texting him to see if he was okay, but didn't want to explain what she was doing to Dylan.

Too many men had never been her problem, but it was

looking as if it might be now. Along with her sister, her mother, the painting, the store and her life, already in progress.

She turned to Dylan. "You have everything together. Why is that?"

He chuckled. "You're giving me too much credit."

"Am I?" She sipped her coffee. "All right, painting-rescue guy. I'll just go for it. Why aren't you married?"

"Is that a serious question?"

She thought for a second. "Yes, it is."

"Okay. I came close a couple of times. Does that count?"

Was she one of the close calls? "With whom?"

"Once in medical school. A fellow doctor. She decided she wanted to be a neurosurgeon, so when we left for our internships, we went in different directions and lost touch."

So not her, she thought. "Anyone else?"

He hesitated, then shrugged. "A woman I met last year. A single mom. But she didn't want to leave, and I knew I wasn't staying."

"You were willing to be a stepfather?"

"Sure. I like kids. I always planned to have them."

"Me, too," she murmured.

"You didn't think Serge was father material?" he asked, his voice teasing.

She punched his arm. "You will not talk about my ex."

"Still pining?"

She reached for her latte. "It was a very short fling with unfortunate consequences. I regret everything about Serge. Especially marrying him."

"I regret not coming home a month sooner."

Nina stiffened, then immediately tried to relax so he wouldn't notice. While Dylan's words were clear, his meaning was not. He'd claimed to have returned to tell her he still cared—only she'd been off getting married. If he'd come a month sooner, she would have been single. So, then what? Would he have said he still cared? Still loved her? And would they have...

She wasn't sure what would have happened next, but she had a feeling everything would have been different.

Before she could figure out what to say, her cell phone rang. She pulled it out of her bag and glanced at the screen. "It's Bertie," she said. "Probably with the bank information."

Dylan nodded but didn't say anything. She answered the call and took down the information. By the time she was done, they were on the outskirts of Seattle and starting to hit traffic. He said something about the rain, she mentioned how Ambrose reminded her of a BBC character, and the moment was lost.

But not the memory of it, she thought. Did Dylan regret losing her as an "oh, darn" moment, or was he thinking he should try to set things right between them? And if it was the latter, what did that mean to her? They were both in different places. She wasn't sure going back was the right thing.

There was also Kyle and how he fit into all this. Too many questions, she thought, and no answers.

"Your insurance company isn't going to be happy if we get rear-ended with a ten-million dollar painting in the back," she said conversationally.

Dylan grinned. "Bet Dad never thought of that when he offered me the Suburban."

As promised, Ambrose was waiting at the bank. They exchanged signed paperwork, then took the painting into the special vault. More signatures were required, then they went to Ambrose's cushy office and he explained the process of getting an appraisal, along with the steps that would need to be taken to bring the painting to auction.

Nina was grateful that he never once mentioned the debacle of her mother sharing her find with the world. She and Dylan stopped for an early lunch before heading north. They were back on the island by three. He drove her to her house, then turned off the engine and walked around the SUV to her door.

"I can't thank you enough," she said sincerely as she slid to the ground and grabbed her bag. "I honestly don't think I could have gotten through this by myself."

"Not to mention the fact that the painting wouldn't have fit in your car."

"Yes, there's that." She glanced at the house. "It's a mess. One that might leave my mom and Bertie in possession of a lot of money, but still a complication." She smiled up at him. "Just think. You got your good deed for the month done early. Now you can relax."

Instead of smiling back, he cupped her face in his hands, leaned in and kissed her.

The contact was warm and firm. Familiar, she thought hazily as she dropped her bag on the ground and wrapped her arms around his waist.

They moved closer, finding a familiar pose. She tilted her head and waited for his tongue to lightly brush her own. Wanting sparked—desire blending with memories into a powerful cocktail designed to leave her light-headed. But before she could figure out what she wanted, he drew back and smiled.

"Take care of yourself," he told her, then walked around the front of the Suburban.

She picked up her purse and walked to the porch. As he drove away, she wasn't sure if she was aroused or annoyed. Maybe a little of both. What was he thinking, kissing her like that, then leaving? What was she doing, kissing him back? She was seeing Kyle. Semidating and definitely sleeping with the other man. Not only wasn't this her style, she had a feeling she wasn't going to be very good at juggling two men. Or was that an acquired skill and one she should think about learning?

Averil sat cross-legged on her bed and hit the enter key with as much force as she could. The screen popped up with an "are you sure" message.

"You bet I'm sure, assholes," she muttered as she clicked yes.

In return the screen posted a message saying she had been permanently unsubscribed from her online writing critique group.

She flopped back on the bed and stared at the ceiling. After the last round of critiques, she'd taken a couple of days to recover from the hostile comments, then she'd gone back into her archives and checked out what had happened the handful of other times she'd submitted her work.

Every comment had been negative, and many of them had bordered on snide or worse. They didn't just seem to hate her writing—it was as if they were questioning who she was as a person. She wrote for a living—articles, but still. She was used to the process and comfortable being edited. Maybe she really was a lousy fiction writer, or maybe they were a really bad critique group. She'd gone back a second time and realized that nearly every comment to every writer was negative. That had made her realize she'd put herself in a position to be discouraged every time she submitted. Was this yet another way she was self-sabotaging what she claimed was her dream? Something to think about.

On a slightly more pressing note, without the critique group, she had no feedback. An oddly freeing thought. She sat up again and grabbed the pad of paper she kept by the bed for bursts of ideas about future articles. She scanned the list and saw there were three articles about falling in love and/or dealing with a relationship, the notes about raiding grandma's closet and a couple of sentences on how to survive a family vacation when it was just you, your parents and your siblings.

Of all of them, the articles she was most excited to write were the ones about love. Falling in love, dealing with a breakup, wondering if he even knew you were alive. She knew she connected with her readers—she had the fan mail and letters to prove it. So maybe the solution to her writing dilemma was to look at which articles got the most feedback and figure out why. Then she could combine that with what she most liked to write and voila. Success. Or if not success, then at least a sense of purpose.

She logged on to her work email and searched for those month-end reports some tech person was always sending. The ones that showed where she got the most hits and responses.

Two hours later, she saw that her readers loved her falling in love articles, too. Most of her fan mail came in the form of questions about relationships—mostly with boys, but sometimes with family. Girls were as confused now as she had been at their age. They were just better dressers.

She flopped back on the bed and wondered what to do with the information. She loved reading young adult fiction but had assumed she had to write a "real" novel about grown-ups. Her last attempt had been about a young woman in her twenties. But her core audience was younger than that. The bulk of demographics for the magazine were thirteen to twenty-five, with the majority of readers still in high school.

She thought about how many questions she'd had while she was growing up. How Nina was her world and yet she resented her as much as she loved her. How she hadn't wanted to go away to college, but also hadn't felt she'd had a choice. That if she'd refused, she would have been throwing Nina's gift back in her face, and then Nina might not love her anymore. While Bonnie had been the fun parent, Nina had been the one to keep their world in order. She could never have risked losing that. She still couldn't.

"Oh, my God!"

Averil stumbled to her feet. Penny raised her head from her bed, as if asking if they were leaving.

"It's okay, baby girl," Averil murmured absently, reassuring the dog even as her mind continued to swirl.

Was that it? Was that at the very center of her problem? That she hadn't emotionally separated from Nina enough to be comfortable making her own decisions on the off chance Nina might not approve? Was Kevin right? If Nina was the voice in her head, then everything had to go through the Nina filter. Any decision that might upset her sister left Averil feeling emotionally abandoned.

As a child, without her sister's love, she knew she would die. Had she forgotten to unlearn that lesson? Because in truth, Nina rarely disapproved. Nina was supportive. Sure they fought and got on each other's nerves, but if she had a dream, she knew Nina would be there for her. So, was it worse than hearing Nina in her head? Was it hearing an abusive form of Nina she'd made up from personal insecurities?

She was stuck, always waiting for approval from someone who didn't really exist. Someone she'd created herself to keep from trying and failing.

Nina cared as much as a sibling could, but this wasn't about her. Averil couldn't put a name to her condition, but she knew it had a lot to do with the dynamics of their family. Of Bonnie refusing to grow up and Nina never being the child and Averil in the awkward position of being taken care of, all the while suspecting the price her sister paid.

She sat back on the bed and pulled her laptop toward her. She opened a new Word file, then started typing. About a teenaged girl and the boy she liked and her crazy family who found a rare coin worth far more than any of them could imagine.

Nina stepped out of Andi's house, grateful the day had ended. She was exhausted. The previous day's trip to Seattle had settled some problems, but it had been two nights since she'd slept well. The first night, she'd been on painting watch. Last night she'd found herself unable to stop thinking about Dylan and that damned kiss.

What had he been thinking, doing that to her? You couldn't just walk up to someone and kiss her and get away with it. Except it seemed you could. Especially when the kissee— her—kissed back.

She didn't know what he wanted or expected. She also didn't know what *she* wanted. Dylan was so different from Kyle. More mature, but also more comfortable to be with. They had a past. Not that she was interested in dating Dylan, or that he had asked, which returned her to the confusing place where she'd spent much of the night.

She turned the corner and saw a man leaning against her car. He was tall and blond and when he saw her, he gave her a slow, sexy smile.

"Hey, gorgeous."

While her brain was busy processing how good he looked and how sweet the words sounded, her body was off with other matters. Her girl parts urged a close encounter, her hands itched to be touching him everywhere and her feet were carrying her toward him as if she had every intention of throwing herself at him.

Confusion brought her to a stop only a couple of feet away.

What was wrong with her? Two days ago, she hadn't wanted to have sex with Kyle. She'd practically decided she was never seeing him again. Yesterday she'd been kissing Dylan, and now she was getting all tingly at the sight of Kyle and wondering if it would be tacky to have sex in her car?

Was it possible she needed some kind of psychological intervention?

"Hi," she said, keeping her distance, even though most of her didn't want to.

He pushed away from the car and closed the space between them, although he didn't touch her. "I missed you yesterday."

"I had to go to Seattle."

She thought about mentioning the painting, but Kyle didn't strike her as the type of guy who watched the local news.

He shoved his hands into his jeans pockets. "I'm sorry about the other night. You were sending me a clear message and I didn't listen. I wanted…" He looked away, then back at her. "We both know what I wanted." He drew in a breath. "The thing is, Nina, I like you. I like being around you. You were right—this started as some quest for me. To find you and make you mine."

And he'd done a fine job of it, she thought. "A fling. You were clear on that. I have no complaints."

His dark blue gaze locked with hers. "What I figured out is that's not enough for me anymore."

Her stomach tightened. What? He was breaking up with her, just when she'd come around to his way of thinking?

"I want more," he continued. "I want to spend time with you. I want to get to know you better. I want us to be about more than sex. I care about you."

Nina honest to God didn't know what to say. "You're talking about a relationship," she said, then waited for him to start pointing and laughing. Because he couldn't mean it. Twenty-six-year-old fighter jocks didn't stand in front of her asking for an emotional connection. Of course, until Kyle they hadn't been bugging her for sex, either, but that was an issue for another day.

"Yes," he said simply. "I want us to be in a relationship. Is that a problem?"

She thought about how, except for a couple of nights ago, she felt free and content in his arms. How he made her laugh and was incredibly pretty to look at. Then she thought about Dylan and their kisses and, for a second, was genuinely confused.

"I, ah—"

The slow, sexy smile returned. "Don't worry, Nina. I'm happy to have to work for it."

She'd barely processed the words, let alone their meaning, when he turned and walked to his car. Before she could blink again, he was driving away. Thirty seconds later, a text buzzed onto her phone.

I'll convince you, was all it said.

Chapter Nineteen

~⁂~

AVERIL STUDIED THE table setting. Until recently they'd mostly used the large dining room set in the store for little more than a giant shelf. Other items were literally stacked on chairs and shoved onto the table. Cindy'd had the idea of using the table for its intended purpose, and displaying dishes on it as if someone were going to sit down to a meal. Averil had suggested they take that idea further to show off *four* place settings.

She and Cindy had put the leaves in the table, expanding it out to its full length, then had artfully draped four different tablecloths. One side showed off the Depression-era glass with its soft tones. An old sterling silver flatware set had been used with those items. Opposite was a more formal setting with beautiful Lennox and Waterford pieces, and so on.

The first weekend after the change, Cindy had sold three sets of dishes. Averil had high hopes for more.

The front door opened, and Nina walked in. She glanced around, as if searching for something, then asked, "Where's Cindy?"

"Out back, spray painting a wooden drying rack we found. We're going to use it to display linens."

Nina still wore her scrubs from work. She looked rumpled and tired—as if she'd had a long day. She reached behind her and pulled off the band at the bottom of her braid, then finger-combed her hair.

"We need to talk," she said wearily.

Averil stiffened. She immediately tried to figure out what complaint her sister had now and how she was going to explain that Nina was wrong. That was followed by the thought that she assumed she was in trouble. In light of her recent semirealization, she wanted to try to stay as in the moment as possible. If she could keep herself from falling into familiar patterns, maybe she could figure out what had gone wrong in her life and then fix it.

Nina sank into an overstuffed chair and covered her face with her hands. "That's not exactly accurate," she amended. "*I* need to talk, and I hope you'll listen." She glanced toward the back door. "Cindy's going to be a bit, isn't she?"

"I think so."

Nina dropped her hands to her lap. "Good. I don't especially want to entertain her with the disaster that is my personal life."

"Understandable. What's up?"

"I'm sleeping with Kyle."

Averil nodded slowly. "Right. The fighter pilot guy. He came to dinner and didn't run screaming when he met Mom and Bertie. He seems nice." Young and not Nina's type, but part of her new maturity was keeping tidbits like that to herself.

"He is nice. Very sweet and a god in bed."

Averil grinned. "You have high-quality problems."

Nina managed a smile. "I wish that was it, but it isn't. Okay, it sort of is." She paused. "I'm so confused. He wants more."

Now it was Averil's turn to not get it. "More, how? Like you tying him up? Because if you want to do that, you need a safe word."

Nina stared at her. "What on earth? No, not tie me up. A safe word? How do you know stuff like that?"

"I live in California. Everybody does bondage in L.A." Averil held in a laugh. "So, what do you mean by he wants more? Relationship more?"

Nina nodded. "He said that when this had started, he wanted a fling, but now he wants more. I think he was asking me to be his girlfriend."

A surprise, Averil thought. Not that Nina didn't have charms, but that she would let herself get close enough to Kyle for him to think that was possible. Being involved meant being vulnerable. Nina didn't surrender emotionally to anyone.

"Is that a bad thing?"

"I don't know," Nina admitted. "It's not what I was expecting. We're having a fling and I was okay with that. I mean, my God, have you seen him? His body, that smile. I have to say when all that attention is turned on a girl, it's tough to say no."

"Do you like him?"

"Sure. I mean, what's not to like? He's the human male equivalent of a puppy. Adorable and fun. He works hard, plays hard and then falls asleep."

"There's more to him than that," Averil insisted. "He has to have emotional depths."

"I guess," Nina said slowly, looking confused. "We don't really talk about things. He talks about his family some. I know he wants to be a Blue Angel."

Averil frowned. "The jets that fly around at air shows?"

"That would be them. He has a plan. But we don't discuss much else. He tells me about his day, which involves a lot of talk about flying. Then we talk about my work, then we finish having dinner, then we have sex."

"Sounds like a relationship to me," Averil told her. "What are you objecting to?"

"I don't know," Nina admitted. "It's just so strange. He's leaving in a few months, so there's a time limit. But it's not as if we're getting married." She rubbed her temples. "I'm getting a headache from thinking about all of this."

"You need to figure out what you want," Averil said firmly. "Do you want to take things to the next level or do you want to keep things light?"

Nina nodded. "You're right."

Averil felt a glow of satisfaction. Words her sister never said to her. Being the calm one giving advice felt pretty damned good.

"Of course, if you're going to try that next-level thing with Kyle, you're going to have to figure out what you're doing with Dylan."

She was mostly teasing, but then Nina stared at her, eyes wide and filled with guilt.

"You're sleeping with Dylan?" Averil asked, her voice rising with each word.

Nina glanced over her shoulder, then motioned for her to be quiet. "Don't shout, and no. I'm not. We're friends. Good friends who have a past. We're not having sex."

"I'm not sure I believe you. You're doing something."

Nina shifted in her seat. "We've kissed. It's nothing."

"Was there tongue? Because tongue isn't nothing."

Nina pressed her lips together. "I don't feel I have to discuss that with you," she said primly.

Averil leaned back in her chair. "You brought this conversation to me. For what it's worth, I think it's okay to sleep with them both. At least until you commit to Kyle."

Nina's mouth fell open. "No, it's not."

"Why not? If you're not in a committed relationship, you're free to do what you want. I'm not saying it's a good idea. I'm not sure you could handle it, emotionally, but it's not wrong. Until you have the talk about being exclusive, you are free to be wild."

Nina covered her face with her hands again. "That is so not me. I haven't been on a date in forever and now this." She straightened and lowered her hands to her lap. "Anyway, it's not an issue. Dylan and I aren't doing that. The kissing was just one of those things. Practically an accident."

"I've never known you to be self-delusional before," Averil murmured. "But, hey, if it helps you sleep at night, go for it."

Her sister stared at her, but Averil didn't care. She'd never seen Nina so rattled, and watching her now was very satisfying. If that made her shallow, so be it.

Nina carefully poured herself a glass of wine. She hadn't eaten much that day. Her stomach was all messed up, and she still had that headache. Although her talk with Averil had helped her feel better emotionally, it hadn't done anything for her physical symptoms.

It was the confusion, she told herself. Confusion about Kyle and Dylan and her life and where she was. The only good part had been leaning on her sister. For once she didn't feel that everything was completely up to her.

She'd gotten home less than a half hour before. After showering and dressing, she had walked into the kitchen for her wine. Now she was going to sit quietly and sip until it was time to deal with dinner. She wasn't sure what everyone's plans were for the night and found herself hoping they would all go out and leave her in peace. Nothing sounded better than a—

Her mother charged into the kitchen and glared at her.

"You had no right," Bonnie began, her face flushed, her glare hostile. "You took my painting. I had a connection with *Evening Stars!*"

Nina felt the slap down to her heart. "Mom, we discussed this. There was no way to leave the painting here. Not after everyone knew about it."

"It's not your painting," her mother reminded her. "It wasn't your decision to make. This is just so like you, Nina. Everything always has to be your way."

Nina quickly looked for an escape, only there wasn't one. The unfairness burned, and she fought against unexpected tears. Crying? Really? Wasn't she used to this by now?

Then she tightened her grip on her wineglass and stiffened her spine.

"No," she said clearly. She liked the sound so much, she said it again. "No, Mom. I didn't take your painting against your will. I cleaned up your mess, the way I've been doing it for my entire life. We had a discussion as a family, and we made a decision. I took care of the logistics. I don't know if you're embarrassed by your behavior or bored or what, but you're not blaming this on me."

Bertie walked into the kitchen and stood next to Nina. "Bonnie, what are you doing? We all talked about this. We all agreed what was best. You said you were fine with it. You shouldn't take this out on Nina. She doesn't deserve it, and you know it."

Bonnie crossed her arms over her chest. "She's so insensitive to my feelings."

"And you're acting like a five-year-old." Bertie sounded disapproving. "Grow up. You're the one who had to go tell the world, and these are the consequences. If you're upset about the painting being gone, you only have yourself to blame, and you know it. Stop taking it out on Nina. She's been your scapegoat enough over the years."

Bonnie turned to her partner, her eyes wide. "Bertie, no."

"Yes," the other woman said firmly. "I love you, but that doesn't mean I'm blind to your faults. You wanted to go on TV with the painting because it made you feel special. But your need for attention put this family in jeopardy. It's a ten-million dollar painting, for heaven's sake. You don't screw around with that."

Nina had heard Bertie upset with Bonnie before, but not like this. She held her breath, waiting for her mother to throw out Bertie or end their relationship. Instead Bonnie nodded.

"You're right," she whispered.

"This has got to stop," Bertie continued. "The bigger issue is that Nina's your daughter. You're the parent. Act like it and stop putting me in the position of having to be the one in charge. I don't want to be your mother, either. I want to be your partner."

With that, Bertie turned and left the kitchen.

Bonnie pressed her hand against the counter, as if that was all that was holding her in place. She drew in several ragged breaths before looking at Nina.

"Well, that was awful," she admitted. "I hate it when Bertie's mad at me."

Nina drew in a breath of her own. "I hate it when you blame me for doing what's right. Especially when two days ago you agreed with the decision."

"I know."

Bonnie walked to the bottle of wine and pulled out the cork. She got down a glass, then poured herself a generous amount and took a swallow.

"She's going to force me to act reasonably," her mother said. "I've tried to explain I don't want to be the responsible one."

"No danger of that," Nina told her. "Mom, sometimes you make it really hard on me. I'm tired of taking care of everything around here. Bertie has offered to help, and I'm going to let her. I don't want to do it all anymore."

Bonnie leaned against the counter. "I think you'll find it more fun to let other people deal with the crap of life."

"I wouldn't know."

She expected her mother to stalk off, but Bonnie only nodded. "I'm sorry I yelled at you before. You're right. I did agree to let the painting go, only now I'm sad it's gone."

At any other time, Nina might have welcomed having the conversation about their twisted past, but not tonight. Her head hurt and she was tired.

"Mom, you and Bertie need to decide what to do about the painting. Ambrose can handle the sale, if that's what you want to do. He has good credentials and recommendations, and his fees are reasonable. We can find an honest financial person to help with the investments. But the painting can't stay in the vault forever. We can't afford it."

Her mother looked at her. "How sad. For you the painting is just one more responsibility to take on. If we don't sell, you're going to have to deal with it for the rest of your life."

"Something like that."

"I only wanted you to be happy," her mother said with a sigh.

"I'm not unhappy."

"But they're not the same thing. I do love you, Nina. And I know sometimes that isn't enough."

For the second time in a few minutes, Nina fought tears. "I know you try."

"Trying isn't the same as succeeding, is it? Then we'll make a decision." Her mother smiled, then kissed her cheek. "And soon. I promise."

Nina watched her leave and wished she could believe that promise. If wishes were horses... But she knew her mother and understood that there was a reason for clichés.

"The thing about G-force is that it sneaks up on you," Kyle was saying as he headed for the bridge the following evening. "You think you're doing okay, then, boom. You're fighting to stay conscious. Not a good thing in a jet."

He'd called the previous evening and asked Nina to dinner. She'd accepted, thinking that after a good night's sleep, she would feel better. She'd gotten through the day okay, but in the past couple of hours, she'd started feeling worse and worse. Her stomach was queasy, and she would swear her head was pounding even more.

"Kyle," she said when they stopped at a light. "I'm not feeling well. Can you take me home?"

She braced herself for a fight or at the very least, a long-winded explanation. Instead he glanced at her once, then made a right turn.

"What's wrong?" he asked, even as he headed back across the island.

"I don't know," she admitted. "I've had a headache on and off for the past day, and my stomach seems upset." She thought about the patients that had been coming through the office and groaned. "Oh, crap. I probably have the flu."

Kyle visibly shrank from her. "Didn't you get a flu shot?"

"Yes, but it's not a hundred percent effective."

He mumbled something about being grounded and drove a little faster into her neighborhood. When they reached her house, he pulled into the driveway and climbed out.

He helped her out and walked her to the door. "Can I help?" he asked. "Get you something?"

While she appreciated the offer, she saw he was careful not

to touch her. She had a feeling he was regretting the kiss he'd given her when he'd first arrived.

"Go," she told him. "Drink plenty of fluids, make it an early night and I'm sure you'll be fine."

"What about you?"

"I'm going to crawl into bed and wait for all this to be over. I'll call you when I feel better."

He hesitated for a second, then kissed her cheek before jogging back to his car. She went inside and shut the door behind her.

Bertie lay on the sofa reading. She looked up. "Back already?"

"I don't feel very well," Nina said. "I might have the flu. I'm going to get into bed and see if I can sleep this off."

Bertie rose and crossed to her. The other woman touched her forehead. "You're very warm. Have you taken your temperature?"

Nina thought about the fever and vomiting that came with the flu. How she would feel shaky and gross and weak. She groaned softly. "I don't want to know," she admitted. "Just ignore me for the next three days."

"As if that's going to happen." Bertie turned her toward the hallway. "Go put on your pajamas. I'll be in with some juice in a second."

Nina did as she was told. As she walked she noticed how the hallway seemed really long and slightly uphill. Her stomach seemed to flip over a couple of times, making her grateful she hadn't eaten anything since lunch.

She made it to her room where she managed to change into PJs. She washed her face and brushed her teeth, then fell into her bed. Some time later—it could have been minutes or hours, she was both hot and shivering. Her whole body hurt. But the worst was the roiling in her belly.

She turned on her side, hoping that would help, and nearly threw up. She pushed herself into a sitting position and told herself to breathe steadily, only it didn't help.

The bedroom door opened. Nina stared at the tall figure for a second before she recognized Dylan.

"What are you doing here?" she asked, and was shocked at how pathetic her voice sounded.

"Bertie called," he told her, crossing to the bed. He touched her forehead, then set a medical bag on the side of the bed and pulled out a thermometer.

"Go away. I have the flu." She eyed the instrument and groaned. "If you stick that in my mouth, I'm going to throw up."

"Not a problem," he said. "It goes in your ear."

She sank back on her pillows and closed her eyes. "Didn't you hear me? I have the flu. What if you get it? Go away."

He smiled at her. "Why did I know you'd be a lousy patient?" He rose and grabbed his bag. "Don't go anywhere. I'll be back."

She tried to tell him not to bother, only instead she had to scramble to the bathroom where she barely made it to the toilet in time to throw up.

Nina staggered back to her bed after her second session of vomiting and told herself that dying didn't seem like such a bad idea. She was both hot and chilled, shaking, weak and generally felt like cat gack. Although thinking about cat gack was probably a bad idea. She'd barely crawled onto her mattress when Dylan appeared in her bedroom.

"Go away," she managed, wondering if she had the strength to roll over and face the other way.

"Sorry," he said, sounding disgustingly cheerful. "I'm here for the duration."

"I don't even know what that means."

She realized he was holding several shopping bags. He set them on the floor and started pulling out the contents. "Soup, crackers, antiviral, soda, juice."

She tried to focus on what he was saying. "You can't just buy an antiviral."

"I'm a doctor. I wrote you a prescription, then filled it at the local pharmacy. When was the last time you threw up?"

She did her best to look fierce and annoyed but had a feeling she came across as pathetic instead. "About twenty minutes ago."

"Let's see if you can keep the soda down before we have you swallow the medicine. It won't do any good if you can't keep it in your stomach. Want some soup?"

Just the image of anything foodlike had her scrambling past him and heading for the bathroom across the hall. She lunged for the toilet and started to gag. Dylan joined her, carefully holding back her hair. Humiliation blended with bile and burned her throat, but there was no way to complain. Not until her tummy stopped contracting.

"Go away," she managed when she collapsed onto the bathroom floor. "Just go away."

"Sorry. That's not going to happen."

He helped her up and then half carried her back to her room.

For a couple of minutes he disappeared. She prayed he was gone for good, but no such luck. He returned with a glass and a couple of washcloths. They were damp and cool as he wiped her face, then her throat. He pulled up the sleeves of her PJ shirt and rubbed her arms, then put the second cloth across her forehead.

"Try to sleep," he told her. "We'll go for liquids when you wake up."

"I'm not going to sleep," she said stubbornly. "You shouldn't be here."

"Stop saying that. You're stuck with me. Accept the inevitable. Now close your eyes."

She did what he said, mostly because she was so tired and felt so crappy. When she opened them again, she knew time had passed because there wasn't any light coming in the windows. The only illumination came from a small lamp on her desk. Soft music played from the clock radio, and Dylan was stretched out reading on the chaise in the corner.

"Hey," he said when he saw her eyes open. "How are you feeling?"

"Awful."

"And your stomach?"

"Less gross."

"Good." He stood and crossed to the bed. He put his hand on her forehead. "Still warm."

He sat on the edge of the mattress and held out a glass. "Can you drink this?"

She sat up and sipped. The sweet soft drink soothed her throat and felt cool as she swallowed. After a few sips, she gave him back the glass.

"I'm okay," she murmured.

"Then you can take your antiviral."

He measured out the dose, and she took it. Then she collapsed back on the bed. Dylan kissed her forehead. "Go back to sleep."

The next time she surfaced, Dylan got her to drink some more soda and take a couple of spoonfuls of chicken soup. Hours later, Bertie was the one replacing the washcloths on her forehead.

"Dylan went to work," the other woman explained.

"He must be tired," Nina whispered. "Did he get any sleep at all?"

"He said he did. Now you rest. Don't worry about anything."

The day passed quickly, in disconnected bits. When it was dark again, she felt Dylan stroking her cheek. She opened her eyes.

"You need to get some rest," she said. "I'm okay."

"Who's the medical professional here?" he asked.

"We both are."

"One more night and then you'll be rid of me."

She nodded, unable to complain about having him nearby. She closed her eyes again.

"Talk to me," she murmured, shifting on the bed to give him room.

"Sure." He surprised her by lying down next to her and putting his arm around her.

Nice, she thought, relaxing against his warmth.

"My mother hates my new sofa," he said.

"Is it black leather?"

"Of course."

"Such a guy."

"That's close to what she said, but she sounded a lot more exasperated. Now she's insisting on going with me to pick out a bedroom set. I gotta tell you, I'm not comfortable shopping for a bed with my mother."

Nina managed a smile. "Remind her you got through medical school."

"I don't think that will help. She says I need color in my life."

"Did she say which one?"

He chuckled. She felt the rumble in his chest. "No, but I'll ask."

He kept talking, but it was more and more difficult to listen and then there was nothing.

Chapter Twenty

❦

THE NEXT DAY, Nina knew she was on the mend. She was able to sit up, eat toast *and* soup, and only napped for a couple of hours in the afternoon.

About four, she wandered into the kitchen and found Bertie putting a pork roast into the oven. The other woman studied her for a few seconds, then smiled.

"Yes, definitely better," Bertie announced, then pointed to one of the bar stools. "Sit. I don't want you getting light-headed. That was some round of the flu." Bertie washed her hands, then walked back over to lean against the counter. "Kyle has been calling to check on you. Your mother had several rather long conversations with him."

Nina groaned. "That can't be good."

"Probably not."

"You don't have to sound so cheerful about it."

Bertie only smiled. "Tea?"

Nina nodded. "Thanks. You don't happen to know what she said, do you?"

Bertie filled the kettle with water and set it on the stove.

"Sorry, I don't. For what it's worth, Dylan was here for two nights and checked on you during the day. A doctor who makes house calls. So rare these days."

Nina rested her elbows on the counter. "I'm still too weak to deal with guilt."

"Why would you feel guilty?"

"Because of Dylan and Kyle. They shouldn't both be worried about me."

"And why is that?"

"Because it's wrong."

"Says who?"

Nina's head still felt a little scrambled. "Kyle wants to take our relationship to the next level. I don't even know what that would mean. Dylan is… I don't know what he is. My friend, I guess." Only there had been kissing. She supposed that simply asking what he was thinking would be a sign of maturity, but she wasn't really there yet.

"I'm sure Kyle would have stayed if I'd asked."

Bertie put a teapot on the counter then filled an infuser with lavender Earl Grey. "You don't think he was worried about getting sick, then being grounded?"

Nina remembered how anxious he'd been to get away from her. "Probably, but it's his job to stay healthy. He needs to be able to fly. Besides, I didn't want him seeing me like that."

Bertie smiled at her. "So Dylan is different?"

"Yes, but don't read too much into that. We're friends. I've known him forever."

"You don't have to choose right now. You can have them both."

"I'm not ready for that," she murmured, thinking Averil had pretty much said the same thing. "I'm going to go lie down before dinner."

Bertie nodded. "I'll bring you a mug of tea when it's ready."

"Thanks."

★ ★ ★

By six-thirty, Nina had napped again and was feeling much more normal. She knew Bertie would say it was the healing powers of Earl Grey and maybe she was right.

She put on fresh sweatpants and a clean T-shirt before joining the others in the dining room, and only winced a little when she heard Barry Manilow on the sound system.

Averil rolled her eyes. "Tell me about it."

Bonnie was already seated at the table and sniffed when she heard them. "I don't care. I love him. And I will always love his music." She turned to Nina. "I'm glad you're feeling better. Kyle has been very worried."

"I heard you two had been talking. Should I be concerned?"

"Only a little."

Averil chuckled. "Just remember the truth is supposed to set you free."

"I'm having my doubts."

Dinner was the pork roast with scalloped potatoes and green beans. Nina wasn't sure how much she could eat, so took tiny portions of everything. Her stomach had been quiet for the past couple of days, but she didn't want to shock her system too much. There was a bottle of Pinot Noir, but she passed on the wine and stuck to her tea.

"I have a list," Bonnie said. "I think we can become a chain."

"Of antique stores?" Averil asked.

"Yes. We could branch out. Imagine how well we'd do in Sedona or New Orleans. I'm very excited."

Nina got the sense this was an ongoing discussion. "You're talking about the proceeds from the painting?" she asked. "What you're going to do with them?"

"If we sell," her mother told her. "That isn't for sure."

Nina felt the beginnings of a headache, but this one had nothing to do with being sick. "You still might keep it?"

How could they? A painting that expensive was a serious responsibility. None of them had the money to pay for the insurance, let alone a safe place to keep it. The bank vault fees alone were more than an average car payment, and what about Ambrose? He wouldn't wait forever for his fees.

Not anything she could deal with right now, she told herself as she put down her fork and pushed away her untouched plate.

"You have to trust us," her mother told her. "We're not idiots."

Bertie glanced at her partner, then turned to Nina. "What she means is we're considering all our options and we're going to make a sensible decision together. As a family."

Averil shrugged. "I'm staying out of this," she told Nina.

Bonnie picked up her wineglass. "No, she's not. Everyone gets an equal vote." Her brows drew together. "And no one gets to tell anyone else no." Her expression brightened. "I was thinking we could buy a racehorse."

Nina pushed back her chair and picked up her mug. "I'm not very hungry," she said. "Excuse me."

Nina checked email on her laptop. She was tired of being in her room, but wasn't comfortable leaving it. She could hear the others talking and knew it was for the best if she didn't know the subject matter. Restlessness stirred inside of her. Nothing about what was going on felt right, she thought. Not the painting or dealing with her mother or being trapped in this house.

Only the problem wasn't any of them, she reminded herself. It was her.

Someone knocked on her door.

"Come in," she called, closing her email program and turning in her chair.

Averil walked in. "How are you feeling?"

"Physically okay. Emotionally battered."

"Mom's being a bitch in that subtle way she has," her sister said as she sank onto the bed and sat cross-legged. "A nip here, a jab there. Nothing direct but you get the message."

Nina wasn't sure if she was being comforted or set up. An unfair assumption, considering Averil was telling the truth.

"Sometimes I think she hates me," Nina admitted.

"She resents how you handle things, but she won't do it herself. She traps you and then complains when you're in charge. It's not fair."

Nina looked at her sister. "At the risk of starting a fight with you, too, you're being very evenhanded in all this."

"I'm outside the fray. I think it's worse now, because you're not willing to simply let Mom screw up. There's too much on the line, so you know you have to push her. She doesn't want to be told what to do, but it's millions of dollars. They could be ripped off or hustled and end up with nothing but a bunch of expenses."

Nina sighed with relief. "Yes, and I don't want that to happen."

"I don't, either. I honestly don't know what to do about her."

There was a second knock, then the door opened and Bertie walked in. "Can anyone join this conversation?"

"We were talking about Mom," Averil said, shifting to make room for Bertie on the bed.

"I figured. She's being difficult."

Nina wondered if Bertie was here to try to make her feel better, too. And if the visit was spontaneous or planned. She was still tired enough not to care either way. As long as the problem got solved.

"Mom sees me as wanting to take the fun out of the situation," she said. "I want this to be fun, but I also want it to end well. This is a massive disaster, waiting to happen. You two could be set up for the rest of your lives. You'd never have to worry about money."

Averil's mouth twisted. "Mom doesn't worry about money now."

"We make enough," Bertie added.

Nina felt her temper rising. "No, you don't. The roof needs replacing. Do either of you have the money for that, because I don't. My savings account got cleaned out last year when the water heater exploded and all that plumbing had to be fixed. You two barely make enough in the store to cover the expenses. With Cindy's new finds, there's finally a chance you might be able to take a small salary. And wouldn't that be nice? Because I've been supporting this household for the past ten years."

She paused to suck in a breath, then exhaled. "Not you, Bertie. You pay your own way." The other woman had a small inheritance and used her monthly checks to pay for her share of the mortgage, utilities and food.

Bertie's dark eyes widened. "I didn't know," she admitted. "Bonnie's offered to make me a partner in the store, but I always refused because I assumed you were all living off that money. I thought it was bringing income into the family."

"It's not," Nina said flatly.

Averil shifted on the bed. "Nina's the one who paid for my college," she said quietly. "Mom didn't contribute anything." She turned to her sister. "Why didn't you say something about the house? I would have helped."

"It's not your responsibility."

"But it's yours?" Averil's mouth flattened. "So only you get to contribute? This is my family, too, and I would be happy to help out."

Nina rubbed her forehead. "No. I didn't mean it like that. You weren't here. I didn't want to bother you."

"No. You want to be a martyr all on your own." She turned to Bertie. "It's not about helping, it's about taking control."

Nina stiffened, unprepared for the attack. "That's not fair. I'm struggling here, and I didn't want you to have to worry. How does that make me the bad guy?"

"I deserved to know what was happening, and you didn't trust me with the information."

"You didn't want to know," Nina snapped, knowing that being less than a hundred percent was weighing on her. But she couldn't seem to keep her mouth shut. "All you care about is yourself. Look at what happened when you came here. You didn't ask if your visit was convenient, you simply announced you were coming back for an unspecified amount of time and showed up. You can see what a shithole this place is, but did you once think to find out why?"

Averil scrambled to her feet. "That's not fair."

"Isn't it? I'm the bad guy for wanting to make sure Bertie and Mom don't get screwed out of a ten-million dollar painting, but it's unfair to ask you to open your eyes and see what's going on here?"

"I didn't know you paid for everything," Averil yelled. "You should have told me."

"Girls," Bertie said, also coming to her feet. "This isn't helping."

"And Nina's all about the helping," Averil said bitterly. "You know what she really hates about the painting? Not you and Mom getting cheated. That would make her happy, because she could be right and still be in charge. If you two have all that money, you won't need her, and then she'll have nothing." She turned to Nina. "My God, you're still living at home. Why don't you have a life? You're the one who's allowed Mom not to grow up. She would have figured it out if you'd let her. But you couldn't stand not to be indispensable."

Nina stood and glared right back. "Sure. I'm the one with problems. You want to look in the mirror, Averil? What are you doing here? Don't you have a husband who's wondering where the hell you are? Don't tell me what I'm doing wrong until you figure out your own life."

The bedroom door flew open, and Bonnie stood in the doorway. "Stop it!" she yelled. "Stop fighting. We're a family. Act like it."

Averil brushed past her. "Give it up, Mom. It's way too late for you to try to be in charge now."

"What's wrong?" Dylan asked, passing Nina a take-out bag.

It was her second day back at work, and he'd shown up just in time for her lunch break. Nina had been in the process of leaving a message for Kyle when she'd seen the other man walking toward the office. She'd hung up quickly, aware she didn't do the "two man" thing well.

They settled on the picnic bench in Andi's backyard. Nina knew there were plenty of windows facing their direction but didn't think their meal would provide much entertainment. She and Dylan were going to eat and talk and nothing else.

"You don't want to know," Nina said as she unwrapped the chicken salad sandwich from the Blackberry Island Inn. "Family stuff mostly."

He handed her a soda but didn't speak.

Nina sighed. "We had a big fight a couple of days ago, and now no one is speaking. Averil got on me, I got on her, Mom showed up and tried to make peace and it all went to hell."

"I'm sorry to hear that."

"Me, too." She stuck a straw in the take-out drink container. "It's that stupid painting. It's changing everything. I just want Mom and Bertie to make a sensible decision where they don't get screwed."

She thought about what her sister had said—that she secretly wanted them to fail so she could be right. Averil was wrong, she told herself. She wanted to break free and be on her own. She wanted to figure out what her dreams were and why she had so much trouble following them.

She shook her head. "Can we please stop talking about me? Thank you for all your help while I was sick."

"You're welcome."

"I'm sorry about the throwing-up part. That was gross for both of us."

He grinned. "I've seen worse. Besides, you were a low-key patient. You mostly slept."

"You stayed with me those first two nights. I would have been okay."

"I wanted to be sure."

She studied his face, the shape of his mouth and once again wondered what would have happened if she'd been home the weekend he'd come looking for her. To think that her entire destiny hinged on her decision to go to a bar on a Wednesday night. That was hardly fair.

Of course, a case could be made she was handing over too much power to Dylan. She could have made her own life-changing decisions if she'd wanted. But as Averil had so eloquently put it a couple of days ago, she was still living at home.

"What did you decide about your bedroom set?" she asked. "Talk your mother out of shopping with you?"

"I told her she was crossing the line. That my furniture was my business."

"Impressive. How did she take it?"

"She started crying, which made me feel like the worst son ever."

Nina stretched her hand across the table and touched the back of his hand. "I'm sorry."

"Yeah, well, we got through it. She's not going to meddle, and I'm going to go over to dinner tomorrow night." He turned his hands so her fingertips rested on his palm, then squeezed them. "My parents are basically good people. But every now and then, an angry estrangement sounds like a great idea."

"Tell me about it."

"Your mom still upset about the painting?"

"How did you know about that?"

He shrugged, and Nina realized that he'd been in her house a couple of days while she'd been sick.

"Bonnie said something," she murmured, both embarrassed and frustrated. While she acknowledged that no one could control her mother, it would be nice if she could at least be reasoned with.

"She complained about you taking the painting," he admitted. "When I pointed out that I'd been the one driving, she got quiet. Then Bertie came into the room and the subject changed. At some point she has to understand why you did it."

"Oh, but that's logical and that's not her thing. It's times like this I think I should have simply gotten away while I could."

The wrong thing to say, she thought. Because talk like that had her thinking about her fight with Averil. *They* still weren't speaking, either. Of course it made for quiet evenings.

"You could still go away," he told her.

"Trying to get rid of me?"

"Wondering if you're happy."

Not a conversation she wanted to be having right now. She pointed to the tree behind them. "Oh, look. Is that a toucan?"

Dylan grinned without turning around. "Fine. I'll change the subject. Maybe some weekend we can head into Seattle

and catch a Mariners game. We could go Saturday and check
out the Chihuly exhibit, go to dinner, then head to the game
on Sunday."

If Nina had been swallowing, she would have choked. He
spoke so casually, she thought. As if his suggestion was completely normal. But a weekend in Seattle with an overnight
stay wasn't normal. Nor was it simple. Was he asking her to
go with him, as in they would be staying in the same room?
Were they going as friends, each responsible for his or her
own sleeping accommodations? Was he asking her out on a
date weekend?

Thoughts crowded into her brain and pushed each other
around. Yes, Dylan had kissed her and she'd kissed him back,
but that wasn't the same as sleeping together. Shouldn't they
start more slowly—like with holding hands or something? Or
was she reading too much into the invitation?

Before she could figure out what to say, the back door to
the house opened. Andi stepped out into the warm afternoon,
a bowl in her hands.

"Hi, I heard you were eating outside and I thought I'd—"
She spotted Dylan and came to a stop. "Oh. Sorry. No one
said you had company."

"Don't run off," Dylan said, shifting to make room for Andi
on the bench. "Join us."

Andi glanced at Nina who nodded slightly, giving her approval of the suggestion. With a third person at the table, an
answer wouldn't be required. Right now time seemed like a
really good thing.

Averil looked at the display on the large dining room table
in Blackberry Preserves and knew something wasn't right.
The linens, she wondered. No, it was the way she'd stacked
the plates. There were too many, and they looked cluttered.

Less is more, she thought, reaching for a couple of bowls. A philosophy her mother would never embrace.

The bell over the door chimed, and she looked up as a tiny Asian woman walked into the store. She was well under five feet, with delicate features. Her clothes were shapeless—a tunic over loose dark pants.

"Can I help you?" Averil asked with a smile.

The woman turned to her and shook her head. Her lips were pursed, as if she'd just tasted something unpleasant.

"Cindy work here?" the woman asked in a thick accent.

Averil did her best to keep her eyes from widening. Was this really the evil mother-in-law? The one who made Cindy's life miserable?

"Yes, ma'am, ah, Mrs. Yoo. She's not here right now. She went to the bank."

Now that they were selling merchandise, there were actual receipts to be totaled and deposited. It was kind of exciting.

The woman nodded. "Good. I'm glad she's not here." She held out a small brown bag. "She forgot her lunch. She'll get hungry. You take it for her and don't tell her I was here."

Averil tilted her head. "You don't want Cindy to know you brought her lunch?"

"No."

"But it's so nice of you. You don't want Cindy to know—" Averil paused to study the tiny woman. She saw how Mrs. Yoo was taking in the store, as if memorizing what it was like here.

"Cindy works hard?" she asked.

"Yes. She's wonderful."

One corner of Mrs. Yoo's mouth twitched, as if she was going to smile, then the stern expression returned. "Be careful. Cindy's lazy."

"You don't mean that."

"I do."

This was the strangest conversation ever, Averil thought. Why would the woman come by if she hated Cindy so much? Why bother bringing her lunch? Unless it was all some strange game she couldn't understand.

"Cindy always speaks so highly of you," Averil lied. "You must be very proud of your successful son and grandchildren."

"Yes. My son is a good boy."

"Yeah, I'm not buying it," Averil told her. "I think you care about her, but for some reason you don't want her to know."

The woman drew in a breath and squared her shoulders. "I don't care about her. She a terrible wife."

"Really? After all these years and two grandchildren? Then why did you bother to bring her lunch? You should be happy that she's going hungry."

"She's too thin. Tell her to eat it all." Mrs. Yoo started for the front door, then turned back. "She's happy here?"

Averil nodded. "I hope so. She seems to be. We would be lost without her."

Mrs. Yoo slowly nodded her head. "Me, too."

"I've decided not to be mad at you anymore," Bonnie announced.

Nina looked up from the book she'd been reading. Her mother stood in the doorway of Nina's bedroom. "Okay," she said slowly. "I guess that's good."

Her mother strolled into her bedroom and sat in the chair by the desk. "I know you've been upset." She smiled. "You don't have to be anymore."

Nina recognized the trap. "You're saying you forgive me."

Her mother beamed. "Exactly."

"Only I didn't do anything wrong."

The smile began to fade. "We don't need to discuss this anymore, Nina."

"I think we do. We had an agreement about the painting. Everyone thought it was a good idea to keep quiet until you and Bertie decided what to do. Only you changed the rules and when that led to consequences, then you got mad. What did you want us to do? Hold the painting in the house so someone could steal it?"

"It would have been fine."

Nina put down her book and sighed. "Do you really believe that? You would be perfectly comfortable leaving an expensive work of art here with no alarm, no nothing?"

"You have to believe in the basic goodness of people."

Nina rolled her eyes. "If you're going to act like you don't get what you did, Mom, I don't want to have this conversation. If you want to say you forgive me, then fine, but I'm not going to say I'm sorry. I took care of things because you didn't leave me a choice."

Her mother's mouth tightened. "I don't know why you're being so difficult."

"I'm being honest."

"That's just an excuse to be cruel."

"And here we go again." She leaned forward. "Why can't we talk? If you believe in the basic goodness of people, why do you see me as cruel?"

Bonnie's hands fluttered, then settled by her sides. "You take everything so literally."

"You're my mom. I listen to what you say and when you talk like that, you hurt my feelings. You want to be free to say whatever pops into your head at the moment and then not have it matter later. We're back to consequences. I wish…"

Nina sank back against her pillows. There was no point in any of this, she told herself. Bonnie would never see things the way a regular adult would. She wanted to be a child forever. It was easier that way. Let someone else take responsibility.

It was part of who she was. Like being tall or female. Some people were good at math, others weren't. Bonnie liked being taken care of, and she was good at making sure that happened.

Her mother crossed to the bed and sat on the edge. "What do you wish?" she asked gently.

"I wish you were more like other moms. I wish you'd admit I did the right thing with the painting. I wish you'd see me as someone who cares about you rather than the person who stands between you and what you want."

Bonnie pressed her lips together. Unexpected tears filled her eyes. "I know you do, Nina." She held out her hands. "I love you so much. It's just…"

"What I want isn't as important as what you want," Nina told her. "You'll never choose what's best for me over what's best for you."

"I can't."

"You won't. There's a difference. You're not going to change." Nina paused as that last sentence spun around in her head. Bonnie was never going to change. If Nina was waiting for the great revelation to alter her mother's behavior, she would find the end of eternity first.

She knew there was more important information in that statement, but she needed more time to think it over.

"It's okay," she said, faking a smile.

That seemed to be enough for Bonnie. She patted Nina's knee. "Are you still fighting with your sister?"

"We're not fighting, but if you're asking about us having a meaningful conversation—not right now."

"You need to be more forgiving of people, Nina. We aren't all like you."

"I get that, Mom."

Bonnie smiled at her. "You've always taken such good care of us."

Which kind of explained the trapped feeling she'd lived with for so long.

Her mother leaned over and kissed the top of her head. "I'll leave you to your book."

She stood and left.

Nina slumped back on the pillows and tried to figure out where the missteps had occurred. She knew she hadn't had a lot of control over what had happened when she'd been a kid, but what about since then? Weren't her actions all her fault?

Her phone buzzed. She glanced at the screen and saw a text from Kyle.

Back in Everett. Miss you. Can I see you?

Nina scrambled to her feet and reached for her large tote. In a matter of a couple of minutes, she'd changed her clothes, brushed her teeth, eaten enough to get her through the night and was heading to the door.

She didn't know what Kyle wanted from her, but right now she didn't care. It was enough that in his bed, she would be able to forget.

Chapter Twenty-One

LATE SATURDAY MORNING, Nina decided to tackle the weeding in the yard. She put on ratty jeans and a T-shirt, along with a big hat that would protect her from any sun seeping through the high clouds. By two she'd made progress and was stiff, but mentally more relaxed. Her family might still make her insane, but at least the garden looked better.

She stood and stretched. She was hot and sticky, and she had scratches all along her arms. All proof of hard work, she thought happily.

Bertie stepped out onto the back porch. "You've done a wonderful job."

"You could have helped."

The other woman smiled. "And spoil your fun?"

"There's enough fun for all."

Bertie laughed. "It's only going to get better. Your mother and I want to have a barbecue tonight."

"Just family?" Nina asked, wondering how much work it was going to be.

"Mostly. You and your sister still aren't speaking."

"We're not *not* speaking," Nina said. "I haven't seen her in a few days."

"You've been avoiding each other."

With good reason, Nina thought. They couldn't seem to have a conversation without fighting.

Bertie picked up the bucket filled with weeds and carried it to the yard waste container. Nina trailed after her.

"I suppose whining that I don't want to talk to her doesn't make me look like the mature sister."

"Not really." Bertie smiled at her. "Tell you what. I'll invite your young man to join us tonight. How's that?"

"Nice. Thank you."

"Good. Now I'll put the tools away. You go shower. We have a lot to do to get ready."

Nina headed for the house. It was only after she stepped into the shower that she had the sudden thought to ask which young man Bertie had meant.

Averil dumped the cooked potatoes into a colander, then turned on the cold water. She'd already diced the eggs and celery for the potato salad. The chocolate cake she'd baked earlier was cooling on a rack and she and her mom had already coated the chicken pieces in marinade.

It was nearly four in the afternoon. Averil couldn't remember the last time she'd spent a few hours cooking. Somehow she and Kevin had gotten into the take-out habit. Or she just threw something together. When they were first married, she'd planned out menus, and they'd gone shopping together. They'd even tried new recipes on the weekends. Like most men, Kevin enjoyed grilling, but he was also pretty decent with a regular stove.

She dropped the celery in the bowl and tried to remember when the cooking afternoons had come to an end. Had she had a deadline? Had he? Then the activity had been lost?

Somehow they'd gone from happy to distant, and she couldn't retrace the journey. She liked Kevin's company. She liked spending time with him—so, what was the problem? Why had she resisted connecting with him?

Bonnie walked into the kitchen. She had on a tunic top over white shorts. Her long, wavy blond hair was loose, and big hoops hung from her ears. "I'm so excited about our party tonight," she said, a bottle of wine tucked under each arm. "I've decided to make my famous sangria."

"Good. Then we won't have hangovers like we did with the margaritas."

Her mother smiled and set down the bottles, then crossed over to hug her. "I'm so glad you're home. I've missed seeing you."

"I've missed you, too, Mom."

"You're so much fun, and we don't have to talk about all those rules."

A slam at Nina, Averil thought, a little uncomfortable with the statement. It was fine when she was fighting with her sister, but Bonnie was the parent—should she really resent the daughter she'd pretty much abandoned to manage on her own?

Now, still pissed about their recent fight, Averil found herself in the annoying place of having to defend her sister.

"Nina takes really good care of things around here," Averil began. "If she wasn't here, you'd have to take on a lot more of the responsibility."

Bonnie sighed. She dug out the wine opener and went to work on the bottles. "I suppose. I'm not really mad at her. I just wish she wasn't such a stick in the mud." She gave Averil a quick smile. "And to prove that, I invited Kyle to join us for dinner."

"Kyle? I thought Bertie said she'd asked Dylan. She men-tioned it when she told me about the party and asked me to make the cake."

Bonnie put down the corkscrew. "Not Dylan. Kyle's the fighter pilot. He's so handsome, with those big blue eyes." She sighed. "If I was fifteen years younger…and still having sex with men."

A fascinating factoid, Averil thought, trying to pull it all together.

"You called Kyle?" she asked.

"Yes. I used Nina's cell phone while she was in the garden."

Averil felt both humor and horror bubbling up inside her belly. She walked to the hall. "Bertie?" she yelled.

Bertie walked in from the living room. "What?"

"You invited Dylan to come over for dinner?"

Bertie's eyebrows drew together. "Yes. I told you before. Did he call? Can't he make it?"

Bonnie covered her mouth with her hand, as if to hold in laughter. Her eyes were bright with amusement. "This is too delicious," she managed to say.

Averil was less sure.

"What's wrong?" Bertie asked.

"I invited Kyle," Bonnie told her.

Bertie's mouth twisted. "But Dylan was with Nina when she was sick. He stayed here two nights. He looked after her."

"Kyle's sexier. He's adventurous. The last thing Nina needs is a man just as responsible as her. She's sanctimonious enough as it is."

"Bonnie!" Bertie's voice was sharp.

Bonnie's humor faded. "Sorry."

Bertie turned to Averil. "We have a problem. Should I call Dylan and tell him the party's canceled?"

"He'll want to know why," Averil pointed out, unable to

believe what had happened. Nina was going to be furious. "So will Kyle. We can't say she's sick again. Kyle won't believe it and Dylan will come over anyway."

"We need a distraction," Bonnie said.

"We're *not* setting the house on fire."

"No. Nothing like that. More people. We should start calling everyone we know. If there are enough people around, Dylan and Kyle won't notice each other."

Averil figured the odds of that happening were slim, but she wasn't sure what else to do. "I need to tell Nina," she said, and wiped her hands on a towel.

Bonnie held up both her hands, then backed up, as if physically afraid of her daughter's reaction. Bertie shook her head. "I don't see this having a good outcome. Why would you invite Kyle?"

"Because she's sleeping with him," Bonnie said. "She and Dylan are just friends."

"He's more than her friend," Bertie said firmly.

They were still arguing when Averil headed toward her sister's room. Nina had showered and dressed in capris and a T-shirt. She'd blown out her blond hair straight and was slipping dangling gold earrings into place.

"Hey," she said when she saw Averil. "I'm clean and prepared to help with tonight. Do you need me to run to the store or do we have everything?"

Averil had been doing her best to avoid Nina and had a feeling her sister had been doing the same. Their last fight had been uglier than most, with accusations flying around. It had also been a lot about telling the truth, she thought. Nina was too proud to ask for help, and she liked being a martyr. Averil didn't want to have to worry about her family, so she didn't bother to ask how things were.

While they were both at fault, she realized she should have

been better about keeping track of what was going on. Of course Nina would support her mother. She always had. Bertie helped where she could, but she wasn't rich. Kevin would have been happy for her to send money every month, Averil thought, fighting guilt.

She opened her mouth to say that, then reminded herself they had a bigger problem.

"We probably will need a few more things from the store," she began. "The party's getting bigger."

Nina slipped on sandals. "Okay. It's kind of last minute to be inviting a lot of people."

"Yes, well, they're here to be a distraction. You know you have a date coming tonight, right?"

"Bertie mentioned she'd invited…" Nina paused. "Bertie invited Dylan, right?"

"Oh, she invited Dylan," Averil told her. "And Mom asked Kyle."

Nina felt the room spinning. It wasn't like when she had the flu and couldn't focus. Her head wasn't foggy. Far from it—she saw everything happening with perfect clarity. Or everything that would happen. Her chest tightened until she found it impossible to breathe.

"Dylan and Kyle?"

Averil bit her lower lip. "I know. Crazy, right? I guess when Bertie and Mom talked about tonight, they discussed inviting your guy over, but they each had a different idea about who that is. I thought you were only sleeping with Kyle."

"I am. Dylan and I are…" She wasn't sure what they were but knew it was about to get uncomfortable on several fronts. This couldn't happen. She had to stop it. "I have to make sure Kyle doesn't show up. I'm going to call him and tell him there's been a change of plans."

"You don't want to try that with Dylan?"

"Kyle's more likely to do what he's told."

She lunged for her phone and pushed the button to dial Kyle. The phone rang several times, then went to voice mail.

She swore softly, then sucked in a breath and dialed Dylan.

"Hey," he said, answering after the first ring. "I'm stopping by the winery now. Your mom just called and said she needs a couple more bottles for her sangria. Then I'll be over."

Nina sank onto the bed. "Mom just called?"

"Yeah. Didn't she tell you?"

"No. She didn't mention it."

He chuckled. "So neither of us is surprised by that. See you soon."

Nina pushed the end button, then dropped the phone onto the bed and covered her face with her hands. "She's doing this on purpose."

"What did he say?"

Nina looked at her sister. "That Mom just called and said to pick up more wine for the sangria. He's on his way. And I can't get Kyle."

This wasn't happening. It couldn't be happening. Both of them here? She had no idea how the evening was going to play out. Kyle would be his usually friendly self.

"I have no idea how Dylan is going to react," she admitted, pressing her hand to her belly. There had to be a solution, she thought frantically.

"Do you care?" Averil asked. "I don't mean that in a harsh way. Just you're sleeping with Kyle."

"I know, but Dylan has been really nice. He took care of me." She stared at Averil. "There was kissing. He doesn't know about Kyle, and he sure doesn't think I'm having sex with anyone else."

Why? That was the question of the moment. Why had this happened?

"He's assuming there isn't anyone else," Averil told her. "It's not like he asked."

"I haven't asked, either."

"So maybe he'll bring a girlfriend and solve the problem."

Nina ignored the jab those words sent into her stomach. "My luck isn't that good," she told her sister.

Bertie walked into the bedroom. "I'm so sorry," she told Nina, her eyes dark with regret. "It never occurred to me that I would ask Dylan and your mother would invite Kyle. It's farcical, but without the British humor." She paused. "How angry are you?"

"Bertie, I love you," Nina said. "But, please, stop inviting my friends over."

"It will never happen again."

Before either of them could say anything else, someone knocked on the front door.

"Already?" Nina moaned.

"I'll get it," Bertie said.

"That doesn't buy us much time," Averil said. "I'm going to call Cindy and see if she and her husband can stop by. If there's enough of a crowd, it should be fine."

Nina stared at her sister. "Do you really believe that?"

"No, but maybe faking it will help."

Unlikely, Nina thought, standing and walking out of her bedroom. As she entered the living room, she saw Kyle handing her mother what looked like a huge box of strawberries. Behind him was Deanna with her husband and five daughters, plus her oldest's best friend, Carrie.

"Hey, you," Kyle said, walking toward her. He took her in his arms and spun her around. "I haven't seen you in a while." He leaned in and kissed her.

They were in public, so it wasn't as if there was tongue or anything, but it was still a kiss between a man and a woman, and Nina didn't think she'd ever felt that self-conscious in her life. She drew back as quickly as she could, but it wasn't fast enough. As she turned, she saw Dylan in the doorway. He had a bottle of wine in each hand and the startled expression of a man who'd just been thumped with a two-by-four.

Averil had never been a huge Dylan fan. When her sister had first dated him, Averil hadn't been all that interested in their relationship. She'd had her own life to deal with. But she did remember when he'd dumped Nina. Her older sister—her emotional rock—had crumbled, and Averil had been both indignant on her behalf and scared of so much raw emotion. All these years later, she figured Dylan had blown his chance, and whatever happened now, he deserved.

But that changed in the second it took him to register that Nina had been kissing some other guy. She saw the emotions pass through his eyes and how his hands tightened on the wine. Kyle was a fighter pilot, the guy with the swagger. Dylan might have bested him in a fair fight, but it was pretty obvious by the easy way Kyle kept his hand on Nina's hip that they were more than just friends.

Bonnie hurried over. "Dylan. You came!" She kissed his cheek and took the wine from him. "Do you know everyone here?" She started naming people and casually mentioned "Nina's friend Kyle" in a list of those attending.

Averil found herself moving toward her sister's old boyfriend and linking arms with him.

"Hey, Dylan," she said with a smile. "Settling in to island life?" she asked.

"I am."

He gave Nina one more glance before walking with Averil into the kitchen.

When they were there, he leaned against the counter and faced her.

"Who's the new guy?"

She thought about pretending not to know who he was talking about, only that was stupid. It wasn't as if he would be fooled and change the subject.

This was just like a situation one of her readers would write about, she thought. Or imagine, briefly wondering if she would use a scene like this in her book. She was only sixty pages in and still hadn't worked out all the—

"Averil!"

She stiffened. "What? Oh, sorry. He's, um, Kyle. Nina's known him forever. She used to babysit him years ago. Well, not him. His baby sister. Funny thing. He remembered her. He's a fighter pilot now and up at Everett. He stopped by to look her up. Small world, huh?"

Dylan looked past her to the living room beyond. Averil could only hope everyone had moved outside. The afternoon was warm, and Bertie had already set up folding tables on the lawn.

She walked toward her still unfrosted cake. "The party just sort of happened. This morning it was going to be the four of us and now it's everyone we know. That's fun."

She hoped she didn't sound as lame as she felt. Dylan folded his arms across his chest.

"Is she sleeping with that boy?"

Averil swallowed. "Dylan, I—"

He pushed off the counter and walked through the kitchen. When he passed through the doorway, he kept going out the front door. Seconds later, she heard a car engine start.

Averil waited until he'd driven away to go out back and

find her sister. Nina still stood by Kyle. She was smiling, but everything about her "aren't I happy" expression was fake.

Bertie saw Averil first and hurried over. "Is everything all right?"

"Dylan had to leave."

Bertie sighed. "Did he say anything?"

Averil shook her head.

"You would think after a decade together, your mother and I would learn to communicate better," Bertie murmured. "All right. I'll tell Nina. Hopefully this is our last disaster of the day."

Chapter Twenty-Two

NINA SPENT MOST of Monday waiting to hear from Dylan. She ducked into her small office whenever she had a moment, mostly to avoid being surprised. Because she knew he was going to stop by. He had to. If nothing else, he was going to yell at her.

She still hadn't decided how she was going to handle his hurt and anger. On the one hand, they weren't even officially going out. He had no right to be upset that she was seeing someone else. On the other hand, they'd been seeing a lot of each other, and she had kissed him back. Would a heads-up have been out of line?

She alternated between understanding and defensiveness. Even with a full schedule of patients, she had too much time to think. But by four it was obvious he wasn't going to drop by.

Nina thought about simply driving to his office and having it out with him. She didn't want the conversation hanging over her head. But maybe work wasn't the best place for them to clear the air. She could wait until he was home. Or call him. Or wait for him to come to her.

After she left work, she swung by Blackberry Preserves. Not that she was hiding out, exactly. It was just that she hadn't been to the store in a long time. Averil had been going there regularly and was always talking about what an amazing job Cindy was doing. And Bertie respected their new employee. But checking on things was smart, too, Nina told herself as she drove toward the water.

As she stopped at a light, she scanned the cars around her, looking for Dylan's familiar BMW. Not that she was going to confront him in an intersection. Besides, she hadn't done anything wrong. As her brain circled back to the "we're not even dating" argument, she prepared herself to cycle through it all for the three-hundred-and-forty-seventh time that day.

There weren't any cars in the lot outside the antique store. Not overly surprising on a Monday before Memorial Day. After the holiday, tourists would swarm the island, but until the unofficial beginning of summer, weekdays were quiet.

She parked and went inside. Cindy was crouched by a hutch on the west side of the store, pulling out stacks of dishes. She stood when she saw Nina.

"Hi," she said with a smile. "We had a run on table settings on Saturday. It must have been something in the air. We sold four complete sets and a bunch of mismatched pieces." Her smile broadened. "We're definitely going to make rent this month. I've been digging out the various remaining sets and trying to decide how to arrange them on the table."

"Are the sets valuable?" Nina asked, still surprised that Blackberry Preserves wasn't a money pit anymore. Had the potential been there all along? Had she simply needed to find the right person? Or had Bertie and Bonnie hit a lucky streak when buying inventory? After all, they *had* found a painting worth ten million dollars.

"Some are." Cindy hesitated. "Nearly everything in the

store was priced under twenty dollars. When people see that, they can easily assume it's all junk."

Nina nodded. "So, you're saying that upping the price from twenty to fifty can make a difference."

"It sure can." Cindy motioned to the dishes. "Even the more modern place settings can be pricey. I sold a retired pattern from Lennox a few days ago. It wasn't that old, but it was in great shape and had a few serving pieces. I got about twenty-five hundred for it."

Nina blinked. "Dollars?"

"Uh-huh."

"I had no idea," she murmured. "I'm going to go check the computer."

"Sure."

Cindy ducked down to pull more stock from the huge hutch, and Nina went into the back office. The computer—still functioning with Windows XP—was on. She went into the password-protected accounting software, then waited while the internet connection gave her access to the latest reports from the bookkeeper they used.

Nina had tried keeping the books herself, but she simply didn't have the time or enough accounting knowledge. Three years ago she'd turned that over to someone on the island. For eighty dollars a month, the handful of bills were paid and the receipts recorded and any employee's payroll processed. All Nina had to do was print out the reports and enter inventory information.

The business's checkbook balance was usually a few hundred dollars. It went up over the month, then dropped when bills had to be paid on the first. Most months, income covered the cost of their part-time employee. Summer was their best time. If she was lucky, Bonnie could pull a couple thousand out of the store each year.

Now Nina scrolled through the various reports. The checkbook balance was— She stopped and stared at the screen. The number seemed to dance and shimmer.

Seventeen *thousand* dollars? Seventeen thousand *dollars?*

Her mouth dropped open as she went back through the register. There it was. Deposit after deposit. There were notes. Linens. Lunch boxes. Dolls. Three chairs and a sofa. The chandelier. The bills hadn't changed. Cindy was working nearly forty hours a week, so she was making more than any other part-time people they had previously had, but still.

Nina looked at the other reports. Inventory had been updated. There were lists and approximate values, which were all a big increase over costs. Bonnie didn't believe in splurging when she went on her trips.

Nina returned to the checking-account balance and stared at the number. This could pay for a new roof. They could replace the carpet. If this kept up, they could pay on the mortgage on the house. As long as she could keep her mother from taking out a second. Something Bonnie liked to do as soon as the previous one was paid off.

The income meant Nina could start saving some of her own money. Put some aside for her future—whatever that meant.

Nina logged out of the accounting system and stood. As she looked around the back room, she realized that what she'd always thought was junk was more. Or it could be. Bonnie would never take the time to figure out what was valuable and what wasn't, but Cindy obviously could.

Nina returned to the front of the store. Cindy had stacked dishes on sideboards and chairs. Now she was playing with different settings and linens.

"Your sister is much better at this than me," she said when she saw Nina. "She gets the colors right." She held up a plate covered with flowers. "I'm pretty sure these are hand painted. Not my style, but still, someone will like them."

Nina looked at the chandelier hanging overhead. "We need to get someone out here to appraise the pieces you think are worth more. Like that. I'll get you some names of people to contact."

Cindy grinned. "That would be great. I've made some estimates myself, but I'm still learning."

Nina crossed to the jewelry displayed in a modified wardrobe. "Does this get locked at night? Isn't some of it valuable?"

"Some of it probably is. Again, I'm not sure about some of the pieces. We haven't been locking the wardrobe. There's no lock."

"Get somebody in and have a lock installed." Nina looked around. "Maybe we should think about an alarm system. We certainly need better locks on the front and back doors. Also, there's too much clutter."

There was more that had to be done, she thought, feeling the weight of responsibility crowding in on her. The whole store needed to be organized. Who knew what else was buried in the piles of crap? Everything had always been so haphazard, but now that needed to change. It was like the painting, but on a smaller scale.

"How is everything being priced?" she asked. "You're checking things online, right? You can't depend on what my mom says. Bertie is sensible, so she might have some ideas. Maybe we should start using a bar code system. Although that would have to be installed."

Once her mother found out about the money in the account, she was going to take it and do something stupid. Nina could feel it. Which would mean there wouldn't be a new roof or paying off the mortgage. Bonnie would find a way to blow it on an endangered turtle or taking six hundred people she'd never met to dinner.

Cindy frowned. "Nina, you seem upset. Are you unhappy with my work?"

"No, not at all. It's just you're not an expert and some of these things are valuable. We have to take care of them."

"I'm doing my best."

Nina nodded absently. "Where's Averil? It's just like her to be gone when I need her."

"She's home, working on her book. We've been talking about it, and she's making progress on the story. It's going to be great."

Nina shook her head. "Right. And will that happen before or after my mother learns to act like an adult?"

She grabbed her bag and headed for the door. "Thank you, Cindy. I need to go think about all this," she said as she walked out into the late afternoon.

The sun was still shining. That surprised her. She felt as if she'd been through some kind of time-space rift and it should at least be night. Or December. She paused by her car and looked back at the store.

The good news was Bonnie and Bertie were able to find valuable items for bargain prices. The bad news was it all had to be managed. Her to-do list had just grown by a dozen items. She had to get someone in who understood the value of antiques to help them price everything. Make sure they couldn't be ripped off by a thief with a crowbar and a couple of free hours. Get Bonnie and Bertie regular paychecks. Figure out a way to protect the rest of the money. Make sure the government was getting its share so there weren't any fines or visits from overly eager IRS agents.

Her head was already pounding, she thought grimly as she got in her car. She needed to talk to Bertie first so they could come up with a plan. At least Bonnie never looked at the store's books. She claimed numbers numbed her creative energy and sucked out her life force. Nina wasn't sure her mother even had a password to access the accounting programs. Which meant there was time. Unlike the painting, this wasn't going to blow up in her face.

If she could just get a system in place, she thought as she drove back to the house. Something simple, that meant the store was covered and Bertie and Bonnie had their money. Then maybe she could start her graceful exit. At least financially.

She pulled into the driveway and got out. Kyle pulled in behind her.

"Hey, beautiful," he called as he got out of his low-slung sports car. "I was hoping to find you at home."

Because he couldn't call first? Nina sucked in a breath. No, she told herself. None of this was Kyle's fault. He was a good guy who liked her and wanted to be with her. She wasn't going to punish him for that.

He walked to her and kissed her. "I want to take you flying."

"In a plane?"

He grinned. "My self-flying skills aren't what they should be. Yes, in a plane. A little one. It's a beautiful afternoon. The sun won't set for another three or four hours. You can see the Sound how it's meant to be seen."

"From the sky?"

"Uh-huh."

She was tired and confused and still trying to absorb what she'd learned at the store. Going inside and making notes seemed to be the smartest use of her time.

Before she could tell him that, he wrapped his arms around

her and pulled her close. "Come look at your world from a different perspective. It will change everything."

"I could use that," she admitted. "Let me go get out of my work clothes."

He walked inside with her. She headed down the hall to her room. As she passed Averil's room, she saw her sister sitting on her bed, typing steadily on her laptop. Penny lay next to her. They both looked up when she paused in the doorway.

"Hey," Averil said. "What's up?"

"I'm going flying with Kyle."

"Sounds like fun. Did you hear from Dylan?"

Nina shook her head. Right now she couldn't deal with him. She pointed at the computer. "Working on your book?"

Averil nodded. "I really am and it's going well. I have no idea if it's any good, but I like it and I've gotten further than I ever have before."

"Good luck."

"You, too. I'll tell Mom you won't be back for dinner."

"Thanks."

Fifteen minutes later Nina had changed into jeans and a shirt. She unfastened her braid and brushed out her hair, then rejoined Kyle in the living room.

He stood when he saw her, then stepped close and kissed her. The feel of his mouth was familiar and arousing. He was uncomplicated, she thought. Not emotionally demanding. Just fun to be with. Easy. Right now easy sounded really good.

She slung her bag over her shoulder and led the way to the front door. As they walked out to her car, she heard her phone ring. She pulled it out and glanced at the screen.

Dylan.

Talk about timing, she thought, pushing the decline button and tucking the phone in her pocket.

★ ★ ★

Flying in a four-seater Cessna was nothing like taking
Alaska Airlines to Las Vegas, Nina thought as she checked
her seat belt and hoped Kyle really knew what he was doing.
Sure the man had *told* her he was a fighter pilot, but did she
have any proof? He could be a mechanic or a janitor for all
she knew.

The cockpit of the small plane was tight on space. There
were what seemed like hundreds of dials and gauges, sticks and
a weirdly shaped thing she assumed was the steering wheel.

"You know what you're doing, right?" she asked, hoping she didn't sound as nervous as she felt. Because no matter how much crap there was in her life right now, she wasn't
ready to die.

Kyle grinned at her. "Trust me."

"I'm not sure I want to."

He covered her hand with his. "This is easy. I was flying
these before I had a driver's license. Now, if you want to feel
power, you should come up in my jet."

"No, thanks."

He motioned to the headset hanging by her door. "It's going
to get loud. Put those on and we won't have to yell. You can
also hear me talking to the tower."

"Am I supposed to talk to the tower?"

"It would be best if you didn't. Ready?"

No! She wasn't ready. She would never be ready. She'd
never thought much about flying, nor did she do it much.
But this was different. This was a tiny flea of a plane, and it
was all that was between her and a long plummet to hard and
unforgiving earth.

"What if I have to throw up?" she asked.

Kyle laughed, then put on his headset. She reluctantly did
the same, thinking she hadn't really been joking.

He checked both sides of the plane, shouted, "Clear," then started the engine. Noise and vibration filled the cockpit. Nina looked around frantically and realized that, yes, there really was only the one engine, so if it went out, it was all over for both of them.

"Should we have on parachutes?" she asked loudly, not sure the built-in microphone could work over the noise.

Kyle shook his head. "You'll be fine. These are safe little planes."

Little being the operative word, she thought.

Kyle moved a bunch of knobs and dials and the plane started to move forward. Far too soon, they were heading down a runway. The plane went faster and faster. Nina tried to believe it was enough. That somehow, magically, they would take flight and not crash into a fireball of—

The plane lifted off. She couldn't say how or why, but suddenly the ground was falling away, and they were climbing into the bright blue sky.

The private airport was on the mainland. After a few minutes they began to turn and head over the water. She saw the twinkling blue of the Sound beneath. The Strait of Juan de Fuca stretched out, and beyond that was the Pacific. It was beautiful—like a living painting. They were free and soaring, like birds.

"Want to violate Canadian airspace?"

The question came through the headset. Nina nodded eagerly. She stared out the side window, straining to see the first glimpse of Victoria Island.

They headed north. Kyle pointed out the various islands in the Sound, then they circled by Victoria. She heard him talking to someone and changing course to stay out of airport airspace. They went east, and he showed her the planes lining up to land in Vancouver, then he dropped lower as they turned south.

The little plane moved smoothly through the afternoon. The engine was steady, and Kyle flew with a confidence that allowed Nina to relax. They buzzed a couple of the tiny uninhabited islands, then flew over Friday Harbor.

"I've saved the best for last," he told her. "Let's take a look at Blackberry Island from the sky."

She watched up ahead until the outline of the island came into view. The loopy, slightly comma shape was familiar, but what startled her most about where she'd spent most of her life was the size. Blackberry Island was small.

Kyle circled the island, showed her the bridge to the mainland and they flew over Blackberry Bay. It all took less than a minute. From up here, the few square miles looked more like a handkerchief than a place anyone could live.

"Can you see your house?" he asked.

She nodded because it was easier than saying she didn't want to.

So small.

The words repeated over and over in her head. She'd lived and laughed, worried and fought, all in a place the size of a postage stamp. Except for a couple of years at college, she'd never lived anywhere else, had never much explored beyond the natural barriers of surf and sea.

He pointed out the Three Sisters, the Queen Anne houses on the hill, then showed her the ferry heading from the island to Seattle. All the while, Nina pressed her hand to her stomach to hold in all the feelings flooding her.

It was like looking in the mirror for the first time. You could imagine what you looked like, get an image in your head, but until you actually saw, you didn't know.

She hadn't known. Hadn't realized how tiny she'd allowed

her circle to become. She was supposed to have gone out and done something with her life. Instead she'd stayed stuck. No one had trapped her, she thought. She'd done that to herself.

They landed as smoothly as they'd taken off. Nina climbed out of the cockpit and looked around at the airport. She wanted to walk into the office and find a plane going anywhere that wasn't here. She wanted to go home and get in her car and drive until she'd reached the East Coast. Then she would get on a boat and let it take her to some foreign port. The where didn't matter, she thought. She had to keep moving.

But even as she wondered where her passport was and how much she could pack in a single bag, common sense took over. Was she really going to disappear with no warning? She had responsibilities. She was upset. This wasn't the time to make an important decision.

"What'd you think?" Kyle asked as he put his arm around her.

"You promised to change my life and you did."

He kissed the top of her head. "You didn't even throw up. I'm proud of you."

They walked to the rental office, and he gave the guy the keys. They talked about the plane for a few minutes, before returning to Kyle's car and heading back for the island.

The drive wouldn't take long, Nina thought grimly. They didn't have far to go.

After dinner, Nina asked Kyle to take her home. She'd been distracted all through their meal, so convincing him she wasn't feeling great hadn't taken much. He'd left her shortly before eight and had promised to call her in the morning.

When he'd left, she started for the house only to turn around and hurry to her car. She got inside and backed out of the driveway.

But once she got to the center of town, she didn't know where to go. The signs for the bridge to the mainland were clearly marked. She could do what she'd thought about earlier. Just drive. Only she wasn't the kind of person who simply walked away without warning. She started to turn left, then went straight and somehow found herself by the marina. After parking, she got out and walked to a familiar condo building.

The concierge recognized her and called up without being asked. Nina had a brief thought that Dylan could simply refuse to see her. She couldn't really blame him if he did. But instead of turning her away, the concierge waved her toward the elevators.

Nina rode to the top floor, then stepped out. She saw Dylan standing in his doorway.

The sun was still high enough in the sky to spill into his unit. He was in silhouette, and she couldn't make out his features. But the second she saw him, something inside of her shattered and tears filled her eyes. She hurried toward him, then stepped inside when he moved out of her way.

She stopped in the middle of the living room and faced him. His expression was tight, his gaze hard.

"Are you crying about him?" he asked.

She shook her head, then sank down onto the black leather sofa. She covered her face with her hands and started to sob.

The cries came from deep inside of her. She felt herself shaking and knew she should probably try to get control, only she didn't care enough. How had this happened? When had she lost sight of everything that was important?

Time passed, and eventually the tears slowed. She sniffed, then opened her eyes and saw a box of tissues in front of her. She reached for a couple and wiped her face, then blew her nose.

Dylan walked in from the kitchen. He had an open bottle

of wine in one hand and two glasses in the other. He poured and handed her one.

He took a seat across from her. He wore jeans and a T-shirt. His feet were bare. It was late enough in the day that he had a little stubble on his jaw, which made him look surprisingly sexy.

She sniffed again and wadded up the tissues, then picked up the glass of wine.

"I'm sorry," she said before taking a sip. "I'm a complete mess."

"What happened?"

"Everything. Nothing." She sniffed again. "I can't keep control of all of it. My mother and the painting. You know that's going to be a disaster. Odds are she's going to be swindled out of the whole thing and end up owing Ambrose for his work and the bank for storage."

"Bertie's there to steady her, and despite how she acts, your mom respects your opinion."

"No, she blames me for being the grown-up in the relationship." She took another sip. "I was at the store today. It's doing really well. I mean, better than any of us ever dreamed. Cindy has organized the inventory. Mom and Bertie do have a good eye for things."

She leaned back against the soft cushions. "My first thought was this was great. We can get the roof fixed and the two of them can take a salary and I can finally start saving money and thinking about…"

She pressed her lips together as her eyes filled with tears. "It's not any of that," she said, avoiding his gaze. "It's not Averil being an idiot about her marriage or my mom or the roof. It's the island."

Dylan frowned. "What about the island?"

"It's so small. I never knew that. Or I forgot. I've been

trapped on something the size of a postage stamp. I thought I had a real life here, but I don't. Look at me. I'm thirty and I still live with my mother. I try to control everyone around me, and it doesn't work. No one listens. I gave up everything for nothing and now I'm stuck."

She stood and moved to the sliding glass door. It was partially open, and she closed her eyes against the gentle breeze. The truth was right there, within reach. If only she was willing to admit it.

"Stuck is wrong," she whispered. "I'm not stuck. I'm afraid. I've always been afraid. Of change, of possibilities. I've told myself I can't leave. At first it was about money. Averil needed to go to UCLA and someone had to pay for that. Then there was my mom. She wasn't ready to be on her own. What if she and Bertie broke up? What if..."

She risked looking at him and found he was watching her, but she had no idea what he was thinking. Maybe it didn't matter. Maybe the point of this was to say the words, not get a response.

"You got away," she continued. "You did what you said. You became a doctor and came back because you'd promised you would. I never did any of that. I've been fooling myself. I thought I didn't have a choice, but I always did. I was too afraid to take it."

She walked over to the coffee table and put down her wine. Dylan continued to watch her without speaking.

"I'm sorry about the party," she said. "I won't apologize for seeing Kyle because I wasn't doing anything wrong, but I never meant to make you uncomfortable. You and I aren't dating or anything romantic. You've been there for me and I appreciate your help. I thought we were friends. You never said you wanted anything more."

He stood. "You're right. I didn't. Who is he?"

"He's a fighter pilot for the Navy. I used to babysit his lit-tle sister. He showed up a few weeks ago." She swallowed the rest of the words. Dylan didn't need to know how Kyle had claimed she was his fantasy.

"Now what?" he asked.

"Are you talking about my life or Kyle?"

"Both."

"I have no idea," she admitted. "I just figured out I've been fooling myself for years. Pretending a self-importance that didn't exist. I've been so busy thinking I was taking care of everyone that I never bothered to notice I was carefully trap-ping myself so I would have the perfect excuse not to leave my comfort zone."

"What are you going to do about it?"

"I don't know. I thought about simply leaving, but that's hardly the mature response. I don't want to change things for the sake of it. I need to live with the revelation for a while. Right now I'm still in shock."

Not to mention battered, she thought. She couldn't believe how stupid she'd been, how blind. A ridiculous figure.

"Hey."

She looked at Dylan, only to find he'd opened his arms. As if inviting her in. Without thinking about the consequences, she walked into his embrace. She wrapped both arms around him and hung on tight.

Chapter Twenty-Three

❧

AVERIL STEPPED OUT of the shower and reached for her towel. She'd gotten up later than usual, mostly because she'd stayed awake until nearly two in the morning, working on her book.

She was making progress, she thought as she dried off, then reached for her lotion. Real progress. She loved the story, loved the characters and had a rough outline for the whole second half. She'd written more in the past three weeks than at any time in her life. Not counting her articles, of course.

She loved the energy she felt, the excitement. Kevin had been reading her pages every night, and he'd offered an insightful, encouraging critique.

This is what she was meant to do. Nothing angsty or literary. Just fun, flirty stories for the teens who read the magazine. She understood them, adored them and connected with them.

She knew she probably wouldn't sell her first book. Most authors didn't. But that was okay. She would keep on trying until she found an editor who understood her and her work.

She dressed, then wrapped the towel around her hair. After

digging through her cosmetics bag, she pulled out her moisturizer and sunscreen, then her birth control pills. She dropped a single pill on her palm and came to a stop.

What was she doing? Averil looked up and stared at herself in the mirror. What was she doing? Why was she working in an antique store rather than at her job? Why was she cooking for her mother and Bertie and Nina instead of Kevin? Why was she talking to him on the phone instead of in person? Why was she still on Blackberry Island? Why hadn't she gone home?

She'd been faithfully taking her birth control pills every morning and for what purpose? To not have a child? But she wanted kids—she wanted kids with Kevin. Fierce longing swept through her as she thought about being with him. Not just making love, but having dinner together, seeing him. Being in the rhythm of their life.

She tossed the pill into the trash, then quickly applied her moisturizer and sunscreen before combing out her hair. She didn't bother with the blow-dryer, but instead gathered up all her toiletries and hurried to her room.

Penny was waiting for her on the bed.

"This is crazy," she told the dog. "What am I waiting for? Kevin to leave me? I'm not sure why I even came here." Penny wagged her tail.

Averil smiled. "Yes, I'm sure part of it was so I could find you. I guess I also needed to take a long look at my past. Figure out my connection with Nina. It turns out my sister is as screwed up as the rest of us."

She knew there was more. She'd needed to prove to herself that she could write. Maybe she'd needed to be by herself to finish growing up. Whatever the reasons, she was ready now. Ready to be the kind of person a man like Kevin would want to spend the rest of his life with. As important, she needed to be the kind of person she could be proud of.

She set her suitcase on the bed and began filling it with her clothes. She barely folded her shirts, instead quickly rolling them into balls and shoving them inside. She was more careful with her laptop and her notes.

When she'd packed up all her things, she collected Penny's belongings. She found Bertie in the kitchen, sipping coffee.

"Where's Mom?" Averil asked, crossing to the pot and pouring herself a cup.

"Out for a walk. She was in the mood to commune with nature."

Which could mean any of a thousand things, Averil thought. "I'm going home," she said. "I miss Kevin and I need to get back to my life."

Bertie smiled at her. "I'm glad. He's a good guy and very sweet to you."

"I know. I got lucky when I found him." She cradled the cup. "What about what's happening here? The painting and Nina and everything else."

"We'll be fine. If we lose the painting, then we're no worse off than we were before. Nina and I had a long talk last night. She's having a bit of a crisis, although she didn't say over what. But she did say that the store is doing well. Cindy has been a find. I promised to get more involved. I'll keep Bonnie from imploding. At least financially."

Averil put down her coffee and hugged her mother's partner. "I'm glad you're a part of our family."

"Me, too. Now go home to your husband."

Averil grinned. "I think I will."

She loaded everything into her trunk. Bonnie rounded the corner just as the last of the suitcases were put in place. Averil explained she was leaving and why.

"It's time," her mother told her, hugging her close. "I loved seeing you, but you need to be with Kevin. You love him."

"I do, Mom." She stepped back. "I love you, too. And so does Nina."

Bonnie's expression tightened. "Your sister," she began.

Averil shook her head. "No. Don't say anything bad about her. She's done the best she could with a really tough job." She squeezed her mother's arm. "You know it's time."

Bonnie ignored the comment and kissed her cheek. "I love you. Drive safely."

"Promise."

Averil held open the back door for Penny. When the dog was settled, Averil got in on the driver's side and started the engine. She had one stop to make before heading home, one last conversation.

Nina's office was in a beautifully restored Queen Anne house on a hill. When Averil had been growing up, the house had been empty and neglected, and a favorite make-out spot. She was sure today's teenagers had found another place for their night activities and was pleased to see the house looking so happy.

"Give me five minutes," she told Penny.

The dog studied her for a second before putting her head down on her paws and closing her eyes.

Averil climbed the stairs, then opened the front door. There was only one mother and her toddler in the waiting room.

"I'm Nina's sister. Could I see her for a second?"

Holly, the receptionist, nodded. "She's not with a patient. Come on back."

Averil followed her to Nina's office. Her sister sat behind her desk. She looked tired and almost lost. Something that couldn't be possible, Averil thought. Nina was always in charge.

"Hey," she said as she walked in. "I wanted to come by and say goodbye."

Nina blinked a couple of times. "You're leaving?"

"Going home."

"Mischief Bay," Nina murmured. "It's beautiful there."

Something was off, Averil thought. "Are you feeling okay?"

"I'm fine. Just thinking about things." Nina looked at her. "What changed your mind? Why are you suddenly ready?"

Averil sank into the spare chair and put her hands on the desk. "I'm not sure. I got out of the shower this morning, and I knew it was time. Maybe past time. I came here because I was confused. Something wasn't right in my life. I like writing for the magazine, but I want something other than that. I think in my heart I always felt that I hadn't made a choice. That I'd been pushed into my choices."

Nina's mouth twisted. "I'm sure now you want to blame me."

Averil thought about all her sister had done for her. All the sacrifices, all the worry. "No," she said quietly. "You held it all together for everyone. You took care of me and loved me and I will always be grateful. Yes, it was your decision for me to go to UCLA, but I could have said no and didn't. I made the choices. I'm responsible. That's what I never saw before. It's up to me."

There was more she could say. She'd handed over the decision-making to everyone around her and then had resented when they'd chosen for her. Even though she and Kevin had talked about having a baby, in her heart, she'd told herself he'd made the choice for her.

"I don't take much responsibility in my life," she admitted. "I need to stop doing that. I want to be married to Kevin, and I need to act like the kind of wife he deserves to have. I want to be a novelist, so I need to get my ass in a chair and write books."

She smiled. "I think this means I'm finally ready to grow up."

Nina nodded. "Good for you. Drive safe. Let me know when you get there."

"I will."

Nina walked around her desk. They embraced.

"Be proud of yourself," Nina whispered. "You've done so much. I love you, sis."

"I love you, too."

Averil blinked away tears. "Come visit us," she said impulsively. "I know you're going to say you can't get away, but please try."

"I will," Nina told her. "I mean it. I'll come see you."

On her way home from work, Nina swung by Blackberry Preserves. She had some fence-mending to do with Cindy.

She parked in front of the store and went inside. Cindy was with a couple of customers. They looked to be mother and daughter and were discussing a pair of chairs. While Cindy showed them the details of the construction and the manufacturer's mark underneath the seat, Nina walked through the crowded aisles of the store.

Every time she came through, the store was more and more organized, she thought. The air was fresh, and there was more light without those hideous drapes. In the storeroom she found information on alarm systems and a receipt from a locksmith for a new set of deadbolts and a lock for the wardrobe. She collapsed into the desk chair and rested her head in her hands.

"You look like you need some tea," Cindy said.

Nina looked up and saw the other woman walking to the microwave.

"I have some oolong my mother-in-law bought for me." Cindy flashed her a grin. "I've been drinking it for a couple of weeks now, so I'm sure it's not poisoned."

Nina managed a slight smile. "Good to know."

Cindy put two mugs into the microwave and pushed the start button. Nina picked up the receipt.

"You got new locks."

"You were concerned about security."

"I was having a meltdown," Nina admitted. "Things have been changing so fast. Or maybe it's just me."

"The painting isn't helping," Cindy said, putting tea leaves into two small infusers and setting them into the mugs. "I wish your mom hadn't gone so crazy with the news crews. They still call here. I tell them the painting has been moved and the family hasn't made a decision. Most of the time that gets them off the phone, but not always."

"You've been terrific," Nina told the other woman. "I'm sorry about yesterday. None of it was about you. I really appreciate being able to relax about the store. I want to give you a raise."

Cindy pulled out the infusers and handed her a mug. "I'd like that."

"Also, if you want to take any classes on antiques, we'll pay for them."

"That would be fun. Thank you." She took a sip. "Want to talk about it?"

"It?"

"Whatever is bothering you. I'm not trying to pry, but there's obviously something wrong."

Nina thought about everything that had happened. "I saw the island."

"Excuse me?"

"I saw it. Yesterday. From the sky. Do you know how small it is?"

Cindy shook her head. "Not in the way you mean."

"I've lived here all my life. I was supposed to leave, but I didn't. I got stuck or scared.... It's so small. I barely slept last night because I was trying to figure out where I got off course. Was it when Dylan broke up with me? Was I afraid to go out on my own? Were there real pressures keeping me here or is that an excuse?" She paused. "Sorry. You don't need to deal with any of this."

"I asked," Cindy told her. "While I'd miss you if you left, you shouldn't stay if being here isn't what you want."

"But that's the thing. I don't have anywhere to go."

Cindy shook her head. "I don't buy that." She sighed. "Sometimes we get off course. Or we start to believe a story that isn't true. Like with me and my mother-in-law. The truth is she can be difficult. But she also loves my husband and my kids, and the other day I caught her putting fresh flowers on my desk at home. It made me stop and think that she's struggling to fit in, too. We all are. Life goes by fast."

Cindy smiled. "It seems like just last week I was twenty-five. Be careful. You'll wake up tomorrow in your sixties. If you're not happy, now's the time to make changes."

Nina got home a little after six. She'd left the store and had driven around the island for a little while, then realized that going in circles wasn't going to help. She needed a plan—something well-thought-out. She didn't want to simply jump for the sake of movement. She needed to figure out what her goals were and then move toward them. It wasn't as if the island was shrinking and she had to go right this second.

She walked inside and found Bonnie and Bertie curled up together on the sofa.

"Hi," she said, then turned toward her room.

"Come join us," her mother called. "We're toasting Averil's decision to return to Kevin."

Nina went into the living room and saw a third glass on the coffee table. She poured the wine, then settled into one of the chairs across from the sofa.

"I'm glad she went home, too," Nina told them. "I think she found whatever she was looking for. I hope they make it."

"They will," Bonnie said confidently.

Nina resisted the urge to roll her eyes. Her mother might feel a spiritual connection to inanimate objects, but she hardly had the gift of precognition. It wasn't as if she *knew* whether or not Averil and Kevin were going to make it. Although a case could be made that assuming the best was a more pleasant way to live.

"I stopped by the store." Nina sipped her wine. All this drinking—first of tea and now wine. At some point she needed to eat. Or not. Maybe being confused about life would allow her to get rid of those fifteen pounds that plagued her. "Cindy got new locks installed on the front and back door. She's also going to lock up the jewelry. She's doing excellent work. She deserves a raise."

"Good idea," Bertie said.

Bonnie nodded. "I like her so much. I want her to stay." She straightened a little in her seat. "We have an announcement."

Nina involuntarily stiffened. "Okay. I'm braced."

Her mother laughed. "It's hardly bad news." She turned to her partner. "You tell her."

Bertie nodded. "We're selling the Stoicasescu. I called Ambrose earlier this afternoon and spoke with him. He's going to take care of getting it appraised. He's already been tracing it, and it seems it's not stolen or missing. Which means the sale should go through."

Nina's gaze swung back to her mother. "You're okay with this?"

Bonnie nodded. "Bertie and I are driving to Seattle tomorrow to sign the rest of the paperwork. We'll stay in town a couple of nights and enjoy the city, then come back."

Bertie cleared her throat. "While that's good to know, the

part that we need you to know is about the trusts. We're setting up four trusts. We'll each get an equal share of the proceeds. There will be fees, commission and taxes, but even
after all that, there's going to be a lot of money left. Enough
for us all to follow our dreams."

The last words were delivered gently, but Nina got their
meaning. While the income from the store would have improved things, the sale of the painting was life-changing.

Nina put down her wine, afraid she would start shaking
and spill. "Are you sure?"

Her mother laughed. "About selling or the money? Ambrose
assures us we'll get a lot for the painting. And if that means
we're all rich at the end of the day, so be it."

She took Bertie's hand. "We're thinking of getting a new
van. A larger one so we can buy more. Who knows what we'll
find if we're really looking."

Nina wanted to believe, but she was afraid. "Mom, are you
sure?" she asked again.

"Yes, very. I want to sell the painting. Averil told me it's
time to grow up. I don't want to, but I suppose she's right."

Nina opened her mouth, then closed it. "I don't know
what to say."

"A rarity," her mother murmured.

Nina smiled. "Probably true." She stood. "Okay, this is a
lot to think about. I'm glad you're selling. You don't have to
give me any of the money."

"We want to," her mother told her. The smile faded. "Don't
you think it's time I acted like the adult in the relationship?
You should savor this moment. It may not happen again."

That was the truth, Nina thought, still dazed. "You'll need
to find a financial planner. Someone with a good reputation
and who is honest. You'll need help managing the money."

Bertie stood and crossed to her. The other woman took

Nina's hands in hers. "Stop," she said quietly. "Ambrose made several suggestions, as did our banker here on the island. We're going to do this right. I'll make sure of it. If you have trouble accepting that, then believe me when I tell you that I want to make sure your mother will be taken care of for the rest of her life."

Nina squeezed her fingers. "You're saying let go."

"Yes. You're free, Nina. Don't be one of those birds who keeps ignoring the open window and banging itself against the mirror."

"That's not me."

At least she didn't want it to be her. She thought about the island, again. Of how she'd realized she was the only one holding on so tight. That everyone else had let go.

She had no idea what to do or where to go. If she wasn't trapped, then what was the next step?

Maybe, just maybe, it was time to find out.

Averil had thought she might have trouble staying awake through the night, but anticipation and excitement kept her alert through Sacramento, then Fresno. She stopped at a twenty-four-hour diner in a truck stop north of Bakersfield for a large coffee to go and a couple of scrambled eggs for Penny. It was just after three in the morning.

Penny gulped down her meal, and then they took a walk together in the silence. The area was well lit and the air cool enough to be bracing. Penny took care of business, then trotted along at Averil's side.

"I hope you like the house," Averil told the dog. "We're close to the beach, and we'll be able to go on long walks. There's a great boardwalk you'll like."

She patted the dog. "I hope Kevin loves you as much as I do."

Penny looked at her with an expression that asked "What's not to love?" Averil hugged her, then they returned to the car.

Two hours later, they were in Mischief Bay. The coastal town, tucked just south of LAX and next to Hermosa Beach, was an eclectic jumble of California chic, beachy casual and a high-tech mecca. There were tiny 1950s bungalows next to ten-thousand-square-foot mansions, a few high-rise condos and, on the east end of the town, a cluster of software companies.

The pier, a smaller version of the one in Santa Monica, drew tourists. The locals knew about the great restaurants tucked away in corners and alleys. Performance artists dotted the boardwalk. At this hour, the streets were still quiet, the sun still only threatening to rise.

Averil pulled into her familiar driveway and parked the car. She took Penny for another short walk, then grabbed the dog's bed and dishes from the trunk. She quietly let them both into the house.

Everything was as she remembered. Kevin was basically a neat guy, so there were only a few magazines scattered on the coffee table. His iPad sat next to the TV remote.

Averil moved to the kitchen and got Penny water. She set the bowl in the corner, then led the way to the master bedroom in the back of the house.

Kevin was already up. The bed was still unmade, but the door to the bathroom was partially open, and she heard the sound of the shower running. She put Penny's bed down, and the dog curled up in it right away. Averil stood in the center of the room, not sure what to do next.

She moved toward the bathroom, then stopped. She looked at Penny. "I'm open to ideas."

Penny wagged her tail briefly before putting her head down on her paws and going to sleep.

Averil returned her attention to the bathroom door, then heard the shower shut off.

"What the hell," she muttered and pulled off her shirt.

She was naked in about thirty seconds and walked to the bathroom door.

"Hey," she said softly, as she knocked. "Good morning."

Kevin turned at the sound of her voice. He had his towel in one hand and a look of surprise on his face. Then his mouth curved into a welcoming smile, and he reached for her.

"You're back," he said, pulling her close.

She went into his embrace, feeling the lanky warmth of his body pressing against hers. Emotions flooded her, battling for dominance. Gratitude mingled with desire. Longing swirled around love. Before she could settle on one, he kissed her.

His lips claimed hers. She parted for him and felt herself melt into him. He ran his hands up and down her back, before squeezing her butt, then moving to her breasts.

He was hard in seconds, which was good because she was ready, too. More than ready. Kisses deepened, hands reached.

"Bed," he said, his voice low and husky.

"Counter," she whispered and stepped back to shift herself onto the cold tile.

He didn't hesitate a second. He moved between her parted legs and pushed into her with practiced ease. At the same time, he cupped her breasts and teased her tight, aching nipples. She wrapped her legs around his hips, holding him deep inside of her.

They made love with fierce abandon. She gave herself over to him, to how he made her feel. When her orgasm claimed her, she let her head fall back as she cried out her pleasure. Not only because it felt good, but because Kevin liked it when she made noise.

When they had stilled, she looked into his eyes.

"Hi," she said.

"Hi, yourself."

"I love you."

His mouth curved up. "I love you, too."

"I'm back for good." She paused, knowing there was a lot more she needed to say, but not sure where to begin.

He withdrew and started out of the bathroom. Panic had her sliding off the counter and following him.

"Kevin?"

He picked up his cell phone. "It's okay," he told her. "I'm calling in sick. I want to spend the day with you, Averil. We have some catching up to do."

Because that was who he was, she thought as tears unexpectedly filled her eyes.

"What?" he asked, moving toward her. "Why are you crying? Did I say something wrong?"

"No," she said, running to him and hugging him as tightly as she could. "I don't deserve you. I'm sorry for what I put you through. What if I'd lost you?"

He kissed her, then wiped away her tears. "You didn't, Averil. You didn't."

He led her to the bed and waited until she climbed in. Then he called his office and said he wouldn't be in today or tomorrow. As he circled the bed to his side, he paused by Penny, bent down and scratched her ears.

"Hey, doglet. Welcome to the family."

Penny wagged her tail and licked his hand.

Kevin climbed into bed and settled on his back. Averil snuggled up against him. Her head rested on his shoulder, her leg draped across his thigh. One of his hands laced with hers and the other played with her hair.

Everything about this felt right, she thought happily. She'd been given a second chance.

She thought about the birth control pills she'd thrown out, but decided that was a conversation for later. As was the matter of the trust fund and how she'd realized that while it was okay to be the princess every now and then, mostly she had to be the queen in her own life. All things he would want to hear, but not now. This moment needed to be about them. About him.

"Tell me, what's going on at work?" she asked.

"We're having some trouble in programming," he said.

She snuggled closer and smiled. "I want to hear all about it."

Chapter Twenty-Four

AFTER ANOTHER SLEEPLESS night, Nina was seriously thinking about calling in sick. Her head hurt; she was foggy. Luck was on her side because Kyle had been sent away on one of his assignments. He'd texted her that he would be back at the end of the week and he wanted to take her to dinner Friday night.

She accepted the reprieve as a sign the Universe was looking out for her, then took an extra-hot shower in an effort to wake up. When she got out she realized that a cold one might have been more efficient. She was still groggy.

Maybe she would go in for a couple of hours and get the paperwork done, then come back home. If she could just sleep, she would feel better.

She swallowed coffee, passed on breakfast, then headed for her car. It was where she'd left it, but as she approached, she saw Dylan leaning against the driver's door.

She came to a stop when she saw him. Heat burned on her cheeks. The last time she'd seen him, she'd been in the throes of a pretty serious breakdown. She was still trying to find her footing.

He walked toward her. "You okay? You look tired." He touched her face. "Not sleeping much?"

"Not sleeping at all. There's something about finding out one's life is a complete fraud to upset the rhythm of one's day."

His green eyes turned knowing. "You always did hide behind humor."

"It's something I'm really good at, but it only works if you don't mention it."

"I won't say a word."

"Thank you."

He nodded. "Made any decisions yet?"

"About my life?" She gave a laugh, hoping it sounded more amused than strangled. "No. Still reeling from everything going on. Averil went home, which is good. I hope she and Kevin can work things out. Mom and Bertie are swearing they can handle the money. They're getting a financial adviser."

"What about you? What are you going to do?"

"I have no idea," she admitted. "I'm torn between running away and becoming agoraphobic. Although I think I'd get bored being in the house all the time." She thought about the trust fund and how that offered financial freedom if nothing else. Which would be a great thing, if only she had a few dreams she could follow.

Dylan surprised her by leaning in and kissing her. His lips lingered before he straightened.

"What was that for?" she asked, to cover unexpected confusion. Dylan kissing her? Wasn't he angry about Kyle?

"To make a point. I learned my lesson ten years ago. I gave you up. I let pride and circumstances tear us apart. There are a lot of other reasons and I could make excuses, but I won't. Instead I'll tell you it was a mistake. I came back to Blackberry Island in part because I'd promised my father, but also because you were here. I wanted to see you again. I wanted to see what would happen when we were together."

She felt her mouth drop open, then carefully closed it. "I…" She drew in a breath. "What?"

He gave her a quick smile. "I let you go once and I'm not going to do it again. I'm going to fight for you." The smile faded. "Let me be clear. I'm not sleeping with you while you're sleeping with Kyle, but I'm also not going to go away."

Okay—she'd officially tipped over the edge and was falling into madness. Dylan was going to fight for her? What did that mean? She had a sudden vision of Kyle and him going at it, like in *Fight Club*. The image wasn't very comfortable.

"I don't understand," she admitted.

"Maybe this will help."

He grabbed her by her upper arms and held her still while he kissed her again. His mouth was warm and passionate against hers, and she had to admit that, despite the madness swirling all around her, she felt serious tingles low in her belly. Just when she was about to wrap her arms around him, he let her go.

"I'll see you soon," he promised, then walked to his car and drove away.

Nina watched him go, then slowly got into her car and rested her head against the steering wheel. "I'm going to need a lot more coffee to get through this day," she murmured.

"Thanks for this," Nina said, as she sat across from Andi at the restaurant at the Blackberry Island Inn. When two appointments right after lunch had canceled, Nina had asked her boss if they could go out and talk.

"Are you kidding?" Andi asked, settling into the chair and sighing with contentment. "I've been seriously craving the chicken salad here. But I worry that all I talk about these days is food, so I didn't want to say anything." She paused, then laughed. "Not that I won't enjoy your company."

Nina grinned. "Good to know I come in second to a sandwich."

"Maybe not. I could order it on a salad."

Their server appeared and took their drink orders, then talked about the specials. When she left, Andi leaned her elbows on the table.

"So," she began. "What's up?"

Nina resisted the need to squirm. "Nothing. Everything. My life is unraveling and I don't know what to do about it."

"I find that hard to believe. You're always so calm and in control."

"Most of that is a façade. I just…" Nina wasn't sure how much to share. While Andi was a friend, she was also her boss. She wasn't willing to discuss her confusion about what Dylan had told her that morning. It simply fell into the "too personal" category. But there were other issues she would really like some advice on.

"I don't know if I ever mentioned this before, but I'd always planned on being a doctor."

Andi's eyebrows rose. "Seriously? What happened? You'd be great. You're the best nurse I've ever had. You're good with the patients and you enjoy problem-solving."

Their server returned with their drinks, and they both ordered the chicken salad sandwich on focaccia bread.

"It was a lot of things," Nina admitted when they were alone again. "I had responsibilities, I was afraid. When Dylan and I broke up, I couldn't face going to the University of Washington and running into him all the time. I went to community college for two years. By then Averil was old enough to be thinking about what she wanted to do. If I went to medical school…" Her voice trailed off. To get answers to her questions, she needed to tell the truth.

"I think I got scared. It was more expedient to become a nurse. Less of a challenge. I told myself it was so there would be money for Averil's education, and while that's true, it's not the main reason."

She paused. "Have you ever seen the island from the air?"

Andi laughed. "No. Have you?"

"A few days ago. It's small. I mean seriously small. You chose this place, I accepted it without much of a fight. I never tried to leave. I never tried for something else."

"Did you want to leave?" her boss asked, her expression concerned.

"I don't know." She paused, then decided to admit the truth. "Yes, I did, but I was afraid to go after my dreams. There were always reasons to keep me here."

"I know you've been looking after your mom for a long time," Andi admitted. "Paying the bills. I wasn't trying to pry, but as you said, the island is small. I heard things. Won't the painting change everything?"

Nina reached for her iced tea. "I don't know," she admitted. "I hope so. If my mom can be responsible and not lose everything. If Averil…" She paused.

There it was. Her go-to emotional place. Taking care of others. Worrying about everyone but herself. Only now she realized what she'd always seen as a virtue was a way to hide out and not take a chance.

"Selling the painting will give all of us financial freedom."

"A nice thing to have," Andi said gently. "What do you want to do with yours?"

Nina opened her mouth, planning on saying she didn't know. But what came out was, "I want to go to medical school."

Andi grinned. "I was hoping you were going to say that."

"You were? Why?"

"Because you'll be great and it's what you want." She wrinkled her nose. "It will make my life sucky because you'll be difficult to replace." She lightly touched Nina's arm. "Please, don't take this wrong, but I do mean difficult, not impossible. I'll find someone."

"I know you meant it in the best way possible," Nina said, a little surprised at her boss's enthusiasm. "Do you think I could get into medical school? I'm not twenty-two."

"And that's to your advantage. You have experience in the medical field. Do you know your specialty yet?"

"I was thinking oncology."

"A tough one," Andi told her. "But you'd be great. Have you taken your MCATs?"

"Last year. I didn't want to say anything."

"And you did well?"

Nina grinned. "I did."

"Okay. Perfect. It's June and you've way missed application deadlines for the fall."

Nina's shoulders slumped. "I didn't even think about that. You're right. I can't do anything until next year."

"Not necessarily. What I was going to say is my mom's best friend is a dean at Tufts." Andi rolled her eyes. "I have to admit, when my mom starts lecturing me, I stop listening. She's better now, but her innate urge to tell me what to do with my life never goes away. Anyway, I'll bet her friend could help. I'll call Mom tonight and ask what she can do. In the meantime, download the application and start filling it out. I'm sure there's a waiting list, but I've learned to never doubt the power of family connections. Especially when my mom is a famous cardiothoracic surgeon."

Nina pressed her hands against the table. "My head is spinning. Do you really think I could have a chance at getting in this fall?"

"Let's find out. If you don't, then you'll apply to a bunch of schools next year. I've seen you in action, Nina. If you want this, you can make it happen."

Nina dressed for her dinner with Dylan carefully. Despite his declaration, she hadn't been sure when she would hear from him again. But he'd called and asked her to dinner. He'd said he would pick her up at six.

Knowing what to wear was a challenge. He'd said dinner, but not where. She'd chosen a simple summer dress with a matching cardigan. The dark pink color of both went well with her skin, and the outfit would fit in at a lot of places.

She was oddly nervous. Or maybe the butterflies in her belly weren't unexpected. After all, the man had declared he was "going to fight for her." Which was perhaps amazing and romantic, but what the hell did it mean?

Thankfully, Bertie and Bonnie had left to have drinks with Cindy. They were discussing plans to renovate the store. Just thinking about that was enough to increase Nina's already jumpy state, but she reminded herself she had to be willing to let go or she would never be free. That she'd trapped herself in her current situation by believing her mother couldn't possibly survive without her. If she wasn't careful, she would find herself at the end of her life and never really having lived it at all.

She walked into the living room just as someone knocked on the door. She opened it to find Dylan standing on the porch.

"Hi," he said with a smile.

"Hi, yourself."

He looked good. Jeans, a long-sleeved shirt. He'd shaved

recently. Definitely a man on a date, she thought, pressing a hand to her stomach.

"I'm ready," she said, as she reached for her bag, then closed the door behind her. "Where are we going?"

"Mansion on the Hill."

"Nice."

Mansion on the Hill was exactly what it sounded like. The big old house had been converted into several retail spaces about twenty years ago. There was a restaurant, a flower shop, along with touristy stores.

"How's work?" Dylan asked as he held the door open for her.

She slid onto the leather seat, then waited until he was next to her before answering.

"Good. For a couple of days we thought we had a case of measles. You can imagine what a nightmare that would be. But it was a false alarm."

"Hives?" he asked as he started the engine.

"Yes. Food allergies, which isn't going to be fun for the family."

They chatted about their jobs until they got to the restaurant and went inside. Nina found herself alternating between talking easily with a man she'd literally known for more than a decade and feeling inexplicably nervous.

They went inside and were shown to a corner table. They had a view of the island and upcoming sunset, yet were a little isolated from other diners.

Nina took the offered menu, but instead of opening it, she thought about what it had been like before—when she'd been in love with Dylan. He'd been everything to her. At eighteen, she'd been dealing with graduating from high school and worrying about her little sister. Bonnie had been flighty, without Bertie's steadying influence. There had been bills to pay and, in the back of her mind, the worry that everything would fall apart when she went away to college.

Dylan had been her rock. They'd talked every day and had emailed even more often. When she'd started to think she couldn't hold it together, he'd given her strength. She'd lived for their weekends. They would spend every second together, talking, studying, making love. He'd been her first time, and it had been wonderful.

By the time they'd actually consummated their relationship, they'd been fooling around for nearly a year. They knew how to please each other in different ways. That night he'd made her come with his mouth and then had reached for a condom.

They'd discussed what they had been about to do in detail. They'd waited until Bonnie and Averil had gone to Seattle for the weekend so they didn't have to rush. Still, his hands had trembled, and when he'd pushed into her for the first time, he'd climaxed within five seconds.

"What are you smiling about?" he asked, drawing her to the present.

She hesitated for a second, then said, "Our first time."

He groaned. "What's the funny part? That I lost it immediately or that you looked at me and said 'I thought it would take longer?'"

"Both," she admitted. "I've been thinking about us a lot lately. Which is totally your fault." She'd been planning on being more subtle in asking him what he'd meant, but realized there was no point. "Our last conversation was intense."

"Why? I thought I was clear."

"I guess I don't know your intentions."

As soon as the words were out, she wanted to call them back. Instead, she pressed her lips together and told herself she was going to sit there and listen.

Dylan studied her for a few seconds before giving her the smile that was designed to make her toes curl.

"I like you," he said, his voice low. "I enjoy spending time with you. We get along and have the same interests. I know what we had before. We've both grown and changed in the past decade, and I want to see if we still have the same spark."

"Good answer," she murmured. "But there's a problem."

One eyebrow rose. "The boy?"

"He's twenty-six and, no. I mean, yes, Kyle is an issue, but not the one I mean. I'm leaving the island."

She watched carefully, but his expression didn't change.

"Where are you going?"

"I don't know. I'm not doing an anywhere-but-here thing. I just know that I'm not happy with the choices I've made. I want to make different ones."

"Like medical school?"

"That's on the list." And the most important item, even though she was frustrated by the fact that she would most likely have to wait until fall next year to get started.

"I hope it's at the top," he told her. "You'll have to work your ass off, but you'll be a hell of a doctor. Let me know if you want to use me as a reference."

"You'd do that?"

"Of course. Why would you be surprised? I care about you, Nina. That's what this is about for me. If getting into medical school makes you happy, then I want that to happen." He frowned. "Did you think I'd want you to stay in a place where you feel trapped?"

"I wasn't sure."

The server came and brought menus. Dylan glanced at the wine list, then ordered a bottle. When they were alone, he stretched his arms across the table and took her hands.

"I'm not trying to trap you or change you or make you uncomfortable."

Words that were pretty hard to resist, she thought. "Wow. That's nice."

"I'm a nice guy." He grinned. "And a doctor. Your mom would be so proud." He paused. "Okay, your mom wouldn't care, but most moms would be happy."

She laughed.

He released her fingers, then leaned back in his seat. "Want to hear what medical school is like?"

She nodded eagerly. "I've heard it's brutal."

"It is. In some ways, the first year is the worst. It's basic science. Gross anatomy, histology, pathology, biochemistry. You learn about the body and all its systems. You'll have a leg up on that with the knowledge you already have, but it's still going to be grueling."

"Lectures and labs?" she asked.

He nodded. "Plenty of both. And there's reading. Lots of reading."

By the time they were done with dinner and walking out to his car, Nina felt she had more of a grasp of what to expect if she got into medical school. She was also very conscious of the man moving next to her.

Dylan had answered all her questions, but more than that, he'd been enthusiastic about her chances of getting through the exhausting four years. He'd been totally supportive of her becoming a doctor, which was great, but also baffling. She simply couldn't reconcile his saying he was fighting for her with the ease with which he seemed to be encouraging her to go for her dreams.

He'd parked at the far end of the lot. The passenger side was in shadows, and as they reached his car, he stopped and drew her close. As he lowered his head, she raised hers. Their lips touched. He tasted of wine and the mint chocolate cake they'd shared.

She let herself lean into him and wrapped her arms around his neck, then gave herself over to his kiss. His tongue brushed her bottom lip before slipping inside.

She and Dylan had made love hundreds of times in every way possible. She knew what he liked...or at least she knew what he *had* liked. Time had a way of changing a person. She knew she was different than she'd been at eighteen.

The realization excited her more. She wanted to touch him and explore the changes. She wanted to find out if she could still make him catch his breath, still make him tremble and cry out her name.

She rubbed her breasts against his chest and breathed his name.

He drew back and looked into her eyes. Desire burned there. Desire and something she thought might be regret.

He reached behind his neck and gently took her wrists in his hands then brought her arms to her sides. "I should get you home."

She stared at him, unable to believe he was doing this. Then she remembered his promise not to sleep with her while she was still with Kyle.

Chagrin made her turn away, even as the logical side of her brain admitted she would feel the same way if she were him. But the rest of her was unamused by the turn of events.

"Home sounds good," she lied.

"I do love these little sticky notes," Bertie said, pointing to the skinny strip with the arrow printed on it. "So convenient."

Nina stared at the stack of paperwork. "I guess you really did visit a lawyer."

"We did and the visit was excellent. She was very patient and explained everything we needed to know." Bertie smiled. "She was very pretty and flirted with Ambrose, which I think both pleased him and made him a little uncomfortable. Next up for us is a meeting with the auction house and the financial planners."

"You're getting this together."

They sat at the kitchen table in the house. Around them were the familiar trappings of their life. Everything was as it had been for years, yet there was the promise of something different just beyond the horizon.

"We are on plan," Bertie said cheerfully. "Your mother and I made a list of everything that has to be done, and now we're working our way through it."

"Really?" Nina asked with a grin. "My mom is checking items off on a list?"

"All right. Maybe I'm more the list driver, but she's listening. I think she sees how important this is to all of us." Bertie's humor faded. "She was very concerned about Averil's time here. That she was responsible for the unhappiness in their marriage."

Talk about unexpected, Nina thought. "She had nothing to do with that. Averil had to find her own way." Or maybe just grow up a little more.

"Despite what you think, your mother is very aware of her flaws," Bertie said. "She knows she wasn't there for you and Averil. You did an excellent job with what you had, Nina, but you were a child yourself. Bonnie feels that both of you are paying for her inability to act in a way appropriate to her role."

Her role? "You mean being a mother?"

Bertie nodded.

Nina did her best to accept the information calmly, but she found herself wanting to snap back that while this was all fine and good, hearing it from Bonnie would mean a lot. After that happened, a flock of pigs would fly by.

"I'm glad she's concerned about following through on all this," Nina said, because she didn't want to fight with Bertie. She motioned to the paperwork. "I honestly can't imagine her sitting through a meeting with a lawyer."

"She did very well. I was so proud." Bertie smiled. "You would have been, too. Now, let's get you signed up for your trust."

Bertie passed over paperwork, and Nina read it. The forms were pretty straightforward. Once the trust was funded, Nina would be able to draw up to sixty thousand dollars a year until the trust was depleted.

The amount was so ridiculously high that she nearly giggled as she signed. Sixty thousand dollars? Who had that much money? It was impossible to imagine. Yet once the painting sold, the fees, commissions and taxes were paid, the four of them would be splitting just over six million dollars. She would have a million dollars in her trust, as would Averil. Bertie and Bonnie were keeping the rest. The sisters had jointly insisted on that.

"We have our meetings with the auction house in a few weeks. We're flying to New York for that," Bertie said. "I can't remember when we're meeting the financial planner, but it's on my calendar."

Nina continued to sign where the sticky-note arrows told her to. "What about the house?" she asked.

Bertie raised her eyebrows. "Is this your way of saying we need a new roof? I've already called for estimates. We're going to replace the carpeting, too. Your mother is saying we should redo the bathrooms, but I like them as they are. We're still deciding."

"You're going to stay here? I thought you might want to move to Seattle or somewhere else."

Bertie shook her head. "This is home. We are going to get a new van, though. A bigger one so we can bring home more treasures." The smile returned. "And we're talking about going to Hawaii once all this is settled."

Nina waited, but that seemed to be all. "Life will just go on as it did before?" she asked. "Even with millions of dollars in the bank."

"Especially because of that. We're happy the way things are. Too much change would jeopardize that."

Nina nodded and continued to sign, but on the inside, her head began to spin. Averil had returned to Kevin, because she wanted the life they had. Her mother and Bertie, upon going from barely making it to having a couple of million dollars each, were going to buy a van and get new carpeting.

She put down the pen.

"What?" Bertie asked. "Are you all right?"

Nina didn't know if she should laugh or burst into tears. "I was so worried about having to hold everything together," she admitted. "But nothing has changed, has it? Despite my concerns and craziness, I was never in charge."

"You did like the illusion."

Nina groaned. "So much wasted energy."

"You cared. There's a difference."

"Is there? Maybe if I'd let go sooner, it all would have worked out sooner."

"Or we would have all been lost. You can't rewrite history, child. You can only learn from it and move on."

Nina stretched out her hand across the table. Bertie took it and squeezed her fingers.

"I'm going to miss you so much," Nina said.

"Because you're leaving?"

She thought about the view of the island from the plane and all the dreams she'd let die. She thought of where she wanted to be in ten years. In twenty.

Maybe she would fail. Maybe she would be bitterly un-happy. Regardless of the risk, she wasn't going to stay stuck anymore. "Everyone has moved on but me," she admitted. "I've run out of excuses. I'm going to go for my dreams and see what happens."

Bertie leaned toward her. "It's going to be wonderful."

Chapter Twenty-Five

❧

"THE FLYING WAS GREAT," Kyle said happily as he drove up I-5 toward Everett. "Perfect weather, light winds and plenty of flight time."

"Your favorite," Nina said lightly, trying to ignore the rock in her stomach. Kyle had returned and called her to set up dinner for Friday night. He'd told her to dress up.

She'd tried to convince him that something more casual would be better, but he'd been stubborn. Which was why she was in a dress and heels when she would have preferred to be in jeans. She wasn't sure why jeans were better, except maybe then she would be in flats, and wouldn't they be better if she had to bolt halfway through the meal?

She'd spent the past three days doing a lot of soul-searching. It hadn't been pleasant or easy, and she'd spent more than a couple of hours in tears. She'd re-created a calendar of the past ten years of her life and made notes of the major events that had occurred. She saw very plainly when she'd given up on her dreams and where she'd settled. If she didn't want to spend the next twenty years like the past ten, she had to get moving.

She'd also realized that while the trust fund had been a catalyst, it couldn't be the reason. She had to make changes for herself—because they were right for her. Which had led to her finishing the application to Tufts.

While it was unlikely she was going to get in this fall, she was hoping for the best. She'd talked to Andi again and then had a long conversation with Andi's mom via Skype. She'd also started researching other medical schools. Tufts would be her first choice for next year, but she would have a lot of back-ups. Averil was lobbying for UCLA so they could be close.

Regardless of whether or not she made it into Tufts, Nina had decided to leave the island. She'd been looking into places where she could volunteer her services for the next year. There were hundreds of clinics in poor neighborhoods in need of help. She simply had to pick one and apply.

All of which meant telling Kyle she wasn't going to see him anymore.

He got off the freeway and drove west. She recognized the route and held in a groan. Not Marianna's, she thought. The beautiful restaurant he'd brought her to on their first date. She didn't want elegant dining and memories. She wanted to make a clean break and escape. But before she could figure out how to make that happen, they were already pulling up to the valet and he was handing over the keys.

They were seated at an intimate waterfront table. Champagne was chilled and waiting. Expensive champagne.

Her heart sank even more. This was not good, she thought, before asking, "What are we celebrating?"

"I'm back with you," Kyle told her before holding out her chair.

Their server opened the champagne, poured them each a glass, then left. Kyle leaned toward her.

"I missed you," he said. "It's tough being away from you."

"I missed you, too," Nina began, then paused. Before she could figure out how to say what she needed to, he took one of her hands in his.

His blue eyes crinkled as he smiled. "I know how this started," he said.

"You mean me being your fantasy?"

"Yeah. And then I came here and you were even better than I thought."

"I'm glad I didn't disappoint," she murmured, thinking there was no way this was going where she thought it was going. They hadn't known each other very long. He couldn't be... There was no way he was...

She swallowed, suddenly afraid and wishing there was a fire exit nearby.

"The thing is, Nina, I didn't have a lot of expectations, beyond living the dream for a few weeks. Then everything changed for me. You and I connected in a way I didn't expect." Emotion filled his blue eyes. "I started to recognize we had something special."

"We did," she admitted, speaking slowly. "Kyle, you caught me in your arms and I didn't know what hit me."

Oh, crap. That didn't come out right, she thought. "What I mean is..."

He nodded. "I know exactly what you mean."

She doubted that.

"I love flying," he continued. "The Navy is exactly where I want to be. You know about my plan to join the Blue Angels. I'm on track for that. But being with you has shown me I want more. I want a wife and a family." He squeezed her fingers. "I want that with you, Nina."

Her mind went blank, and she had a bad feeling she looked as shocked as she felt. Even thinking that he might possibly propose had in no way prepared her for the actual words.

He continued to smile at her. "I know it's fast, but I love you, Nina. My mom always said I'd know when I found the real thing, and she was right. You and I are great together. We have so much in common, and you're going to love being a Navy wife. We can live all over the world. There are so many advantages. You don't want to stay on this island forever, do you?"

"No," she said, relieved there was a question she could answer. "I was going to talk to you about that. I want to leave." She pulled her hand free of his.

"We can do that together. We'll travel and explore together. You'll like the other wives. They really stick together, especially when their husbands are gone. It's like a sorority. When I'm deployed, there's still email and Skype. We'll have a true partnership."

"How is it a partnership when you're gone for six months at a time?"

"We'll still be in touch."

"But you won't be there. When you're gone, I'll be the one taking care of the house, the kids. You can't be a partner when you're half a world away on an aircraft carrier."

She wasn't sure why she was saying all this. She didn't want to marry Kyle, so it wasn't an issue. But she couldn't seem to stop talking.

"I'd be responsible for everything," she continued. "Taking the kids to school, dealing with them when they're sick. I'll have to do everything. It'll be just like it is here, only in a different location. I don't want that. I don't want to be the one in charge."

"You wouldn't be the only one. Okay, I'll be gone for a few months, but you'll have the other wives."

"I won't be married to them. I don't want a part-time marriage. I want…" She shook her head. "Kyle, I want to go to medical school. I want to be a doctor. There's a chance I can get in this fall, but it's not likely. I'll be applying to other schools for next fall."

He didn't look the least bit daunted by her statement. "That's great. You can go to school and be married to me. While I'm gone, you'll have more time to study."

She stared at him, taking in his eager expression. He'd been good to her. He'd literally saved her life or at least kept her from breaking a few bones. But he'd rescued her in other ways. He'd brought her back to life when she'd been in danger of losing herself. He'd made her laugh and had reminded her what it was like to be desired. But even without him being in the Navy, she couldn't spend the rest of her life with him.

"Kyle," she said quietly. "I don't love you. I'm sorry."

His smile faded. He was quiet for a long moment. "You don't? Are you sure? Maybe you need some time to think this through."

She felt as if she'd been kicked in the gut. "I'm sorry," she murmured.

"You're not going to change your mind?"

She thought about saying she wished she could, only that would be a lie. Nothing about the life he described sounded the least bit appealing. She didn't want what he could offer, and she knew that, in the long term, she couldn't make him happy, either.

"I'm not going to change my mind. This has been wonderful. I'll remember you always. But you're not the right man for me. Our life wouldn't be the right choice for me."

His jaw tightened, and he looked away. When he turned back to her, there were tears in his eyes.

"I thought we had something special," he said simply.

She bit her lower lip. "We did, Kyle. I can't thank you enough for this summer. For your passion. For a lot of things."

He nodded once and stood. "Come on. I'll take you home."

"I can get a cab. It'll be easier."

Kyle was a gentleman to the end. He waited until the cab arrived, then helped her into the backseat. She watched him as they drove away, waiting to feel an emotion that would tell her she'd made a mistake. There was regret—mostly for hurting him—but also a sense of anticipation. She'd taken the first step of her new journey. There was no going back now.

She leaned forward to speak to the driver. "I'm going to give you a different address. It's still on the island, but it's by the marina."

The evening concierge smiled a greeting and immediately called up to Dylan's place. A few seconds later, she was waved toward the elevator.

She rode to the top floor with her stomach doing backflips and her knees threatening to give way. But at the same time she was filled with a sense of having done the right thing. Power was sexy, she thought as the doors opened and she stepped out onto Dylan's floor.

Once again he was waiting for her, the door open. He wore jeans and a T-shirt, and he was barefoot. When he took in what she was wearing, he raised an eyebrow.

"Hot date?"

"Sort of."

He stepped back to let her in. "With the boy?"

She put her purse on the small table by the door. "Kyle asked me to marry him."

Nothing about Dylan's expression changed, although a muscle tightened in his jaw. "What did you say?"

"No."

She was going to say more—explain what she'd realized, how she could never be happy with him. She wanted to discuss the merits of various schools and the volunteer opportunities. But before she could start on any of that, Dylan moved toward her. He cupped her face in his hands and kissed her. She rested her hands on his shoulders and parted her lips for him.

His tongue pushed inside. She welcomed the steady stroking, the heat that poured through her, the sense that she'd been waiting for this moment for a literal decade. She wanted to be with Dylan. She wanted to feel the way she had before, when being touched by him, making love with him, had been the best part of her life. She wanted to surrender and know that she would always be safe with him. Not taken care of, but safe.

He drew back enough to kiss her cheeks, then her nose. He kissed his way along her jaw, following the path to her neck. When he reached her collarbone, he inhaled deeply, as if drawing in her scent. Then he straightened and looked at her.

"God, I've missed you," he said.

She stepped out of her heels and reached for the zipper of her dress. It fell to the floor. He pulled off his T-shirt. She undid her bra. He unfastened his jeans, then pushed them down, along with his briefs. She stepped out of her panties.

They studied each other. He was a little broader in the shoulders than she remembered. More muscled. Extremely erect. She was aware of the ten or so pounds she'd put on but couldn't summon enough energy to care.

He took her hand and led her into his bedroom. He threw back the covers with one jerk of his wrist and then pulled open the nightstand drawer and grabbed a box of condoms. Finally he turned to her and pulled her close.

She went into his embrace easily. As she moved next to him, she took his hands and placed them on her breasts. Then she began to kiss him.

They explored each other's bodies while standing, then moved to the bed. He touched her as he had before and when

he stroked her between her legs, she found the glorious promise of her release was exactly as she remembered.

But as she got closer, as she trembled, she had him stop and
put on his condom. Just as they'd always done. When he entered her, filling her, watching her as intently as she watched
him, she quivered on the edge.

"Dylan," she breathed, barely able to keep from coming.

"Sweet Nina."

He filled her and withdrew, then pushed in deeper. She
cried out, so nearly there.

"Ready?" he asked, obviously remembering what they had
done together before so many times.

She nodded once and braced herself. He increased the speed
and intensity of their lovemaking. Faster and deeper. On the
third stroke she lost herself to the pleasure pouring through
her. She wrapped her legs around his hips, holding him as deep
as she could, crying out her release, but careful to keep her
eyes open. He came seconds later, allowing her to see down
to his soul. As he always had.

Later when they were snuggled together under the covers,
she rested her chin on his shoulder. "I can't stay."

"I know."

"I don't mean tonight. I mean I'm leaving Blackberry Island."

"I know," he repeated.

She looked at him. "You're letting me go?"

"It's what makes you happy."

"What happened to fighting for me?"

He smiled lazily. "I have a plan for that."

"Want to share?"

"It's a surprise."

"You have a call," Holly yelled, running into Nina's office.

Nina stared at the office receptionist. "Why do you have
my cell phone?"

Holly shook it at her. "Answer it!"

Nina took the phone. "Hello?"

"Nina Wentworth?" an unfamiliar female voice asked.

"Yes."

"I'm Marian Underwood, at Tufts University School of Medicine. I'm calling about your application."

Twenty minutes later, Nina put her cell phone on her desk. Her hands shook, and there was a faint ringing sound in her ears. She was conscious, so she knew she had to be breathing, but it didn't feel like it. Air wasn't necessary.

Andi burst into her office. Her very pregnant boss danced to her desk. "I've known for two *hours!* It's been a nightmare not to say anything. I had Holly get your cell phone and keep it on her desk so you wouldn't miss the call. I hate you for abandoning me, but you were going to go do volunteer work anyway, so I'm not going to be bitter." She paused. "Nina? Are you okay?"

"I got in," Nina said, barely able to form words, let alone believe them. "I got in!"

She stood, then walked around her desk. She and Andi jumped up and down before hugging.

"You got in!" Andi laughed. "I knew having medical phenom parents would pay off at some point. And it has. At least for you. Are you in shock?"

"Beyond shock."

She'd spent the past month figuring out what she wanted to do and waiting to hear on her application. She hadn't contacted any of the clinics she'd identified, mostly because she hadn't wanted to say she wanted to work there only to have to call back and explain she couldn't make it after all. She'd hoped, she'd worried, but she wasn't sure she'd actually believed…until this minute.

"I have a million things to do," she said. "There are forms

and they want money. A lot of money." A problem because the painting hadn't sold yet.

Andi squeezed her shoulders. "Don't worry. I'm going to loan you what you need to get started, and you'll pay me back when you're rich. It's only for a few months, and I can totally afford it, so don't try saying no."

Nina hugged her. "You're the best."

"Something my husband tells me all the time. So I'm starting to believe it." She grinned. "When do you have to be there?"

"Classes start in six weeks."

"That soon?"

Nina nodded, then realized all she had to get done. "I need a place to stay, I have to figure out what I'm taking and—" She looked at Andi. "I don't want to leave you in the lurch, right when you're going to have a baby."

"The baby is still a couple of months away, and I'll start interviewing within the week. I can do this." Andi drew her eyebrows together. "You're not using me as an excuse not to follow your dream, kid. You're out of here. Go home. Make lists. We'll be fine. Just remember, there's going to be a party for you before you leave."

"I can't wait," Nina said, still in shock over everything that was happening.

Nina drove home, careful to keep her attention on the road. She had a lot to do, but getting into an accident wouldn't help. It was mid-July, and there were tourists everywhere. Some of them had been to the various wine tastings.

She pulled into her driveway and raced inside.

"Are you two here?" she called, grateful her mother and Bertie had gotten home the previous day from their trip to New York.

Bertie stepped out of the kitchen while Bonnie walked out of the den. She had reading glasses in her hand.

"Nina? What are you doing home so early?" Bertie asked. "Is everything okay?"

"I got in," Nina breathed. "I got into medical school. I start in six weeks."

Both women screamed, then lunged for her. There was group jumping followed by hugging.

"I have so much to do," Nina said. "I don't know where to start. Packing and housing and I'm going to need supplies and I don't know what. Should I sell my car? Drive it to Boston? I should call Averil and I want to see her on the way. What do you think about a trip out there right away? And Dylan. I have to tell Dylan."

And while medical school was her dream, telling him she was leaving was going to be difficult. Because over the past month, she'd been spending most of her spare time with him. She was at his condo several nights a week. He said this was what he wanted for her, but…

"We'll start a list," Bertie said, heading for the kitchen. "I'll get a pad of paper. Once it's all written down, it will be easier."

Three hours later, Nina had a plan. The to-do list was several pages long, but that was okay. At least she knew what she had to get done. She sat at the desk in the room where she'd grown up and wondered how different she would be in a year or four.

She'd already called her sister, and they'd arranged a visit. Nina was going to go see her on her way to Boston in late August. She was driving. In the next week she would go to find housing. That trip would be by plane. All the big stuff was planned—except for telling Dylan.

"How are you feeling?"

Nina turned and saw her mother walking into her room. "Stressed. Wide-eyed. But I'll be okay."

Bonnie, tall and beautiful in shorts and a tank top, all lush curves and easy smile, kissed the top of her head, then settled on the bed.

"I'm so proud of you," her mother told her. "Not just of you getting into medical school, but all of it. You're a wonderful daughter."

"Thank you." Nina bit her lip. "You're only going to have Bertie now, Mom. You're going to have to take care of some things on your own."

"So I've been told." She scooted back and sat cross-legged on the mattress. "Bertie and I had a wonderful time in New York. I'd never been there before. We did all the touristy things and saw two shows. Then we met with the auction people. Did I tell you Ambrose joined us?"

"No. But I'm glad he helped you."

"He did. He's very restful, for a man." Bonnie smiled. "I think the young man at the auction house was a little disappointed. He knew that Bertie and I are together, and I think he was a little excited about us being lesbians." Her smile widened. "Unfortunately I'm fairly sure he was expecting two hot girls, not a couple of middle-aged women."

She leaned toward Nina. "Regardless, the auction is scheduled. They're as confident as Ambrose that we'll get at least ten million. So you'll have your money for your education."

"Thanks, Mom. You're being really generous."

"No. I'm doing what's right. I haven't always." The smile faded. "I never wanted to grow up. Peter Pan was my hero. I liked letting other people take care of me. If they didn't do so good a job, it was still better than having to do it myself. But my mom stepped up and then you. I never had to be more."

"And now?" Nina asked.

"I don't like it, but I'm doing it. People can change, I guess. I have so much, Nina. A wonderful woman who loves me, two beautiful and successful daughters who love me." One corner of her mouth turned up. "Because it's always about me."

She drew in a breath. "I'm so happy. Even without the painting and all that silliness, I was happy. But you weren't. I see that now. You were trapped because I wanted to be Peter Pan. I'm so sorry."

"Mom," Nina began, emotion tightening her throat.

"Don't say it was okay, because it wasn't. I want you to promise you'll do exactly what you want from now on. Find work that you love, a partner you can care about. Maybe children. I want you to have it all."

"I want that, too," Nina admitted, her thoughts immediately wandering.

"Dylan?" her mother asked.

Nina nodded. "I'm going to miss him. A lot. We've gotten close again, but now I'm leaving."

"Maybe he'll go with you."

"He's in practice with his father. That's what he promised and what he was always going to do."

"People change," her mother repeated.

"Not that much."

"You did. Look at how different you are from just five or six months ago. You've learned to let go. You're doing what is important to you, the rest of the world be damned."

Nina smiled. "I wouldn't go that far."

"Keep trying. You'll get there." Her mother studied her. "You're my daughter and I love you. Accept that I'm going to make mistakes. Trust me to fix them. Trust Bertie to watch out for me. It's time for you to go, Nina girl. Take my love with you and bring it back when you visit us."

"Oh, Mom."

Nina stumbled to her feet, tears filling her eyes. Her mother hugged her close.

Averil picked Penny up from the groomers right at eleven. She'd already been to the grocery store to get steaks for that night and a bottle of Malbec. Kevin and Nina both liked it and she couldn't stand it, which would make watching them drink it a little easier to take.

"You're stunning," Averil told her dog as they walked to the car. "A real beauty. All the boys are going to want you."

Penny yawned as if to say she'd been spayed and boys really weren't her thing, but she would take the compliment.

They drove home, and Averil went to work on the salad she was making for lunch. A little before noon she heard a car in the driveway and headed for the door. Nina was already walking up the walkway.

They hugged tightly.

"Hey, sis," Averil said, leading the way inside. "Someone is very excited to see you."

Sure enough, Penny raced toward Nina, her tail wagging as she barked and yipped. Nina dropped to her knees and hugged her.

Averil took a second to take in the changes from the last time she'd seen her sister.

For one thing, Nina had cut her hair. Gone was the long straight hair hanging down her back. Instead she had a short, layered cut that barely covered the nape of her neck. Also missing was the slightly disapproving air, as if she was waiting for anyone within a six-mile radius to screw up.

"Love the new hair," Averil said as Nina rose.

"Thanks." Nina touched the back of her head. "I thought

it would be easier to take care of. I just have to towel it dry and comb it. When it dries, it looks like this." She shrugged. "I know it's silly, but I'm trying to streamline everything before I start school."

"Whatever the reason, it looks great. Come on, you must be starved. I have lunch waiting."

They went into the kitchen, and Nina leaned against the counter while Averil continued fixing lunch.

"How are things?" her sister asked.

"Great," Averil told her. "There's an envelope right there. Why don't you open it and read it?"

Nina did and studied the email Averil had printed out. "I don't understand," she said, looking confused. "It's a rejection."

Averil grinned. "I know. From a *publisher*. I finished my book. I finished it, polished it and got an agent. That's my first-ever rejection. I'm thinking of having it framed."

"You finished your book?"

Averil nodded. "I know. Pretty damned impressive, if I do say so myself. Kevin's so proud. He told everyone about the rejection, then had to explain why we were happy about it. Obviously I'd rather sell, but it's still out at a few places, and my agent has faith in me. I'm not giving up. I've already started a new book."

She glanced toward the table and pretended dismay. "Oh, darn. I didn't clear all that stuff away. Can you grab some of the crap and move it to the counter?"

"Sure," Nina said and walked over. She reached for the thick book right in the middle.

Averil waited as her sister glanced at the title. She'd considered wrapping baby booties in a box, but thought leaving out a copy of *What to Expect When You're Expecting* was better. Certainly more normal than Kevin hovering beside her while she sat on the toilet, trying to pee on a stick. Eventually her bladder had come through, then they'd both waited breathlessly for the test to tell them the good news.

Nina looked from the book to Averil. "Are you—"

"Pregnant? Yes! Seven weeks. I think it was right after I got home." She grinned. "Things were hot and heavy that first week, let me tell you."

"Oh, my God! A baby. Have you told mom?"

"I thought we'd call her this afternoon. We can use the speakerphone. Then we're going to celebrate tonight. Kevin is so excited. I am, too."

Nina hugged her. Averil hugged her back. She'd had a really good summer.

They ate salads and caught up with each other. The painting had ended up selling for nearly eleven million dollars. They grumbled about the cut the government got and how weird it was they were now trust-fund babies. Well, not babies, but still. After lunch they took a walk on the beach. Penny trotted ahead, tugging slightly on her leash, always pleased to be a part of things.

"What about Dylan?" Averil asked. "How did you leave it with him?"

"He said we were still together, and he's going to come visit me." She didn't look completely convinced. "We're going to talk on the phone and stuff. I don't know if it's going to be enough. I'm afraid I'm going to lose him. But I can't stay on the island just in case. This is my chance, and I'm taking it. I've waited too long as it is."

"Do you love him?" Averil asked, aware her sister could easily snap her head off for the question.

Nina surprised her by nodding. "I do," she admitted, her voice a little thick with emotion. "It really sucks that, to do what I've always wanted, I have to leave someone I really care about, you know?"

Averil put an arm around her. "I'm sorry."

"Me, too." She sniffed and tried to smile. "But I'll figure it out."

"I'm glad you got into medical school." Averil grinned. "My sister, the doctor. You're going to save us a fortune in medical bills."

Nina stared at her for a second and then started to laugh.

Nina waited for the light to change, then crossed on the green. She shifted the weight of her cross-body tote, wondering if her relatively short walk from campus to her apartment was going to seem a lot longer once winter arrived.

It was early fall now. The leaves had barely started changing. But three weeks after the start of classes, she didn't have much time to admire the beauty of nature.

As Dylan had promised, there was a ton of reading and plenty of memorizing. The labs were long and sometimes confusing, but she'd made friends and joined a great study group.

She turned the corner and hurried toward her apartment. It was Friday. She had big plans for the evening. Takeout and a pay-per-view movie. A treat she hadn't had time for since moving to Boston. But she'd read ahead, done well in her lab and was prepared to reward herself. At ten she had a call with Dylan. Hearing his voice always made her feel she could do anything.

She headed into her building. It was fancier than she'd expected, and the monthly rent had made her blanch, but it was close to school with plenty of shopping nearby. Convenience mattered these days. Besides, she had a snazzy trust fund to cover expenses. Change sometimes came with unexpected bonuses.

She walked through the foyer, pausing to get her mail. Another resident, an elderly Russian woman, smiled at her.

"Hello, Mrs. Volkov," Nina said as she unlocked her mailbox.

"Nina! I met your husband earlier. So handsome." She winked. "I can see why you've been working so hard, eh? Wanting to be caught up for when this one came to town." Mrs. Volkov touched the side of her nose and smiled again.

Nina blinked at her. Husband? Then she slammed her mailbox shut and raced for the elevators. "Thanks, Mrs. Volkov," she yelled as she rounded the corner.

Dylan. It had to be Dylan. He'd shown up for a surprise visit. She hoped it was just for the weekend, because she had classes on Monday. But even so—two days with him would be a miracle.

When the elevator doors opened on her floor, she ran down the hall and let herself into her apartment. Sure enough, Dylan was there, but he wasn't unpacking a suitcase. Instead, he was kneeling by an open box, surrounded by stacks of more boxes. Dozens of them. And there was some new furniture in her place, including his large, black leather sofa.

She dropped her bag to the floor. Her coat followed as she stared at him.

"Dylan?"

He stood and gave her a sheepish grin. "Yeah, I know. I should have talked to you first. Only I thought you'd say we should wait and I'm tired of waiting. I want to be with you."

He was here? As in *here?* "You're moving to Boston?"

He stepped toward her. "I know you're in shock," he said. "Just tell me if this is a good surprise or a bad one."

"Good." Having Dylan around all the time? It was great. But could he do that? "What about your dad? You're in practice with him."

Dylan shoved his hands into his pockets, then pulled them out again. "Yeah, well, that's a funny story. Once he found out I'd rather be here with you than on Blackberry Island with him, he decided to sell his practice. He already has three good offers. He and Mom are looking at retirement homes in Arizona. You know how Dad loves to golf."

"I've heard rumors," Nina said, unable to fully grasp what was happening. "You didn't want to tell me what you were thinking?"

"I wanted it to be a surprise." He crossed to her and cupped her face. "And I wanted to make sure I didn't get in your way. I was afraid if you knew what I was thinking, you might put off starting school. I wanted you to make the choices that were right for you. You need to do this, Nina. You want it and I want it for you. If you don't like the idea of me moving in, I'll understand. I can get my own place and we'll go back to dating. I just thought…" He hesitated. "I love you. Still. Always. That part never went away."

"What about your work?"

"I have interviews with two Boston hospitals. And there's a fellowship I'm looking into." He kissed her. "I moved back to the island partly because I'd told my dad I would but mostly because of you. I could never forget you, Nina. I mean it. I love you."

She leaned against him, letting his words settle into her heart. Tears filled her eyes, but they were the happy kind. The best kind. Everything about this felt right. She flung her arms around him and hung on as if she would never let go, because that was her plan.

"I love you, too," she told him, staring into his green eyes. "I don't think I ever got over you."

He smiled and kissed her. "Good to hear because I was

thinking when you graduate we'd talk about opening a practice somewhere. Dr. and Dr. Harrington."

"I hear it's beautiful in the Appalachians," she told him.

"It's beautiful anywhere you are. What's that line? *Stay with me and be my love and we will all the pleasures prove.*"

She grinned at him. "Wow. A doctor who recites poetry. Can it get any better?"

He nudged her toward the bedroom. "I think it can. Let me take on that challenge and we'll see where it leads."

★ ★ ★ ★ ★

EVENING STARS

SUSAN MALLERY

Reader's Guide

Blackberry Chipotle Chicken Tacos

1 lb boneless, skinless chicken breasts
Olive oil
1 cup Blackberry Chipotle Sauce
(recipe at www.BlackberryIsland.com)
Flour tortillas
Ranch salad dressing (optional)
Onions
Tomatoes
Lettuce
Cheddar cheese

Chop raw chicken into small chunks. Heat oil in ten-inch sauté pan, brown chicken and cook all the way through. Pour the Blackberry Chipotle Sauce over the chicken and cook for another few minutes, until liquid is reduced and chicken is sticky. (Note: You can start with precooked chicken and simply warm together with the Blackberry Chipotle Sauce.) Warm the flour tortillas and assemble the tacos with the remaining ingredients.

1. Why did Nina stay on Blackberry Island so long? Why did she put everyone else's needs ahead of her own? Do you know any women like that?

2. If you have a sister, how is your relationship similar to Nina and Averil's relationship? How is it different? In general, do you think brothers' relationships are as emotionally complex as sisters' relationships are?

3. One of the themes of *Evening Stars* clearly related to taking responsibility for one's own life. How were different facets of responsibility explored through the characters of Nina, Averil and Bonnie? Is it possible to be too responsible? Where do you fall on the responsibility spectrum?

4. What other themes did you think about as you read *Evening Stars*?

5. Were you on Team Dylan or Team Kyle? Why? Did your allegiance change as you progressed through the book? Were you satisfied with the choice Nina made?

6. What did you think of Averil's relationship with her husband, Kevin?

7. Early in the book, when Dylan drives Nina home, she sees the house through his eyes. How did her feelings about her home reflect her feelings about how her life had turned out? How would you feel if your first love visited your house?

8. Do you think Bonnie will change? Why or why not?

9. What caused Averil and Nina to begin to see each other differently? What caused them each to see themselves differently, and to take positive steps in their lives?

10. Explore a metaphor from *Evening Stars*.

*Visit www.BlackberryIsland.com for a wealth of bonus content
about the quaint island and its inhabitants.
You'll find a map of the island to print out for your book group,
recipes, a history of the island and more.*